Cindy Darling

ANDERS GATE

A novel of Taela

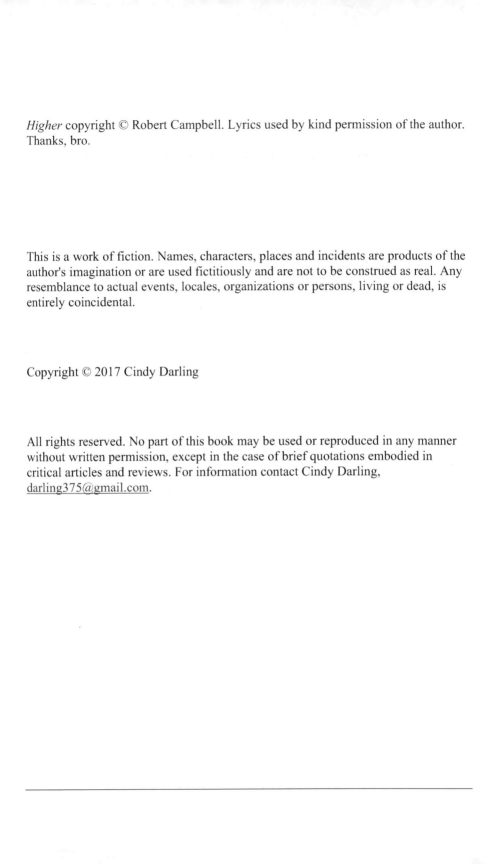

For the circle, in all its incarnations. With much love.

It was midsummer.

The early morning rain had left the air thick with a warm, green smell. Tendrils of mist were rising in fragrant ghosts while thousands of droplets adorned pendant branches and tips of pine needles, multiplying reality into a profusion of tiny, elegantly curved copies.

Benjamin Agante hung his knapsack from a low branch, took out his sword, and became someone else altogether.

The broadsword he held was heavy, but he began his attack with a seemingly effortless overhand spin. Swing, parry, swing, jump, a two-handed block, holding the sword overhead like a quarterstaff. Very little in the way of elegance - since a broadsword could easily weigh twenty pounds - yet this character he had become, this *Hotspur*, moved with serpentine grace.

The grip of his weapon was wound with fine brass chain, over-wrapped by narrow strips of soft red leather that were sweat-stained, molded by time and use to his hand. The fluttering ends trailed between his fingers like drops of blood after a kill. The dark ruby that graced the pommel was chipped where it had slammed into an enemy's helmet, and gleaming silver ran in Celtic cables around the guard to cradle a blade that danced with ancient engravings. He glanced at it for an admiring moment before lifting the sword high over his head, ready to -

Abruptly, Hotspur stopped. He frowned as distant music caught his ear. *A minstrel?* But this was wrong. It was a melody he had never heard before, pulling oddly at his concentration.

Benjamin was on the verge of stepping out of character to investigate when the music stopped as suddenly as it had begun. He shrugged, took a breath, and settled easily back into the exercise when a twig snapped ten feet behind him. A smirk twisted his lips as his head turned. Only a fool would threaten this warrior during a private workout. He spun on his heel, knowing that in two paces he would be at the intruder's throat.

"There you are," the intruder said, wiping her hands on stage-dirty jeans. "We're ready to start working the second act."

Hotspur frowned, blinked, and pulled back a step.

"Ben? You okay?"

It was the actor who nodded, almost compulsively. "Ah, yeah. I'm fine, Jan. Fine." His smile seemed a little too bright.

"Good. Five minutes?"

"Got it. Five. Thanks." He smiled again, nodded again, and looked around for something to focus on other than the stage manager, who sighed as she turned to walk back down to the outdoor theatre.

The actor stood quietly until she was out of sight. Taking a deep breath, he looked again at the stage sword in his hand.

Bolts showed at the join between the silver-painted wooden guard and the battered aluminum blade, which was chewed like a hacksaw. The grip was wrapped with friction tape, more likely to grace a well-used hammer then a warrior's weapon. Lightweight, worn, simple. The suggestion of a broadsword rather than a replica.

He shook his head. With a quiet laugh, Benjamin Agante grabbed his things and walked down to rejoin the cast.

1

The outdoor stage nestled at the base of a gentle, grassy slope, forming a natural amphitheater. With its cedar finish and large scale, the stage easily gave the impression that someone's deck project had gotten completely out of hand. Both the acting space and the tall metal light towers were open to the sky, leaving the productions at nature's mercy – which also meant that rain, lightning, and a well-practiced tech crew could shut down a show in less than ten minutes.

Ben shrugged off his knapsack near the front of the stage and wandered over the grass to where Jan was checking lists. He looked toward the band platform as he spoke. "Sorry I'm late, I got distracted up there."

The stage manager automatically searched her clipboard. "It's fine, Paul's having a chat with 'Oberon' about the damn staff, anyway."

The actor nodded a grin, he added, "Where's Ray?"

"Music Ray?" she flipped a page, "looks like we start with the band tomorrow."

"Really? Then who was playing before?"

"No one. Well, the soundtrack recording, but that's just the piano line."

"No, not that. When I was up there", he turned, pointed toward the woods. "I heard someone playing - guitar, I think - and now there's this song I can't get out of my head."

Jan scanned the prop table and shook her head at two young female apprentices who were trying rather obviously to get Ben's attention. "You two. The lantern, and the wrench for the bower. They should be here. *Now*." Her finger tapped the table where two taped-out squares were conspicuously empty, and the girls dashed to the lockup like frightened deer. Jan kept her drill sergeant expression on when they looked back, but spoke calmly to Ben. "Could have been anyone. This *is* a public park, you know."

The actor frowned and looked thoughtful, an expression that made one of the apprentices sigh heavily. The stage manager gave her an exasperated 'hurry up' gesture, and Ben's eyes followed the two as they scurried away. Jan growled quietly. "Those two will be the death of me. Watch out for them."

He shrugged. "Right. Where were they when I was sixteen?"

She returned his thoughtful frown with some sarcasm. "Kindergarten?"

Ben barked a laugh and brushed the grass from his jeans. "Gee, thanks. I was thinking at least grammar school."

"No problem. Just remember you have a contract."

"Come on, Jan. Like I'd go looking there."

She patted his head. "Good actor. If only all of you were so sensible." Walking with a grin toward the trailer, she called back to him. "What's the song?"

"Hmm? Oh." He shook his head. "I don't know."

She stopped, looking back over her shoulder. "Come again?"

"I don't know. I've never heard it before."

"But it's stuck in your head."

"Well, yeah." Ben glanced away sheepishly.

Jan gave a deep laugh. "I can check around," she said smoothly, "if it's bothering you."

"No." He smiled at the back of her head as she walked away, recognizing all too well her 'crazy actor' voice. "I liked it."

"Ah. Well, I'm sure it liked you, too."

A shiver ran up to the nape of Ben's neck and his grin vanished, making him shrug his shoulders and turn back toward the woods with a frown.

*   *   *

They broke for lunch, and Ben carefully dodged the interns as he headed up the backstage hill. He was eating an apple and struggling to read his own scribbled notes from the director when a softly singing rustle made him look up nervously. He let out his breath when he saw who it was.

"Oh, sorry, love", the woman smiled when she saw him, the faintest Irish lilt warming her voice. "I didn't know you were here. D'you mind?" She was walking easily through the trees, tying back her long, coppery hair.

"No problem, Annie. Pull up some grass and sit down."

She obligingly pulled up some grass blades and tossed them at him before sitting and taking a long drink from her water bottle. "How's stayin' with Dave going?"

"Fine. A cross between a bed and breakfast and a dorm, now that the second show people are coming in. But we all have different schedules, so… it's fine." She chuckled as he opened his lunch sack and her gaze became more thoughtful as she watched a dragonfly dart between the trees.

"D'you think it works?" He grinned at the assumption that he'd know what she was talking about. They'd known each other for so long, and been married so often on stage that even her husband joked about it.

"I think so." He tore a small loaf of homemade bread and brushed the crumbs off his shirt. "Course, if they don't fix the mics downstage right, we'll have to change the blocking anyway."

"Oh, Kate'll take care of it. Always does." She looked toward the stage, the sun dancing metallic lights through her hair. "And the new cross isn't a problem?"

"Nope. You run, I chase. You could do that line halfway up the hill and I'd be right behind you." He lifted an eyebrow. "Just don't slow down."

She closed her eyes as she chuckled, tilting her head back to catch the sunlight. "You're a chore, Agante, but you're my chore and I love you." Ben toasted her with his bottle, and returned to deciphering his notes when she spoke again. "So." He looked up at her with a slightly puzzled frown.

"So?"

The actress pushed her hair back and looked around in what - for an experienced professional - was a completely failed effort to act casual. "I understand Lara's in town. Max called her in for his show."

"So I hear." Benjamin looked back to his notes.

"Did you… call her?"

"Annie…" He shook his head, stared off into the woods without seeing. "It's done. It's been over for -"

"But three years -"

"Is a long time."

She paused. "Sorry, love. I just -"

"I know. You just want me to be happy." The sun brightened the blue in his eyes as he looked at her. "I appreciate it. I do." He opened his mouth and then shrugged, not finishing the thought. After a delicately awkward moment he frowned at the remaining bread in his hand, and tore it in half. "Here. Try this. What do you think?"

Annie accepted the bread along with the change in subject, chewing critically. "Is this the new recipe? It's lovely." Her laugh was as welcome as it was sudden. "Did I tell you? Sean and the girls made dinner last night..." Ben smiled and nodded as she told the story, but music began echoing in his mind. And this time, he thought he could hear words. He realized he must have frowned in concentration, because Annie looked mildly offended. "Well, it wasn't that bad, really. If you ignored the colors, the mashed potatoes were -"

Ben cut her off. "Can you hear that?"

Annie stopped instantly, listening, then shook her head. "I'm hearing nothing. What am I supposed to be hearing?" He stared off into the trees as they sat silently for a few moments, the stirring of the leaves and a few birds the only sound.

"Nothing. I guess it's in my head." He sighed and gave his best forlorn look. "I've got this song that won't go away."

Annie shuddered appreciatively. "Ech. I hate it when that happens. Although I read somewhere it means your subconscious is tryin' to tell you something." She stood and walked toward him, brushing a few stray crumbs off her loose cotton pants and nodding toward his sword. "Fight call today?"

Ben glanced at the weapon shining dully in the sunlight. "Nah. I'm just working on Hotspur for next show."

"Really."

"Paul practically told me the part was mine. With Mike stuck in the city, he said that I'm next in line..." He looked up at her expression, and his tone became flat. "You know something."

"Can't imagine what –"

"Annie."

She sighed and took a step closer to him. "Darlin', Paul said Phil's coming back. He's getting Hotspur."

Ben's jaw tightened. "Ah. When did you hear this?"

"Just this morning, love. I'm sorry."

He stared down at the grass, his eyes narrowing. "Well. Doesn't that just figure."

"C'mon, Benjamin. You did get Demetrius this year. And you know it's an old boys club."

"Sure it is. And I've been a certified combatant for five years. When do I get to be an 'old boy'? When do I actually get to *do* something?" He threw the scrap of his bread angrily into the woods, where it failed to hit anything. "Damn."

"Sorry, love. Maybe I should have kept my mouth shut."

"No, no. I'm glad I heard it from you. If Paul told me, I might have punched his face in."

She grinned in spite of herself. "Probably not the best way to get into that *club*, dear." He gave a shrug and she leaned over, patting him once on the head. "You're it," she whispered, bolting down the hill as he automatically scrambled to follow.

Ben was walking confusedly through his Grandfathers' house, trying to find his script to Henry IV. *The house was largely as he remembered it as a child, but in the front hall was a door he'd never seen. Puzzled, he pulled it open and saw a staircase rising to a landing with three doors - one slightly ajar. With a sinking feeling he realized familiar music was wafting down from the room. Climbing the stairs, Ben inched the door open and saw a man sitting on a wooden stool, playing a guitar. On the floor just past the doorway lay his missing script next to his sword, which sparkled in the dim light. The man lifted his eyes when Ben entered the room, but didn't stop playing.*

"There you are. Finally." The musician managed to look relieved and annoyed at the same time. "Find the way." Curious, Ben walked toward him, but the man vanished into mist. Ben took a few more steps but abruptly stumbled, overcome with the sensation that he had fallen off the edge of a cliff.

The actor woke with a gasp, kicking his toes hard against the wall next to the bed. He grunted and lay panting until his heart accepted the fact that the fall was only a dream. Sitting up slowly, he rubbed his hands roughly over his face and back through his hair.

"Perfect. Now I'm *dreaming* the damn song." He shuffled his legs off the bed, deciding more sleep was unlikely, especially the way his toes were throbbing. "Ow. Damn it. This is *definitely* not my week." Limping out of his borrowed room, Ben packed some food and a change of clothes in his knapsack and headed for the park, hoping that some exercise would help him settle down before another marathon day.

His practice clearing felt different in the gray light before dawn. The grassy circle, wet and beaded with dew, could have been the throne room of an old ruin, with pillars of tall dark trees reaching brokenly to a faded denim sky. Centering the space was an oak tree stump three feet across - the tree it once supported must have been huge.

The actor slipped into the circle silently, as if he didn't want to disturb it. Loose pants and a hooded once-black sweatshirt gave him the flexibility he needed for practice, while over his shoulder a faded olive green knapsack had carry loops sewn down one side to hold his practice sword. In the scooped neckline of his undershirt a pendant of stained glass flashed burgundy just below the hollow of his collarbone.

Ben scratched his fingers through his thick mane of brown hair and stretched. Personally, he thought his hair and beard were barely long enough for the look of the play, but it seemed to be the norm for him. Always in the process of growing one or the other for a part, and never quite feeling he had reached the right image before the show was over. A director once told Ben that he was such a chameleon, no one would know he was the same actor. He said it was probably why he got so many commercials.

Ben had a drink or two over that 'compliment'. He'd been pegged early on as 'dependable supporting actor'. He knew he had talent for more, but the leads he longed for - and even the combat choreography gigs, were few and far between. And now, he'd lost Hotspur… He blew out a breath. "Damn."

The sky was warming like a backlit scrim when he sat cross-legged on the stump, trying to relax his breathing. As he closed his eyes he heard birds singing, and noticed that morning traffic was getting louder on the nearby expressway.

It was odd about the park. It seemed to have been dropped into the middle of the city while roads that curved around it were held back, perhaps by some mysterious force that this bit of protected nature possessed. It may just have been smart planning on Olmstead's part, but it felt good. Ben's mind was wandering over the peacefulness of the greenspace when his eyes snapped open.

"Damn it." The song was back. The actor sighed, trying not to lose the calm. Breathing deeply, he stood and stretched. "So much for meditation." Staring at his weapon for a moment, he shrugged, picked it up and started a broadsword routine.

Stage combat was one of his favorite things, especially sword work - an intricate dance complicated by the simple addition of having the participants swing heavy, pointed metal objects at each other while trying to stay in character and not actually hurt anyone. He got through three moves before the song started up again.

"All right. This is ridiculous." The music was like a fly buzzing around his head on a hot day. He spit on the ground, relaxed his arms and dropped his head back to look at the sky.

The sun was lifting in a tawny red smudge over the trees at the eastern edge of the park, and Ben watched as the sky made room for it, making the lake sparkle with rubies. He could still hear his grandfather saying, 'Red sun at night, sailor's delight. Red sun at morning, sailor take warning.'

He wondered if his grandfather knew about the ominous sensation that phrase always gave him when the sun came up red, even to this day. He absently stroked the pendant at his neck, and sighed in defeat as the song carried on.

"Fine. I'll get some breakfast instead. Stupid -" He grabbed the knapsack angrily and slung it over his shoulder. But as the actor turned, sword still in hand, a squirrel jumped in fright, running up a nearby maple and chattering wildly. Something in the absurdity finally broke through, and Ben couldn't help laughing. He leapt onto the oak stump, waving the sword in mock challenge.

"Come out, vile song, come out and fight. I'll hear what you have to say if it's the last thing-"

An odd feeling tickled over him, like windblown mist from a waterfall. He closed his eyes and listened as the song cycled back to a beginning, more quietly now. It had begun as a demand, but now... now it was more like a request. Someone was calling, and he could hear the words.

> *light the way*
>
> *begin the rhyme*
>
> *yours is all to know in time*

Ben realized that the more he strained, the harder it was to hear. If tension hindered it, then maybe -

> *find the center*
>
> *strike the balance*

With a blink, Ben realized he was doing just that. "What the hell?" His voice was a bare whisper. He had automatically slipped into the state he thought of as 'actor's ready' - relaxed but focused, able to react. Ready for anything.

yours to choose

accept the challenge

you alone decide what it is you are to be...

Ben shook his head, frowning. "Who are you? How are you doing this?"

...and all you have inside

is more than you will ever need...

In the strained pause that followed, a weary voice spoke.

"Finally. You're it."

"What?" Recollections crashed into each other in Ben's mind, trying to find a context.

"Come." And then, sounding a quite reluctant, the voice faded more with, *"Please"*.

"But who are you? What's this about?"

"Just... come. You can do this." The voice sounded faint, as if speech was more difficult than singing.

"Come where? To do what?"

The voice was growing fainter. *"To do something."*

Ben's eyes jerked open and he glanced down the hill toward the stage. He was tired, he was stressed, he was probably imagining the whole thing... and the way his dreams had been going lately, he could even still be asleep.

Now the voice was barely audible. *"There's a place for you here."*

"Where?" Ben closed his eyes again and saw a strangely familiar pearly mist. Something urged him toward it, trying to hear the voice, and he felt himself running. "Where are you?" He stumbled and lost his balance, but when he tumbled forward, he never hit the ground.

2

The first thing he saw was the quilt.

A log cabin pattern of greens and browns, made by his grandmother for him when he started college. In one corner, a carefully embroidered signature. 'God bless you Benjamin, and keep you warm. Love, Nonna'. Ben smiled as he pulled it up under his chin, then frowned, looking around his old room. He'd had this dream before, but there were never so many doors. And the sword, his dream sword, was hanging on the wall. The changes took him back.

He was three weeks short of fourteen when his parents died in the accident. Nonna and Papa had taken him in, and been as kind as two people could be.

It was hard when Papa had the heart attack, forcing Ben to leave rehearsals of his college production of *The Cherry Orchard* to get home for the funeral. It was worse when the second one came just two weeks later.

"Don't worry, Benjamin," Nonna had said, patting his cheek. "We belong together, Papa and I. We'll keep an eye on you."

Ben thought that it was grief talking, but she passed quietly in her sleep that night. The fire in this house that ended it all just months later seemed strangely connected, and far too final.

He dropped his head back against the headboard, and his left hand reached for the pendant he wore, his fingertips smoothing across it. The curved teardrop of glass was from a Tiffany lamp that held a place of honor on the grand piano downstairs. When the house burned down the lamp was destroyed, but when Benjamin had to walk through with the insurance adjuster, he found this piece shining in the ashes. He had worn it ever since. Sometimes, when he had this dream, the lamp downstairs was whole – but always missing this one piece.

A door opened and a tall, distinguished man with round spectacles and wavy silver hair walked in. Ben sat up and stared. "Papa?" His grandfather stepped closer and hugged him, then straightened up in a business-like manner.

"Get out of bed, son, you can't sleep all day. Things to do." He stood to leave as Ben reached toward him.

"Wait." His grandfather gave him a stern look as Ben smiled, hugging his knees to his chest. "Don't go yet."

"You know I can't stay. Get movin'."

"Papa." The older man turned, looking resigned but fond, as if he had lost similar arguments before. "Papa, why are there so many doors in here?"

The man looked around. "Don't you know? It's your room."

Ben shook his head.

"Well then," his grandfather said, taking off his glasses and polishing them with a handkerchief. "I guess it has something to do with choices. Looks like you've got more than enough." With a grin he turned to leave. "Be true to yourself, Ben."

The younger man chuckled. "And it must follow as the night the day thou canst not then be false to any man," Ben finished the quote. "Give Nonna my love?"

The tall man nodded and was gone; Ben's vision was too blurred to say how. As he wiped a sleeve across his eyes, the sword's weight in his hand pulled it down.

His eyes snapped open and he gasped, suddenly awake.

Sword?

Frowning down at the ground, he realized he was still standing on the oak stump. *I dozed off?* Ben glanced at his aching sword hand. His fist was clamped so tightly on the grip that he couldn't feel his fingers. *How long have I been standing here?* Then he looked at the sword again, and pain or no, his hand jerked open as if the grip had burned him.

The weapon tumbled once over and stuck, easily, into the flat top of the stump. Woven bands of silver shimmered in the morning light, and the red leather strips were stained burgundy with dew and sweat. Ben stared as if it might rebound and attack him

It was *real*. The weapon that stood shivering in the sun was one he had often *imagined* using and he stared, focusing on every detail that he had built into it over the years. Not as heavy as a broadsword, or as thin as a rapier. It was perfect for him.

Ben blinked in shock, first acknowledging only those things that made sense. The stump. *That's still here; I'm standing on it.* The sword. His mind reeled drunkenly away. *No, better not try to explain that now.* The traffic noise. *Good, that's good, mundane and typical and* - Ben stopped with a little shudder. *That's not traffic.* Stepping unsteadily off the aged wood, he scrambled toward the sound and over a small rise in what should have been the direction of the park lake.

What his mind had interpreted as the distant rumble of traffic was actually the sound of water tumbling over a rocky outcropping before relaxing into a shallow stream. Far beyond there was no road, but forest that stretched to the horizon.

"There's no stream here," he said, a little louder than he meant to. The stream remained, unperturbed. "I said," he shouted, just a touch of hysteria piercing through, "There's no stream -" As if to correct him, the breeze shifted and sunlight brightened his view, filtering through leaves to shimmer on the water. In self-defense he stumbled back to the oak stump. "Dear God," he whispered hoarsely, squatting to huddle on the edge like a frightened child. He pounded his fist against the wood, not really surprised when it hurt. For a moment he stared at the blade, his hand reaching toward it, considering. "And what would that prove? A dream sword cutting me in a dream?" He pulled his fingers back, wrapped his arms around his chest.

From where he sat there was nothing but soft green twilight as far as he could focus. A peaceful, whispering hush was punctuated by birdsong and mumbling brook. Ben blinked and worked the glass of his pendant between his left thumb and fingers. Suddenly, and without any visible provocation, he gave a slightly manic laugh.

"I don't think we're in Kansas anymore, Toto -"

A noise from the dense vegetation to his right stopped him. Without stopping to think he yanked his sword free and crept toward the sound. When he pulled the brush away to see what was there, a large equine head pushed through from the other side.

"Gah," Ben said, jumping back. The horse regarded him for a moment with liquid brown eyes, then snorted and turned away, chewing. Ben tried with limited success to unclench his adrenal glands and stabilize his breathing simultaneously as he hissed quietly. "Wake up, Agante. Wake up! This is just… it's just…" Closing his eyes, he took a deep breath and let it out. When he opened them he felt better, but only for a moment. He could see beyond the hedge now, through the space the horse had cleared.

A man was lying there, near a spent campfire. Ben's mind, free associating with reckless abandon at this point, pulled Annie's lines when she finds Lysander in the wood.

But who is here? Lysander, on the ground? Dead, or asleep?

As he pushed through the undergrowth, the actor's eye registered details without trying. The man was breathing easily, the neck of a guitar resting across his hand. *Alive.* He looked to be close to Ben's height, and just as fit even though he might be ten years older. Brown tunic and pants appeared to be well worn, and a scored leather gauntlet was tied over his left forearm. He was unarmed, unless the guitar was dangerous, but a sword and bow hung with a pack from a nearby branch. Since there was no immediate threat, Ben slipped his own sword back into his knapsack's carry loops, not noticing as the sharp blade sliced one halfway through.

"Hello?" A draped forearm half hid the man's face, but as Ben stepped closer he could make out a square jaw and broad cheekbones. There was something native in the features, with a hint of that olive complexion. Dark hair fell past his shoulders with only a few strands of silver at the temples. *Nearly a Robin Hood,* Ben thought, playing casting director for the moment, *but not quite.* He eyed the weapons nearby. *Still, not too anxious a fighter, or the sword would be closer than the guitar.* Picking up the instrument, Ben startled when the man spoke.

"Hey."

Ben looked at him. "Are you all right?"

"Put it down."

The actor blinked and rested the instrument back onto the grass. The man eased himself to a sitting position, stretching his neck and taking a moment to inspect his instrument for any damage, or perhaps, contamination.

Ben's shoulders dropped. "Look…" The actor tried unsuccessfully to formulate a sentence with his hands. "Can you tell me where I am?"

The man straightened up and exhaled noisily. He wore a squarely cut goatee that gave him, when a serious expression crossed his dark, hooded eyes, a distinctly malevolent aspect.

"Yours is all to know in time." He stood and walked over to his pack, slipping the guitar into a leather case before walking back to the fire, moving some sod, and throwing on a pile of tinder. In moments embers had flared up, and he added larger branches. Ben blinked in recognition.

"Wait. You were in my dream. You played the song."

The man rubbed at his eyes with one hand. "Yeah. That's me. That's what I do."

Ben stared. "That's what you do? Bring people here?"

"No." The minstrel looked annoyed. "You brought yourself, I just put out the call. You made your own choice." Ben's jaw dropped in disbelief.

"But I wasn't trying to go anywhere! I was fine there."

"If you say so." The man waved off Ben's expression. "You hungry?" He poked at the fire with a long stick.

"But where -" Ben stopped as he heard the panic in his voice, and attempted to collect himself. A quick vision of his grandmother looking at him with an expectant frown flashed through his mind and he nodded, strangely relieved at the memory of protocol. Formally extending a hand he said, "My name's Ben. Benjamin Agante."

For a moment it looked as if the musician would ignore the gesture. Then the thin ghost of a smile passed over his eyes, not reaching his lips. He brushed his palms together and grasped Ben's hand briefly. Even in the short contact, Ben felt a tickling sensation that ran over his body, as if lightning had struck nearby.

The minstrel seemed unfazed as he pulled a knife from the leather sheath on his thigh. "Nice meeting you. Let's eat." Grabbing a root from a nearby pile, he trimmed the ends, slicing a spiral line the length of the vegetable. Spearing it on a long stick, he held it out.

"Here. Roast it 'til it's black. Slowly. The skin'll come off easy enough." Without waiting for Ben to acknowledge, the minstrel repeated the process with another root and held it over the fire. Ben followed suit numbly, trying to get a feel for this stranger who seemed to welcome and shun him simultaneously.

It wasn't easy.

The last rays of sun twisted sideways through the space over the brook, and the forest's silky green twilight faded to solemn grey. The fire held back what darkness it could, but over time the circle it defined grew smaller, until the world was bounded only by fuzzy firelight, enclosing the minstrel on one side, Ben on the other.

Between roots, the minstrel retrieved a skin from his pack. He drank from it and passed it to Ben, who sniffed it, sipped, and blinked surprised approval. The wine was good, honey-flavored without being too sweet, and had a faint aftertaste of strawberries. He drank more deeply and passed it back to the minstrel.

"So what is this place?"

"You'll feel better after you get some sleep. We'll talk in the morning."

"You know I need answers."

The minstrel raised the skin mockingly in toast, took a swig. "Fine. *In vino veritas.* What're the questions?"

Ben felt the wine encouraging his exhaustion. Part of his mind calmly registered the statement *you're in shock, you know,* and he nodded to himself as he drank again, then stared at the skin. "What is this?"

Raising an eyebrow, the other man answered. "It's perriwine. Topaz." Ben's frown urged him to continue. "Made with perri – that's a kind of fruit - and honey. Other stuff. I drink it, I don't make it." He paused, seemed to consider, and went on with more than a touch of sarcasm in his voice. "I didn't think the questions would be this tough."

Ben shrugged. "Look. I'm tired and confused and sleep will probably help a lot. But at least tell me…" He paused for his mind to decide what question was most pressing. His mind wanted no part of it. *This must be the worst case of jet lag in history.* "Okay," he said, trying to relax. He looked at the minstrel and opened his mouth, hearing the question as it left his lips. "Who are you?"

Dark eyes met Ben's across the fire. It was only with the shock of connection that Ben registered how little this man used direct eye contact. Its power was startling. He also felt tension coming from the minstrel that puzzled him, as if every word said further committed him to something he wasn't sure of.

"Hawkins. Connor Hawkins. They call me Hawk." The man stuck out his hand. Ben clasped the proffered hand with his own, blinking at the tingle in the air.

"And what do you call yourself?" Ben grinned, but backpedaled as Hawkins tensed visibly. "Sorry, it's just a joke…" The minstrel cut him off with a wave.

"I know." He shook his head. Then, almost as if the idea surprised him, he smiled tightly and added, "I guess I call myself Hawk as well. But I don't always answer to it."

"Connor, then," Ben repeated, realizing that this was the first time he had seen the man smile. The expression held powerful charisma, and Ben wondered how this Hawk used his.

"That enough to get you to sleep?" Connor asked, giving a broad yawn. He stood, moved a few steps out of the fire lit circle and whistled. Ben heard nothing for a moment, and then the soft thudding of hooves on the forest floor as two horses appeared out of the shadows. Connor murmured softly to the animals as he untied packs, tossing a bedroll to Ben. "Here. We'll be roughing it for a few days." He unrolled his on one side of the fire and Ben followed his example.

"Connor."

"Yeah?" The minstrel spoke absently, distracted by the ministrations he was working on the fire.

"How long've you been camped here?"

Connor took a weary breath and squinted into the dark. "Two days, maybe three," he said at length. "Why?"

Ben pointed at the fresh bedroll. "You haven't slept in three days?"

The minstrel snorted, his glance flashing toward Ben for only a moment. "I've been busy."

Ben laid back in the sleeping bag, his knapsack and sword by his side. Overhead, the canopy of leaves left interesting spaces defined by a bright dusting of stars. His eyes were dragging shut out of sheer exhaustion when a thought struck him. Pushing up on his elbow, he looked across the fire. "Hey."

A sigh. "Now what?"

"Two horses? Two bedrolls?" He paused for a moment, not sure exactly what he was feeling. When no response came, he spoke again. "You said I chose to come. But you were pretty sure, weren't you."

Hawkins sighed and pushed himself up on one elbow to mirror Ben. For a moment, raw charisma slipped from its armor once more. "You were the one that fit the call. The only one, evidently." He stopped for a moment, looking out past the dim light of their circle. "It was your choice. But I felt it from here."

They stared at each other. Then, without further comment, they lay down in a continuing mirror of movement, and were sound asleep within seconds.

*   *   *

Morning dawned, the sun lifting the misty blanket that covered the water with parental care. Birds fluttered around the campsite, curious about crumbs and bits of grain the horses dropped from their feedbags.

"Ow." Ben jerked awake to a sudden pain in his head and a chattering squirrel. Rolling onto his side he opened his eyes cautiously; saw the acorn that had beaned him and rubbed his forehead as he glanced upward. "Thanks a lot." He looked around, a little afraid of what waking might bring.

High above him the morning sun was turning the forest canopy into a golden-green screen, while to his side the brook held a complicated conversation with itself. Ben shook his head. The bedroll across the way had been repacked, the fire revived, and the horses were grazing peacefully. A touch of mint scented the clean morning air as Ben called out.

"Hello?"

"Yeah."

"Good morning."

"So far."

Ben sighed and shook his head. The sparse response already seemed normal. He chuckled in wonder at his own defensive ability to adapt. *Good thing I took those improv classes.*

Walking over to the stream, Ben stripped off his shirt and tossed it to the side. The bank was carpeted with moss, and the blocky stone outcropping that made the waterfall was a good spot to perch. Ben admired it as only a devout camper could, feeling the warmth of the sun on his back.

The water, however, was like ice. This clearing must have been the first time it saw the sun for miles. He lay down on his stomach and scooped up a double handful of the liquid crystal, splashing glittering droplets over his skin, some turning crimson for a space as they ran across his pendant. Another splash across the back of his neck elicited a primal scream.

"Wow." Ben shook his head like an Irish setter. He wiped the water out of his eyes when an electric tingle rushed up through his chest to his brain. *I'm not alone.*

Like Hotspur in the clearing he whipped around and froze, his hand reaching for the hilt of a sword that currently was on his bedroll, and found himself almost face to face with Connor.

The minstrel's expression wavered between disbelief and anger, his knife in a white-knuckled grip. For a brief, adrenaline-soaked moment, Ben was absolutely positive Connor was going to kill him.

"What?" Ben said, sounding angry when he was really frightened out of his wits.

Connor spoke quietly, his words measured out like rosary beads. "*Why* did you scream?"

Ben frowned and barked a response. "Cold water."

The minstrel stared at Ben for a few seconds before dropping his eyes to the knife in his hand. "Look," he said, as he slipped the weapon back into its sheath. "I'm pretty sure this place is safe. But warn me if you plan on doing that again." The taut tone of his voice made it clear that it was not a request. As he turned to walk away, Ben called after him.

"Connor." The minstrel stopped without looking back. "I plan to do it again." Without waiting for a reaction, Ben knelt by the stream, ducked his head, and yelled. It was freezing. And, he inwardly suspected, as good an excuse for screaming as he would find.

By the time he dried off and walked back to the fire, Connor had made breakfast. They ate in silence as the morning unfolded around them. Ben nodded in a conciliatory fashion to the minstrel as he downed the last of the mint tea, and said, "This is good."

"Thanks"

Connor stirred the fire down, and Ben's eyes dropped to his knapsack. To the sword still held in the carrying loops. *The sword.* Rubbing the bridge of his nose and closing his eyes, Ben took a deep breath. "Why am I here?" He looked up into the silence and was surprised to find the minstrel's eyes meet his. For a long moment their gaze locked, before Connor looked off towards the stream.

"You chose to come here."

"I'm not accusing you of anything, I just -" Ben stopped as his anger surged, trying to pinpoint what he was feeling, what he wanted to say. He rested his elbows on his knees, staring at the mug between his hands. Finally, he said, "What's going on? Just tell me." In the pause that followed, the minstrel nodded, looking across the fire. There was a discomfort in his eyes that Hawkins obviously wanted to keep to himself.

"Fine." The minstrel took a moment, decided where to begin. "You know you're not in the same world anymore."

"I gathered that," Ben said hollowly. He had known, somehow, but hearing it spoken so matter-of-factly sent a tingle up his spine. "So where are we?"

"Taela."

"Tay-la?" The word slipped over Ben's tongue. "Is that the country?"

"The world."

"Ah." He glanced around, tried to toss off an unconcerned laugh. "Looks a lot like Earth."

"And you look like a smart boy. So I won't bore you with my opinion of multiverse theory." Ben's eyebrows lifted but the minstrel went on. "Physically, the world and the people are pretty much like us. I thought they were more primitive when I first got here-"

"First got here? You're -?" The minstrel waved him silent.

"The arts are important here. Creating is almost… a religious practice." He paused to finish his cup, shake out the last drops on the fire. "And the people I've met are peaceful, for the most part." Connor stood, stretched, and began to gather together the bits of their camp.

"For the most part?"

"For the most part. This is no paradise, although some places - well, some people, anyway…" Pulling a roll of paper from his pack, Connor spread it on the ground.

It was a map, done in ink but largely unfinished, with streams and roads that ended far before the paper did. Details, names, and dates were noted abundantly along specific lines, almost nonexistent elsewhere. Ben was impressed by the concise artistry of the work, almost like a journal and map combined.

"You did this?"

The minstrel shrugged. "Yeah. Maybe one of these days I'll get a chance to finish." His eyes wandered over the map with an almost wistful expression. "Anyway, this is where we are, this is where we're headed first." He pointed to a castle on the edge of a large, black area that reached the paper's edge. Nearby, north of the castle, were neat letters.

"*Anders Gate*", Ben read, and then, seeing smaller letters closer to the castle, "*Lady Anders.* Who's she?"

The minstrel looked away, trying to compose his answer in the trees. He scratched his beard line with his thumb and shrugged. "Hard to describe. Her family's been prominent in the area for generations."

Ben nodded. "So she's what, a queen? Empress?"

Connor looked annoyed. He opened his mouth to speak, then stopped and shook his head instead. "No. It's not like that." He gestured to the map. "But she's important. The whole region looks to her for direction, and protection, I suppose. She's powerful - not in the sense you'd think. You'll see."

"But I won't be able to describe her," the actor said. He was enjoying the minstrel's company in spite of himself, although he was still fighting a surreal sensation. As if he were in the first moments of an improvisation, when he didn't know if the scene was a comedy or a tragedy yet. But still - that was a sensation he lived for.

"Probably not."

Ben shook himself mentally, blinked his attention back to the more concrete information of the map. "What's the black?" He pointed, although his finger avoiding brushing the paper. "Water?"

"No," the minstrel said in a flat voice. "I don't know what it is."

Ben lifted his eyes without moving his head. Inconspicuously, he looked from Connor to the map again. By tilting his head slightly to the side and changing the angle of the light, he could make out impressions of lines in the black. Something had been written or drawn there and inked over. Ben glanced back to Connor. "Oh?"

The minstrel exhaled. "As far as I know, it's the other side. Anders Gate is a kind of doorway between a force of darkness and the Lady's dominion."

"Force of darkness?" Ben's voice was skeptical.

"I know how you feel. It sounds strange, but trust me," the minstrel met Ben's eyes and the hardness there chilled him. "Once you're in, you'll believe it." Ben looked at the map, then back to the

Hawk. He did believe. The tingle at the back of his neck was convincing enough.

"Wait a minute. '*Once I'm in*'?"

The minstrel reached over and pulled another paper from his bag. "You should read this." The sheet he handed over was much older than the map, broken and frayed but still legible. "It's part of the story. Passed on from parent to child in stories, songs, books," he motioned for Ben to read it. "Go ahead. I'll finish packing up." Ben took it, stared at the paper until the minstrel spoke again. "The Lady thought you should read it." With a shrug, he walked away.

The actor blinked. He wandered back through the trees to the oak stump, which he found somehow reassuring. As he sat down he saw the deep cut his sword had made in the flat surface of the wood, ran his finger along its edge. Taking a breath, Ben centered himself, carefully unfolded the paper. The sentence on the torn-out page began in the middle.

the lord of all Anders dominion, stood high on the ledge looking out toward Anders Gate. Raising his hands to the Artist he cried out:

In the time that will be the time that is

the One shall come to save this place

although not from us

for us

although stranger we shall know him

by the way his power flows in the time of creating

his strength shall come from within

and protection from the Artist's minion

then shall the darkness be broken

and once more the light of creation

shine on the barren plain

A cold rock formed in Ben's stomach. Something in this touched him, and he didn't know why. He studied the paper in an attempt to catalogue it logically, trying to avoid the emotional reaction.

The text was like something out of the book of Kells. Gold leaf, although dulled with time and folding, glimmered in dots and on crinkled capitals outlined in lapis blue. On the right of the page, a stylized hawk soared majestically from the palm of an open hand. *What does this have to do with me?* Ben reread the text for the third time. *And why are my hands shaking?* He stood up and found the minstrel without the help of his eyes.

"Connor!" Ben heard himself bark and stopped, trying to calm at least his voice. "What's this about? What does it have to do with me?" *And why does it feel so…real?*

The minstrel squinted at Ben, gauging his reaction. He appeared to be satisfied. "Look, kid. I don't know who you are or what you can do." The minstrel paused, tried to sound reasonable. "But you're the One."

Ben looked at him, confused. Was that sarcasm or regret in the man's eyes? "I'm the One." Ben felt the truth even as he said it, even though he didn't know just what it meant. "And what are you?"

The minstrel dropped his head back to stare at the sky, clearly holding his feelings in check. He saw something high above, and abruptly his expression changed. A harsh laugh escaped before he turned, giving a shrill whistle. Ben took a step backward, trying to figure out how he could get to his sword from here. He glanced to his knapsack and back just in time to see Connor raise his left arm straight out from the shoulder.

A flurry in the leaves high above preceded a dark missile that dropped like a stone toward the minstrel's head. Ben had jerked forward instinctively to push Connor out of the way when the missile banked, broad wings outstretched, and landed gracefully on the leather gauntlet at Connor's wrist. Ben gasped, stepping back. Connor turned to look Ben in the eye.

"I suppose it makes me the Hawk."

Ben stared for a moment at Connor, then at the red-tailed hawk perched regally on his arm, which looked huge at close range. Clearing his throat made an extraordinarily loud noise in the suddenly hushed wood. "She's beautiful," he said in a halting voice. "Is she yours?" The minstrel shook his head, and Ben exhaled in exasperation, his hands outstretched. "Connor, you've got to help me here. I don't know what's going on."

The minstrel stroked the bird's chest lightly with the back of his hand. "This is W'kai." She looked fearlessly at Ben, with an expression strangely similar to the man who held her. "Old language. Kai means 'messenger', and the prefix connects it to the one God. The *Artist*." Ben's brow furrowed as he looked down at the paper still clutched in his hand. "Birds of prey are special messengers. You can see." The minstrel's free hand pointed at the page.

The actor's gaze was thoughtful when he lifted his eyes once more. "And the *Artist's minion*?"

Connor and the hawk both regarded him gravely, but said nothing.

"I see," Ben said, afraid he actually did. He turned, stepping away emotionally as well as physically. "So. You're the Hawk, the Artist's minion, who will protect the One." Ben said it calmly, as if it made perfect sense, as if it were the kind of thing he said every day. "Me." The minstrel nodded.

"As far as I can tell, yes." Connor stroked the bird once more, and then, with a quiet word and an upswing of his arm, sent W'kai flying.

"You're joking."

"You don't believe that. You know yourself better than that."

Ben shook his head and held his hands up, fencing himself off. "Connor, look. I'm no savior. I'm a good actor, I'm a decent person, I think. But –" He looked around abruptly. "I should be getting home. I don't see what I can do here."

"Neither do I." Ben's eyes snapped back to him in surprise. "But I *know* that you're the One. You know it too, somehow, or you wouldn't be here. Here we can make a difference." He dropped to one knee and pulled the sword from Ben's knapsack. "We can do things here."

"Christ, I'm no warrior, Connor. I don't have it in me." Benjamin found himself nearly shouting while somewhere in the back of his mind, Hotspur bristled. The minstrel rose and stalked the distance between them until their chests were a mere hand's-breadth apart.

"I think you're missing the *point*," he said, his voice dropping to a growl. "Tell me. Did you have that sword before?"

Ben gave ground a step, frowning, and braced himself to look. The intricate metalwork, the fineness of the chain. It was beautiful. It was his. "No. Well, I had a sword, but -" he stopped. "But I only imagined one like this."

"Right. And I only imagined *really* being able to touch someone's mind with a song." Connor stepped back and tossed the sword to Ben, who caught it like it was part of him. "I'm guessing you were as frustrated as I was. As fed up with how things were. I'm telling you that things can happen here," he gestured at the sword. "And we can do more than most."

Ben stared at the weapon in his hand for a long breath. Then, lifting his eyes to the minstrel, he touched the blade lightly to his forehead and whipped it down in salute.

He turned to walk toward the water, his left hand brushing the glass of his pendant against his chin as he looked down at his reflection in the stream. For some reason, he was almost sure he would see someone else. He glanced back towards the minstrel.

"You realize I have no idea what I'm getting into."

"Probably more than you imagine." Connor stepped up and put his hand on Ben's shoulder. "But all you have inside is more than you will ever need." Searching the actor's eyes he added, softly, "Believe."

3

"Connor." Ben brushed a fly from his horse's neck, his voice weary. "How much farther?"

The minstrel glanced over his shoulder and slowed his horse. "Why, you getting anxious?"

Ben looked dourly at him, refusing to be baited. "Actually," he said, shifting in the saddle, "I'm a little out of practice. And hungry. Can we take a break?"

Connor considered. "Yeah. There's the remains of an old cabin along here somewhere. Shouldn't be far. Not much there, but it's flat. We'll eat something."

It was their third day out. They had been traveling since daybreak up a small stream that eventually ran into the brook they had camped beside that first morning. Without recent rain the stream was tiny above ground, vanishing in places only to reappear when the trail dipped down. At times it seemed to exist only to define the gently winding path between tree-covered hills that rose steeply from it, limiting their view of the sky to a long blue corridor.

As Connor had predicted the valley ahead broadened a bit, and halfway up the hill on their left a broken stone foundation wall surrounded a mossy flagstone floor. It was only about four by five paces, but flat and dry. They scrambled up the slope, scavenged some wood for a fire, and put water on for tea.

Ben used the time to stretch his aching muscles, and after avoiding it, tried working with his sword. The metaphysical strangeness of the weapon gave way to sheer enjoyment when he used it. Almost as if it was - he shook his head at the thought - made for him. He'd used real swords before, but none compared to the balanced perfection of the weapon of his imagination. After a while he stopped to breathe, looking at Connor. "You know, sometimes I feel like I've been here before."

Connor looked up from his guitar case, startled. "You mean Taela?"

"No, I mean… this life. Didn't you ever start doing something and feel like it was too easy? Like you'd done it before?"

Connor smirked as he picked his guitar. "Yeah, but I don't buy the reincarnation bit. Too pat. Too easy."

Benjamin considered the minstrel for a moment. "So what *do* you believe?"

For a long moment the minstrel looked past Ben into the trees. "I *believe* that there's a perri tree back there. You should grab a couple." His expression made it clear that this was the only answer Ben was likely to get. Leaving it for the moment, Ben began to turn toward the trees and stopped.

"I have one problem with that," he said. "I have no idea what 'perri' look like." He paused as he looked at the musician, folding his arms on his chest. "And since you know what they are…"

The minstrel looked up again, his eyes a more mossy brown in the sunlight. "I'm warding. Protection is my job, remember?"

Benjamin tilted his head sideways and peered at this strange man that had become his companion. "Warding," he said quietly. "I've heard of that." Connor tipped his head dismissively. "You're doing it now?"

"I *believe*," the minstrel paused on the word, drawing it out as he played, "that I am."

"How?"

"By trying to create a safe place around us. By… believing."

Ben watched in silence. Then he squatted across the fire from Connor, watching the minstrel pick unconsciously at the guitar as he stared into the trees.

"Is the power in the instrument or the music? Do you use words?"

A breeze flew in to fan the flames and then left again, pausing only to artistically ruffle their hair.

"Guitar came with me," the minstrel muttered. "So not that. Most of the music did, too, though I've found more since I got here." He shrugged before going on, reluctantly. "Frankly, I think the power is in *me*, and whatever control I have of that power comes from creating. Whatever works to bring it out, works," he shrugged. "Maybe." He paused and stretched his hands, shaking them out and taking a sip of tea before he started playing again. "Music and lyrics work together for me, usually." Ben watched him curiously.

"But you've made things happen?"

"With either." He stared past Ben with flat, distant eyes.

"Does it matter what you're playing? What the subject is?"

"Not so I've noticed. If I feel it, I can make things happen." Then, with a sudden and unexpected sparkle, he smiled. "First time scared the hell out of me."

Ben looked from the minstrel to the sword in his hand, and laid it carefully across his knapsack. "I know what you mean." Standing and stretching, the actor turned back toward the trees. The hill rose steeply again from the foundation's landing, but was thick enough with saplings that climbing was no problem, as long as he didn't depend on solid footing in the slippery layer of decaying leaves. As he started to climb he heard Connor's guitar again behind him. Then his voice.

"Pomegranates."

Ben turned, sliding a foot downhill and nearly losing his balance. "What?"

"Perri. They look like pomegranates, only bigger. And these should be more yellow."

Ben shook his head, a breathy laugh escaping. "Thanks."

The tree in question was scattered with softball-sized fruit that did indeed look like oversized pomegranates. He picked a few that he hoped were ripe as he called down to Connor.

"You know, the first time I saw one of these, a real pomegranate, I mean, I told my grandfather that someone was trying to sell fake apples." A movement caught his eye and Ben looked higher up the hillside, not sure if it was a deer or something else. Setting the fruit down at the base of the tree, he worked his way higher up, not noticing that the music had stopped.

"Ben!"

The sudden cry made Ben spin around, his fingers slipping as he lost his grip on the sapling he had been holding. As he slid he saw Connor braced against a tree staring up the hill, an arrow at the ready. It was the last thing Ben registered before he ungraciously slammed to a stop behind the bulk of a fallen tree trunk. He heard *thwp* and *thwp* again, followed by a crashing noise higher up the hill.

Ben scrambled to his knees, hanging on to the log. "Christ, Connor. You didn't have to kill it. You almost scared the-" the actor stopped short as he noticed his view of the minstrel was partially obscured by an arrow imbedded in the other side of the fallen tree. It wasn't one of Connor's. The minstrel's arrows were fletched in black, and this one was mottled brown. Ben stared at it. Then he stood unsteadily and looked at Connor, who was panting as if he had just finished running a marathon.

"Shit." The minstrel clutched his abdomen and leaned back into the tree. After taking a few deep breaths, he turned toward Ben with concerned eyes.

"You all right?"

"I'm fine. You?"

"Yeah." Connor slung the bow over his shoulder and worked his way up the hill, Ben following behind. They came to a crushed brake of undergrowth and the crumpled body of a man, a bow still clutched in his hand. On the ground next to him was a quiver of five arrows, and when Connor carefully pulled one out, its point glistened a sickly green. The minstrel nudged the figure over with his boot. Protruding a good two inches from the man's back was the point of Connor's arrow.

Benjamin stared in shock. "That's a hell of a bow."

"Shit," Connor repeated softly.

"Do you know who is he?"

"I met him. Once." Connor picked up the green-stained arrow, smelled the tip and drew back sharply. "Veridin. Poison."

"But you know him?"

"We disagreed about something."

"Must have been a hell of a disagreement. He was trying to kill you!"

"I doubt it."

"Seriously? He's hiding in the woods with poisoned arrows, and you think he was what, trying to scare you?"

"No."

"Then what? Look, Connor, you're not making -" Ben stopped as another possibility seeped slowly into his consciousness, reinforced by the minstrel's steady gaze. He looked down at the body, and back up to Connor, who looked older somehow then he had before. "Not you. Not trying to kill *you*. It's me, isn't it?"

Connor gave a weary sigh. "There are some people who don't believe the One is a good idea. Who think the whole legend is-"

"It's me," Ben cut him off, "It's me he wanted to kill, because - anything to stop me." The momentum of his feelings had his emotions spinning out of control. "This is *insanity*. Get me *back home*." The actor's eyes were wide.

"Look, Ben -"

"Take me back! I'm don't know what they think I am, but they're wrong. I'm just a man, I'm an actor, damn it, not a-" he stopped, slumped against a tree as adrenaline collected its toll. The dead body of his would-be assassin lying so close brought bile to his throat, and he swallowed hard. "I want to go home. Please."

The minstrel's voice was uncommonly gentle. "Ben -"

"No." The actor slid down the tree as his knees gave out, his hands held out as a shield. "Please. I just want to go home."

"Stop. Damn it, you knew this was serious when I called. You *must* have." He paused, looking away from the nearly weeping boy.

"And I don't even know if I can get you home." When the actor made no response, Connor squatted down next to him and spoke more quietly. "Listen to that part of you that believed from the beginning."

"People want to kill me, Connor!"

"Knock it off. There're crazy people everywhere, you know that. Even back home. Maybe more so back home." Connor took a breath. "This guy's a renegade. You're not alone in this. Just settle down for a minute." Gradually, more out of habit than effort, Ben found himself centering as Connor went on.

"Somewhere in your mind is a door, and everything you believe is stored behind it. Everything you've ever known about yourself, all the potential that would overwhelm you in everyday life. If you look behind that door, you'll know if this is part of your path."

Ben pressed his palms into his eyes and shook his head. *Still… there was that familiar room from his dreams… and doors. All the doors, all the choices. And suddenly, the sword that hung on the wall seemed more important…* After a slow minute he took a deep breath and exhaled carefully. He looked at the minstrel, then rubbed his palms against his face and back through his hair. Connor sat down beside him and they remained silent in their thoughts for several minutes.

"So." Ben said quietly. "If this is part of my path, I can just imagine trying to forage through the rough." Connor shrugged, broke the twig he was absently worrying. "I don't know, Con. But… something about this feels like… I don't know. I'll play it out for a while, anyway. See where the story's going."

Connor gave half a grin and helped Ben to his feet. "We'll make it through this," he said, meeting the younger man's eyes.

"Or die trying."

Connor considered for a moment and shrugged. Then, looking down at their attacker, he added, "But not today." Bending toward the still body, he placed his palm over the man's chest. "I release you," he said in a whisper. Ben felt an unusual shifting of energy, and took a step backward.

"Are you sure he's the only one?"

Connor straightened up and shook his head. "No. Let's eat while we ride. There's a village a few hours off." He laughed humorlessly. "So much for resting the horses."

Ben moved unsteadily down the hill. "So much for resting the riders." Halfway down, he stopped, sliding a few feet before he turned back to Connor. "What ever happened to the wards? I thought they kept danger away."

"Away? Nah." Connor frowned as he passed. "Not all the time. But I knew he was there, didn't I?"

In ten minutes time they were packed and back on their horses, riding hard upstream out of the valley. The steep rise of the hills that seemed so idyllic to Ben an hour before now glowered with potential dangers at every pass.

After a half hour of pushing their mounts, the valley broadened into a wide clearing around a narrow waterfall, a white ribbon of water that spilled thirty feet before curling into foam in a gently cupped basin. They stopped at its base, watered the horses and shared one of the perri. Then they rode for ten minutes along the base of the escarpment, coming to a steep but negotiable trail that wound back and forth up the hill. They led the horses to the top rather than ride, and Ben's tension slowly leveled off with the landscape. In two more hours they were riding across a grassy plain, in the company of grazing cattle.

Ben pulled his horse up alongside Connor and they slowed to a walk before he gave a rueful chuckle. Connor turned to him and frowned. "What?"

"I feel like I'm surfing."

"Never tried it."

"I only got it right this one time. There was this incredible wave. I knew, once I was on it, that it could kill me. I mean, I *knew* it. But by then there was no choice but to ride it out or be dead quick." Ben looked at Connor. "You know what I mean?"

Connor looked into the distance, squinted at the far-off trees. "You could have done both."

Ben rolled his eyes. "Thanks for the vote of confidence," he said, matching the minstrel's tone so closely that Connor grinned in spite of himself.

After a few minutes of walking the horses, the sound of chimes tinkling gently in the breeze wafted toward them.

"What's that?" Ben asked.

"Overlook." The minstrel spurred his horse on, and Ben had no choice but to follow in his wake, wondering who or what this Overlook was.

4

The pair rode in the shadow of tall trees that bordered the pasture until a wide pathway opened, then picked their way along a mud-churned trail that was apparently used to move cattle. After a few soggy minutes, Connor turned them onto a narrow path that snaked between the trees before dismounting briefly to open a gate, putting them on a firmer road.

"So. This is Overlook." Ben's terse tone didn't seem to faze the minstrel.

"Yeah."

Ben reined his horse to a stop. "Connor."

The minstrel looked back, raised an eyebrow, and turned his mount so they could talk face to face. "What's up?"

Ben shook his head and smiled thinly. "That's my line. Can you say why we're here? Or am I still flying blind?"

Connor spit the dust from his mouth. "I thought it was surfing." Looking annoyed at Ben's expression, he shrugged. "This is a good stopping place. What's the problem?"

The actor barked out a short breath. "Gee, Connor, I don't know. Maybe today I'm crazy enough to be worried about going into a strange town. Maybe, and here's a laugh, I'm afraid of getting *killed*."

Ben's voice rose, and by the end of his speech had shifted from sarcasm to panic. The sudden release of emotion surprised them both.

Ben could feel the minstrel's guard go up like an iron gate. His horse, sensing the sudden tension, stomped its feet and whinnied.

"Sorry." Ben closed his eyes and took a deep breath, pushing the image of *himself* dead in the woods away yet again. "I'm not used to this."

There was a loaded pause as the minstrel shook his head. "And you think I am." Connor drew his horse closer to Ben. "I may have stronger feelings about this little adventure than you right now, but I'm not blind. I'm as mortal as you are. Maybe more so." Ben opened his mouth to speak but the minstrel cut him off with a sharp wave, eyes glittering. "At least you didn't have to kill anyone. Yet."

With a cold stare he turned and galloped toward the town, shrouded in a cloud of dust. Startled, Ben took a moment to collect himself. Then he kicked his horse to a gallop, calling the minstrel to wait. By the third try he was too close to ignore. "Connor!"

The minstrel slowed, stopped. "What now?"

"You never killed anyone before."

Connor stared into the wood and exhaled briskly. "You sound surprised."

"No. Well," Ben struggled for words, gave up and started over. There was no comfortable way to say it. "You looked… it seemed so…"

The steel flashed in Connor's eyes before he dropped his head and gave a short, bitter laugh. "What, easy? Did it look that way?" He pulled at the lacing of his shirt and looked into the trees, focusing as far away as possible. "I did what I had to do."

Ben stared at the man before him, who had abruptly become a stranger once more. With sudden comprehension he dismounted and slowly walked the few steps between them. He stared up at the minstrel before extending his hand.

"Thank you," he said, "for saving my life."

There are moments on stage when an actor opens himself completely. When it is so clear that his soul is exposed and undefended, people in the audience will gasp without knowing why. When it's honest, it can be devastating.

Occasionally it happens off stage as well.

Connor's focus returned to Ben, unflinchingly connecting with the intensity of the actor's expression. Slowly, he reached out and grasped the outstretched hand.

A shimmer in the air around them went unnoticed until it had blossomed into a faint blue-green aura that encompassed their hands, continuing to expand outward in a slowly fading spherical wave. When it met the trees they stirred as if in a breeze.

What was that? Ben thought as the sensation faded.

"That was power," Connor said. He released Ben's hand and looked around as the wave dispersed.

"What did you say?" Ben's mind raced, out of gear. "Were you answering me?"

"What?"

"I didn't say anything out loud." Uncertain fear thrilled through him. "Can you hear me thinking?"

Connor stopped for a moment, tilted his head. An expression came to his eyes that Ben didn't recognize, but might have been surprise. "I guess I did." He squinted appraisingly and then peaked his eyebrows. "We must have connected."

"Connected?"

"Yeah. People who are aware of the energy, who can use it… sometimes they call it that. It's one of the things that Alious is doing, only he's, well… using *people*."

"Alious." Ben felt hair rising on the back of his neck as the name slipped over his tongue, and turned instinctively to see if anyone was behind him. "Alious," he said again, tasting the word. "He's the one I'm supposed to stop." Connor nodded, looking thoughtful but not surprised. "Why do I feel that?"

The minstrel shook his head. "People here would say that the Artist wouldn't send you unprepared."

"Who?"

"The Artist. The Creator. *God*. Come on. The town's only about twenty minutes from here. We'll talk while we ride."

Ben swung back up onto his horse. *I may need more than twenty minutes for this.* Then he shot a quick look at Connor, who gave no indication that he had heard anything. The minstrel set the pace at a slow walk and Ben took a deep breath, trying to relax.

"I will try," Ben said, "to ask one question at a time."

"Fair enough."

"That glow, or whatever we felt -" he looked up suddenly. "You saw it, didn't you?" The minstrel nodded impatiently and Ben continued. "You called it power. I don't know what you mean."

"Yeah, you do." Connor paused as Ben looked exasperated. "You've felt it, I'm sure of that. You just haven't *seen* it before because where we come from, the power's diluted. We don't believe. We push to make things happen and there's no guarantee anything will actually change. Not even a hint. That's why so many people give up." He shook his head and looked at the actor. "It doesn't mean the energy isn't there.

"People who use it tend not to think about it at all. That is, until a moment when something important is at stake, and you put all of yourself into it." He paused and stretched his neck, unaccustomed to long speeches. "Some might call it 'heart'.

"Back there, it was important to you that I understood how you felt." He shot a look at his companion. "What we saw was spillover, I guess, of the power that was more than enough. And could be why we connected without trying."

Ben nodded, and rode in the silence of his thoughts. *I don't know if I actually want to try, then...* He glanced at Connor again, then shook his head.

The road became smoother, and a few villagers appeared along the way. Ben heard a young voice yell, 'They're here!', as a boy of perhaps nine swarmed down from a treetop lookout, excitement bursting from every pore. "Hawk!"

"Hey, buddy, how's it going?" Connor grinned and reached down to ruffle the boy's hair. Ben watched, curious.

The group of villagers grew as they drew closer what appeared to be a well at the center of town. Hanging from the support over it were a row of shining metal bars in graduated lengths that chimed softly in the breeze; a man from the crowd grabbed a stick, running it across the bars several times in an obvious, although strangely musical, signal.

The minstrel appeared completely relaxed in the midst of the chaos. The actor tried to follow Connor's lead, but felt like he had walked into a scene from someone else's play. *Too many people, and I don't know any of them!* When they finally reached the well, Connor swung down and walked through the crowd into the welcoming embrace of an older, bearded man. They spoke quietly for a moment before Connor clambered up onto the well's edge, his hand sweeping toward Ben.

"People. This is Benjamin Agante. The One." He stared toward a few reluctant faces in the back of the group, and his voice hardened. "As I promised."

Ben felt more nervous in front of a crowd than he had since he was a freshman in high school. Drawing on years of experience, he straightened his spine and focused on appearing confidant and at ease. Acting came in very handy when his emotions were screaming.

While he tried to look calm, a girl of no more than fifteen stepped up to Ben's horse, looking nervous but determined. Ben recognized the brightness of her eyes and the speed of her breathing and gave her a tight smile, one panic to another. Taking a stone cup from the edge of the well, she filled it, bowed over it, and carefully handed it to Ben. Then she began to sing.

It was glorious. He didn't understand the language but he could tell, somehow, that she was singing about him. About the One. Legends unfolded in her melody as the people around her reacted with wistful smiles and tears. As the last note faded away on the breeze, he lifted the cup toward her in tribute, and drank the sweet water in one go.

Dismounting, he took the girl's hand and formally brushed a kiss over it. "Thank you."

The girl, who was positively glowing with relief at this point, made a low bow to Ben and pushed falling strands of dark hair back from her face. "In the Artist's name, we welcome you to Overlook. I am Aletia."

Ben nodded at her practiced formality. "Aletia. I'm Benjamin Agante," he leaned closer and whispered conspiratorially in her ear, "but you can call me Ben."

Her eyes widened, and she nearly giggled. Looking into his clear blue gaze she impulsively, "Can you really help us?"

Ben heard the collective murmur of the people near enough to hear her question. He looked at the nervous, hopeful faces that surrounded him, then back at Aletia.

He bowed his head gently. "I'll do what I can," he said in a quiet voice. "I promise." For a shining moment, even he believed.

"Ben." The actor turned to Connor and the older man with him. "This is Taas. He's leader here." Ben nodded, not sure of how to greet the head of the village. Sensing his uncertainty, Taas reached out and when Benjamin did likewise, they grasped forearms instead of shaking hands.

"Welcome, Benjamin," he said, clapping his other hand on Ben's shoulder. "It would be an honor to have you in my home. The two of you must be hungry after your journey."

Ben blinked, and his stomach registered its vote. "That would be great."

The road to Taas' house was busy with people. Many of them pushed forward only to nervously back off once more before the Hawk's forceful glance. Taas walked at a slower pace behind Connor and next to Benjamin, not even trying to talk amidst the crowd. His silent presence was comforting for Ben, who attempted to look confident until they reached the leader's house. Once there, the door shut safely behind him, Ben let out an audible sigh of relief. He wasn't sure why he felt safe here, but the change was so welcome that he didn't care to question it.

The cool shadows of the grey fieldstone house felt quite dark compared with the raw sunlight outside. As Ben's eyes adjusted, they were greeted by a woman with silvered auburn hair and a warm smile. Taas kissed her, and the expression they exchanged told of a lifetime together.

"This is Ahna. My partner." With an affectionate smile he added, "Ahna listens."

Feeling like there was a response expected, Ben glanced at Connor, who nodded. He bowed low and took Ahna's hand. "Thank you for taking us in. I suspect it is no small inconvenience."

The woman's mouth pursed in what Ben guessed was an attempt not to laugh, the kind of expression an adult might take with a child who is trying very hard to be polite.

"It's no bother." Her hand reached out instinctively to ruffle his hair and stopped just short, touching his cheek instead with strong, gentle fingers. Ben found himself liking this couple on instinct, although there was a curious intensity to Ahna's gaze, one that made Ben step away, ostensibly to look around the room.

As his eyes adjusted to the dim light, Ben saw carvings of a reddish wood in various niches around the open main room. Some of them apparently used two woods together and looked more alive than not, entwined in impossible positions, as if they had grown that way. He turned to Ahna, still feeling slightly self-conscious. "Is this your work?" He knew it was part of her, but he couldn't explain why.

Ahna stared at Benjamin with warm, green-brown eyes, as if she was waiting for the result of some test. After a moment she nodded, and said, "Yes." Then she stepped forward and hugged him like his grandmother used to. For a moment Ben was overcome by a wave of homesickness for a house, and a place that no longer existed. She smiled, her hands on the sides of his face, and looked into his eyes before a small frown creased her brow.

"You need rest. And food. Wash the road away and we'll have a meal." Looking at Connor, she made a *tsking* noise and shook her head. "You too." Her hand rested on his cheek affectionately for a moment and he smiled, a more open smile than Ben had seen on the minstrel. "Go." She motioned toward a basin and pitcher on the far end of the room, and Ben obediently walked over to do as she said. Halfway there he realized he was smiling broadly.

The noon meal was more like a dinner, and afterwards the group sat in back of the house on smoothly worn wooden benches. Directly in front of them was a large herb garden wound with flagstone paths.

"Was the journey difficult for you?" Taas refilled Ben's goblet with the garnet-red perri wine as he spoke.

Ben smiled ironically at the older man and laughed, more air than sound. "You mean besides getting shot at?"

Taas shook his head as he sipped his wine. "I mean the first journey," he paused and looked at Ben once more. The clear pale blue of his eyes seemed to see through him. "The one that brought you to Taela."

Ben stood uncomfortably and looked out across the trees, which were swaying gently in the breeze. The rising scent of lavender and sage tickled at his nose. Part of his mind seemed determined to forget that he was not from this place, that he had a normal life back home. *Back home.* An oak sapling on the garden edge pointedly dropped an acorn onto the path ahead of him. He shook his head and thoughts back into place. *A scene, that's it. Think of it as a scene that happened to a character you were playing. That, you can handle.* He took a deep breath to center himself and looked through the memory of the last few days.

"It was all right once it began. The hard part was before. Connor was calling and, well, I didn't know what was going on." Ben sighed, his blue eyes darker in the afternoon sun. "This kind of thing doesn't happen where I come from."

Taas looked up at Ben with a mischievous grin. "But it did, didn't it?"

Ben gave a short laugh and yawned. "'S'cuse me. Yeah, I guess it did." He looked down at the wine in his glass with a frown. "Is this perri too? It's stronger than what Connor was carrying."

Taas nodded, holding the glass up in the slanting sunshine to examine the ruby glow of it. "There are three kinds of perri - topaz, garnet and sapphire. Topaz wine is common, garnet more respectable for friends and family. Sapphire is most rare, because the sapphire perri are hard to grow. Even Ahna has only managed to grow one on our land, and she can plant a pebbles to harvest boulders." He smiled at his wife when she laughed. "Truly gifts of the Artist."

Ben frowned hazily. "Sapphire wine? Is it really blue?" Somehow the image made him chuckle.

Ahna got up and moved toward the house. "All right, you two. That's enough for now. Benjamin, Connor, you need some rest if you're joining the circle tonight." She was the first person in the village that Ben heard use Connor's given name.

His thoughts became more sluggish as the food and wine settled in for a rest. Without quite realizing it, he followed Ahna inside, and into a smaller room of the house. There were two low beds made up there, and Ben was quick to flop down on the nearest one. He was only vaguely aware of gentle hands covering him with a warm quilt, and quiet, gentle humming as he drifted off to sleep.

He woke to the rustling sounds of Connor dressing. For a moment he felt the disorientation that accompanied waking in a strange place; then he remembered, and sighed. As he stirred, Connor turned toward him, tying the lacing at the neck of his shirt.

"Better get moving. The circle starts at moonrise."

"The circle?"

"Yeah." Without elaborating, Connor walked out of the bedroom.

"Thanks," Ben called after him sarcastically. The quilt over him was soft and warm, and smelled lightly of rosemary, a quiet echo of the garden outside. He took a deep breath and heard a knock on the doorway. "Yeah?"

Ahna looked around the door. "Benjamin. The circle -"

" - Starts at moonrise, got it," he finished her sentence dourly.

She tipped her head down at him, giving him a gently reproving look. "Yes, it does. If you need to prepare, you might want to start now."

Ben frowned as she started to walk away. "Ahna?" She turned back to him and walked into the bedroom, sitting comfortably on the edge of the bed. She smoothed his hair with maternal ease as she leaned closer to study him.

"You look troubled."

"Well, I am." He decided it was not nerves as much as feeling unprepared. He knew the difference between the nervous excitement of going on and the sickly anxiety of not knowing all his lines when he should. This was definitely the latter. He paused and waited for the words to come. "What is this circle? How can I prepare when I don't know what it is?"

Ahna took a deep breath and watched him for a moment. "Benjamin. I can't pretend to understand everything that's happening. It wouldn't be true, and wouldn't be fair." She stopped and her smile became more solemn. "But I have faith in this creation. I feel the rightness of you being here. And I know," she said, rising from the bed, "that no one is going to be able to tell you why the Artist wants you here now, or what you are supposed to do - not even Connor, for all his talents, because only the Artist knows that." She paced over to the window and pulled back the curtain, letting the soothing dim light of dusk into the room.

"Right." Ben shook his head and motioned helplessly. "But what am I supposed to do?"

Even though she wore smudged working clothes, simple leggings and a loose tunic, she swept back to the bed in an amazingly graceful way, with a posture that spoke more of ruling than gardening. "You must do what you do." It seemed to make perfect sense to her, but he frowned in confusion.

"And that would be...?"

His comment made her laugh in delight, like a mother reacting to an infant's far too adult expression. Catching herself, she stopped and stared at him. "For creation's sake, Benjamin. What do you do?"

"You mean - for a living?"

She shook her head thoughtfully. "No. That doesn't feel right. What makes you alive? What makes you feel most like yourself," she struggled to find a way to explain. Her hands danced in front of her until they posed as if they were holding a mallet and chisel. She looked at them and smiled as she recognized the position. "Like you're a tool being used for the right purpose?"

Ben stared. She was looking at him like he should know how to respond, and it didn't make sense. It was like - "Acting." The word came out without him thinking.

"Acting?" Ahna looked at him curiously.

"Acting. It's what I do. Creating a character is the most satisfying thing…" The expression on her face told him she didn't quite understand. "You must have actors here."

She seized the pause. "No. What's an 'actor'?"

Ben stopped. How could she not know what an actor was? *They must call it something else.* But that's not what he felt when he looked at her. There was more going on than that… and a creeping dread that climbed strangely through his chest. Something that had used the moment of his confusion.

"Benjamin?"

He was barely aware that he had moved to the window and was staring out at the gathering darkness. Feeling like something in the darkness had entered his mind.

Yes, the something said, in rolling, deep tones. *You should forget this insanity and go home. I will help you escape.*

Ben startled at the clarity of the voice. Stronger than Connor ever was, it pulled hard at his mind, dragging him toward something dark and vast, but a gentle hand on his shoulder pulled Ben back in the direction of reality. He turned his head slowly to look at the hand, then let his eyes travel up the arm to a shoulder, a neck, a face with eyes that seemed to look through him and into his pain. Slowly he felt calm settle over his fears. The *something* faded reluctantly to the perimeter of his mind.

"I'm sorry, Benjamin," Ahna said quietly. "You can't give in to fear." Her eyes softened as she felt him regain control. Ben wondered how much she could sense of what had just happened to him, but the moment was already fading.

"I'm not familiar with your creating, but there's much in creation I'm not aware of." She smiled, projecting her own calm onto him. "Tell me what it's like, where you're from, to be an actor."

Benjamin stared at her. He felt the pressure of the last few days. He felt the burden of expectation coming from all around him. And he felt the lingering sensation of a strange darkness in his mind. Looking into her calm, hazel eyes, he shook his head and exhaled a laugh.

"Actually, it's a lot like this whole trip feels. We call it living truthfully in imaginary circumstances. It's pretending. Becoming someone else, using a personality -"

Ahna's eyes widened. "A soul-shifter?" There was an ominous sound to what she said, and Ben was sure that whatever a soul-shifter was, he didn't want to be one.

"I don't think so," he said carefully. "Nothing that dismal-sounding. Actors entertain people, educating or challenging their way of thinking. We try to open people's minds to other realities," he said, shrugging in resignation, "most of our creating is figuring out how to do it well." Ben shifted uneasily. "What's a soul-shifter do?"

Ahna seemed torn between telling him and not wanting to discuss it at all. Her calmer sense finally won out. "This is difficult."

"Look, if you don't want to talk about it..."

"No, you need to know. I'm surprised Connor didn't tell you about this." Her eyes widened. "Does he know that you're an - actor?"

"I think so. Yeah."

Taking a deep breath, she closed her eyes and made several fluid hand movements that were similar to the gestures she had made earlier. While his eyes couldn't interpret them, something inside of him felt it. *Wards*. There was a safe space around them, and it was the most comfortable he had felt since the *something* had unsettled him. He found he was breathing more easily, and was relieved without knowing he had ever been in distress.

"What was that?"

"I'm not going to expose either one of us to these ideas without protection." She rushed on. "A soul-shifter can take someone, use their life energy, use them up without draining themselves." She barely stopped a shudder as she went on. "It's evil. To take talent without regard for the living being that they're stealing from. And Alious is the most powerful one we've ever heard of." Ben felt a familiar tingle down his spine. "His forces are taking power in this world, spreading." She paused to take another deep breath, making direct eye contact with Ben. "We've always been told that when evil walked freely in our land, the One would come. 'Not of us, but for us'-"

Ben stopped her with an outstretched hand. "So I've heard." He walked to the window and looked out over the garden, one hand on the sill, the other holding his pendant. "Tell me something." He took deep breath. "Do you really think I'm the One?"

Her voice was steady. "Yes."

He nodded, looking heavenward out into the darkness. "Great."

5

The sweet smell of damp stone tickled Ben's nose as he leaned over the waist high wall of the well. The moon had not yet risen, but the stars were shining with an intensity that seemed to indicate they were more than up to the challenge of the night alone. He watched their pinpoint reflections on the water waver as a breeze touched the surface, then heard the same breeze brush the metal chimes over his head, creating a crystalline sigh of anticipation in the soft evening air.

Taking a centering breath once more, Ben wondered if it would hold this time. He had been trying to settle himself for half an hour, and was seriously considering the possibility that he had forgotten how. *Not helpful,* he told himself. *Relax. There's not much else you can do. Actor's ready,* just like he had told Ahna later in their conversation. *Be prepared to react without having to know what you'll be reacting to.* He grinned as he finally felt the familiar sensation of that readiness sink in and surround him, always more obvious in its absence than its presence. *En Garde.*

Looking up from the water, he saw that a few people had gathered nearby, while even more were clustered beneath the huge willow. There was subdued conversation all around, but whether it was hushed out of deference to him or out of respect for the sanctity of the night and the upcoming ceremony, he didn't know.

Plucking at the shoulders of his tunic, Ben grinned in spite of himself. Ahna had insisted he change after the long trip, and he had to admit that he felt more comfortable being dressed in the same manner as the villagers. Moss green leggings were bound at the ankle by soft brown leather boots, and a matching tunic laced at the neck covered a long-sleeved creamy cotton shirt. He sighed as he looked down at himself, feeling like some other, as yet unknown character. The only thing that remained of 'Benjamin Agante' was the glass pendant, which once more caught flashes of starlight.

Ben looked for a place to stretch, something a little more private than the well at the center of town. While he had no trouble warming up in front of *civilians*, it seemed a good idea to find a quieter spot. Even in his world, people who weren't familiar with the idiosyncrasies of actors could be a little taken aback by how they worked. Walking to a grove of aspen opposite the willow, Ben began his usual routine.

Standing with his feet shoulder width apart, his head dropped forward onto his chest as his spine slowly curled over. Then he reversed the process to stand upright once more. Ben grinned at the familiar feeling - he always swore he was taller after that one. A series of odd vocalizations followed, as he warmed up his lungs and voice. He wanted to feel ready, whatever this night would bring.

Comfortable within his instrument, Ben sat against a tree, willing his mind to slow down. This was so familiar, so comforting, that part of him wished that he could just stay in this relaxed state. Indeed, if he hadn't been so relaxed, Ben might have jumped right out of his skin when he heard the voice.

"You all right?" The voice came not from in his mind, but from directly in front of him, about where someone's face would be if they were squatting down. He responded without opening his eyes.

"I'm fine. Where the hell have you been?"

"I had things to do."

"Terrific. I thank you for your confidence in me -" a derisive noise cut him off.

"You don't need my confidence. You ready? They're afraid to come anywhere near you while you're doing this stuff." The sarcasm was faint but clear. Benjamin took a deep breath and opened his eyes. Although it was dark and shadowy beneath the trees, the minstrel's eyes glimmered like stars in the well.

"Like you don't have to do anything to prepare yourself to perform."

"This isn't performing. Besides, once the guitar is tuned, I don't have to 'prepare'. That work was done long ago."

Ben shook his head. Something was bothering Connor. *It would be nice if I could trust his reactions a little more.*

I can *trust him,* something inside responded calmly, *but his actions, not his words. His words hide him.* He looked at Connor with an expression of sympathetic understanding that actually made the minstrel fidget in the darkness.

"Well, Connor, I'm just tuning myself. I'm the only instrument I have, and it can get kind of complicated in here." Not waiting for a response, the actor almost stood up before he paused, frowned, and changed the subject. "And I'm wondering. How do I ward myself?"

The minstrel blinked, and his voice became strained. "Why? Who told you that you need wards?"

"No one. I just felt a little strange, that's all. Earlier, when I was talking with Ahna. Interesting conversation, by the way."

"Always is, with her. What happened?"

"I felt like there was something, I don't know, watching me, I guess. Listening in?" Ben exhaled and shrugged. "Maybe I'm just tired -"

The minstrel reached out and put his hands on either side of Benjamin's head.

"What-?"

"Shut up." Staring into his eyes, Connor took a deep breath and seemed to be listening.

"Connor." *You're starting to scare me,* Ben almost said, but something kept him from actually doing it.

"Shut up. Please. Just think… good things. Strong, healthy things. Don't be afraid. And be quiet."

Ben frowned at the minstrel in amazement. Feeling like he'd stepped into a production of *Peter Pan,* he closed his eyes and concentrated on happy thoughts; friends he had back home, his grandparents, the show he was working on only a week ago. He thought about the song that called him here, and realized that he was hearing another one. The minstrel was singing words Ben couldn't quite understand. As he tried to keep his mind clear, the dark fog became obvious only to disappear a moment later. In its place, a pale blue-green light shone peacefully. Somehow Ben felt more unnerved than before.

"Connor?" His voice was almost a whisper. "What's happening?" He opened his eyes and saw the dark outline of the minstrel kneeling in front of him.

"My fault." The minstrel's hands slipped to Ben's shoulders. "You're strong, but you can't fight what you're not looking for." Ben felt the pressure on his shoulders increase momentarily before Connor released him. "That dark feeling. The foggy someone's watching you feeling. It's not good. Alious -"

"-Is trying to steal my soul?" Ben thought his voice didn't sound quite right. Of course, it was saying things that he never dreamed he would say outside of a rather bizarre script. The minstrel shrugged.

"I don't know about that. I do know he can take control, because I've seen it happen. And being open is good, but be careful. You're okay now. Remember how it feels." Connor's gaze dropped down to the pendent at Ben's neck. Taking it in his hand, he said, "Do you wear this all the time?"

Ben nodded shakily, and his voice matched it. "Yeah, I do. Why? Is that bad?"

Connor frowned at him in one of his more typical expressions. "Take it easy. Does it mean good things to you?"

Ben looked down at the small piece of glass. He thought about the intricate Tiffany tree that his grandmother had once told him was made by fairies. He thought about all the years he lived in the old house reading under that lamp, everything from Dr. Seuss to Shakespearean scripts. More carefully, he remembered going through the house after his grandparents were gone, and yet again after the fire. He remembered walking through the rubble with an insurance adjuster, seeing the morning light glimmer on this one piece of glass that he picked from the debris, marveling that it was unbroken, a lone survivor of all it had been part of. Somehow it had resonated with him more than he thought possible.

"Ben," the minstrel said quietly. "Feel for it. Does it have any power?"

Ben looked up from the pendant. "Yeah," he said, brushing across his eyes with his palms. "Yes. All good."

The minstrel gave him a reassuring nod. "Good. Then let's make it better."

"How? And do we have time?"

"For this, we make time." Connor sat back on his knees, still resting the pendant lightly in his right hand. "Make something."

"What do you mean?"

"Like the sword. Create."

Ben thought for a moment and shook his head. "I can't. I mean, I've got no focus. What am I trying to create?" He expected an exasperated response, but was surprised to see the minstrel look thoughtful.

"How about - something that means strength for you. Good energy. Do you have anything like that?"

Ben frowned, and hesitated for just a second before responding with something that was clearly personal. "Okay. I use an image of liquid white light when I'm centering, or trying to, well, purify myself, I guess is the idea. Something like that?" Ben waited to see if the minstrel would scoff.

"Sounds good. Make up a handful of that liquid light. Don't think, just do it." Ben shook his head and shrugged. Closing his eyes, he cupped his right hand between them. The minstrel nodded. "Go ahead." He began humming softly as Ben concentrated.

The one exercise was a manipulation of space. Use the space around you to make what you need, to help you do what you had to do. The other was recognition of the energy within, visualizing so that you were more aware of potential. Ben used the two to see in his mind his cupped hand filling with the familiar energy. His hand felt pleasantly warm where the liquid touched it.

"Good," Connor said softly, with what Ben could have sworn was respect in his voice. "Now let that get soaked up by your pendant, okay?"

Ben opened his eyes and gasped. His hand was filled with a liquid that literally brought sunlight to the space between him and Connor yet didn't hurt his hand, or his eyes. Fear tried to get hold of his mind, but awe was filling the space already. Besides, he *knew* this stuff. "This is a lot, Connor," he whispered softly. "I use this a drop at a time."

"Good. That's exactly what we're going for." Ben accepted unconsciously that the minstrel had something to do with why it had been so easy to create the energy pool. "Now just soak it up with the glass."

"Can it hold it?"

"Of course it can. Just let it."

Ben moved his cupped hand closer to the minstrel's, where his pendant laid flashing in the miniature day, leaving a crimson shadow on Connor's palm. He thought for a moment, and smiled. The liquid reared up like a leaf unfurling and leapt smoothly to the glass, running into it like water falling into a lake. He shivered at the sudden shift in energy, and blinked to re accustom himself to the night around him. He looked at Connor and shivered a laugh, unable to contain it. "Like that?"

The minstrel, out of character, laughed as well. "That would be it. Now remember what you have here, that it can protect you and keep you aware, okay?" Ben nodded. "And another thing. Anytime you have, I don't know, extra energy or any good feeling - after you're full - send it there."

The glass didn't look any different, but when the minstrel released it Ben felt it tingling against his chest. The quiet energy warmed him as he stood and began walking.

They crossed to the huge willow, which was leaning gently this way and that, whispering elaborate confidences to the wind about powers and potential. The people beneath the tree, some fifty in all, were echoing those sentiments, looking at Connor and Ben with a combination of excitement and apprehension. Aletia was there, one of the youngest of the group, and Ben smiled at her as she strained to catch his eye. Something about her shy attention reminded him of the apprentices in the park, and for a moment his thoughts flashed back toward his other life. He felt like he was dreaming. *Or maybe,* he thought as he rubbed the pendant between his fingers, *I'm finally awake.*

Quietly, Taas walked out of the shadows with a tall young man on one side and Ahna on the other. "Benjamin," Taas said, "this is Tomas. He teaches here."

Ben reached out instinctively to shake hands, but remembered and followed the teacher's lead when he grasped his forearm instead. His immediate impression was of height. The man was easily six and a half feet tall and powerfully built, yet a calm radiated from him that displaced any possibility of fear. At first glance he would have made a quite satisfactory angel Gabriel. Their eyes met and Tomas smiled. "Are you ready?"

"As ready as I'll ever be," Ben responded honestly. "Am I supposed to do anything?"

"Only what you feel is right," Tomas said. "The legends say - well, the legends say a lot of things, but they aren't specific about your first circle."

"Then this is a regular event?" Ben had been wondering about that, but wasn't sure he wanted to know the answer.

"Oh, yes," Ahna answered. "We that trust in the Artist join often to share our creating and take strength from it." She looked around the gathering fondly. "There's a story that in the beginning the Artist found this creation most frustrating. Looking into a mirror he saw his own struggle, and smashed the glass. The shards of that reflection blended with his creation to truly give it life." Turning to look at Ben, she smiled. "Every living thing carries a reflection of the Artist, and when we join those pieces, we reflect a larger image." She looked at Benjamin, placed a hand gently on his chest. "You carry a shard within you, too."

He stared at her, not knowing what to say. "Thank you."

The moon was nearly free of the horizon; faces and shadows became better defined as Taas turned in place to address the group. "May the Artist who created us protect this circle." Reaching out his hands, he added. "We begin."

The community formed a large ring near the willow. Benjamin was relieved that they didn't ask him to take a place in the center. In fact, they didn't ask him to do anything. They seemed content to let him do wherever he wished, although he felt many eyes making sure he was there. With some relief he stood between Connor and Tomas, the minstrel once again holding his guitar.

The teacher leaned over with a whisper. "Let me know if you need anything, or if I can explain anything. I'll try." He looked intently at Ben, who nodded.

"Thanks," Ben said, and meant it. He looked around at the community and tried to figure out what they were doing. At first, all that was obvious was a certain striving for calm; stilled breathing and closed eyes. Soon, out of nowhere, a voice began. Not exactly singing, but vocalizing. Benjamin blinked. *Hey, I know this exercise.* Other voices joined in, waiting for the energy to be right, waiting for the proper moment of unity.

It was always fascinating for Ben to see a freshman class do this exercise, because it made them realize that there was a connection between people that was innate, waiting to be used. This circle already knew. Voices began to branch off into intricate melodies, harmony and counterpoint to each other, instinctively knowing when to step forward and when to back away. It was a dance.

The guitar began before Ben realized Connor had moved. Some of the villagers had small drums, and at least one played a wooden flute.

Ben joined in without realizing exactly when he started. He opened his eyes for a moment, and stared in surprise. A soft blue light was bathing the circle, giving the moon an azure halo. He closed his eyes again and found he was overflowing with the joy of the moment, laughing with delight, and even his laughter was woven into the tapestry of sound when the feeling was picked up by those around him.

A crisp run in G made him open his eyes. The minstrel had somehow shifted from accompanying to leading in easy steps. Fascinated, Ben watched as Connor centered the faint glow of the circle, eyes closed and lips twitching as if he had to call upon certain notes and chords to appear personally. Driving rhythms pulled the group until their own momentum carried them, then he would settle back, sweeter, softer lines supporting them gently.

The minstrel amazed him. Ben had experience with the magic of performing, and he knew the best times involved a reciprocation of energy, the audience giving as much to the performer as the performer did to the audience. That was the case tonight - no line between energies, only a constant tidal flow between parts of the circle, individuals, and somehow, tempering and adding to it, the moon. He reveled in it.

When it began to wind down there was no disappointment, just a quiet resolution among the members of the group. As voices had joined in they faded out again, sometimes with a flourish, and sometimes in a gentle hum. The air was soft and warm, and a breeze cooled them as the energy relaxed. There was a heightened awareness, an openness that was almost physical in nature. Ben exhaled slowly and wondered how long he had been holding his breath. It was glorious, it was wonderful, it was drawing to a close but not yet ended.

In the quiet, not quite finished moments of the joining, a flute began to play. Alone, in a haunting minor key, it led the circle somewhere else.

Benjamin frowned.

This was different, and didn't feel right. He opened his eyes and saw the minstrel putting his guitar down, grabbing something in the darkness. *Darkness?*

A dark fog was settling over the circle, swirling to the rhythm of the haunting music. Most of the villagers had their eyes closed, were still being led by the lone flute. The minor key evolved into something thicker, something that clawed at the senses. A few of the people broke off, but the vast majority simply went along with the strength of the song.

In the gathering fog the minstrel brushed by Ben.

"Connor? What's going on?"

"Don't listen."

"What?"

"Don't listen. It's him." Ben realized that Connor had his bow in hand, and was listening for the source of the sound.

"Connor?" In the swirling darkness the music swelled, added to by some misled part of the circle. Ben clutched his pendant, and the smooth cool energy steadied his spirit as Ahna appeared by his side.

"Do something!" Her eyes flashed as he turned.

"Like what?" He shook his head. The flute became louder, forcing itself on their thoughts, impossibly strong for one instrument. "I don't know how."

At that moment there was a quick whirring noise, a pained cry, and sudden, dead silence. The flute had stopped, and the dark mist ebbed with the sound although it hovered around the circle still.

"Ben!"

In the shifting darkness Benjamin saw the minstrel standing over a man who had an arrow imbedded in the left side of his chest. The man was scrabbling in the dust for the fallen flute and the mist was weaving closer once more, gathering strength as it did so.

Connor motioned toward the lowering darkness. "Do something!" Ben stared at the milling confusion that the crowd had become. He saw Aletia crying over the fallen musician, the arrow bending against the ground at a sickly angle as he struggled. Confusion danced around him, people being hurt, in danger, and too many of them looking at him, expecting him to do – *something*.

Without knowing exactly what he was doing or how he was doing it, Benjamin swept his right arm into the air. He held his hand straight up, palm open, and released a shining blue-white burst of light.

The light spread like liquid energy, streaming out from his palm and arching down to the earth again in a graceful dome that completely encompassed the circle. As the dome touched down, the man who had been shot collapsed limply. For a moment the only sounds were a clean, crystalline whisper that seemed to come from the energy dome itself, and the more human noise of Aletia weeping.

Ben gaped at his creation. The soft whispering sound went well with its translucent alabaster appearance. Slowly he relaxed his arm, dropping it to his side, but the dome remained intact. With a glance he saw Tomas sitting cross-legged on the ground, and Ben knew instinctively that the teacher was supporting the creation that he had begun. Several others joined the teacher. Ben nodded gratefully as exhaustion gripped him, leaving him lightheaded.

"Ben," Connor called into the hushed air, "Get over here." Pushing dizziness aside for the moment, Ben half stumbled across the grass to where the minstrel stood. The first thing he registered was Aletia; tears falling silently down her cheeks as she cradled the musician's head in her lap. She looked at Ben, her dark eyes swimming.

"Can you help him?" Her beautiful voice was cracked and brittle. "Please. He's my brother."

Ben looked at Connor, who shook his head in resignation. "I'm lucky I didn't hit anyone else." The minstrel looked away, and Ben could feel guilt close like a curtain around him.

"Can I?"

Connor turned and frowned. "Can you what?"

"*Can* I help him?" Benjamin felt a heady surge of energy from the group surrounding him. He watched Connor as the minstrel looked down at the musician and back to Ben's eyes.

"I don't know. I think he's clear now. I mean, he's himself again, no matter what happens." Connor reached toward Ben and shook his head. "But I know him, Ben. He's a good man. If he dies… if I've killed him…" Connor looked away again, but not before Ben saw the helpless anger in his eyes.

Benjamin Agante looked down at the musician panting in the dust. He was handsome, bearded, no older than Ben, with fine dark hair swept back from a high forehead. His breath was coming in wet gasps as he lay on the ground. Ben looked at Connor again. "I have to try." His hands opened in supplication. "Can you help?"

The minstrel nodded. "I'll do what I can. What's first?"

Ben took a deep breath as he squatted down. "Watch my back."

"You got it." The minstrel traded his bow for his guitar once more, using it to pull his scattered energies into line.

Looking at Aletia, Ben spoke quietly. "What's his name?"

The girl looked at him through red-rimmed eyes, still hopeful. "Perahn." She paused and gasped out a cry. "If he-"

Ben placed his hand gently on her shoulder. "Aletia. I'm not sure what I can do. But I'll try." He paused before he went on. "Try to focus on good, give him your best energy, okay?" Without waiting for a response, Ben leaned close to the musician. "Stay with me, Per. I'm going to need your help."

Carefully, Ben ripped the bloody tunic back from the wound. It should have been a clean shot, but the skin was torn open from his struggle after the fall. Benjamin swallowed hard and took the shaft of the arrow in his hand, trying to ignore the moans coming from Perahn in semi-consciousness. "I'm sorry," he whispered. He pulled gently on the shaft, and it broke nearly flush with the skin of the musician's chest. "Damn."

Connor winced. "That has to come out."

"I know." For a moment Ben thought that he would have to give in to the protests of his stomach. Then a strange calm floated over him, enveloping him like a gossamer blanket. *I can do anything. I can feel it.* Reaching down with his fingers into the flesh of the man's chest, Ben carefully grasped the broken shaft. His attempt was thwarted by blood that was flowing freely now.

Calming himself, he managed to get a firm hold, and began to pull the broken stem out. He lost it once more when Perahn's body jerked spasmodically in revolt against the pain. Ben took a deep breath and went after it yet again, ignoring the feeling of flesh, hot against his hand, the pulsing of blood vessels against his knuckles. He almost had reestablished his grip when a hand grabbed Ben's wrist, holding him back. Ben found himself staring into dark brown eyes, pained beyond anything physical.

"I have to get this out of you."

"I know," Perahn whispered. He gasped, coughed blood, and cried out in pain at the spasm. "I'm sorry. Make sure she's all right." Benjamin shook his head.

"Work with me. Don't give up now." The musician nodded weakly and closed his eyes. He took a shaky breath, trembling against the pain.

"Yes."

With as smooth a movement as he could manage, Ben grabbed the piece of arrow and pulled it out. He could feel tissue catching and tearing, and gasped at pain he could swear he was feeling himself. Perahn held steady as long as he could, then jerked back as he cried out and lost consciousness. *Just as well,* Ben thought. He threw the broken arrow down and swallowed the emotional reaction. A ragged hole in a human being lying in front of him. Blood everywhere. On him. On Aletia. Everywhere. Perahn turning a pasty grey behind brightly contrasting smears of crimson. *What the hell are you doing? He's going to die!* Deep breaths that smell of copper and fresh meat. A look at Connor, who nods. *Center. Hang on. He needs you.* Holding a bloody hand over the oozing hole in the musician's chest, Ben tried to concentrate.

Reconstruction. Energy. Enough to remake the space under his hand. Enough to fix the lung that was surely hit, enough to reknit the muscle fibers. Enough to repair the artery that was cut nearly through. *How do I know that?* Enough to repair the shoulder blade that cracked as it stopped the arrow from going out his back and still enough left over to close the skin.

He wasn't sure where it was coming from, but knew he had control of seemingly limitless energy. It was as simple as seeing the man whole and healthy, or as complex as telling the cells what to do to make it happen. It didn't matter. When his energy had settled, and he felt the process was complete, he lifted his hand and looked at Perahn's chest. The wound was *gone.* Blood still ran down his fingers, but the wound that the blood had come from was already healed. He blinked at his hand as if it was someone else's and looked into Aletia's eyes. The expression that met his was filled with awe.

"You really *are* the One."

"I thought you knew that," he panted, nearly intoxicated with power and the sheer joy of its success. She bowed her head to kiss her brother's forehead, looking years older than she had that morning at the well.

"Thank you."

Sitting back on his knees, Benjamin looked at her brother, whose eyes were fluttering open. He was *alive*. The feeling swelled in Benjamin until he could hardly bear it. "How do you feel?"

Perahn took a deep breath, bracing against a pain that never came. "I – I'm…" He tried unsuccessfully to struggle to his feet.

"You don't have to do that," Ben said quickly. "Take it slow. You still need time."

"I'm sorry." Perahn spoke loudly enough to carry across the circle as he slumped back against Aletia. "I'm sorry."

He turned to where his flute lay, the instrument dirty and spattered with blood. Picking it up, he stared at it with utter contempt before dropping it again, looking away in disgust.

"No." Ben easily restrained him in his weakened state. "No. It's not your fault. I felt it. Don't abandon your creating." Lifting it, the actor examined the wooden tube wrapped with red fibers and - beneath the blood and dirt - worn to a honey gold color. He held it out to Connor.

"You know instruments. What about this?" Connor stared at the flute for a slow count of ten, then turned away with a wrenching sigh. Taas was there, holding the guitar that Connor had nearly dropped when Perahn tried to get up.

"You need this."

Connor looked at the leader with a weary nod, took the instrument. "Thanks." He slung it over his shoulder before taking the flute from Ben. Wiping it carefully with his shirt he held it out to Perahn. "Take it, Per. You have to be part of this." The musician sat weakly with his back against his sister, unable to raise his eyes until Taas put a hand on his shoulder.

"Perahn, know that you're not alone."

Perahn looked around to see that the circle had joined once more, watching him with unwavering support. He pushed back feelings of guilt and took the flute.

Connor nodded. "Good. Now follow me until it feels right."

The minstrel sat, took a deep breath and began to play. At first his expression was almost contemptuous, as if it were so ordinary that he didn't even have to think. Then he merged with the music, his eyes half closed, and when they opened, they focused on things that weren't there. Perahn followed his lead, still leaning on Aletia.

Ben stood still and listened. Quite different from doing nothing, he felt the power that Connor was sending out and radiated his own feelings back into it. The yin and yang, as Annie used to say. Neither one whole without the other. *Annie. What would you think, old friend, if you saw me now?* Ben almost smiled at the memory when the flute begin to play.

It sang an apology. It sang of thanks. It sang of peace returning and wonder at the way things were.

Ben watched Perahn carefully, feeling a slow but consistant change as the song grew, until there was no darkness in the melody at all, only a swelling joy. The meandering strain seemed to repeat and echo on itself once or twice, before breaking into a song that both he and Connor knew. Seeing the half-grin emerge on Connor's face was enough to tell Ben that his job tonight was finished. Exhaustion triumphed at last, and he would have hit the ground if Tomas hadn't appeared at his elbow to catch him.

The last thing he remembered was watching the dome around them fading like frost in the sun, feeling safe in the knowledge that it was no longer needed.

For now.

6

It was midday before Benjamin dragged himself out of bed. He had stirred once, when sunlight brightened the homespun curtains, but his body had cast the deciding vote, and he rolled over into unconsciousness once more. Memories of Connor describing a long journey made some part of him realize that this could be the last time he slept indoors for quite a while. *Or just the last time,* some part of his mind volunteered with chirpy brightness. He sighed and pushed the thought away.

In its place, memories of the circle the night before flooded back. It was dream-like, yet he could physically remember the feeling of setting the warding dome, of the energy coursing through him and being able to direct it. He remembered too, with a queasy flutter, how it felt to reach into Per's chest and take out the broken arrow. The healing itself was harder to wrap his mind around, whether it was because he was exhausted already or because he had given over to the process, he didn't know. There were times on stage when he really didn't remember his performance, and this felt painfully familiar.

He finally sat up, took a few deep breaths, and stretched so hard he thought he might hurt himself. The cool air on his bare chest made him wonder how he got to bed last night, but the process of trying to remember that triggered something else. He approached it slowly, like the wisp of a dream, not wanting to scare it away. It was about Connor.

Connor. That's right, I remember now.

It had been early morning when Connor got up quietly, dressed, and sat on the edge of Ben's bed.

"Hey," the minstrel said in a bare whisper. "You okay?"

Ben answered without opening his eyes. "Yeah... I think so. You?"

"Yeah. Look, I'm not trying to wake you up. I want to thank you. For Per. He's a good friend, and..." Connor stopped, sighed it out. "I did what I had to, but - I don't know if I could keep this up if I'd killed him."

Ben lifted his right hand, and Connor clasped it with his own. "Anytime, Con." Enhancing his exhaustion with just a little acting, Ben rolled over and made Connor's exit as easy as possible. When the minstrel left, Ben had grinned and drifted almost immediately back to sleep.

Now, the actor threw back the covers and pulled on his pants. It was quiet in the house. He looked through the front window, and there was no one in sight. *Back home, it would have been a media circus after last night.* An unusual feeling swept through him, and he tried to decide whether it was disappointment or relief. Relief seemed the more respectable choice.

He washed and finished dressing before slipping out back to the garden. Ahna was there, tending her plants. A young woman walked away from the garden with a bouquet of herbs in her hand and a smile on her face, and Ben wondered once more just what Ahna's position in the community was. He watched the sun sparkle on the silver in her chestnut hair, making a faint halo in the sun.

"Good morning."

"Ah, good morning, Benjamin." She looked up at the sun and chuckled. "Or perhaps 'good day'? Are you rested?"

Ben returned her smile warmly. "I hope so. I've run out of sleep, as my grandfather would say. Where's Connor?"

"Getting supplies for your trip." She patted his cheek with a basil-scented palm. "I'm supposed to tell you, 'when and if you wake up', that you should go see Tomas." She looked at Ben fondly as he grinned at her impression of the minstrel's voice. "Do you know where to find him?"

Ben shook his head as Ahna brushed off her hands. "Well, no matter what Connor says, you have to eat first." Pausing to pinch a few sprigs to cook with, she shooed him back into the house.

Inside, Ben sat at the large wooden table as Ahna hummed snatches of songs and cooked. The smells were wonderful, and he had the overwhelming feeling that he was nine years old again, sitting in his mother's kitchen.

Benjamin soaked up the comfort of that for a while, his chin resting on crossed wrists against the table, elbows splayed out. For just a while, he felt settled, peaceful. He could even imagine a different world than this one, one with more technology, less intimacy, less realization of true power. One where he wasn't as important as he seemed to be in this world.

Or did I just not see it?

He shook his head as he let the complications creep back, and sighed at the loss of the moment. Ahna turned, as if she could feel the shift in his mood. He smiled at her, pushing his hair back out of his eyes. *It's getting long enough now. Annie would be happy.*

He let his gaze drop to the satiny reflection of the table, and looked at himself. *Who is this guy? And what is he going to have to do before you're through with him?* Ben squinted at the unknown character, and was gratefully distracted by the wood of the table.

The grain looked like a cross between cherry and oak, the lighter and darker colors flamed against each other. It was similar to the wood Ahna's sculptures were made of. "This table is beautiful," he said, rubbing his palm against the worn smoothness.

"Taas cut the top for me." She smiled as she stirred. "I have a hard time directing the wood instead of listening for what it *wants* to do. I took the top where Taas was leading it, but the rest is mine."

Ben looked under the table and saw the pedestal base was a large, sinuous mass, and for a moment he saw it as two bodies, intertwined and supporting the table. It was smooth as the top, almost glowing in the daylight, and Ben could only imagine how many hours it would take to finish such a piece. He looked over the edge of the table at Ahna once more, his respect increasing.

"What kind of wood?"

"Perri. An ancient garnet tree from the back woods that fell in a storm a few years ago. I can feel its presence through the house." She looked into him, gauging him once more. "It has so much of so many in it." Ben looked at her. He wanted to dismiss it, but he could feel what she meant.

She proceeded to set a huge breakfast and lunch before him, and to his surprise, he ate everything in reach. *This expenditure of energy must take a lot out of a person.* The fact that she was a marvelous cook didn't hurt.

"Ahna," he said, between mouthfuls of an egg and herb mixture, "What happened last night?" He paused, not knowing how to describe what happened. "After I passed out."

Ahna paused. When she spoke, it was gently and quietly, as if she could feel his discomfort over the loss of control. "Tomas brought you here when the song of Per's healing was done. Perahn wanted to come along, of course, but Connor took him home and put him to bed before coming back." She paused to put another thick slice of dark bread on Ben's plate. He nodded his thanks as he chewed.

"Poor Aletia." Ahna shook her head with a sympathetic chuckle. "Connor put her in charge. I suppose it wasn't fair, but all his sister has to do is look at him with those big brown eyes and he'll do anything." Her laughter danced in the quiet. "Once Connor was here he insisted on setting wards. I think he was worried about you being as vulnerable as Perahn was, but I believe you're fine now."

"For now." Ben saw her expression tighten, and tried to shrug off his comment. "Hey, with all the people I have looking out for me, what could happen?" She shook her head as he reached over to pat her hand.

Ahna drew herself up, shoulders squaring against an invisible challenger. "I feel you will be fine. Fear is the greatest weapon against us, and I won't give in to it." Her eyes met his, and he could see steel behind the warmth there. "You shouldn't either."

Ben had no chance to respond before the door opened and Connor walked in, looking like he had already put in a full day's work on too little sleep, which he had.

"Glad you could join us," the minstrel said, showing none of the sensitivity that Ben recalled from their morning encounter. For a moment Ben felt Connor scanning him, as if he were looking for some sign of damage.

"Me too. Want some lunch?"

"No thanks, I ate already. You been to Tom's?"

"No. Give me a minute." Ben cleaned the plate before him one more time, grabbed one last chunk of bread and stood up. "Thank you, that was wonderful, I shouldn't have to eat again for a week," he said rapidly to Ahna, bowing theatrically to kiss her hand. She laughed just as he hoped she would, and he grinned as he followed Connor out of the house to Tomas' studio. Ben glanced sideways at the minstrel as they walked briskly down the path from the house. "You look beat."

"Thanks."

"You're welcome. Look, I think it's important for you to be rested if-" Ben stopped as the minstrel whirled on him.

"Look. Don't tell me how to do my job. I'll make sure nothing happens to you, don't worry."

Ben shook his head. When he spoke again, it was in a soft voice. He owed this man his life, if a life was something you could owe.

"What I was trying to say, is that I know how hard a long ride can be if you're tired. I know how worn out I was this morning, and you worked as hard as I did last night." The concern in his voice was clear. "I would never suggest that you weren't 'doing your job', because I still can't quite believe that you're putting yourself on the line for me. I'm sorry if it sounded that way." The minstrel looked away.

"Don't do that."

"Don't do what?"

Connor ran his hand through his hair. "Don't apologize when I'm being a jerk."

Ben laughed, surprised by the minstrel once again. "Well, okay, but warn me next time." Connor shook his head with half a grin and Ben felt him relax, like a knot being loosened, as they began walking again.

The sunshine trickled golden-green through the leaves overhead, and sparkled in the dust clouds that their boots kicked up.

"So," Connor said after a minute, "you feel any different?"

Ben shrugged. "Yes. And no. I don't know. It seems like a dream one minute, the next I'm scraping Per's blood out from under my nails." He looked at his fingertips and is mind clicked over to his friend Cassie doing Lady Macbeth. *Would these hands never be clean?* After a moment he said, as casually as he could, "Is he okay?"

"He's fine. He's going to be fine. He's lucky you found yourself just then."

"Weren't we all." Ben stopped abruptly, picked up a stone from the road, and whipped it into the wood. Connor could almost see the nervous energy streaming off it like a comet in flight. When it was gone, Ben avoided the minstrel's eyes. "Is that what I did? 'Find myself'?"

Connor picked up a stone of his own. "I'd say a door opened." He pointed to a large oak and threw the stone, hitting it easily. Ben snorted a laugh at the implied challenge and took a turn at it.

The two stood, throwing stones. For a few minutes they were ten years old, and the most important thing in their day was the ability to hit a tree with a rock, glorying in limitless strength.

When they ran out of suitable stones and nervous energy, they walked another twenty paces to the structure that housed Tomas' workshop. Connor called hello at the door, and a distracted voice from inside called back an acknowledgement. They stepped in, and Ben was instantly taken aback.

The right hand wall was covered with landscape paintings of water. At least one Ben recognized as the waterfall that he and Connor passed on the way to Overlook. The mist looked as if it was hovering above the canvas, and Ben resisted an impulse to touch it to see if it was wet. Another, in deeper purples and white, showed the same fall in winter, ice and snow freezing the movement in the same way the painter had. Ben moved from picture to picture in the humble gallery, marveling at the images that were captured as much as the craft.

In the center of the studio, the tall teacher was packing his case. Distracted by the artwork, Ben refocused in time to hear Connor say, "You're going to Lintock?"

"Yes. There was an attack three days ago. Their leader and teacher are both gone."

"I'm sorry, Tom. At least we can travel together. That's on route to Anders." Connor shook his head as Tomas rolled a set of brushes in a canvas case. "Do you think you'll have time to paint?"

Tomas sounded philosophical. "If he's defeated then yes, I will, and if he's not, I'll need my creating to remain strong enough to help Lintock." He shrugged, muscular shoulders shifting under a worn, paint-stained shirt. "There's no choice, so I don't have to make one." The smile that flew across his face was real and Ben found he was nearly jealous. This was a man at peace with himself.

Ben extended his hand. "Thanks for the help yesterday. Both during and after." The teacher grasped his hand firmly, proving to Ben that painting on a large scale does wonders for upper body strength, and answering once and for all how he got back to the leader's house.

"I'm glad I could help. Your creation was strong. It was clear what had to be done to sustain it." He grinned. "I think you convinced a lot of people last night."

"Convinced them? That I'm the One?" Ben shook his head. "Who's going to convince me?" The teacher's expression never faltered as he shared a look with Connor.

"No one has to." Tomas looked at Benjamin, and Ben could feel the energy behind the sea grey eyes. They sparkled with it, and with a certain excitement in spite of the dangers that were manifesting themselves. "These are days of prophecy. Exciting times to be alive." He walked toward the back wall of the studio and projected loudly toward them, his deep voice booming in the space. "If you have time, I want to show you some paintings. Some are my own creating. I see what I want to paint in the world, and mold it as I like." He motioned toward the waterfall on the wall that Ben had been studying, twisting his hand as if shaping the rocks and water, forming the mist that hung ghostly above. "There are times, though, that I feel an image is sent to me, and I have to be the hands of the Artist so others can see it too. Take a look."

In the back of the studio, there were several large canvases leaning against the wall. The first was of a stream through a forest, golden sunlight tinted through green leaves to sparkle on the water, dancing in intricate tendrils where mist rose from the water's surface. Nearby was the smooth grey top of a large tree stump. Ben recognized it instantly. "Ah. This is where I came in."

"Yeah." The minstrel spoke with a quiet reverence in his voice. "Tom and Per helped me find the right place. Tom got this after we talked for a while. Then it was a matter of figuring out where it was, once we knew what it looked like. Per nailed it down - he gets around, and he'd been there before, a couple years ago."

Tomas moved to the next picture. "I was hoping you might recognize these. The images were strong as they came to me, but no one here knows them." The second painting showed a tree stump again, this time in a clearing ringed by smaller trees. There was no thick forest, and off in the distance was a broad lake, edged by a hazy dark line. "Do you know this place?" Ben stepped back, hit by a wave of homesickness so strong that Connor and Tomas felt it too.

It was his workout space, up the hill backstage at the park. Imbedded in the tree stump was a sword, strips of blood red leather wrapping around the grip and catching the breeze.

"That's -" he paused and swallowed, his voice breaking slightly. "That's where I'm from. I never had my sword there, though. I mean, I had it, it just didn't look that way." Tomas nodded as if it made perfect sense while Ben continued to stare, not quite believing. Next to the stump was a thick book, and while he couldn't be sure, the reddish brown led him to believe it was the Riverside Shakespeare that Annie had given him for Christmas three years ago. Tomas moved on to the next one before Ben had finished processing the second, and perhaps that's why it caught him off guard. At least he liked to think that's what it was.

"Then what about this?"

The canvas was as tall as Tomas and had been covered with a sheet, or Ben couldn't have missed it when they walked in.

The picture was of a man from behind, looking down over - *wait a minute.* Ben realized in an instant that it was *him*, looking down the hill toward the stage in the park. The supports for the second level had been rendered as trees, but it was still unmistakable.

His eyes widened as he took in the details. Even the costume was right. In fact, he partially recognized himself by the blue and silver-gray doublet that he would have worn as Demetrius - a costume that he had only seen renderings of. He barely whispered, "Wow."

"What is it?" Tomas asked, and Connor looked as if he would like to know as well.

"This is - it's the stage in the park. Where I was working on a show before I came here. Where I should be working now." He took a deep breath and fought with the sudden emotion. Blinking a few times, he clutched his pendant like a lifeline.

Tom pointed to a rectangular black shape in the trees. "Do you know what that is? It doesn't make sense, but I felt it there."

"Speakers. New sound system last year. It was a grant." Ben spoke distractedly, absorbed in his other life. Tomas looked more puzzled then before, but a gesture from Connor told him to let it go for now as Ben continued to gape at the painting. "This is amazing. Back here," he explained, pointing to the distant circle of trees with a slight tremble in his hand and he tried vainly to ignore, "Is what the other painting shows. I used to warm up there." Shaking himself free of the memories and feelings for the moment, Ben turned and looked at Connor, expecting him to understand. "Have you ever been here?"

The minstrel shook his head as he stared at the painting, his arms folded on his chest. "I don't even know what state we're in."

Ben stared at him in shock. "New York." Connor nodded. For some reason that he couldn't quite identify, Ben felt like a reference point had been taken away from him. "Connor, where the hell are you from?"

Connor raised his eyebrows and looked surprised. "Colorado. Near the Springs. Why?"

"I - I guess I just thought that we were - well, I suppose that doesn't make any sense." The actor paused, shook his head. "Colorado?"

"Yeah."

Ben looked thoughtfully at the minstrel and a memory stirred. "I was Mercutio in the Denver Shakespeare Festival once, about five years ago. Did a commercial for a bank while I was there, too."

The minstrel laughed shortly. "I don't get to Shakespeare much. And five years ago, I was… well. I have a sister who probably knows who you are." The mention of family made Connor's focus change to something too far away to see, and Ben understood the feeling. He wanted to tell the minstrel that, to ask him about the people he left behind, but maybe when they were alone again - or, knowing Connor, maybe never. Tomas looked at them questioningly.

"Shakespeare?"

Ben had to grin at the way Tom said it, more like an instruction than a name. "He's a writer."

"A friend?"

"No, but it feels that way. He lived hundreds of years ago, but his writing lives on, kind of like your prophecies. He wrote plays and poetry... some people think he's the greatest writer in our language."

"Poetry I know. What's a play?"

Ben couldn't resist. "The play's the thing wherein I'll catch the conscience of the king."

The teacher's eyes widened, and Ben had a sudden sensation that he had stepped into water over his head. "I'm sorry, Tom, that's a quote." He took a deep breath and tried to respond seriously. "A play tells a story. Actors, people like me, take the parts and try to bring the story to life by acting out what happens." He paused and frowned, feeling like that didn't explain it at all. "I don't know if that helps or not."

Tomas nodded, and Ben felt a familiar artist-to-artist connection. "Ah. There are players on Taela, but not everywhere. I should warn you that there are people who would be frightened by what you just told me."

"I know. Ahna told me a little, I think I made her understand." He stopped, looked at Tomas quite seriously. "What about you? Do you think I'm dangerous?"

The artist laughed, a genuine sound in the face of concern. "No more than any of us. I feel no fear in you of what you do. That's enough for me. You must have felt it in Perahn last night. The fear was the first thing I felt, before the darkness, and before the pull."

Ben shook his head; his hands open in front of him. "I know what you mean. There was a kind of lull, and then a feeling of going downhill too fast." He frowned his eyes shut, experiencing the sensation of the night before. When he opened them again, he was sitting on the floor, with both Tomas and Connor holding him upright. Connor spoke first.

"What the hell was that?"

The teacher stared at Ben intently before answering. "I think he hasn't finished this, and that's important. Especially being his first experience and his power being realized so fully." He leaned in to Ben, speaking quietly. "When you think of last night, what do you feel?"

Ben rolled his eyes. "What don't I feel?"

"Okay. What's strongest?"

Ben nodded and tried to concentrate. "That's easy. Blood. I've never …I was… it was hard." He stumbled over the words, frustrated at how even mentioning the image caused his sense memory to bring it to perfect life, years of training helping him to recreate the smell of blood and something more sickly - fear, his and Perahn's. The texture of flesh and tendon and the roughly shattered edge of a bone, hot to the touch, all pulsing with life, with pain. He shuddered and swallowed hard.

"All right. When you see Perahn in your mind, how does he look?"

Ben paused a moment to expand the view on his sense memory. "Bad. Bloody. In trouble." His fingers rubbed against each other, still feeling Perahn's lifeblood congealing on them.

"But he isn't anymore, you know that." The minstrel spoke, the concern in his voice tinged with annoyance.

"I know. Maybe you'd say I don't feel it."

The teacher helped Ben to his feet, and still towered over him. "That's easy, then. You have to see Per before you leave, connect with him in a way that makes you believe. If you don't feel complete, he can't either."

Ben shook himself out experimentally. "But what just happened? Why the blackout?"

"I know it happens sometimes, usually to those who discover a great potential at a young age. I think it protects them from hurting themselves when they can't control the power yet." As Tomas studied him, Ben recognized the artist slipping into teacher mode. "The power is there. Our own control comes through creating. Experience is the best teacher for someone with your talents."

Ben considered being called a child prodigy, and let the thought go. "What can I do, in here," he said, smacking his fingertips against his forehead, "to keep it from happening again?"

Tomas took a deep breath and blew it out slowly. "First of all, relax. Gain control of your body, because it's the most simple. Then be aware. Be conscious of where your thoughts are going, and realize that you can give yourself trouble by recreating difficult moments recklessly. Know that you are always in control of where your thoughts are focusing. We are given that, and many of us give it up far too easily." He looked around and re-covered the large painting of the park. "I'm not saying that you'll never think about difficult or painful things. I'm saying that you need to be aware that you're doing it. Like stepping on a rock instead of tripping over it. You have the power, you have the control. Use it."

Ben nodded thoughtfully. "I think I know what you're saying. Responsibility, using what we have responsibly, for our own sake, as much as for anyone else's-" He shook his head and exhaled a laugh. "Not that I'm able to make it make sense out loud, but I think I get it in here." He tapped his forehead again, grinning wryly, and Tomas nodded.

"Good. It's important that you realize that with all your potential, all your talents, you're still new to this. Get help, ask questions, let us fulfill our parts." He sounded so teacher-like that Ben had to suppress a smile as Tomas put a hand on his shoulder. "You must know that there are many who would throw down their lives for you."

Ben looked into the sea grey eyes once more, and with a humbling flash realized that he was looking at one of the many.

"I understand."

Tomas finished gathering his things together, and took a last look around his studio. His eyes misted over like one of his paintings, and he whispered something under his breath as he turned to leave. Ben and Connor followed him silently. They headed back to the grey fieldstone house, where Ahna was talking to a tall, nervous looking man, speaking gently to his fears.

Connor spoke as they walked. "We'll drop your stuff off here and then head over to see Perahn. Can't stay too long if we're getting to sleep early." The minstrel nodded to Ahna as they walked in, not wanting to disturb her. She nodded back without losing eye contact with the man.

Ben looked confused. "Aren't we leaving soon?"

The minstrel shook his head. "No. Important journeys should always begin at dawn." He turned to Tomas. "Isn't that what the prophecies say?"

The teacher nodded and smiled. "Actually, 'In the new light of dawn'. Funny you should choose *that* one to live by."

"Hey, everybody's got to do what they've got to do." They exchanged an amused look that made Ben realize that this was part of a debate so old that it had become a joke between them. In the comfort of the moment, something else crossed his mind.

"Hey."

The two turned and looked at Ben expectantly.

"Can you tell me what it is that Ahna does?"

Connor and Tomas turned back to look at each other, and Tomas frowned in confusion. "What do you mean?"

"I mean, she's always talking with people, and I just realized that I was one of them. I have a sudden feeling it was no coincidence I was taken to her place to stay."

The teacher shrugged. "Ahna's skill lies in understanding the weavings of confusion. Of being able to see, and to help others see the images in them. To read the mapping there that shows us where to go."

Ben turned to Connor. "Shrink?"

The musician barked a laugh. "Sort of."

They smiled at their intentional simplification and turned to Tomas, who had raised an eyebrow as if they were unruly students.

By the time they approached Per's house on the other side of the village, the day was settling into afternoon. The breezes were soft and fair, and the sky was a brilliant aquamarine mounded with white clouds. People working stopped when they walked by, sometimes to look suspiciously at Ben, and sometimes to smile and nod. Ben didn't know how to respond to either, but kept focused on Connor and Tomas, who were talking briskly about the route to Lintock and how long it would take. Before he knew it they were at Perahn's door. Aletia answered their knock, looking tired but glad to see them.

"Welcome. I'm sorry I can't offer you much -" Tomas stopped her with an outstretched hand.

"You need only ask us in. How is he?"

Aletia smiled, weary and a little nervous. Ben realized that on top of everything else, Tomas was her teacher. He tried to imagine the variety of feelings she must be dealing with and smiled with new admiration.

"He's doing fine, but it's hard getting him to rest. Maybe you can help. Tell him it's for his own good." She looked more mature than Ben remembered, more poised. "Please, come in."

They followed her into the main room and a concerned voice came from a door off to the right. "Who is it, 'Letia?"

The girl rolled her eyes and smiled at her guests. "He worries." She called softly at the door, "There are friends here to see you. Can they come in?"

The pause that followed was filled with strange sensations for Ben. He could feel reluctance on Perahn's part, actually *feel* it. Something in his head acknowledged that the problem was not with him or with Per individually anymore, but a matter of whatever passed between them last night not being finished. What that meant, he really wasn't sure. He only knew he dreaded doing anything that might bring back the sense of horror and fear, the sensation of helplessness. Even more strongly than that, the thought that he might feel the darkness settle in on him again, the loss of control. That he could see the people who trusted him caught up in an evil creation that used his talents, that was truly his but not his, and then the pain on top of the pain - Ben gasped. *My God, this isn't mine.*

His stomach twisted as he considered it, and he knew that he had to face it once more. He turned firmly to Connor and Tom. "I'm going to see him first."

It wasn't a request, and the two men looked first at each other, then back at Ben. Neither one moved. Connor said simply, "Okay."

"I'll try to figure it out. But please," he said to them in earnest, "stay close." Without further comment, he walked into Per's room.

It was dim, and Ben's eyes took a minute to adjust. Only a faint echo of the afternoon sun backlit the curtains. Once he could make out shapes, he moved toward the bed and stood over it with his arms crossed, trying to figure out what he should be doing. After a time, Perahn spoke.

"What?"

"I'm trying to figure that out." Ben looked at Per in the half light and finally sighed. "Did you ever meet someone and feel like you knew them, but couldn't for the life of you figure out from where?"

The figure in the bed nodded. "I feel it too."

"You're from Taela, aren't you?"

Per laughed in spite of himself, a warm, surprised chuckle. "Of course I am."

"Then where do I know you from?"

The man sighed, sounding serious once more. "I've heard stories about what you do. About acting, and how you use souls without stealing them. Maybe you borrowed mine once." There was a cynicism in his voice that the actor didn't like the feel of, and he shook his head in annoyance.

"No, it's nothing like that, and you know it if you're feeling anything like what I'm feeling. I don't use anyone but me." He sat down on the edge of the bed.

They looked curiously at each other. Finally Perahn shrugged, as if there was no way Ben would understand what he was going to say. "The prophecies say that there are others, in other places, who share our space. That anyone can have a shard that once touched ours. They say that when we meet those people we recognize them, because our spirits have always touched." He twitched the curtain back and squinted briefly at the bright afternoon sky.

"Really." Benjamin felt the truth brushing up against him like a friendly dog that would not be denied. "Is there a word for people like that?"

Perahn held up his right hand with the palm facing Ben, and Ben, without thinking twice, mirrored the movement with his left so that their palms touched. In an internal burst of light, mimicking the physical contact of their hands, he felt another mind touch his.

Ben knew that he didn't have control of the connection but still, like a static shock that equalized an imbalance, he felt a harmony that he couldn't even describe to himself. He realized that Per felt the same way, and they shared in the surprising *rightness* of the moment before it slipped like a raindrop into the sea. Per grinned at Ben, his eyes brightening.

"In the old tongue," the musician said, "we call them W'hentali." He paused and smiled. "Artist-brothers."

7

They stayed with Perahn until sunset, when Aletia quietly suggested that he needed his rest and genteelly shooed the three out. They walked back to the grey fieldstone house, where Ahna served them soup with cheese and loaves of crusty bread that they ate as if it were their last meal. Ben attempted to push that thought away - along with his third empty bowl - and turned his focus across the table to Tomas.

"So what happened?"

Tom broke off another piece of cheese and frowned. "What do you mean?"

"You know. With me and Per. What was that?"

"You were the one there."

"Wait a minute. You told me this afternoon that if I had questions I should ask. I'm asking." Ben's eyes flashed in the firelight.

The tall teacher smiled, obviously unthreatened, and raised his hands in surrender. "Fair enough." Rubbing his palms together, he steepled long fingers. "I thought you were asking me what happened. You want to know why it happened, and what it meant. Right?"

Ben thought for a second and sipped his wine before answering, the liquid cool and pleasantly biting on his tongue. "I think that's a fair assessment."

"All right. *That*, maybe I can answer."

Connor, who had been eating quietly to this point, chuckled. "This should be good." He smiled dryly as he tore his bread into his soup.

Tom gave him a very teacherish look before he went on. "It's an accepted belief that someone would have to fall for the One to prove himself, and that's always been a subject of debate - why would the Artist hurt a trusting soul just to show that the One was here? And being chosen, why shouldn't the One know what to do without having someone fall into darkness?" The teacher paused to refill their glasses with the garnet wine, making ruby sparkles across the table in the firelight. "I was one who questioned the need. It seemed like a test, an unnecessary one. Now I understand." He took another bite of bread and cheese, chewing long enough to make Ben restless once more.

"Great. Can you explain it to me?"

"It should be obvious, if you feel for it." Brushing the crumbs from his hands, Tomas looked carefully at Ben. "Think for a minute. Did you ever believe you could have done what you did last night?"

Ben shook his head and gave a rough laugh. "I don't have to think to answer that. I still have a hard time believing I did it." He looked at his hands as if they belonged to someone else. "But I know I did."

Tomas nodded. "And if the need had not been so great, if it had not been friends that needed you so desperately, and if it had not been a good man that was suffering - one that even the Hawk, as skeptical as he is, sees as a good man - would you have been driven as strongly to take action?"

Ben tried to imagine what he would have done if things had been different, but he couldn't picture it any other way. "I see what you mean. But if that's the case, then I'm being manipulated. Is that fair?"

Tom's eyes brightened in amusement. "And is it fair if I make one student do more work, knowing they can do better; but not another, knowing they've already done their best? If you're on the Artist's path, you'll be led to your best."

Benjamin sighed, then finished his glass a bit too quickly. His own religion, the one he had been raised in, was a little used thing for him now. But the sense of spirituality that was a part of him, as natural as centering his breathing, accepted the metaphysics easily. "I need to sleep on it."

Tomas grinned. "Good idea. We could all use a full night's rest before we leave." Looking pointedly at Connor, the teacher began to clear up the dishes. As he did so, Ahna and Taas came in from the other room, the latter with an armful of blankets.

"Tomas, I assume you're staying tonight." The way Ahna spoke it was a statement, not a question.

"If it's all right."

Benjamin looked at the two of them and blinked. For a moment he could have sworn the teacher was a boy of fifteen, and Ahna younger as well. By the time he blinked again, the image had faded back to the present. He looked into his wineglass as Taas handed Tom the bedding. Ahna gave a somewhat forced smile.

"The other boys are in your old room, and you may want to join them. It would mean using the floor, but it would keep your energy together, and before your trip -" She stopped and exhaled strongly.

"That's what I'll do. Thank you." The teacher leaned over to kiss her forehead. "Thanks for everything." She reached up and took his face in her hands, and Ben saw her eyes shining before she turned away. Taas smiled and put his arm around her, walking her out of the main room as she called over her shoulder.

"You boys get to sleep. It's late, and you'll have plenty of time to talk on the road."

In impromptu chorus, the three said, "Yes ma'am." Then they started laughing, and for some reason could not stop until their eyes were watering helplessly, random giddy giggles that kept returning and thankfully, would not let them focus on anything serious for the rest of the night.

*   *   *

The next morning dawn wandered tentatively through the forest, like a cat in a strange barn. Shafts of light spun out through the trees onto the path as the travelers moved along, their horses cautious in the shrouded glow. Benjamin looked up at the grey sky overhead, took a deep breath redolent with earth scents, and tried to make sense of what Tomas had just said.

"Well, wait a minute. Does that mean that the One is actually supposed to fight the evil? It almost sounds like he's supposed to train someone else to do it, this 'Inca'ti'."

Tomas shook his head and continued to look at the book in his hand as they rode. "I don't know if it's clear one way or the other. It could be part of your creating." He looked over at Benjamin and grinned broadly, knowing by now that it was exactly this kind of statement that was making the actor crazy.

Ben nodded as he felt the echo of a giggle well up in him. He stopped at a smile, but his horse whinnied as if she could feel it too.

"Okay. Give me that last one again. About the leading prince. Inca'ti." The word felt odd in his mouth.

Tomas flipped back a few pages in the book he was holding, cleared his throat, and began to read.

"Out of nowhere, out of here, the One shall come. It is he who shall find the Inca'ti, who will lead and gather. The Inca'ti will draw even the One with him into darkness. He must find his way, or all may be lost"

Benjamin shook his head in exasperation. "Fine, but what does that mean? 'Find the Inca'ti'? I'm supposed to, what, look for him?" Connor, who had been riding point, reined back until he was alongside Ben.

"I think it means that there's someone that needs your help, someone who has a place in all this. You help him find his way."

Ben shook himself in frustration and shrugged. "If I can find mine." Stretching back to look up at the sky, he noticed blue was slowly winning out over the grey. "I'm beginning to feel like I'm not supposed to know what happens next." He took a deep breath and closed his eyes for a moment, centering. "So then after I help him find his way, he draws me on – does that mean I go with him to get the bad guy?"

"Sounds easy enough." Connor and Ben exchanged a look, and Tomas turned a page.

"There's something else here that I find interesting. It's always been called a message to the One."

Ben's eyes shot open. "To the One? Why?"

"Don't know. Except that the One is new to us, and maybe the Artist has to tell him something that he wouldn't have grown with, as we have. Or, maybe the Artist just wants the One to know that he's not alone."

Ben frowned and muttered under his breath, "Great. A note from God. For me." He shook his head. "Do you understand the message?"

"No, of course not," the teacher grinned once more. "I'm not the One." He looked at Ben with a familiar sparkle, and the actor rolled his eyes.

"Thanks. Well, let me have it." Then the actor lifted his hand. "Wait a minute. What if I don't understand this message?"

"It may not be yours. Legends grow up around the One like weeds in a garden. You'll feel if it's for you." He looked at Ben with calm, grey eyes. "Do you want to hear it or not?"

The actor stared at his horse's mane, took a breath. "Okay. Let's have it."

The teacher cleared his throat once more.

"The One shall come, with power to control his soul, to splinter without harm, to create anew without destroying. There are those who will not understand, those who cannot, and those who will try to destroy him.

"I will be with him, though he does not know me. I will be with him, even if he cannot unseat the true enemy of light, the one who in the balance can never be destroyed, that my creation may turn away.

Even this One, the child of my art, has the right to choose. "

"Wow," Ben said, his voice shrouded in subdued sarcasm. "No pressure."

Tomas shrugged. "This next part is more vague, which I suppose is why some say it's the message. It's always easier to say something is divinely inspired, rather than trying to figure it out." He took a breath before reading.

"Some are born great, some achieve greatness, and some have greatness thrust upon them." The teacher lifted his eyes to glance at Benjamin before he continued. *"The One will understand."*

Ben jerked up so suddenly that his horse stopped with a whinny. He stared again at the back of his mount's head, as if he were reading something there. *I know that quote.* He stared at Tomas, then at Connor.

In a split second, his mind had found where he knew it from, and also told him where he was when he heard it last *the park* and what he was wearing *that awful, hot, red costume with the scratchy neckline* at the time. *That can't be right,* he thought, and opened his mouth to say it, but nothing came out. Meanwhile his brain, having opened that particular file, continued to spit out random information about the show. The director's address. *526 Lincoln Park.* The stage manager's marital status. *Single, looking, interested.* The night that Malvolio stepped wrong and fell down the stairs. *Sprained ankle, standing ovation.* The review that made it sound like he hadn't even been in the show. *Stop!*

"Ben?" Connor turned back as he realized Ben had stopped moving. "What's going on?" The minstrel looked around, one hand on his bow, concerned that he had missed something.

Ben shook his head, tried to make his hands say something, and failed. He felt like he was sliding down an icy hill, committed to the run but unable to focus his thoughts on how to steer. He took a deep breath, pinched the bridge of his nose and closed his eyes hard, as if that might squeeze out the confusion in his mind. He found his voice and turned to Tomas.

"Let me ask a question, Tomas. Is there any significance to -" he paused, not really wanting to ask. "The *twelfth night* of this month? Or maybe the next?"

Tomas stared at him for a moment, before letting his gaze drop back to the book in his hand. He looked up again, this time at Connor, who rubbed his hand back through his hair, relieved that it was only the prophecy bothering Ben and not an attacker. The minstrel shrugged. "He didn't hear it from me."

The teacher took a breath. "Among many, it's called the day of darkness. Twenty years will have passed, to the day, since Alious took the Castle of the Stone."

"Twenty years? That long?" Ben shook his head in confusion. "How could this have possibly been going on for twenty years?"

"For a long time, it was quiet. Some thought the castle was all he wanted. We later found he was gathering power from other places, we don't know where. Only in the last few years have we struggled against him ourselves, and some think that it has to do with the Lady's son coming of age."

"The Lady Anders? She has a son?" Ben tried to sort out what information he needed now. "What would that do?"

"If he can't sway her, maybe he feels he can control her son. There are prophecies that point to that, but even those are confused, speaking of his own heir, as opposed to hers." Tomas began to shuffle through the book in his hand, the teacher again, then stopped himself. "Why did you ask about the twelfth?"

Ben paused, unsure about how to answer.

How will it sound to say that one of the prophecies is a quote from a Shakespearean comedy? Or did Shakespeare quote a prophecy and use it in his play? And if there is some sort of cosmic force at work here, one that wants me to come out and play, what do they mean by this?

Ben took another deep breath and blew it out slowly.

"The plays I told you about yesterday, the writer called Shakespeare? He wrote a play that has almost that exact quote in it. 'Some are born great, some achieve greatness, and some have greatness thrust upon 'em.' I did that show three years ago. They weren't my lines, but I was in the show."

Tomas nodded calmly, and actually looked pleased by Ben's revelation. "That would explain why the One would know it."

"Yeah, I guess so. Anyway, the name of that play is *Twelfth Night*."

Connor and Tomas exchanged a look, and Connor shook his head as if nothing could surprise him right now.

"Do you think it has anything to do with our journey, or is it a message from the Artist that speaks only to you?"

Ben scratched the back of his head and frowned. "I really don't know. I'll think about it. And can I see that?" He motioned toward the book. The teacher nodded, and then the three, with Connor riding point and Ben and Tomas following side by side, headed down the road once more.

The sun had slowly risen to almost directly overhead when Ben and Tomas heard a whistle from Connor.

"Hey," He called out from ahead of them. "Lintock dead ahead." The minstrel sounded almost cheerful as he pointed off into the distance. "I told you, Tom, it couldn't be that bad –" his sentence was cut short by a shrill scream, still far off. "Damn. Ben, find some cover. Tom, you're with me!" He yelled instructions as he simultaneously nocked an arrow and spurred his horse forward. Ben stared after him in shock for the briefest of moments, then kicked his horse to follow.

As they drew closer, the sounds became louder. Shouting fought for attention over the clashing of swords, and the sobbing of children punctuated them in a way that made Ben's stomach twist in a knot. The minstrel only noticed him as they came up on the edge of town. "Dammit, Ben, I told you to get out of here!"

"Shut up, Connor. This is my fight, too." Ben yelled over the chaos that confronted them. He pulled a pair of black leather gloves from his pack and drew them on quickly, adjusting the gauntlets over his cuffs with the practiced ease of a hundred quick changes.

From the height of his horse's back, he could see that the fight was a collection of smaller scuffles, with a force of perhaps twelve against a somewhat larger grouping of villagers who were hampered in their efforts by the presence of children. It was like the enemy had invaded a school outing, here on the edge of town. And, he noticed uneasily, it appeared to have begun just when they were close enough to hear it. Anger trickled through him, releasing its chemicals into his system. "I'm supposed to help these people, aren't I?"

"Don't you get it?" Connor pulled close to Ben and grabbed his horse's bridle as it shied against the noise. "I don't know if I can protect you and fight at the same time. This is dangerous."

Ben looked the minstrel in the eye. "Then I'll have to protect myself, won't I?" Somewhere inside of him a warrior stirred. Words came to his lips unbidden, learned in another time, in what might as well have been another life.

"Tis dangerous, my lord, to take a cold, to sleep, to drink."

He reached down and pulled his sword from a leather sheath Ahna had given him in Overlook. As his hand tightened around the grip he felt an electric tingle, as if the sword itself were anxious for a fight, and something inside of him relished the role he had to play to get through the next scene. As if Shakespeare's Hotspur was there with him, acting for him. He looked with different eyes at Connor, felt the unease of this man who would fight to save his life. Hotspur respected it. Lines from *Henry* leapt unbidden to the front of his mind.

...let my soul want mercy if I do not join with him! Yea, on his part I'll empty all these veins, and shed my dear blood drop by drop in the dust... The actor nodded to his inner voice and spoke quickly, unsure of how this would end, yet feeling the moment draw him on like the swift current of a waterfall. "How do we know who's on our side?"

Connor's frustration spilled over onto Ben, nearly tangible in its intensity. He looked briefly off into the fray and accepted that there was no way to talk Benjamin out of it. "You can feel it. But if you're not sure, look at their eyes."

"Their eyes?" Ben frowned at the minstrel in disbelief. "You're kidding."

"Trust me on this one. If they come up empty, they belong to him."

Ben shifted his grip on the sword. His eyes were still locked with Connor's when an arrow cut the air between them, heading toward the fight. In startled unison they looked where it had hit, in the drawing shoulder of a darkly dressed and briefly surprised looking man holding a bow of his own, and back to Tomas, who looked grim.

"Perhaps you two can work this out later," the teacher called ironically, as he headed into the midst of the fight. Ben and Connor glanced at each other once more, the minstrel pulling his horse hard to the right.

"Fine. But there'll be hell to pay if you get yourself killed."

"You can count on it."

The two wheeled away from each other, Benjamin heading through the attackers toward the village, Connor alternating between hitting distant targets with arrows, and nearby ones with fists. As for Tomas, he proved to be stunningly accurate with the bow, choosing his targets in an almost laconic fashion, hitting every time. Ben noticed their progress as he pushed on, and felt a wave of nausea wash over him. He wasn't ready to kill anyone. Not even these warped humans, who would have killed any one of them without thinking twice. *Does the fact that I'm thinking twice make me better? Or is it that when I kill them it's different because my cause is just?*

His abstraction was stopped by the appearance of another attacker, this one on horseback and coming directly at him. He watched in a detached way as the man raised his sword overhead, ready to swing down into Ben's shoulder. Without thinking, Ben moved his own sword to parry the blow. *Target number three. Parry with number three.* His perceptions shifted into high speed, while at the same time, every movement around him drifted into slow motion. Ben could see the emptiness in the man's eyes, and realized with a chill that the minstrel was right. His mind raced.

Can I stop this? He looked for a bare instant over to Connor, who was off his horse now, and fighting hand to hand. A small child was watching, cowering and screaming in terror, as Connor pushed back briefly and brought his knee into the man's midsection. He doubled over, the wind knocked out of him, and the minstrel slammed joined hands into the back of his neck as if he were a headsman wielding an axe. The man collapsed like a rag doll, but Connor had already dropped to one knee at the child's side, making sure he was all right. Just beyond, Ben could see Tomas, who was yelling to the small group of villagers that remained standing, rallying them into a reasonable defense, helping to get the children into one place. The cries never stopped.

The force of a sword hitting his sent a shock up Ben's arm, right to his shoulder. He drew back and swung at the man, who parried the blow with some difficulty. This was not a trained warrior, no matter what he was being led to do.

Ben pushed the attack, and actually had his assailant backing up when he realized that none of his moves were designed to kill. They were designed instead for the carefully intricate choreography of stage combat. Cursing softly, Ben watched as he automatically aimed his attack where the man had the best chance of deflecting it, his eyes telegraphing the move. At least his attacker didn't know that, but Ben was buying time, nothing more.

He wanted to turn and check on Connor and Tomas again, but he didn't dare. The man was swinging wildly now, his blade aiming horizontally across Ben's neck. Raising his sword vertically, Ben blocked the stroke. He looked at his attacker, panting, the cruciform of their swords between them. Out of nowhere, a fight staging fell into Ben's mind. He knew there was a good move out of this. He found he was arguing with himself, with no time to do it. *From where? That doesn't matter - I won. What did I do next? But where? Damn. All right. -It was a class. That's right, second semester combat. Okay? But what did I do? I...*

There it was. Ben pivoted his blade under the horizontal crossbar that his opponent's weapon created. With a swift movement up and forward, he slammed the pommel of his broadsword into the man's jaw.

In the fight choreography of the scene in class, his partner was ready for it, fell back as if hit before Ben's weapon came close enough to touch him. This man wasn't ready. He was hit full force by steel wrapped in a fist, and jerked his head backwards so violently that Ben was afraid that his neck might have broken. He also got a quick lesson in how to look like you've been hit hard, as the man fell backwards off of his horse to land in an ungracious heap on the ground. The horse, sensing its freedom, reared and ran for the woods. For an absurd moment, all Ben could think of was how far his fight partner's fall had been from what really would have happened. *I told him it would -*

"Ben!" Connor's yell startled him. As he wheeled his mount, he saw the minstrel and child trapped, surrounded by three remaining attackers. The actor looked for Tom, saw that he was too far away, helping the other children.

For a moment, confusion left him helpless. Then the power within began to build once more, spilling out over his fears. *Good. I can use this. All I have to do is -* the dark soldier nearest to him was reaching out with his sword. Not towards Connor, whose blade was lifted, but at the child peeking fearfully out from behind. *No!*

Ben shot his hand forward, fury spilling from his palm. The force of the energy hit the closest attacker in the back, who cried out as he fell. The rocky ground accepted him with a sick thud, and Ben tried to ignore the echo of pain that spasmed across his own back as he lashed out at the man on Connor's right. This time the force was weaker, but it still had the desired effect. Ben felt the energy drain out of him as Connor spun to snap a kick into the chest of the only remaining attacker. Then, as the minstrel turned towards him, everything went black. He heard Connor yell, but his consciousness was fading fast.

Damn, Agante, you've got to learn to control this better. He collapsed forward, burying his face in the warm musk of his mount's mane, hoping that he wouldn't lose his grip on the horse as well.

*   *   *

"You all right? Ben?"

The words appeared through a foggy haze, clear but not translated by his brain into something he could respond to.

"That was stupid."

Slowly the translation circuits in his mind began to function again. The effort of connection and the memories it triggered made his head hurt. He groaned softly.

"He saved your life. And the boy."

"I don't care. He could have-" an exasperated sigh punctuated the sentence - "damn it, Tom, you know what could have happened."

The throbbing in his head eased slowly as Ben unclenched his thoughts from the last images he had seen.

"Trust."

"You know -"

Ben figured out where Tom and Connor were standing over him by the content of their phrases, more than by the sound of their voices. He tried to open his eyes but they instantly began to water. With a grunt of pain he winced them shut again. He took a deep breath and cleared his throat. The abrupt silence convinced the actor that he had their attention.

"What happened this time?"

"What do you think?"

"I'm assuming that we're all right, Connor, because you wouldn't be this mad if we weren't." Ben turned his head to the right, where he sensed Tomas. "Do you want to tell me what happened? Or do you want to yell too?"

"I'm not going to yell." Ben could hear the humor in the teacher's voice. "How're you feeling? You've been out for a while."

"I ache all over. And my eyes hurt." Ben opened his eyes and squinted at Tom, water blurring his vision, but able to make out the broad-shouldered height of the teacher. "The kids okay?"

"The kids are okay. Pretty shaken up."

Ben felt him not saying something, and didn't have the heart to pursue it. The minstrel's voice went on, still angry.

"You could have -"

"Connor."

Ben was surprised at the teacher's voice. It had dropped with suppressed anger into a rich bass that Ben felt in his gut, and the word stopped the minstrel in mid-sentence.

"He's alive. That's the important thing right now."

Ben rubbed at his eyes and blinked out the remainder of whatever was irritating them. The room came into focus in time for him to see Connor walking away, Tom shaking his head after him. When the teacher turned back and saw Ben staring at him, his expression changed to one of genuine warmth. "Glad you're okay."

"Thanks. What's he talking about?"

"You know Connor. He's just worried -"

"Tom. Please. I'm not stupid. What could have happened?"

Tomas sighed and sat back in the chair. He pushed the long mane of hair back over his shoulders and looked at Ben, the teacher unsure that his student was ready for any more lessons today.

As he waited, Ben distracted himself by looking around the room. It was entirely possible that the teacher was calmly reviewing every prophecy he knew about the One.

Besides, the actor noticed unsteadily, there was something wrong with this place.

It took Ben a few minutes to figure it out. It was a log cabin; maybe a hunting lodge, or maybe the people in Lintock just lived more humbly than the roomier dwellings he had seen in Overlook. The log walls were dark, and more than dark, they were irregularly mottled in color. And strangely familiar. As if - *oh God. A fire.*

The image of his childhood home flashed through his mind, the way it was as he walked through it, the last remaining adult of his family. *Adult. Alone is more like it.* Even now, years later, he didn't feel the title fit. A familiar rush of insecurity tried to take hold in his heart, and just as quickly, died away. It was so sudden that he took a test run to see if it would happen again. He looked at the charred patterns on the walls, felt the prickle of sweat on his scalp. In no time at all, his mind superimposed the wallpaper that his grandmother had put up in the foyer, blackened almost beyond recognition, then - nothing. While he wasn't proud of it, he knew that the memory of the ruined house was his Achilles' heel. He used it when he could in his work, and fought it when he had to in his personal life. His right hand drifted to the pendant at his neck, and he concentrated on the energy in the room.

When he centered he could see, or perhaps feel was the better sense, a soft blue-green glow. Warded. Maybe the entire cabin. He was being protected from his own thought processes.

At first something in him resented it, wanted to know just how bad things were, or how bad they could be. Then a more sensible part of his mind took over, and he realized how asinine it would be to keep poking the sore tooth. He consciously relaxed into the safety of the place, and perhaps the teacher was aware of it. A long moment passed before Tomas began speaking.

"Connor was concerned," he began, "because you let loose with enough energy to down a man from ten yards away. I've worked with a lot of people who are strong in their creating, and I've never seen anything like it." He paused to take a sip from a mug sitting on the small table near the bed. "The first danger is that it was completely unfocused." Ben raised his eyebrows.

"No it wasn't. I hit him, didn't I?"

Tom frowned thoughtfully. "True. That's probably a testament to the Artist more than to you. I wouldn't count on being able to do that often." He leaned forward, intensity crackling in his voice. "There was no creation involved. Without creating, our powers are more potential than effective."

Ben frowned at him, blue eyes glittering. "But I *was* creating. I didn't have time to think about it, but there was some kind of -" he paused, almost embarrassed. "Some kind of character thing going on. Something that might have required special effects to work, but that I had to see anyway, had to believe in, make real for myself. Like doing Puck, or Ariel. Maybe Prospero. Or maybe," he said, staring at his hands thoughtfully, "the One." Ben looked back to Tomas, not wanting to have to explain, and felt the teacher trying to understand. For a long beat they stared at each other, and the only sound in the room was the rhythmic flapping of the faded cloth hanging at the open window. Tom finally nodded and continued.

"Well, that would explain why something that appeared out of control to us was focused for you. But there's another problem with using your power that way, and I think you know what it is. It's the same reason that Connor didn't want you involved in the fight to begin with."

Ben took a deep breath and tried to relax. "What?"

"The energy never flows in only one direction. When something goes out, something has to come back. There's a balance. Do you remember, in the circle? The people in the group supported your creating not by giving you more strength, but by completing the pattern of energy. Their potentials added to yours by being part of the balance, by raising the total." He locked his hands together, long fingers entwined as he tried to express the concept. "When I paint, there's a series of circles. My hand and the brush. The brush and the paint and the canvas. And the painting isn't truly complete until someone else sees it. Then, they add their energy to what they perceive."

"The yin-yang. I know it. A creation isn't complete without the response it causes. A play isn't finished until it has an audience." Ben sighed. "What does that mean about today?" He wondered briefly if it was indeed still today, or if he had, as he felt, slept 'round the clock.

"It means," Tom said in a flat tone, "that when you use your powers to affect someone else's being, that will be reflected back at you. All you need is two. That's one reason that the villages get together in large groups. If there's any dangerous potential, it's diluted by the sheer number of beings involved, and the overall desire for good." He stopped to see if Ben was following. "Do you see? The more you give that is good, the more you get. The opposite is true as well, especially if you have connected with someone whose aim isn't toward 'good'. To interact with someone is to connect with them, and learning to protect yourself from unwanted influences can take years of training." He paused for the information to sink in. "So. How are you feeling?"

Ben stared at him, realization dawning across his features like a fast light cue. "Wait a minute. You're saying that when I connect with someone that way... with the raw power, I'm hurting myself as well?" The memory of pain searing across his back as the man fell leapt to his mind. Then, in a more curious and hesitant moment, the memory of connection with Perahn, and the sickening sensation of an arrow shifting in his chest.

"How am I supposed to do anything to get rid of Alious when the more strongly I try to hurt him, the more I'll hurt myself?" Anger and bewilderment sang in his voice. "What am I supposed to do, Tom? Is the One just a sacrifice? Am I supposed to kill myself to kill him? Or is there another way to use the energy?" The teacher waited patiently, his expression unchanged, while Ben vented his anger. "Why didn't you tell me?" Ben stopped, closed his eyes and took a deep breath. There was too much traffic in his brain, too much might be and could be.

He concentrated on his hands, the soft, well-worn fabric of the blanket drawing the perspiration from his fingers as he collected himself, the breeze from the window that cooled them. He felt himself calming, his pulse steady.

"Okay. I know. You didn't tell me because I already knew. I felt it with Per. I just didn't know how far it went." *Connor isn't mad at me for saving him, or even for the way I did it. He's mad because I could have gotten myself killed, and there was nothing he could do to stop it.*

"It's all right." Tomas smiled kindly at Ben, looking more relaxed himself. "But at the same time, I want you to know that I personally don't think that the One is meant to be 'just a sacrifice'. Perhaps it's just that using the power 'raw', as you said, isn't the way. The more creation that is involved, the safer it may be for you." The teacher gave Ben's shoulder a gentle squeeze before he went on. "I think you might need a little more rest before you meet the village." He put his hand on Ben's forehead. "Sleep now. Dream in peace."

"Thanks, but I don't know if -" A yawn stopped his sentence. "Well, maybe I do. But just for a while, okay?"

The teacher smiled. "Sure."

"And Tomas? Tell Con I'm sorry. And that I'm okay." With another yawn, Ben felt himself drifting into unconsciousness, a sensation of sinking and bobbing that he was aware of for only a few seconds.

The teacher sat for a quarter of an hour watching the fulfillment of the prophecies, the possible sacrifice, the One – as he sank into sleep.

With a little sigh of relief, he whispered, "I will."

8

Ben stood on the beach as a huge tidal wave reared up from the sea, a wall of water so high that it looked as if the ocean was standing on end. From his vantage point on the sand he could see familiar houses suspended in it, as if it were thicker than water but still greenly translucent. He felt with a strangely calm certainty that this was it, he was going to die, and there was nothing he could do.

Closing his eyes, he felt his toes dig futile braces into the sand. Yet just as the wave touched the shore, it dissolved abruptly into air and mist, hitting him with nothing more than a stiff breeze. He heard a chuckle, turned around and saw his grandfather smiling behind him. "Nice work," the older man said, and vanished as quickly as the water had. Confusion engulfed him, and the aftershock of adrenaline made his body tremble as he stood alone on the beach.

Out of the sudden emptiness, a voice softly said

"Ben?"

Ben's eyes fluttered open.

"Hey. You okay?"

"Connor." Disorientation played over his perceptions. Then, abruptly awake, he was sure of the place, the cabin, the minstrel sitting there, and the surge of adrenaline that had been generated by nothing less than a tidal wave.

"Wow." He rubbed his eyes, shook himself, and blinked. "What's up?"

"Not you, that's for sure." The minstrel smirked as Ben registered the morning light through the cabin windows.

"Are you kidding? I slept through?"

"Yeah. How do you feel?"

Ben took a minute to honestly consider his condition. His back was better, though it felt a little sunburned. The rest of him felt much more solid. "I feel good." He took another minute to study the minstrel, who looked peaceful and relatively well-rested himself. *How am I supposed to keep up with this guy?* There was none of the anger that Ben had imagined the night before. "So where's Tom?"

Connor's expression changed fluidly to one of annoyed frustration. "He's out there trying to convince these people to defend themselves. Most of them think now that you're here, they don't have to do anything, and that display of yours didn't help. Not to mention the fact that the people who did see it are making it bigger than it was, and by this time the story is that Tom and I were cowering on the sidelines while you took on forty men."

"Only forty, eh?" Ben shook his head and exhaled a laugh. "That's crazy."

"No kidding." The minstrel got up from the chair and walked to the open window. Sunlight pushed against his chest and bounced back onto the mottled walls of the room. In the bright morning light, Ben noticed more details than the evening before.

The cabin had two beds, a table with a couple of chairs, and a wood stove that probably served for both cooking and heating. Hanging over his bed was an ancient looking bow of gnarled wood, and over the other was the matching quiver of arrows. Skins that had seen better days were draped across both beds, which were nothing more than thick mats on log frames. He half expected to see the head of some dead animal hanging over the door, although he sincerely hoped that Taela wasn't familiar with that tradition.

Sitting up, he threw his legs over the edge of the bed and waited to see if his head was as cooperative as it seemed to be. It held. Encouraged, he stood and walked to the washstand by the cold stove. The water pitcher was terra-cotta glazed inside with lapis blue, and he noticed an intricate series of designs running around the belly of it. "Connor." The minstrel turned away from his thoughts at the window.

"What?"

"What do you make of these? They look kind of like runes." Connor glanced at the markings and nodded.

"I think they *are* kind of like runes. You see them in the prophecies here and there. Some ancient version of their writing." Almost as an afterthought, he added, "Tom can read them."

Ben nodded. "Figures. He seems like a bright guy."

The minstrel snorted. "Yeah." If he hadn't been looking at Connor when he said it, Ben would have taken his response for jealousy. As it was, no matter how it sounded, it looked more like respect.

"Something about him doesn't work for you."

The minstrel looked at Ben and narrowed his eyes. "Let's just say that I'm not used to working with people who don't have a personal agenda, and I wasted a lot of time waiting for his to appear." He glared for a moment at Ben, as if daring him to take offense. The actor only shrugged, so he took a deep breath and continued. "Let's also say that I know from experience that I can trust him with my life. You can do the same."

With some difficulty Ben hid a smirk. "I know how you feel. It's tough to trust a person on their terms instead of your own. But sometimes," he paused and shook his head sadly, "it's all you can do." The minstrel gave him a shocked look, and then laughed.

"All right, wiseass. Clean up and we'll see if we can talk some sense into this town."

"Sense? What if they're right?"

"Are you kidding? Not even the clear prophecies promise a free ride when the One is here. Hell, they don't even guarantee that the One will come out on top. Chew on that, and tell me you don't want to convince these people that you're just a man."

Ben poured water into the bowl and scooped it up to splash his face. "You've got a convincing way with an argument, Con. Why don't you talk to them?"

The minstrel shook his head. "Tom's the one who's got to lead. It wouldn't be right, and it probably wouldn't work anyway, coming from an outsider."

"Not even the Hawk?" Ben waited for only a moment, figuring that Connor wasn't going to respond to that. "What do they need to do?"

The minstrel blew out an exasperated breath and scratched his freshly trimmed beard. "Right now, they need to realize the danger. It was stupid to take those kids out." Ben quietly dried his face as he watched the minstrel glowing in the sunlight at the window, his hands clenching and unclenching as he spoke. "What good is it if by the time we get to Alious, his people have killed half the population without a fight? What good is that kind of sacrifice?"

The actor walked over to the minstrel silently, put a hand on his shoulder. "We'll make them understand, Con." The minstrel turned, and their eyes met in an instant of connection. "We will."

The sun was bright and cheerful in a clear blue sky, a direct opposite of the group of villagers gathered around Tomas. Ben and Connor watched for a while from a distance, saw the teacher try once more to explain what was happening, and heard the villagers again fly at him with anger and accusations of heresy or worse. In an interesting change, Ben was quiet while the minstrel fidgeted.

"I think I know how to do this."

"What've you got?"

"This town isn't like Overlook. Their creating is just to survive. That hunting lodge is right there, and this is the center of town. And look, you can see fields of crops from here, too. It's less sophisticated. What do you think?"

"Looks can be misleading."

"Connor, if you know something, tell me now. I'm trying to come up with a plan here."

"All right, maybe they're less sophisticated. What does that give us?"

"Tom's trying to convince them philosophically. Maybe we need to be more concrete."

"Those guys showing up wasn't enough? Three people getting killed? How can we make them see anything if that didn't?" The anger in Connor's voice was no surprise.

"I'm not sure. If I'm the heart of the problem, I suppose I need to show them what I'm really like… Get my drift?"

The minstrel nodded slowly, one eyebrow raised.

"Okay. You've been awake at least part of the time since we took out that gang. What are they expecting?"

Connor sighed and squinted off into the distance. "A great warrior. One who can down whole armies with bolts of lightning." He made a hand motion complete with sound effect that could only have been an imitation of Ben. "That kind of thing."

Ben frowned and nodded. "Okay. Is the One - am I supposed to be vengeful as well?"

"I suppose. How would they feel if you weren't angry for them?"

"Okay. I think I've got it." He repressed a shudder as he thought through what he was going to do. "Tough part. I hope I can pull it off. Any of Alious' men still here?"

"Yeah, they got five of them, and they're holding them in the old teacher's house. At least they've got men guarding them." Connor looked at Ben, trying to follow his line of thought. "What do they have to do with it?"

"Are any of them hurt?"

"Sure, it wasn't like we were pulling any -" Connor stopped as something of Ben's plan touched him. "Can you do that? I mean, can you…" He made a vague motion on his chest that expressed more about feelings and decisions than his words ever could.

"I better be able to, or the prophecies are completely wrong about the One." Ben gave him gave a grim smile. "Otherwise, I'm not the One at all, but I really don't want to go over that again right now." A curious look crossed the minstrel's face.

"Okay. Let's do it."

They strode down the road to where Tomas was surrounded by the villagers. Stopping a few yards back, Ben boomed out with projection that would have made his voice teachers proud. "What's going on?" There was a spark of anger in his delivery, just a touch of shock at the impudence. "Tomas?"

The teacher's eyes widened, and he came close to questioning what was to him an obvious act. *Come on Tom, improvise. Follow me.* Their eyes met, neither one changing expression. Then Tomas shook his head with an obvious sigh.

"I've tried to tell them, oh *just* One, that the battle isn't over. They don't believe me. They think that you will save them, without them so much as lifting a hand."

Ben nodded. "Do they know I must go beyond Anders to fight the evil at its root? Or do they want me to stay here and protect them, while the rest of those who wait for me suffer?"

A rustling of discomfort grew in the crowd. *This is where I have to be careful. I have to be in character enough to make them a little afraid of me, but not so afraid that they don't want to back me up.* Ben shook his head sadly, as his eyes swept the crowd. "That can't be what you want." The villagers looked sheepish and a little scared. Mob mentality was in full force, and Ben ran with it. "Where are the dark warriors that were captured yesterday? Who can lead me to them?"

For a long count nothing happened, and Ben was afraid he might have overestimated. Then a man with shaggy dark blond hair and a full beard stepped forward. Faded blue pants that ended just below the knees and a simple off-white tunic open at the collar gave him a more casual look than the rest of his fellows. Casual, but not haphazard. To Ben, it seemed that the man was more comfortable with himself. His observant gaze bordered on suspicious, but it was kept skillfully under control. The actor saw something in the calm, pale blue eyes that he could trust - self-confidence and its best companion, compassion.

"I'll take you to them."

"What's your name, friend?"

The response was strong. This villager had no fear of the One, or none that he cared to show. "Berke."

"Thank you, Berke. Are they alive?"

"Yes. For the moment. One may not see tomorrow."

"Show me." He turned and beckoned for Tomas and Connor to follow. "I'll need your help."

The villagers milled behind them, and Ben could hear bits of conversation as he followed his guide. " *...he'll get rid of them now ... no, I don't know if he can ...why would he need help ...why should I be quiet? I've heard that the One can hear what we think... "* Ben repressed his exasperation at the gossip, and tried instead to focus on the task at hand. Connor and Tomas fell into step on either side with a protective air. Berke walked a few paces ahead, and the rest of the crowd kept a respectable distance as they followed.

Ben spoke quietly to Tom as they walked, not turning his head. "You talk to Con?"

"Yes."

"Well?"

"Well what?"

"Am I on the right track here?" The actor risked a quick glance at the teacher, and was rewarded with a look as bright as sunlight.

"I believe you're on the One's path."

"Thanks." Ben's expression hardened. "I hope so."

They reached the house and went inside. Four of the prisoners were all right physically, but sullen and quiet. The fifth lay on the ground on a thin mat, breathing heavily and covered in sweat.

"I'm the healer here," Berke said, motioning toward the herbs and oils that were the tools of his trade, "But this is beyond my skills."

"Or your desire." Ben raised his hands to soften his comment in the face of Berke's expression. "I mean no offense, this village has been wounded. But trust me, we often do things we don't expect that we can." The healer nodded, feeling something of Ben's truth in his statement. "Will you help?"

"Help you?" The healer looked skeptical. "I wouldn't expect you to need anything from me."

"Live and learn, Berke. I'm a lot newer to this than you are. If we work together..." As he spoke, Ben knelt down next to the man and gently pulled a bloody dressing away from his abdomen. Beneath it a dark red gash was swollen open, the skin surrounding it a sick yellow.

"Ben."

Ben gladly looked away from the infected wound and up at Connor. "What?"

"I don't know if it's safe to do anything with them here." He motioned to the other prisoners, sitting against the wall with their hands tied.

Ben looked at them and sighed. "Can we help them? The way you helped Per? Were they ever normal?"

"I don't know. Normal's a state of mind, and I don't know if I'd be helping or not." Ben looked at the floor to hide his surprise at this admission of the minstrel's limits. "Maybe we can just ward them off."

"I don't know if we want to spread that thin. We need enough energy to get through this without me sleeping for a week to recharge." Berke looked puzzled but said nothing, watching them like a line judge at a tennis match as Ben turned back to him. "Is there anyone else in town that you trust? That has strong control?"

"There's no one here like you, if that's what you mean. We've been fighting for subsistence."

Tom spoke up. "Is there a circle?"

"There was. But we haven't met in months. There's no confidence." Berke trailed off, frustrated and resigned. The flash in his blue eyes faded a bit. "I'm sorry. I wish there was."

Ben took a deep breath and sighed. "I don't see that we have a choice. This might help, if we can pull it off." He stood up and walked to the door. "Wish me luck."

The minstrel nodded. "Break a leg."

Berke turned and frowned. "What's he doing?"

Tomas watched as he left. "He's going to get their help."

The healer shook his head. "Does he think he can convince them to support this?" He looked down at the patient he had sincerely tried to save, and crossed his arms on his chest. "Out of nowhere, to gather the circle for a man like this?" His expression was sincerely questioning. "Do you think he can talk them into it?"

Connor thought for a brief moment, and shook his head enigmatically. "Ben? No. But maybe the One can." He looked at the wounded man. "Let's get him cleaned up." The healer nodded and moved over to a pitcher of water and pile of clean cloths.

Outside, the villagers were restless, but they stopped and stared when Ben walked outside towards them. "Listen. I need all of you. I need the energy that comes from your circle. I'm trying to save a man's life." He watched as realization dawned across the group. "Will you help me?"

The people murmured among themselves, and for a long moment nothing happened. Then a few women stepped out together, looking significantly at the others. The gathering began to connect in groups of two or three, which in turn strung together into a line. There were not enough of them to stretch around the house, and Ben was wondering about that when the group spaced out evenly into a circle. It looked a little spare to Ben, but then the drums started.

The village here did not focus their circle through vocalization. They used movement. Slowly, the circle moved to the right, deliberate, measured steps moving in rhythm to the simple beat of a drum. Then, smoothly, a woman of the circle broke the beat by adding to it, clapping a syncopated triple that changed her step. Other percussion added her movements into their pattern, and the circle went on. It built in that way, by bits and leaps, until the power was overwhelming. It reminded Ben of a Greek folk dance, contagious in its energy. He tore himself away and headed inside, almost distracted from the task at hand.

"You did it." Berke was staring out the window in surprise.

"They did it. All I did was ask." He turned to Tom. "How do we ward this place?"

The teacher squinted for a moment, as if he was trying to picture something. Then he nodded. "It's done. They're doing it." His eyes opened wide once more, and he smiled at Ben. "Nice work."

Ben frowned, remembering where he had heard that last, and shook his head. "This is just an infection, right? No internal bleeding?" He stared at Berke, who looked puzzled.

"The wound isn't clean, if that's what you mean. It won't heal this way."

"That's what I mean. Tom, can you keep an eye on the others - I think you know what to look for better than the rest of us." The teacher nodded, and took up a station between the other soldiers and his friends. "Connor, can you help me with this?" The minstrel looked dubious for a beat, and then smirked at Ben.

"There is no try, only do," his voice made Berke take a small step backward.

Ben grinned. "Then let's do it."

With Connor singing quietly next to him, Ben found the place within himself, within the One, that could heal. He closed his eyes and felt the heat drain out of the man's skin along with the infection, and made sure that the wound was closed well. Within what seemed like minutes but was closer to an hour, the man was resting comfortably. Connor wound his song to a close, and Tom rejoined them. "He's well?"

"I think so. And I don't feel like I'm going to collapse, although I could eat a horse." Berke's eyebrows shot up. "I'm kidding, Berke. But I am hungry."

The healer looked at Ben, considering him carefully. "I'll tell them what you did. How you did it. They'll want to know why."

Ben looked Berke in the eye and took a deep breath. He appeared to stand just a little taller as his shoulders relaxed back, and was filled with a calm that spilled out into the room. "Why do you think I saved a man who tried to kill us?

Berke's eyes flashed as he looked at the three strangers before him. "You did it," he said evenly, "because it was the right thing to do." Ben smiled and put out his hand, which Berke gripped at the forearm as he spoke. "They'll understand. I'll make sure of it."

With a short backward glance Berke walked out of the house and moved to the small group of percussionists. He took what looked to Ben like two nicely finished cylinders of perri wood, and by altering the rhythm, added himself to the circle before he began to spiral the energy down.

Tomas watched Berke through the window and nodded. "He's a natural focus for them. We're fortunate to have found him so quickly." The teacher shook his head and looked at Ben. "I think we may have found the true leader for this place. Do you know how unusual that is? This quickly? I can teach after all." He smiled, a broad and more relieved expression than Ben would have expected.

Benjamin shook his head. "All I did was ask."

The celebration went late into the night. Because the One inferred that Berke should lead, he was accepted as the leader of Lintock. Berke, in turn, asked Tomas to stay on as teacher while they rebuilt, to protect and guide the wisdom of the village. It was going well, and Ben was beginning to feel the relief ease into exhaustion. He was leaning against a young tree and sipping topaz perriwine when Tomas walked over to him.

"How are you?"

"Tired. Is this going as well as I feel?"

"I believe so. You did well, Ben."

"Thanks." The wind whispered in the silvery leaves above, leaving a sweet scent behind. They stood for a long time looking into a sky just beginning to release stars from hiding, and Benjamin laughed quietly. "I can hardly believe it. I think I'm finally getting a handle on this One character." Tom gave him a puzzled look as Berke and Connor walked up to join them, both carrying bottles of topaz. Berke refilled their goblets with the bottle he carried, while Connor just drank out of his.

"To the One," Berke said in toast, downing his wine in one go. Benjamin smiled and sipped more cautiously. His head was already spinning from what he had drunk this evening, and what he had done that afternoon.

"Can you stay with us a while?"

"We leave at dawn." Connor sounded determined but a little slurred, unless it was Ben's hearing.

"Dawn? Are you kidding? I could sleep-"

"Important journeys start at dawn."

"So I've heard."

"He's right, you know."

"We'd be glad to have you stay longer."

The conversation blurred in Ben's mind, and he looked up into the night sky. Without any conscious effort, he saw his favorite constellation. The familiar hourglass shape with three stars tilted across its center caught his eye, and a joyful cry erupted from his chest. "Orion!"

The conversation around him stopped dead.

"What?" Even the teacher looked startled at his outburst.

"Orion. There." He pointed a bit unsteadily at the sky. "Orion. That group of stars. My favorite, always has been, so easy to find." The other men peered up into the sky. "That one, the one with three stars in a row for his belt, and the three hanging down for his sword. See it?" Tom and Berke looked at each other and smiled, as Berke began to laugh soundlessly. Ben frowned over at them. "What?"

"That isn't called Orion," the teacher said, in a very teacherly way.

"No," the healer and new leader of Lintock added, shaking his head and then nodding. "That's not what it's called here."

Ben groaned inwardly, wondering if he really needed to hear this. "What is it, then?"

Berke smiled and took another swallow of wine, his eyes sparkling in the starlight. "Everyone knows that. It's called the One."

9

Although most preparation had been done the day before, it was still a good hour past dawn when the two travelers finally stood by their horses, ready to leave. Both Ben and Connor were feeling the after effects of wine and a late night, and neither was in any hurry.

The previous evening had progressed smoothly from the celebration to planning to general conversation, and Ben remembered the sky deepening beyond midnight by the time he closed his eyes. The four who talked the latest - Tomas, Connor, Berke and Ben - did not sleep until they had determined the path that the two going on would take, and the path that the two who stayed behind would take as well. They probably would have talked until dawn if they had the strength. Ben was reminded of a wrap party after a show - no one wanting to let go of the rare magic of connection.

Berke had been reluctant at first to take on the role of leader, but by night's end was beginning to look forward to the challenge. He still had the disconcerting habit of catching himself in the middle of a sentence to Ben, as if he realized that he was speaking to the One and felt the implications that went with it. At moments like that his pale blue eyes would change their expression without taking the rest of his face along.

While it didn't change anything he said, it gave Ben a peculiar feeling. He knew that particular sensation - seeing the abruptly serious cast of Berke's normally smiling, accessible eyes - would stay with him for a long time.

"You ready?"

"Yeah." Ben came out of his reverie and tightened the packs on his saddle. He couldn't believe that this was anything but stalling, and tried to find a good reason why. When he stepped back to consider that he had little idea of where he was going or what he was to do, it seemed almost reasonable. He shook his head with a laugh and turned to see the minstrel staring at him.

"What's so funny?"

"I am." Ben walked over to where Connor stood in front of his own horse, adjusting the bridle. "Did you ever find yourself in a situation where you expected more of yourself than you would of anyone else, if your life was their story and they were telling it to you?"

Connor blinked and frowned, then blinked again, brushing distractedly at a fly buzzing near his head. "Are you still drunk or am I?"

"No, I mean it. I get upset with myself for reacting in a way that I would find perfectly normal for anyone else. Don't you?"

"Yeah, but that's because I expect more of myself than I do of anyone else."

"Okay. Why?"

"Because I do."

"Because you're better?" Ben looked the minstrel in the eye, a slight grin showing that he had thrown down a gauntlet and was enjoying every minute of it.

"Maybe." The minstrel looked away seriously, but there was a sparkle that Ben recognized as appreciation of the verbal sparring, a chance to bring his brain back into action. "Or maybe it's just that I know myself better than I know anyone else, I know what I'm capable of at my best, and I expect my best."

Benjamin made a derisive noise. "Fine. Expectations are fine, Connor, and being my best is what I want, but how fair is it to beat myself up for struggling when I would understand anyone else having trouble?" The minstrel opened his mouth to speak but Ben went on. "For example. This morning. I'm nervous about this trip. I'm sorry that

Tom won't be coming with us. And oddly enough, I'm missing how comfortable I was in Overlook. Can you believe it? I'm taking my time getting going because of all that. That makes sense, doesn't it?"

The minstrel nodded and smiled wryly. "Sure it does, if *you're* doing it. If *I* was doing it, it would be really annoying." He turned away to check on his saddle pack, and Ben was left with his mouth open as Tom approached them.

"Good morning." The teacher's smile was a bit weary. "Do you need anything?"

Ben grinned. "Another five hours of sleep would be terrific."

The minstrel walked over to the teacher and they clasped forearms. "Thanks, Tom. I think we're set." Connor slapped Tom's shoulder and stepped back, frowning as he tried with limited success to avoid the emotion of the moment. In a quiet voice, he said, "Be safe."

"We'll see each other again."

"That in the prophecies?"

The teacher smiled widely. "It's in my heart." He turned toward Ben and reached out his hand. "Be well. Come back to us. And if you need anything, create a way to let us know. We'll do what we can."

Ben felt warmth spreading in his chest as they grasped arms. "Thanks. I know. We'll see each other again." Ben heard himself say it, and something in his mind acknowledged it as truth. "I know that much."

With a nod and a smile, Tom stepped back as they got on their horses, and raised his right arm in what looked like a benediction. "May the Artist protect you, and return you to us safely."

Ben's hand went to the pendant at his neck, feeling the energy connecting. *Amen.*

The rising sun cast spears of light at them as they rode away from the town, making Ben's eyes water as he squinted into the distance. At least he told himself that's why they were watering. They rode in the quiet of their thoughts for close to an hour, recognizing the passing of this part of their journey, and thinking forward to the rest.

"Is there another town between here and the Lady?" Ben had heard Lady Anders referred to so many times the night before that now saying it almost seemed natural.

"No, no towns. But there's the occasional house, and a small farm I know. Trou lives there." He gave a fond grin. "She plays with words, too."

"She writes?"

"Poetry. She's been okay. At least she was when I was here three years ago."

Ben frowned in concern. "Meaning?"

"Meaning that living this close to the border on your own, anything can happen. But she's tough. I'm sure she's doing fine."

Ben felt tightness in his chest when he thought about her, a suspicion with no facts whatsoever to support it. *No, that's not right. It's when I feel Connor thinking about her.* He sighed. Taking a few deep breaths, he focused on the road ahead of them, and tried to relax. He felt like himself this morning, which unfortunately at this moment meant that he was nervous about what was ahead for him, tired, and experiencing some free-floating anxiety. Connor, not noticing his discomfort, didn't let the moment of attempted relaxation last long.

"So."

Ben waited. "Yeah?"

"You're an actor."

This was as far from anything Ben expected as he could imagine.

"Yeah, I'm an actor." There was a moment, which turned into a pause, which eventually led to a pregnant silence. "So what?"

The minstrel shook his head, pulled the lacing of his collar tighter against the coolness of the morning air.

"Nothing."

"Oh, come on."

"What?"

"You know I'm an actor. I've talked about it. It's -" he made futile circular motions with his hands. "You know I am. Why the sudden surprise?" Ben was taken aback by his own defensiveness. And *was* that a vaguely condescending tone in the minstrel's voice, or were the words simply too close to sounding like someone else?

"Look. Don't get worked up. I just never thought the One'd be an actor, that's all."

"I just never thought my son would be an actor, that's all, not if he had intelligence and strength."

Ben could see every detail in his father's face. The strong, square jaw line and echoing blue eyes. He could smell aftershave, feel the heat in his own cheeks as he reacted. Outside, the sun was slanting in orange lines through the dusky sky, kids were laughing and playing in the magical last days of summer. Ben had never before questioned his father's opinion.

"What's that supposed to mean?"

"Well, you're a natural athlete, for one. You could get a sports scholarship to any med school you wanted. I had such high hopes for you."

"Don't get worked up? I'd be careful about telling other people what they should or shouldn't feel, given how you'd respond to the suggestion." Ben felt himself flush as his feelings spiraled out of control. A familiar sensation of his cheeks burning.

"It's what I want to do. It's - I feel good when -"

"What do you know about what you want to do?"

"Look, Dad, you don't get it. They don't give kids like me chances like this. This isn't some school show. This is the real thing!"

"The real thing? It's a local theatre. And I'm not going to have you tie up your school nights with some stupid show when you're just starting high school. For God's sake, Benji, you're only thirteen! Go to college first, and get this nonsense out of your system. Then-"

"Don't call me Benji!"

He willed himself to take it easy. He was not a thirteen year old running out of the house and into the backyard, climbing blindly up to his tree house pretending the tears weren't really there, trying to think it didn't matter if he didn't do the part. Trying to deny the passion for what he wanted to do more than anything in the world.

Easier said than done.

Not really, some other voice in his head said. He tried to breath normally, but a wave of guilt washed up like the tidal wave in his dream.

What am I guilty about? There's nothing - and out of nowhere, the reason spilled out, in a nasty little tone reserved only for himself, with a clarity he had never fully appreciated before.

If my parents had lived, they would have convinced me to become a doctor. They would've kept me from my dream, and some part of me is glad they're dead, glad they couldn't stop me, because - a sound caught in his throat as his body automatically took over the breath that he had been holding. *No, that can't be true. I can't be that much of a bastard that I would be glad my mother and father are dead. No.*

And then the other voice in his head, one that was him and something more, spoke again. *No.*

His thoughts stopped dead for a blessed instant and posed a simple, straightforward question. *What would the One say about me?*

How could I possibly be the One when I'm capable of -

But the actor had already begun the technical process. He found himself in a dialogue, just as he had been with other characters in the past.

Why do you assume that you would have given up your dream for your parents?

They would have convinced me - Ben took another breath and thought he might have heard something on the periphery of his awareness. *All right, let's say I didn't give up my dream. Let's say I fought it out with them, and went on anyway, without their approval. Without their support.*

Yes.

Then why do I feel guilty? There was a long pause.

Guilt always serves a purpose.

Purpose? What possible purpose - and with a flash, as if someone had opened the curtains in a long closed room, he saw it. The guilt lay like a thick blanket across his feelings of loss, and as long as he played with the blanket, he didn't have to look under it. A vacuum formed in his chest, and this time a shocked gasp sucked in as reality flooded his feelings.

Damn! I wanted them to see me work. I wanted to show them I was good at this. I wanted to prove they were wrong. I wanted...

Know this, Benjamin. They are proud.

A familiar energy swelled in his chest. The broken lock of guilt had opened a room of unbelievable grief and sorrow, yet it was accompanied by a glow, strengthening and comforting him. A profound understanding that the energies that were his parents on earth did not cease to exist with their physical bodies. That they didn't need physical bodies to know him, to understand the importance of his work... or to be proud of him in a way that the humans might have struggled with.

"Ben?" Connor's voice on the edge of his awareness was soft.

The actor opened his eyes and blinked, aware that they had stopped. "Sorry." He wiped his hand across his face and motioned that they should go on. Connor grabbed the reins before he could start moving.

"Right. As soon as you tell me what the hell just happened." The minstrel stared intently into his eyes, genuine concern on his face.

"I'm not sure." He frowned at Connor. "This sounds strange."

For a moment the minstrel almost laughed. "Strange? With what we've already been through?" But the look in the actor's eyes made it clear he had encountered a whole new variety of strange. With a carefully modulated voice, the minstrel spoke. "Go ahead."

Benjamin shifted in his saddle, feeling like he had been sitting there for years. "There are things, unresolved things, with my father, especially." Unable to sit any longer, Ben swung down off his horse, and stretched. In a moment he was leaning back against his mount to steady himself, the sweet smell of hay and leather mixing with the warm scent of the animal itself. Ben forced another breath so deep into his chest that it began to hurt, and then let it out slowly. "And," he paused again, emotions he didn't yet have a handle on coursing through him, "I think the One may be helping me. Trying to show me the path to – God, I don't know. It sounds crazy. Healing myself."

Connor sat back and stared at Ben for a long time. Then he looked out past the trees on the roadside, and finally to his hands as they rested on the saddle. After a very long time, he looked Ben in the eye and spoke quietly.

"I guess I can accept that. I don't understand it, but it won't be the first or the last thing that I've had to accept without understanding." He looked away, breaking the intimacy of the link, and then back at Ben, the windows with curtains properly in place. "Are you okay? Okay enough to go on?"

"I think so." With a graceful movement, he was on horseback once more. The experience trembled through his memory, and he knew he wasn't done with it. At the moment, though, the strongest urge was not to touch it, to leave it alone. His mind swam slowly back to the conversation that started this particular incident, anxious to feel more comfortable ground beneath his feet. Hindsight, however, gave him a clear view of how he had sounded. "Sorry if I, ah..."

The minstrel waved his hand in a vaguely dismissive way, looking into the trees. "Don't worry about it. We're fine."

Ben nodded gratefully, then turned to look at his companion. "Didn't you know I was an actor when you called?"

Connor frowned at the sudden jump, and gave an amused grin at Ben's single-mindedness.

"Hell, no. As far as I knew I was calling a warrior. 'The One'. I pictured everything from a marine to a ninja." He shrugged, pointedly looked Ben up and down. "Who knew?"

Ben laughed, but this time it was genuine. They rode quietly through the trees for a while before Ben spoke again.

"I don't understand why this hit me now. I mean, I've been dealing with feelings about my folks - especially my dad - since I was a kid. Why now?"

Connor nudged his mount towards an open, wider path. "Do you want my answer, or Tom's?"

Ben exhaled and led his horse alongside Connor's. "Yours first."

"Simple. You're more stressed out than you've been since your folks died. This brought out the similar stress-level incidents of the past for your mind to compare it to."

Ben nodded and tilted his head sideways. "Seems to make sense."

"Yeah."

"What would Tom say?"

The minstrel paused a moment as an unusually roguish smile touched his lips, then proceeded to do a passable imitation of the teacher.

"The Artist knew that you had this wound within you, and it has to be healed before it can be used against you. This was simply the first chance to do it."

The actor looked at Connor with wide eyes.

"Connor."

"Yeah?"

"That feels like it makes sense too."

The minstrel sighed, his eyebrows shrugging. "Yeah. I know."

They traveled in silence for several hours, until dusk fell and they made camp. They talked lightly then about the food and the weather, and anything that didn't make them think too hard. Anything that didn't make it obvious that they were in touch with a greater power, a metaphysical link, or a path they couldn't quite see. By mutual, unspoken consent, they unrolled their packs early, and gave every appearance of falling quickly to sleep.

10

"Hear that?"

The whisper in the darkness brought Ben to full consciousness in a heartbeat, even though he had a suspicious feeling that he had fallen asleep only moments ago.

"Hear what?" He spoke so quietly he could barely hear himself, but somehow knew Connor caught every word. By the flickering remains of the fire, he saw the minstrel string his bow and nock an arrow in place.

"Them."

Ben looked around. In his sleepy state, with a completely unconscious effort, he expanded his awareness to the forest around him. There were people there. Maybe half a dozen. No good intent. "Hawk."

"Quiet."

"They're after me."

"No kidding."

The minstrel slipped out and away from the reddish circle of light so quietly that Ben would not have known he was moving if he hadn't been watching. As the actor reached for his blade, he heard a bowstring twang and a stifled cry in the night.

His awareness registered the hit without noticing that he was doing something he didn't know how to do.

Five. Taking his sword, he rolled away and crouched farther from the fire in a smooth, graceful movement. The sword eased into his palm as if it belonged there, as if it were merely an extension of his arm, another part of his body. He felt his eyes adjusting to the shadows, heard Connor moving softly some yards away. Every sense was reporting in so much detail he could hardly keep up. He could *feel* the five that remained. *Feel them? What the hell does that mean?* The part of him that was still largely asleep tried to wake up enough to get the upper hand. *It doesn't make sense.*

Ben turned his head as another wave of *something* hit him. An attack. He was sure of it. He saw no one, heard nothing, yet - His sword was in front of him in an instant, *parry two,* blade pointing down in front of him, grip nearly at eye level. A foil fencing move, it was a showy but awkwardly inefficient block, one that took far too long to get out of in close-quartered swordplay.

The force of the arrow hitting his blade would have knocked it out of his hand if he hadn't been braced for contact.

Benjamin Agante, abruptly fully awake, gasped as he looked down, watched the polished smoothness of the shaft gleam as it tumbled through the firelight to the ground, realizing he had been saved from an arrow through the heart by a piece of metal the width of his blade. Fear welled up, separating the character of the One from him like oil from water. *No. Stay with me. We can do this.*

Ben ducked behind a tree, panting like a chased animal. From across the wood he heard Connor, felt his alarm at hearing the arrow flight and clang of the sword being hit. Even though he knew it located him for the others in the party, he couldn't let Connor expose himself. "I'm all right!" The announcement was met with a series of arrows flying into the night, most of which buried themselves in the tree he was sheltered by. Panic leapt through him like an electric shock. Petrified, he cringed in the darkness, his arms covering his head as he crouched low against the tree. *Home. I want to be home. I just want to wake up, and...*

There were multiple rustlings in the wood now, as shadows jockeyed for position in the darkness. Ben couldn't make out which one, if any, was Connor, and he strained to listen more closely. What he finally heard was a song, faint, and in his head alone.

The words were too hard to make out. In desperation, Ben fought with himself, tried to get in touch with the character of the One once more. *Technique*, a voice from his past whispered in his ear. *When all else fails, technique your way through.*

Taking a deep breath, he centered and straightened his shoulders. The One would be alert, relaxed but ready. Ben made his body do just that. Knees slightly flexed, shoulders down, eyes open, sword *en garde*. The One would be looking for Hawk, trying to find a way to help him. Ben scanned the woods as far as he could see them, an efficiency to his search born of calm. The One - *was there.* The song became clear. It was a bridge between them, clear as a bell.

Stay down and I'll get as many of them as I can.

No, Con. There's five more. I can tell where they are.

I don't give a damn what you can tell. Stay down.

Ben smiled darkly as he ignored the minstrel's order. He felt one of the attackers sidle up to the tree that sheltered him. Slipping quietly around the trunk, he wrapped his left arm around the man's neck from behind, tightly enough to stifle the cry in his throat.

In an instant, he could feel the possibilities unfold before him. With this close contact, under this strain, the man's mind was an open book. There was a heart problem that could easily be manipulated. There were lungs that could be encouraged to stop with little more effort. There was a multitude of brain functioning - Benjamin recoiled in horror, nearly losing his grip.

No. I can't kill him.

What would you do? Let them kill us? And the Hawk?

There has to be another way.

In the space of time it took to inhale once more, Ben saw the possibilities unfold again. This time he searched instead of simply being overwhelmed by the choices. Relief washed over him as he discovered what he was searching for.

Sleep, that's it. Just sleep.

Sleep? A faint rustling as his soul brushed against the warrior spirit of the One.

Yes.

With a minimal effort, the One reached into the man's mind and found the spot that would render him unconscious. Now. For quite a while. A faint sensation of amusement washed over Ben. *Sleep. I never would have considered that. Yet with these simple, compromised minds, it works.* In stealthy steps, Ben circled around two more of the attackers and used the same technique to put them under. Understanding and not understanding. The One and yet still Ben.

Connor moved steadily through the wood, knowing he had killed one of them. If Ben was right, and there were five more, then that shape must be - he drew back silently and let fly. The only target that he could be sure of was the man's head. If it had been light, he would have seen the arrow pass through his would-be assassin's left eye. The man hit the ground dead, never knowing what hit him. The minstrel called out to Ben on the line he had established with a song.

You still here?

Yeah. Three down.

Two here.

Good.

The link was ruptured when they both wheeled at the sound of a horse bounding through the woods, toward them, past them, away from them, passing close enough to Benjamin to kick up a rain of leaves and dirt from the woodland floor onto his arms as he shielded himself.

That's it, then, was the last thing that Ben felt coming from Connor. Again, the strange oil and water separation. This time he didn't fight it.

"You okay?" Ben called softly across the darkness that separated him from the minstrel.

"Yeah. You?"

"Yeah. What do we do with them?"

"What do you mean?"

"I knocked three of them out."

There was a pause as the minstrel fought with his reaction. "You didn't kill anyone?"

An equal pause for the actor.

"No."

"Just what the hell did you do?"

Ben let out a sigh. "Let's just say they're asleep."

Connor nodded, exhausted, not really wanting to know, and made a circling motion. "Let's get the fire built up and bring the ones who're left over there. Maybe they can tell us something."

Ben headed back to the camp to work on the fire, and Connor walked unsteadily to the two he had killed. Holding his palms out over them, he muttered quietly, "I release you." Then, into the subtle shifting of energy and more quietly still, he said, "and may the Artist forgive us all."

While Ben built up the fire with some of the wood they had saved aside for breakfast, Connor dragged the three unconscious attackers nearer the circle of light. The minstrel looked at Benjamin carefully as he stared with a rather stony expression. "You okay?"

The actor started and stopped a sentence, as nothing more than a broken fragment of sound came out. Then he forced his features into some semblance of calm and looked back at Connor. "Gimme a minute." He sat with his elbows cradling his knees and stared into the fire, trying to slow his breathing.

Connor nodded, watched curiously as the actor obviously sank into a meditative state. He worried briefly about more attackers approaching them, and found himself humming a warding under his breath, giving Ben time to collect himself. After a moment Ben spoke quietly, with difficulty, but needing to explain.

"I'm not quite myself yet."

The minstrel shrugged. "Don't push it. Do you think they're out until morning?"

The voice lifted slightly. "I think so. It's kind of new to me."

"All right. Just relax, do what you have to do. I'll set a warding, and we'll wait until it's light to deal with the rest of this. Okay?"

"Sure." Ben didn't really know how he felt about it. But he knew that he needed time to settle down after what had happened. He leaned his head against his knapsack, realized he was still clutching the sword, and closed his eyes. He heard the fire crackling, felt the warmth against his face and the cold of the night on his back. From a little way off, he heard Connor singing softly in the darkness. He shifted his grip on the sword without letting it go, and quietly fell asleep. The last thing he remembered was a voice in his head that sounded like him and yet not, but sounding more like him all the time. *Nice work.*

In his dream, Benjamin was flying. The air rushed by in a wild symphony of sound as his wings guided him effortlessly through the moonlit night. Far below, he could see a castle in the darkness. With a subtle shift of wing, he dropped toward a high tower that sparkled in the moonlight. A woman stood there, her arm outstretched. He studied her; deep green eyes and dark hair that fell in ringlets across her shoulders and down her back.

Banking against the air, he landed gracefully on the waist-high wall at her side, and they studied each other openly. Her voice was soft and calm. "Be safe." He studied her for another moment, then was off again, flying east into the star-flecked night.

Ben awoke in exactly the same position he had fallen asleep in, with the unexpected addition of a tucked blanket. Releasing the leather wrapped sword hilt gave him a brief wash of deja-vu, but it passed along with the stiffness in his fingers. He stretched and yawned, shivering into the morning cool. Sunlight filtered through fog into the wood, closing up the world around them in an oddly comforting manner. A surprising scent wafted toward him.

"Coffee?" Connor held out a steaming mug to Ben.

"Coffee?" Ben blinked. "You have coffee? Where did you find it?"

"It's not exactly coffee. It's an herb. There's a bank of it over there." He nodded at the wood behind him as he passed the drink over. "Same effect, though. Careful. It's hot."

Ben accepted the mug gladly. "Wow. Thanks." The first sip verified that it really did taste like coffee, with a slight vanilla tinged cinnamon edge. As he drank, he looked around the campsite. Across the fire from him were three bodies, draped over with horse blankets. Ben froze as he realized that some of the memories stirring inside of him weren't from any dream.

The minstrel shrugged, misunderstanding Ben's sudden silence. "I did it after I set the wards. I might have killed them if I had to look at them all night, and I'm assuming you had a reason."

Ben looked over at him, confused, and shrugged. "I don't know, Connor. The reason may be that I just can't. I struggled with the One about it, he almost -"

"Wait a minute." Connor gave him a flat stare. "What do you mean, you 'struggled with the One'?"

Ben sipped and pulled the blanket closer, waiting for his thoughts to weave themselves into something recognizable. When he finally spoke, it was as if he was hearing some of the ideas for the first time, and putting words to them gave a reality he hesitated to bestow.

"I think I'm figuring it out now. Creations here have their own power. The act of creating releases power, and the creation itself, if that's possible, retains it. At home, I might have worked on this character, used him when I needed him. Here, the character of the One really exists. I've anchored him to my soul. We're stuck with each other." Ben paused to sip his coffee before going on. Connor frowned. "I've played with characters outside a show before, but this is the first time I've ever really felt a power struggle with one." He looked over at the minstrel, waiting for a response.

After a thoughtful pause, Connor shrugged. "It makes sense to you?"

Ben nodded, surprising himself. "Pretty much. Hard to explain, but it feels right."

"You feel safe? You won't lose track of yourself?"

"A part of me is part of the character. I can't lose track of myself." Ben stopped for a minute, considered. "And I know that I'm the one creating, I'm the one in control. I suppose it might be possible to lose that, but I don't really believe it. It's my *job* to control characters."

"All right." The minstrel stood and brushed his hands off on his thighs. "I don't get it. But then, I won't try to explain to you how I compose something here that lets us think to each other, and you can pretend to understand, or understand a little, or just forget about it and let me deal with it when I have to. Fair enough?"

Ben smiled broadly. "You got it."

"Good. Then let's see what we got here." He moved to the nearest lump of blanket and pulled it off. A slender figure in black was crowned with short, dark red hair. "Oh my God." His voice was a hoarse whisper.

"Con?"

The minstrel was pulling the figure over onto its back, moving more gently now than he had before. It was a woman. She was pale, and her high cheekbones and features might have been carved from ivory.

"Connor?" Ben moved over to where the minstrel crouched at her side. "Do you know her?"

"Yeah. It's Trou. Damn! I should have stayed, I could have -"

"You could have been taken right along with her." The actor's tone was logical, but he felt incredibly cold saying it.

"But she -" The minstrel's face was a stone mask, but somewhere deep in his eyes he looked like he might cry, or scream, or perhaps kill someone.

"Connor." Ben clamped his hand firmly on the minstrel's shoulder, hoping to anchor him somehow. "I can wake her up, but she's probably not going to be whoever you remember. Can you handle that?"

Connor took a deep breath and blew it out slowly. "Do it. Let me check the wards first." He closed his eyes and seemed to be listening for something. After a moment he nodded, satisfied, and opened his eyes. Ben's curiosity overcame him.

"Can you actually hear them?"

"Yeah. You might too, if you knew what to listen for."

"Maybe."

"So. Let's do it." The minstrel's brusque tone was belied by the gentle way he brushed the hair from the girl's face.

The actor settled into a cross-legged position above her head, closed his eyes, and relaxed over a series of breaths. Now that he was sure the One was a character he was working to create, he knew where to go within himself to find it. *I need you here. Let's do this.*

He opened his eyes and looked at Connor as himself and more. It was a powerful feeling. He felt there was a world of things he could do, but didn't yet know how to do them. A smile played over his features as he felt the minstrel's concern.

"Ben?"

"I'm here." Ben looked down at the woman, and saw her with the One's eyes. She was damaged. A haze around her eyes and across her chest spoke of the touch of darkness. He placed his hands at her temples and reached into the practical workings of her mind, undoing what he had done the night before. She moaned softly as he released her.

"I think it may take a minute for her to come around."

They sat silently for a few minutes as she began to stir.

Suddenly, and without warning, she sat bolt upright and screamed. As if she were being tortured. As if her very being was torn apart. Her eyes focused on nothing, and still she screamed. Connor grabbed her shoulders and yelled into her face. "Trou! It's Connor. C'mon, Trou."

A wave of guilt hit Ben, that somehow he had made this happen, that it was some kind of side effect of not knowing what he was doing and having the supreme arrogance to tamper inside someone's brain. But she stopped as abruptly as she started, and sat there, panting.

The minstrel was staring into her face, talking softly, the way one would reassure a small child. Gently he wrapped his arms around her, and after a moment's hesitation, she collapsed into them. Connor looked over and met Ben's eyes.

"Night terrors. She said it used to happen a lot."

"She okay?"

The minstrel shrugged in frustration. "You tell me."

Ben looked at them again, with eyes that could see more than he could alone. Against the minstrel's rich, blue-green aura, Trou looked like all the color had been leeched out of her. The haze of black remained, but beneath it what he saw was dark and bruised, a scarring on her spirit that had been there for a long, long time. This was a woman who had suffered within herself for most of her life.

"She's been touched by darkness, that much is clear. But Connor -" Ben hesitated, knowing what the One sensed, but feeling the connection his friend had to this woman. "She's fairly dark herself. Not evil, but… you must realize the potential is there."

Connor continued to hold Trou, rocking her gently and stroking her hair. "I know. She always struggled with that. I thought she was okay when I left, or I never would have."

"I know."

The minstrel sat quietly, Trou nestled in his arms. Finally, he got out a question.

"Can you heal her?"

Ben's eyebrows lifted as he studied her once more. "I don't know. I can remove the shadow, for a while, anyway. I'm not sure what that will do. I don't have any way of knowing what's actually going on inside her mind."

Yes, we do.

Shut up. I'm not going there.

Trou moaned and shook her head. Her eyes opened again on the two of them, her expression wrapped in fear and pain. Abruptly it changed, and her senses seemed to snap into place. Malicious laughter rolled from somewhere deep in her chest.

"You thought you could help me? Fools. You should have killed me when you had the chance."

Connor spoke in a soft voice. "Trou." Slowly her head turned until her eyes met the minstrel's, and the pain washed out as far as

Ben. Tears gathered until they brimmed over, spilling down her cheeks, a bizarre split of anger and the desire to connect with her friend. Connor continued to look into her eyes as he spoke to Ben.

"Do you think whatever you do can help her?"

"I don't know. But it might let you talk to her. I don't know for how long."

"Do it."

"Okay." Ben motioned for Connor to lay her down once more. She grimaced, as if in pain, as he released her gently onto the blanket. A flutter of movement shook her, and Connor's eyes pleaded with Ben to do something quickly. It was such an uncommon expression for the minstrel that Benjamin was nearly startled out of character. Getting hold of himself, he took a deep breath and put one hand on the poet's chest. He could see the sooty black mist that clung to her there and tenderly, with a touch of energy, pushed it away. After doing the same to her eyes, he looked again at the bruised light that surrounded her.

He had never seen anything like it, but neither had the One. There was so much power there that had never been reconciled. As if the power itself, being ignored or restrained, had bruised her. He took a deep breath, shuddering within himself. *Dear God. This could have been me.* He realized that there was nothing he could do to actually heal her. This was her own doing, her own path. In the intimacy of the moment he hurt for her, and for Connor as well.

It was the minstrel who spoke first.

"Trou?" He whispered into the morning mist. "Talk to me."

The poet's eyes opened once more. This time she only looked tired, and smiled softly. "Hawk. I'm glad to be able to see you once more." Tears spilled down her face, although her voice remained stable.

"Once more?"

"I can't do this any more. I can't hurt anyone else. And I can't keep him out."

"Listen. You can come with us. I-" He stopped and glanced briefly at Ben. "*We* can protect you."

"I've seen the path, my friend. You couldn't. But thank you. Thank you for wanting to." Her left hand wrapped around his and held tight.

"But we can at least help-"

She smiled at that, and touched Connor's cheek with her other hand. "No. No one can. And I'm too tired. Don't worry, Hawk. I believe that the next world will be better -" She arched her back in pain, and Ben saw the black mists curling around her once more. With an quick movement he brushed them away, as if he were brushing away a fly. Trou's body responded by falling limp again, but she was panting hard, and it was clear from her eyes that she didn't expect it to last.

"I'm tired of fighting him. I know he wants me, my abilities, and I'm just too tired. Thank you, for everything, my friend." She turned then to Ben, grabbed his arm in her pale, slender hand. "Please. Just keep him away from me for a few more minutes. I know you can." Ben nodded and put his hand over hers. It was cold, and yet there was energy there, a phenomenal power - and a fine white sparkling that surrounded her like windblown snow. Ben heard Connor say something, his voice rising in the still morning.

"No. Trou, come on… don't give up." But the poet only smiled at him, and touched his cheek once more.

"Goodbye, Hawk," she whispered.

Ben felt something within, heard a voice that he only realized after the fact was his own. *I release you.* And then she was gone, the pale hand falling limp onto her chest.

It happened so suddenly that Ben couldn't quite register what had happened until he felt the subtle shift of energy that he had learned to associate with death in this world. He looked up at Connor, and saw tears flowing down the cheek that she had touched just a moment before. "Connor. I - I'm so sorry."

The minstrel said nothing. Silently he brushed her hair back, laid her hands together on her chest. He knelt there beside her for a long time. Long enough for Ben to shed the character and feel for himself the pain of loss.

"I tried." The agony in Ben's voice broke Connor out of his reverie. He stared at the actor and saw, perhaps for the first time, just how young he was. Ben and Trou were probably the same age.

"No one could help her," the minstrel managed to whisper.

"But the One should have been able to." Frustration tangled through the grief.

Connor wiped a hand over his face. "Don't. Just- don't." Leaning over he kissed her forehead gently. "She never had it easy, but I didn't think she'd give up."

"She didn't give up, she…" Ben's mind was writhing in anger when a quote struck him.

Vex not his ghost. O, let him pass! He hates him that would upon the rack of this tough world stretch him out longer.

The quote from Lear flooded through him with all of the meaning it had acquired for him when he did the show. And something more from the One.

It was her choice. We did what we could. We gave her the peace to escape.

They sat in a weary tableau, and Ben had no idea how long it had been when the minstrel rose and covered her gently. He spoke quietly, without looking at Connor.

"Should we bury her?"

Connor shook himself and leaned against a tree. "No. She wouldn't like that." He looked around, a little lost, and then found what he needed. "There was a clearing back there. Maybe if we built a fire."

"And them?"

"Leave them. Let whoever leads them, find them."

They moved out from the campsite, gathering wood, building a pyre. Hours later, as the flames died down, the sun proceeded to give up for the day. It surrendered, eventually, to a cool grey rain that both washed and hid their tears.

11

On the high peak of a castle that shone in the new light of dawn, the Lady Anders stood. Tears glistened on her cheeks as the breeze played with her long, dark hair. She watched the west, feeling for the One that was coming with the Hawk at his side, feeling his frustration with the role he had been given.

"Have courage," she whispered. "You will need all your strength. Remember that all you have inside is more than you will ever need." Silently she asked the Artist to send whatever energy could be spared toward the travelers.

The faint whisper of soft-soled leather boots made her aware of her son. She steeled herself against the dull pain she felt coming in waves from the two she waited for, and focused instead on the more familiar intensity of the one who stood behind her.

"Mother?" His voice was low, a benign growl. He walked to her side and looked out to the west with her, breathing deeply of the morning air. "Are they here?" Something in his tone betrayed a far greater anticipation than he would openly portray.

"Soon." She turned and looked up at him as he stared out over the fields and forests beyond the stony landscape of her keep, reaching up to smooth the dark hair that fell in curls to his shoulder. Exercising her right to mother her son even when he had reached his twenty-first year. He stood unmoving, showing neither pleasure nor disapproval at her attention.

His complexion had always mimicked her own, but the contrast of fair skin and dark hair was made more obvious in him now by the thickness of his brows and the finely trimmed line of his beard. His eyes were so dark as to appear black - far different from her deep green gaze. She knew that while he was off at the safe haven of the Core, studying to prepare himself for the duties that came with being heir to Anders Castle, he had developed other, less obvious differences as well. She had expected it, yet when it looked her in the eye she wasn't really prepared. He turned, still deep in thought.

"Today?"

"I'm not sure. They've been - delayed." The words brought an echo of the pain she had touched. "I feel they'll be here within two days." She sounded more certain than she really was. Her son frowned.

"I'd feel better if I knew what to expect."

"I know that. If I could tell you, I would." She felt his anticipation, along with something else that she couldn't define. "Be patient, Jhaun. I know it's difficult for you."

"I'm fine, Mother. Just curious."

There had always been that reluctance to make himself seem vulnerable. Now, as an adult, he was able to put a polite veneer over it. Make it look like a choice instead of a necessity. There were times she wanted to see what he was really thinking - but that would be a breach of privacy she could never justify. He would find his own way. And if there was one thing Lady Anders knew, it was how easily potential could be hidden. *Especially from ourselves.*

Her son leaned his forearms on the parapet, looking down. "Do you think he'll be what the prophecies say? What we've been waiting for?"

The Lady looked down at the view as she collected her thoughts. "He'll be himself." A curious emotion surfaced in her eyes, something she *almost* felt. After a moment she lost the thread of it, shook her head. "I'm anxious to meet him too."

Jhaun glanced at her, and deep in his eyes there seemed to be an abrupt touch of fear, like lightning at midnight. The Lady, still looking outward, didn't notice.

"The weather's with them. They shouldn't have any trouble crossing the dominion." He nodded at her small talk, returning his eyes to the west, as if by searching long enough he could cause them to materialize.

The Lady smiled softly as she looked back at the young man beside her. She wondered if he dressed purposely to accentuate his coloring, or if it was habit that led him to dress in black, save for the white shirt beneath a velvet tabard. From his wide leather belt a fine sword hung in a black and silver scabbard, a trophy he had returned with proudly from his last days at the Core. Black leather gloves tucked beside it completed the picture of this new son of hers, the one who had been gone to study for five years, who had returned for good just weeks ago.

The only real touch of color on him was an oval of malachite set into the pommel of his sword, currents of green on green. The Lady felt an innate pride at the stone of their house being there, and her hand unconsciously went to the familiar drop of malachite and silver at her ear. She wondered if it was his idea, or Cento making sure he remembered his heritage while he was away, so that nothing was left out while he was remaking the boy into a man.

She'd seen him often during the first three years, before it became more difficult for him to get away, and more dangerous to travel. Before he came home, nearly six months had gone by with only the inconstant contact of letters. *And, of course, the music.* She tilted her head and wondered, the words coming out before she could really think about them.

"Did you ever hear me play?"

Jhaun turned, frowned, and shook his head. "What do you mean, Mother? I've heard you play all my life." His bemused expression brought a smile to her lips.

"I mean when you were gone. Sometimes, I would play to you." She looked into his eyes, trying to read there anything that would help her to recognize him.

At first he met her gaze with a practiced stoicism, revealing nothing. Then he slowly smiled in spite of himself, a crooked half smile that she recognized, that told her this really was the boy she remembered. He looked at the stone floor with something akin to shyness on his face.

"There were times," he said quietly, "when I was by myself, and I would feel my spirits lifting. It seemed to come out of nowhere." He raised his eyes to hers, briefly, and looked back down, his fingers tracing designs on the hilt of his sword. "I asked Cento about it, if it ever happened to him. And he said", Jhaun shifted into the accent of the southlands, the voice of his teacher, "That means, lad, that someone's thinking about you. And sending good, too. Use those moments, because you've more energy there than you would ever have alone."

A laugh bubbled from the Lady, more so at the reemergence of her child than at his story. She pressed the moment close to her heart, a blossom of memory to preserve. "You speak him well." His smile faded, his gaze became distant once more, and the Lady Anders felt a tightening around her heart. Before the space between their words could lose all its light, she spoke again.

"How is Cento?"

"He's well, Mother. I told you he sent his love, didn't I?"

"Yes, but it's good to hear it again. When will we see him?"

Jhaun paused and looked out to the west and south again. "I suppose that depends." He shifted back to his quiet contemplation of the landscape.

There's more to him now, more going on inside. But he's still Jhaun. She sighed, relieved, and stroked his hair once more, indulgently letting her hand linger on his cheek for a moment. "I have to play for them now. If you'd like to join me…" She let the question hang unfinished in the morning air.

"I'd like to get some riding in."

She was disappointed but not surprised, as he hadn't joined her in music since his return. He must have sensed her feelings, because he gave her a smile again - not the crooked one that she loved, but an adult one, a polite one, laying his hand on hers. "I'll be in for breakfast. I promise."

The Lady returned his smile and walked through the stone arch to the steps that would lead her spiraling down to her rooms, to the harp that was key to her creating. As she passed through the wooden doorway within, she looked back at her son, this man that she knew so well, yet didn't quite recognize. *The Artist protect you, dear one, as you find your way. The Artist protect us all.*

12

Ben and Connor traveled quietly. There was nothing they really wanted to talk about - and certainly not Trou, or how her own potential power led to her death.

In their speed the first day out they didn't bother to stop for a midday meal, but watered the horses at a small stream and went on. Ben took the short break to reach back in his mind and free the remaining attackers from his influence; it was disquietingly easy. It had been finding the One within himself that was the difficult part, since touching that character meant feeling his way through the ordeal once more.

They slowed their pace somewhat after that, stopping to sleep long after the sun was down and the breeze was cool, traveling by the light of the full moon and hoping that they could wear themselves out enough to sleep through the night. It worked. Not even the rocky ground they camped on disturbed their exhausted slumber.

It wasn't until dawn the second day that they felt a subtle change. Not exactly cheer, but a kind of peace settling in. There was a fresh scent in the air as well, of growth and distant wood fires. Ben thought it was affecting him alone until Connor started humming.

"You too?"

"Yeah. I just figured it out."

There was a pause while Ben waited. When nothing happened, he shook his head. "Care to let me in on it?"

"We've crossed the border. We're in Anders Dominion." Connor saw the blank stare that the actor was giving him and continued, with some annoyance. "It's the Lady."

"Oh." Ben let that rest for a minute. "What does it mean?"

The Hawk stretched his neck, looking up into the sky. "It means we're safe. Everything this side of the Gate is safe, if she approves." He took a breath and exhaled slowly.

There was something different about the way the minstrel was carrying himself. It seemed to Benjamin that it was the first time he saw Connor truly relaxed since they left Overlook. The actor studied him with professional detachment for a few minutes before realizing that Connor wasn't *listening* anymore. *He's been keeping up the wards all this time, and now he's not concerned.* Ben realized at that moment just how much Connor trusted this Lady. "How much farther?"

The minstrel squinted off into the distance, the sun partially obscuring his vision. "If we take our time, a day and a half. Less if we push." He looked at Ben, his eyes asking the question.

The actor nodded. "I think, if it's okay with you, I'd rather take it easy. If we're as safe as you say we are, it would be nice to catch my breath again."

"You got it."

"How can she possibly keep this large an area safe?" Ben's thoughts went back to the energy dome that he had created when Perahn was hurt. To keep that up, constantly, would have killed him.

"I don't think it's the area, it's the people. She just can." Then, with a little wonder, "I don't know."

Ben looked up. "Not your problem?"

"Nope. It just works."

*   *   *

When they stopped to eat, Connor got out his guitar for the first time in days without needing to. Ben put on water for tea while the minstrel sang songs the actor had never heard. He listened, stretching out on the soft grass and closing his eyes. By the time the tea was ready, Ben felt more grounded than he had in days.

They decided by default to camp there until the next day, Connor taking the time to hunt some small game birds for their dinner, and Ben reorganizing their supplies, refilling their water skins at a small stream. The sense of safety became more obvious by how alien it felt.

That night, as they finished eating and passed the last skin of topaz perriwine back and forth between them, they began to talk. As always, there was something about sharing a drink that broke down the usual guards. Ben had seen it happen time and again at bars back home. Conversations were most vulnerable or volatile there, after a difficult show or rehearsal, while the next day you could easily pretend that you were too drunk to know what you were saying, or that you were too hung over to remember. Ben was first to leap into the space separating them.

"How long did you know her?" He didn't have to say who. The ghost of Trou was a silent companion on their journey. The minstrel frowned thoughtfully.

"I guess …four years. She was one of the first people I got to know here."

"You've been here that long? Four years?"

"Actually, five." His eyes glazed over, as he stared into the fire. "God, she'll be twenty-two."

Ben frowned. "Trou?"

"No. Karen."

"Karen?" The actor blinked, wondering what he had missed.

"My daughter." A minute passed in silence. Both men stared into the fire as thoughts sparked and wove like the flames. "Trou was something. I wish you could have known her when she was…" Connor stopped, shook his head. "She was about your age, or close enough. She wrote the most incredible poetry. Make you feel, make you see. Incredible." The minstrel shook his head and drank, passing the wine back to Ben. "She reminded me of Karen in a lot of ways. Independent, searching. But Karen is a lot more stable. Or was, anyway."

Ben took a swig from the skin again before speaking. He wanted to get more on the subject, but it seemed easier for Connor to talk about Trou than his daughter. Ben felt like he might frighten the moment away if he moved too suddenly.

"You have a family?"

"Had. A wife. My daughter." He turned from the dancing light to look Ben in the eye, and then away again. "I left them there."

Again, a silence passed.

"Why?"

Connor shook his head, shrugged. "Because I thought I could do something here. Because I knew I couldn't do anything there. Because I had to." He took the wine back and drank deeply, emptying the skin. "I don't know why."

"Did they know you were leaving?"

"No."

Ben paused, feeling the loss of his own parents. "That sucks."

"No kidding."

Connor got up and walked over to his pack, and for a moment Ben was worried that he had pushed too far. Instead, the minstrel brought out another skin, walked back to the fire. "Garnet," he said by way of explanation. "From Taas. I've been saving it."

Ben nodded and accepted the offer. They continued to pass it back and forth as they talked, their speech coming a bit more slowly as time went on. The actor decided that if Connor was willing to answer the last question, he could answer anything.

"Con?"

"Yeah?"

"Did someone call you here?"

Connor tilted his head to one side thoughtfully, the breeze teasing his hair. "I don't know. I don't think so." He looked at Ben with a slight frown for a moment, as if he were trying to merge in heavy traffic, and then plunged forward. "It was a bad time for me, that's why

I took off alone." He paused, staring into the firelight. His voice was quiet, almost fragile, when he spoke again.

"You ever feel like you knew you could do something, knew you had talent, and the world just didn't seem to care? A time when you feel so insignificant, that even the things you manage to do, and manage to get credit for, don't feel like they matter?" The question, the statement, hung in the air between them, and Ben could taste the echo of his own bitterness.

"Yeah," Ben said quietly. "I have."

They took a moment to breathe before Connor went on, sounding slightly annoyed and matter-of-fact once more. He swung the skin blithely. "Anyway, I spent the week climbing during the day, singing at night. I was frustrated, and I was wondering about my place in it, as compared to being a speck clinging to a rock. And I wondered, from time to time, if I should just… let go. I was singing it for about three nights, and then it hit me."

"What?"

"I was in the middle of working on a song, and it's… flowing, you know? No effort."

Ben nodded in understanding. "Like it was already there and you were just playing what you heard."

"Exactly. Exactly like that. And I'm playing, and singing, and I notice what's happening. It's so intense that it makes me dizzy. Like the-" he struggled for the word. "The power was there in front of me. Like a road. I could feel it. So I followed it. I threw out a line to a place, a place where I could be - " He shook his head. "I followed where that song was taking me, that had all my desire to make a difference wrapped into it, and it brought me here." Connor looked over at Ben and shrugged.

Ben frowned and looked at him, remembering his own experience of crossover. "Do you remember the song?"

The minstrel shrugged. "I lost it. Like waking up from a dream. You know you dreamt something, but," he shook his head, made a face at the feeling that caused. "Frankly, I'm not sure I want to chase it down."

They sat quietly for a while before Ben broke the lull, his thoughts blurring slightly. "D'you think it was the Lady?"

"Don't know. Don't think so. She'd have told me by now. If someone called me here, I haven't met them yet."

"Huh." The actor turned over the story in his mind, amazed that Connor was sharing so much, wondering how much he was leaving out. Wondering what it cost the minstrel to give up what he had, and if following his desire had been worth the sacrifice.

"You said Trou was one of the first people you met here?"

"Yeah."

Ben looked at the minstrel, a frown creasing his brow. "How did you survive? I mean, if you hadn't been there when I came through, I could have wandered for months. I might have gone crazy." He trailed off as he noticed the flat look on Connor's face.

"Yeah, you might have." The minstrel took a long drink and threw another piece of wood on the fire. "It was two weeks before I ran into Per."

"Perahn? Where?"

"He was - get this - climbing. He needed to get away for a while, he was curious about the Gate." The branch he threw on to the fire sputtered and crackled, too fresh to burn cleanly. "I was sitting on this rock one night, ready to just start walking in some direction in the dark and if I went over, well, fine. Then I hear this flute. It was amazing." His expression warmed at the memory. "If it wasn't for him, I'm not sure what would have happened." Silence descended once more, one of them reliving the experience, the other trying to fit all the pieces together and look at the picture. This time it was Connor who stepped into the dead air, gesturing with the skin.

"So I suppose you didn't leave anyone to come here? No family, no wife, no ...dog, nothing?"

"Nope. No one." Ben frowned as names and faces began to race through his mind, in direct opposition to what he had just said. *Annie. Marie. Diane. Tim. Cassie. Christian.* The list went on, the images of faces, scenes, conversations, coming faster and faster as his brain slid slowly down the hill.

"Okay," he said, a bit more loudly than was necessary to stop the flow. "That's not quite true. I was in the middle of rehearsals for a show. They must be wondering what the hell happened to me." He scratched his head and shifted his bedroll between his back and the tree he was leaning against. "I wonder who they got to fill in. I know there was this grad student, what was his name? Marco. Right. That's it. He could have done Demetrius. And he was crazy about Annie."

He shook his head and stopped quickly, not liking the sensation the abrupt movement gave him. "But he couldn't do Hotspur." A wave of disappointment washed over him, spiced lightly with something else, perhaps jealousy. He had really looked forward to that show. But could it compare with what he was living now? What character could compare with the One?

From somewhere deep inside, some part of him automatically said *Hamlet*. It made him chuckle. *Always the role to compare to.* The character of the One stirred at this, and Ben couldn't help thinking at himself.

Shakespeare. It's all in there. You better get familiar with it. He chuckled again, the wine making him feel pleasantly warm. *If I were you, which I sort of am, I'd start with Hotspur. But try Prince Hal, too. And Edgar.* Connor looked up at him, distracted from his thoughtful haze.

"But that's not *family*. That's co-workers."

The actor blinked himself back into the more human conversation.

"No. It's more than that. At least it can be. 'Less than kin but more than kind', to get it completely backwards." He snickered at himself, took a deep breath and yawned. "They were a good group. It was working. I hope I didn't screw them up too much."

"But no folks? No brothers or sisters or anything?"

"I had some older cousins, I guess, out in California. But I haven't seen them in years. My folks died, car crash, when I was fourteen. God damn drunk driver. I stayed with my grandparents, and when I was a senior in college -" he stopped, ostensibly to sip again, collecting his voice.

"When I was a senior Papa died, heart attack. I came home, and Nonna died two weeks later. They said it was her heart, too, but I think it was really more like..." He stopped and stared at Connor. "Really, it was more like Trou. Just tired of being. Trusting that there's something more than what's here. There. You know." He reached for the pendant at his neck and clutched it in his hand. "Anyway, I've been pretty much on my own since then. Good friends. Not a lot of consistent connections, but good ones. Really solid unstable ones." He paused for a minute, waited for the ground to steady itself. "What about your family? Do you think they're okay?"

"My wife's strong. If she could put up with living with me, she'll do all right living without me. And since I was on a rock climbing trip... well, they probably got the insurance by now."

"After five years, I should think so."

"Yeah. Karen's another one. Tough. Tough as nails, but sweet as anything, and beautiful." Connor watched memories in the flickering light of the fire, until his expression darkened suddenly. "I bet she hates my guts by now."

Benjamin frowned. "I doubt it."

"Why?"

"A feeling."

The minstrel didn't respond.

"And let's put it this way. My folks were never exactly supportive of my acting. But when they died, I mean, hell, they were still my parents." Ben turned and punched his bedroll several times, ostensibly to make it more comfortable to lean on. Connor drank again, wiped his mouth on a sleeve.

"I wish I could let her know what's going on here. That I'm alive. How important it is. How much it means to me."

"Have you tried getting a message to her?"

Connor's brows knotted, some of the old, familiar annoyance seeping into his eyes. "How?"

"What do you mean, how? The same way you got to me. The same way." The actor shook his head and yawned again.

"I don't think it would work."

"Have you tried?"

A pause. "Kind of. But maybe she's better off thinking I'm dead." The minstrel suddenly needed to add wood to the fire, and stood to get some.

"Right." Ben blinked blearily at his retreating figure, trying to keep thoughts together. It seemed the minstrel was more accustomed to perriwine than he was. "Look, Connor." He called after him into the gathering darkness. "Maybe when things calm down we can try together. You know? If you want?"

The minstrel's eyes sparked for a second, before the light died once more. "Maybe. But I'll wait until this is over, one way or the other."

Ben shrugged, yawned again. "Suit yourself. But let me know if you change your mind." As he spoke he yanked his bedroll open, flopped down onto it and pulled the blanket around himself.

The minstrel stepped out of the circle of light and stood silently for a long moment. He glanced back at the companion this 'One' had become; frankly amazed at just how much he had let the actor in. "Yeah. I'll keep it in mind."

The actor would surely have been touched by the surprised quiet of his tone, if he had only been awake to hear it.

*   *   *

Ben woke with a start. His mind, after dwelling on the theatre the night before, and his body, hung over enough to assume that he had been out drinking with his friends, decided that it must be the weekend and he had a matinee to do. It proceeded to pump in enough adrenaline to get up, dress, and perform a three-hour show coherently. The morning light was interpreted as coming through his bedroom window, and that had to mean he was running *really* late. His body kicked in a little extra to make up for lost time. He was standing upright next to his bedroll, clutching his head and swaying like a tree in a storm before he was able to figure out where he really was.

Several birds who were filching the crumbs of their dinner flew off in a panic at his movements, inadvertently triggering his fight or flight mechanism, causing him to jerk away and shield his face with his hand. When he realized they weren't coming after him, he took a deep breath, stretched out his arm to lean against a tree, and closed his eyes, wincing at the dull throbbing in his head.

"You okay?"

Ben opened his eyes to see the minstrel across the fire from him, propped up on one elbow, staring at the spectacle Ben had become in open curiosity. "You get stung or something?"

"Aah. No. Just woke up thinking I was somewhere else. No. That I had to be somewhere else. Ouch." He rubbed his head, yawned, and shivered. "Do we have any coffee?"

Connor smirked as he rolled out of his sack and put some more wood on the embers of the fire. "Probably. Put the water on and I'll look."

"Thanks."

Ben filled the pot, put it on the fire and sat down on his bedroll once more, taking the opportunity to down half a skin of water. He looked up at the sky, which was the palest shade of blue at this early hour, and took a deep breath. The short version of his meditation sequence was all he had the capacity for today, but he knew that he needed it. Although he was loathe to admit it, there was something about the prospect of meeting the Lady that made him feel like he was auditioning for a role way over his head - and she was the producer. By the time Connor returned and the coffee was brewing, he felt reasonably human. A cup of coffee later, he was fairly sure of it.

The minstrel had walked a few paces out of the camp to whistle the horses back, when he suddenly crouched down, staring into the grass. "Hey. Look at this."

"What?"

The minstrel put something into his mouth. "Wild strawberries. Bring your coffee over and we'll have breakfast on the patio."

Benjamin grinned and joined him, sitting on the grass. The berries were tiny, sweet and tangy, and so juicy that they practically exploded in his mouth. "Man," he said, shaking his head. "I haven't done this since I was a kid at my grandparents cabin."

"It's been a while. I haven't had them since… well, since the first time I was here." He shook his head. "At least three years. Back when I met the Lady."

They ate and drank, and enjoyed the peace around them.

"So. Will we make it there by sundown?"

"We could. Why?"

Benjamin sighed, trying to ignore the tension that was attempting to wind its way into his gut. "I have this fantasy of sleeping in a real bed."

Connor shook his head disparagingly as he popped another berry. "City boy."

The actor looked at him, playing a fit of pique thickly enough for any melodrama. "Fine, Connor. Fine. You come backstage with me to any theatre around, and we'll see who can sleep better when they have a forty-five minute act to sit through, a hard chair, and exactly eighteen point five inches of counter space." He tossed another bright red berry into his mouth, his eyes wide. "And then, when you've *finally* drifted off, have an assistant stage manager wake you up by whispering in your ear, 'Sorry to bother you, but it's time for you to die, Mr. Agante.'"

The minstrel raised an eyebrow but kept his expression in check. Instead, he stood up, brushed off his hands and whistled through his fingers, an ear-splitting tone that was surely intended to make Ben's head fall off.

"Oh, thanks." Ben shifted his jaw to pop his ears, and headed back to pack up. Connor loaded up the horses as soon as they came to his call, and the actor noticed he couldn't help sporting a victorious grin.

13

"There it is." The minstrel pointed at the rocky outcroppings that had taken over the horizon once they rode out of the trees. "Anders Castle." With the sun skimming across the wood behind them, the landscape flashed white on peaks and faded into dim terra cotta everywhere else. The full moon hovering in the sky above looked fragile as a soap bubble against the power of the stones.

Ben stared at the fractured display of rock in scale beyond reason, stretches of open field accenting their proportions. *Like the Artist dropped a sculpture the size of a mountain. I wonder what it was of?* It took him a minute to find the castle that Connor was talking about amidst the rose and toffee-colored rock. "Well camouflaged."

Connor looked out over the fields with a fond expression. "Yeah. Legends say that it 'grew with the rocks', but I've been there, seen the stonework. It's just weathered with the rocks. Cut from the same stone." The Hawk hadn't sounded so cheerful since he'd heard the chimes at Overlook.

"Connor."

The minstrel looked back at Ben, frowned, turned his horse and walked back to where the actor had stopped. "What's up? You okay?"

Ben shifted uncomfortably. "Is there anything I should know before I meet her?"

"Like what?"

The actor sighed. "Look, I've been getting the story in bits and pieces. If there's a big surprise waiting for me, I want to know." He motioned off toward the castle and waited.

The minstrel looked at him for a moment, and scratched his beard with his thumb. "Fair enough." He stared into the back of his horse's head long enough for Ben to wonder. "No," he said finally "I don't think so. Nothing I should tell you, anyway." Ben rolled his eyes and the minstrel raised a hand defensively. "You know I haven't said much about Alious, or what we can do against him. That's because Miran understands all this better than me, and she'll give you better advice." He looked at Ben's confusion and clarified. "Miran. The Lady. You can trust her. Okay?" Ben nodded, but didn't move.

"What else?" The minstrel said wearily, pulling his horse around. He frowned again at the actor who seemed, more than anything at the moment, embarrassed.

"Well, I'm just wondering if - if there's any protocol that I should know, meeting her. If she's as important as you say, I don't want to..."

Connor blinked and barely concealed a smirk as he looked down at the grass. "If you're worried about that, I guess we're doing all right." He cleared his throat and said in mock seriousness, "You do know how to behave in polite company, don't you?"

"Connor -"

The minstrel waved him off with a short laugh. "She's not the type to stand on ceremony, if that's what you mean." He looked up again, met Ben's eyes. "You'll be fine. Be yourself. Trust me."

It took Ben a deep breath to settle his thoughts, but then he nodded. "Okay. But look," he said, as he urged his horse into a walk once more, catching up to Connor. "Don't vanish on me this time, okay?"

"I'll do my best."

The path became rougher as they approached the first outcropping of rocks. Ben looked at the horizon from this new angle and shook his head.

"Hey."

"What?"

"Do these look familiar to you?"

The minstrel looked around. "These what?"

"These rocks. There's something -"

"Yeah, they look familiar to me. I've been here before. Been known to stay around here." Connor gazed up at the formations with a fondness that made Ben think twice. Then he remembered.

"Oh my God." Ben pulled his horse to a dead stop, making it snort and back up at his unintentional command.

"What? What's wrong?"

Ben gaped at the minstrel. "Connor, come on. You know. This is the Garden of the Gods. I've been here. In Colorado. Not far from the Springs. I went during a break in Hamlet. I remember, because they were working on Cassie's - on Ophelia's mad scene, and they finally told the rest of us to go away, 'cause we were making her crazy', which I thought was kind of ironic at the time, but still…" He watched the minstrel drop his eyes to the path between them, then look up at the moon hovering higher over the rocks in the still blue sky. "Is this where you were rock climbing? When you came here?"

Connor looked off at the castle once more, then back to Benjamin. "Close." He shifted in his saddle, stretched his neck and gestured into the distance. "Yeah, I was here. *There.* A few miles south. It was confusing when I passed through - things had changed, things hadn't changed." Benjamin was nodding in agreement.

"I know what you mean," the actor said quietly. He stared at the massive rock formations once more, and shook his head. "This is a hell of a similarity, don't you think?"

"Oh yeah. But there're a lot of differences if you know the place. The castle's just the most obvious one."

He peered into the gathering dusk before pulling his horse ahead between two angular boulders. A path appeared almost as if by magic, and they moved on in thoughtful silence. The ground became more barren, the path itself flat areas of stone or packed dry clay that alternately made their horse's hooves ring with hard echoes or deadened thuds. They rode easily for another hour, winding between shadows and bright angles, trotting over unexpected stretches of field and around the occasional dwarfed tree until the path wound itself up to a large open space before the castle proper.

"What do you think?" The minstrel broke the reverent silence that had enveloped them.

"Wow." The castle, at least the front section, had been built on a foundation that could have been one of the larger stones cut off flat. Ben shook his head as he studied the design. "Is it possible that they carved up one of these and rearranged it to make the castle?"

"It makes sense. There's no quarry around, and the stone is right here. And I know at least part of the keep was carved from solid rock."

"Wow."

The footprint of the castle had been determined by the mini-mountain that was its base. It was roughly square, although the angle outward in the front wall made looking up dizzying. The broad point of that side was graced with dark perri-wood doors, inlaid with serpentine paths of green and silver.

The structure narrowed as it extended upward. Towers rose into spires as if the stone had slowly grown into the delicate looking formations. High above, a central tower formed a sweeping line into the sky, and Ben could make out a balcony near the peak, an ideal lookout point. He thought he saw a figure there, but it was gone before he could be sure. Guards posted at that height would be able to see for miles.

As they moved toward the castle doors, Ben saw a few people tending crops in garden patches that had been stolen from the rocky ground. He noticed them in passing, but his attention was soon focused on the massive doors. The green inlays of sensuous lines were actually solid malachite. Silver accents highlighted the vines in some places, in others blossomed into flowers of moonlit beauty. The design of the two doors wound into each other and focused into a medallion that bridged them, at least a yard across. Ben was so taken by the complexity of the mandala that he was caught off guard when the doors swung open.

A man appeared, tall and thin with pale blue eyes and a dusty brown cap that somehow matched him perfectly. He looked out at them and nodded, speaking more out of an obligation to be polite, it seemed, than anything else. "Come on inside. Let me take them in and rub them down, it's a long trip for an animal." He spoke quickly, and appeared to have little regard for how the humans perceived him. He made a preliminary examination of their mounts, stopping to talk quietly to each horse, checking their feet and massaging the lines under their bridles.

Ben looked across at Connor in bemusement, perplexed by the greeting. The minstrel just shook his head and grinned. "Hey, Wesp. How's it been?"

The groom looked up at Connor, changing gears with an effort. "About the same as last time you were here. Too many people, not enough horses." His eyes crinkled in a smile as sun-browned skin slivered into well-worn laugh lines. They both chuckled, and Ben relaxed into Wesp's no-nonsense attitude.

Connor had swung down off his horse by this time, unhooking his packs. He moved to undo the cinch strap, but Wesp stopped him. "No, no. The Lady's waiting," he said, in an animal training singsong. "I'll take care of the rest."

Ben found he was strangely reluctant as he dismounted, and was surprised to realize that he didn't want to give up his equine traveling companion, or turn her care over to someone other than himself or Connor. Slapping her flank lightly in thanks for a trip well done, Ben murmured to her under his breath. He looked back at the groom after he had done so, and found Wesp staring at him. The actor looked back at him and handed the reins over, a bit ceremoniously, as the groom nodded in approval. "I'll take care of her," he said softly. "Don't worry."

Ben smiled, surprised to find that he was truly relieved. "Thanks." He retrieved his knapsack and saddlebags, and followed Connor across the broad, stone flagged courtyard. Several people smiled as they passed, and more than one stopped what they were doing to greet the minstrel.

Past the courtyard they walked into a hallway of cool stone, the arch over their heads filled with relief carvings of men and horses, of women and stars. The actor caught greedy glimpses of them as he struggled to keep pace with the minstrel.

He followed a winding maze of halls until they came to a stairway leading upwards in a gentle curve. At the top of the stairs were two doors, smaller sisters to the ones at the castle gate. If anything, these two were further embellished, protected here from the elements. The stone vines stood out in relief an inch deep, and small stones of exquisitely cut emerald picked out the centers of silver flowers. *This has to be it,* Ben thought. He took a deep breath and tried very hard to center himself as Connor pushed the doors open. He was not prepared for what he saw.

The room was large, open, and except for a few chairs and benches, empty. Windows cut into the stone radiated a soft, delicate light as Ben stared wide-eyed at them. They lined two walls, and looked like stained glass. His hand automatically went to the pendant at his neck as he looked more carefully.

Either the glassblowers here put all their energy into creating faux stone, or the windows he stared at in shades of rose quartz, aventurine and amethyst were slices of the semiprecious stones that they appeared to be. He shook his head and whistled quietly. Connor glanced at him with a smile.

"Beautiful, aren't they?"

"Amazing. Is this her throne room?"

The minstrel snorted. "She doesn't have a throne room. Hell, she doesn't have a throne. This might have been someone's, once. Now it just gives people a place to wait and calm down. Come on." He walked to a heavy tapestry hanging on the far wall. Pulling back the fabric, Connor uncovered a door. He knocked briskly, opened it, and they walked in.

The Lady of Anders Castle stepped out from behind the broad wooden table that dominated the room, more of an office than anything. She wasn't tall, but an easy elegance in her posture made her seem so. Long, loose ringlets of nearly black hair fell in a dark cascade down her back, accented by a brushstroke of silver on the right of her hairline. Over her left ear a clasp lifted the raven curtain, and appeared to be there for the sole purpose of revealing an earring made of the same malachite and silver that graced her doors. Her eyes were the darkest hunter green Ben had ever seen, and matched the velvet of the simple gown she wore.

Ben stared as Connor stepped forward, kissed her hand, and stepped back again, all in the smoothest movements that he had ever seen the minstrel use outside of playing the guitar.

"Milady," he said, "I'm back." He gestured back over his shoulder with his thumb toward Ben. "And I brought him with me."

For the first time, the Lady looked at Benjamin. She looked calmly, steadily into him, and he could feel the energy flow between them. Slowly a smile grew in the space. "Milady." He waited, more calm than he had felt in days, for her lead.

"The One is welcome, and I hope will be a friend to Anders." Before he could quite grasp it, she had dipped into a low curtsy, as deeply as Connor had bowed to her. While part of him accepted it gracefully, another part did not.

"Milady, I trust it is so. But whatever else I may be," he said with a formal bow, "My name is Benjamin Agante."

There was a moment as the Lady studied him once more. Then her expression softened. "Benjamin," she said, holding out her hand. He took it easily and brushed a kiss over her knuckles. She looked at Connor with an expression that balanced between wonder and relief. "He *is* the One." Connor sighed, as if he had been holding his breath for a week.

"Yeah. I know."

The Lady led them out of her workroom and up another flight of stairs to a large, bright space that looked out into the courtyard. "You must be hungry after your trip, and tired," she said as they walked. "Which is more pressing?"

"It's a dead heat," Connor said with a grin. "But I need to clean up before either."

"Done. Your rooms are ready." She turned to Connor and tilted her head thoughtfully. "Your room was only aired last night, as some students were our guests. I hope," she said, with a mischief touched grin, "it will be all right."

"It'll be fine. I could sleep on the floor."

"I'm sure that won't be necessary."

Ben half listened, watching as the Lady and Connor fell into the easy banter of friendship. There was something calming about this woman, something safe and caring. Part of him felt, oddly enough, that it was good to be home.

"Here we are," she said after a short walk down the hall. Turning to Ben, she motioned to an open door. "This is for you. If there's anything you need, anywhere you want to go, my apprentice is in your service." She smiled again, somehow knowing that he would understand. "She's a little young." The Lady's eyes darkened slightly. "But I trust her with my life." Turning away from the two men, she called, "Cyrin. Our guests are here."

Out of the dim hallway a young woman appeared. She was tall, with long hair and dark eyes, and looked quietly self-conscious. Ben felt her unease and was trying to find a way around it when Connor spoke, surprise in his voice.

"Cyrin? Really? You've grown six inches since I saw you last. How are you?"

The girl blushed slightly, and smiled. "I'm fine, Hawk. I hoped to see you." The minstrel stepped forward and gave her a hug. He brushed her hair back with easy familiarity, one that suggested he had known her when she was much younger. She still looked embarrassed, but having Connor recognize her seemed to help, as there was a glow about her smile. Ben took advantage of the moment to slip into the familiarity.

"Hey, Cyrin. I'm Ben." He stuck out his hand, and she stared at it for a moment like a deer caught in headlights, wavering between the curtsy she had rehearsed and the polite, in-kind response before shaking it. As he grasped her hand, her eyes met his at last, and again he felt her comfort level grow, as if she saw something in him that made her less nervous.

The minstrel spoke again, still reveling in his re-found friend. "What are you now, sixteen?"

She nodded as she looked back at him, her nervousness never making her break eye contact. "Seventeen summers, actually. And then some."

"That's amazing. You look great." He stopped, corrected himself. Taking her hand, he kissed it formally and said, "You are lovely, Cyrin of Anders."

Benjamin nodded in agreement. The girl had an easy beauty about her, and a demeanor that made her appear older than she was. And her height was close to his own, putting her more than half a head above the Lady.

Connor's comment, however, had her blushing in shocked earnest. Ben smiled in what he hoped was a comforting manner, and gave her a job.

"Listen, Cyrin, could you show me my room? I'd like to wash up before we eat."

"Of course." She nodded a smile to Connor and turned to lead Ben into his quarters, a hallway away. The room was small but comfortable, containing little more than a bed, shelves scattered with books, and a low dresser with a pitcher and basin. Richly colored tapestries in browns and greens warmed the stone walls. Ben moved to the window and looked out at the view.

"If you need anything, let me know." The girl spoke with barely a touch of her former nervousness. "I'm usually around, and my room's just down the hall."

"Thanks. This should be fine."

"I'll let you settle in, then-"

"Cyrin." Ben turned away from the window and looked at her.

"Yes?"

"The Lady called you an apprentice. Apprentice what?"

"Apprentice what?"

"Yeah. What are you an apprentice to?"

Cyrin frowned for a moment, and then spoke carefully. "I'm an apprentice to the Lady."

"Okay. What does that mean? What do you do?"

Cyrin frowned again, raising one dark eyebrow, and her expression made Ben wonder if he had suddenly grown another head.

Then her face brightened as she realized what he was asking. "Oh. I'm learning to do what the Lady does. But I don't think I'll ever do it as well."

Ben nodded. "Okay. But what exactly does the Lady do?"

"Ah. Well, more than anything she understands. She sees potentials and brings them together. And she takes care of - well, of all of us." Her gaze unfocused just for a moment, and she smiled. "I'm fortunate to be here." Ben stared at her and tried to understand.

A voice at the door spoke quietly. "Thank you, Cyrin."

The girl nodded formally to the Lady, smiled briefly at Ben, and was gone. The Lady shook her head with a small laugh.

"The young amaze me. As if I'm doing her a favor by letting her work as hard as she does. And she has more focus at her age than I do now. All she needs is time, and a chance to find herself." She sighed peacefully and turned her attention back to Ben. "I need to talk to you, Benjamin. Do you wish to eat or sleep first?"

"Milady," Ben said with a weary grin, "I don't think I'd be able to do either before talking to you. Here?" He swept his hand in a gesture that took in his room.

"This is fine." The Lady paused, deciding where to begin. After a moment, with a resigned shake of her head, she stepped closer and looked him in the eye. "Do you know your mind?"

"What?" Ben blinked. It was as far off topic as he could have imagined. "What do you mean?"

"I mean, do you know your mind. Do you know how to explore within it?"

Ben stared at her for a long moment before responding, realizing that she was quite serious. "Maybe not the way you mean. But I've done a lot of meditation, and my work can be very philosophical, some would say an almost spiritual undertaking."

She nodded with some satisfaction. "Well, let me tell you what we are trained in here, from an early age." She settled down on the bed, drew one leg up underneath her, and motioned for him to sit down. "The mind," she began, "is your home. This home will come to an end with the physical body, but the things our spirit learns while living here will be part of us forever. The mind is a link, a crossing point, if you will, between the physical body we occupy and the greater whole of the Artist's creation."

"A crossing point?"

"Yes. There is more within our true, spirit selves, than we can imagine. More potential, more power..." The lady sighed. "But I feel you know a lot of that already."

Ben nodded and shrugged and shook his head, in that order, and the Lady smiled when he did. Her smile made him chuckle, breaking through his concentration. "Sometimes I feel like I haven't learned anything. Other times, I feel like I'm just remembering things I knew once, and forgot." He ran a hand over the soft woven blanket and shrugged. "There's more in heaven and earth than is dreamt of in our philosophy. Does that sound strange?"

"Not at all. From what I've heard, and I usually hear what happens in this part of the world, you've done well. Amazingly so, given that this was thrust upon you."

The actor startled a bit at the quote, pushed it aside, and went on. "So what is it about this 'home' that you want to tell me, Milady."

She tilted her head thoughtfully. "Your true self creates a space in your mind to live, to organize, to be. Often your physical home will resemble it, which is only natural if our true selves lead us."

Ben shook his head, warming to the discussion. "I would think it would work the other way around, the mind home looking like what you were already comfortable living in physically."

"I've seen it happen. But it's not healthy. Let your true self lead, and this life makes sense. Try to conform your true self to what you experience in this life, and all you find is chaos."

Ben took a deep breath, trying to let her words settle within him. "All right. But how do you find this place? This 'home'?"

The lady looked into him. "It's just inside. Many people find it easily. Some I have led."

"Just you?"

"No," she smiled. "There are many who can. But I believe," she paused, looking carefully at him, her eyes narrowing, "that you have already found yours. Years ago."

Benjamin stood up and walked back to the set of drawers, playing idly with a small bowl of round stones. He picked up a particularly vivid blue one, an inch and a half across, and held it up in the light between his thumb and forefinger. "Lapis?" The lady made a small smile and nodded. She waited. Ben tried for a few moments to be distracted by the stones and failed miserably.

"Okay. I think you're right. It's something I've used in my meditation for years. But it's an exercise." He stopped, scooped up the stones and let them trickle slowly through his fingers. "Do you see these houses as *real* things?"

The lady watched him for a long moment, then spoke as if he had never questioned her. "There must be a way in, if we are to share our homes with each other. Some people have a courtyard, some a few steps leading to the door. Personally, I have an open field to meet friends in, with a garden path up to my house." Her eyes misted over as she saw what she described. Then she looked at Benjamin expectantly. "And you?"

Ben shook his head. "I don't know."

Her eyes sparkled just the slightest bit. "Then look."

The actor sighed, unwilling.

"Benjamin," she smiled. "Don't be afraid of this."

He looked at her and knew that she was right. He felt the fear distracting him so that he wouldn't have to see if there was even more to himself than he had already discovered. More that wasn't odd, wasn't *strange*. With a resigned shrug he closed his eyes, centered, and found the familiar space within.

The room was large and rounded. Honey-colored hardwood floors glowed softly in a light that came from nowhere in particular. High arched wooden doors stood three to the left and three to the right. A larger door was directly ahead, and behind him, a wide archway with broad steps leading upwards. The door before him, he knew, was the front door they had talked about, although he had never tried to open it. He walked to it, put his hand on the brass doorknob and pulled it open with surprising ease.

Gently, he heard a distant close voice say. *There's no hurry.* Stepping slowly across the threshold, Ben looked out onto an inviting, rustic porch. A wooden rocker and porch swing, padded with fabrics that matched the quilt his grandmother made him. The railing was white, and the pillars were overgrown with flowering vines. Ben leaned on the railing and looked out, breathing in the delicate fragrance.

The steps led down to a flagstone path that wandered through a grassy garden patch, and faded away. Twice he thought he saw something there, but couldn't quite make it out. He frowned and rubbed his eyes. When he opened them again, the Lady was standing on the path.

It's beautiful, Benjamin.

Would you like to come inside?

No, but thank you. She gave a wry smile. *It is... an intimacy. Or an honor that is earned.*

Ben shrugged. *I didn't know. Can we sit here?*

Of course. A near visit is something friends do.

He motioned for her to join him in the swing, and they sat for a long while, not talking, not thinking, just being together on the front porch of his mind. Finally the Lady spoke. *Then you know this place?*

Yes, but outside is new to me.

I think it's lovely. Have you ever explored the rooms inside?

Some of them. Mostly I work in the main room. I can bring things there. Is this the only door?

The lady blinked, caught off guard by how much he knew and didn't know. *It would be rare to not have a back door. But that one doesn't lead to the same place. It goes to... the backyards, I guess you would call them. The rest of the spirit world.*

You mean there's more than a home here? And more than one... world?

Yes. But only masters have found more, and the temptation to explore that world has led more than one to abandon our physical world entirely. And why would we have physical bodies if we were not to explore our physical world?

But if we have the capacity to explore more, why shouldn't we?

The Lady paused. *Having the capacity to do something doesn't always mean we should do it, or need to do it now.* She stood up and walked back to the steps. *We should take care of food and rest.*

I'm not hungry or tired.

I know, she said with a smile. *But your body is.*

With that, she turned and walked down the steps. As she moved along the flagstones into the mist, she turned back once more. *Thank you, Benjamin. Thank you for sharing this with me.* Then she was gone.

Ben stood up, walked into the house and closed the door behind him. Taking a deep breath, he opened his eyes to physical reality. The Lady was sitting on the bed across from him, her hand placed delicately on his.

"Is physical contact necessary?" Ben nodded at her hand.

"It helps. In fact, it's a necessity for most people." She smiled and gave his hand a gentle squeeze before letting it go. "Personally, I find it reassuring." She stood gracefully, smoothing the blankets that she had not really disturbed. "Now. Let's find Connor and feed you both, before he takes over the kitchen."

He followed her down the hall and through the courtyard, finding Connor literally singing for his supper. The actor smiled and thought about the minstrel that he knew, and the different roles people play in their lives. As if he knew what Ben was thinking, Connor glanced up at him. Their eyes connected briefly, and Ben chuckled aloud as the minstrel winked.

He sat where the Lady led him and was served quickly. As he finished the bread and stew put before him, he felt his eyes blinking more and more slowly.

"Milady," he said, barely suppressing a yawn. "I think sleep is winning after all."

The Lady smiled and Cyrin appeared like magic to lead Ben back to his room. He was asleep between soft sheets before she shut the door.

*   *   *

Something in the twilight before dawn woke Ben up. In what was becoming the norm, he wasn't sure of where he was. *On tour? Cleveland again?* The room was small, sparsely furnished, and there were these stones - *Oh.* Slowly, Ben sat up in bed and swung his feet down to the stone floor. It was cool but not cold, invigorating in a subtle way.

Staggering to his feet, he moved to the dresser and splashed some water from the pitcher into the stoneware bowl. After a prolonged yawn he washed his face and dried it. He listened, but heard nothing. Frowning, Ben pulled his pants on, moving quietly as the breeze through the tapestry covered window. Out the door, back the way the Lady had led them, to the open hallway that opened onto the courtyard.

From here he could hear plenty - animals from below in the stables, a baby crying, and the kitchen help calling to each other over the noise of falling water. The air was fresh and clear, with the sweet smell of wood smoke and baked bread added into it. Standing there, barefoot and bare-chested, Ben felt like he had walked onto an elaborate medieval set.

He took a deep breath, planning to walk back in the direction of his room - but something drew him farther. Past the room that was Connor's, around a corner and past an ornate door that was surely the Lady's. His feet moved on evenly, unhurried, but with such determined focus it seemed that he was on a path he had walked hundreds of times before. He came to another short hallway, with a door on either side and another on the end. Standing there half dressed was hardly the way to pay a call on someone, but before he had a chance to think, the actor found he was standing in front of the door at the hall's end.

It was decorated very much like the doors to the castle, but there was a profusion of black with the silver, onyx replacing much of the green malachite and giving it a more serious appearance. Here and there were veins of lapis, standing out in bright contrast. In the center of the door was a starburst some six inches across, malachite beautifully figured and worked into a nine-pointed star, centered with a low dome of lapis blue. Curiously, Ben moved back a step and looked at the doors on either side. They both had designs almost childlike in their simplicity. One even had a small malachite frog in the corner, a whimsical touch of nature that appeared nowhere else. The door with the star drew him back, and without thinking, Ben lifted his hand and rapped his knuckles lightly on it.

It opened quickly, as if someone was waiting. The face that appeared was a study in black and white, fair skin with dark hair and eyes, thick brows, a beard cut low on the jaw. Ben thought automatically of what a great headshot the man would have, reflecting on how his own medium coloring - blue eyes and golden brown hair - all faded to average contrast in his black and white photos. Then the eyes drew him back. There was something about the eyes.

"You're him?"

Ben frowned and looked at the man, younger, he realized, than he had thought at first. There was confidence and composure in the portrait that lessened when he spoke. An insecurity that was felt more than observed.

"*Him*? I mean, who is it that you think I am?"

"You're the One?" There was a touch of desperation in the question.

Ben glanced briefly at the figure before him, observed the tension that radiated like heat from a fire. Then he looked deep into the obsidian eyes, deliberately keeping himself loose, his tone casual. "So they tell me. Who're you?"

The young man stared for a moment, teetered on the edge of uncertainty, and exhaled loudly. "I'm the Lady's son." He said it as if it had been his defining tag all his life, more than a name or title. Ben felt it, and with a deep breath relaxed into the moment.

"Okay." The actor stuck out his hand. "My name's Ben. They say I'm the One." He shrugged. "But my name's still Ben."

The young man looked into Ben's eyes, realized what he had done. "I'm Jhaun." There was some pride, and just a touch of fear in his tone.

"Jhaun." Ben shook his hand gravely, and tried to figure out how old this kid was.

"I have twenty-one years." Jhaun paused as if that would make something clear to Ben. "I'm of age."

"Oh. Right." For a brief moment Ben was back on horseback, riding through dappled sunlight as his mind scrambled to remember the conversation with Tomas. Something about the Lady's son and how it related to Alious attacking now. With some surprise he felt the character of the One stirring.

We must connect with this one. He is pivotal.

Dangerous?

Perhaps. Still, we must experience the outcome. There was a hesitation that Ben was surprised to find in the confident nature of the One. *I don't know what will happen. I only know that it must.*

Ben sighed. "What do you want from me, Jhaun?"

For the first time, the heir to Anders castle broke eye contact, walking back into his room and implicitly inviting Ben to join him. The actor followed, and as Jhaun sat on the edge of a table Ben stood with his arms crossed easily over his chest as Jhaun spoke. "I understand you're a different kind of shifter."

Ben shrugged at the description. "I'm an actor. An artist who creates other personalities, other characters, and uses them to describe other realities." He frowned at the words, as they didn't quite seem to be his. Then he waited for the expected misunderstandings to surface in the young man's face.

"I see."

Ben was surprised at that, even though somewhere in his mind a voice that sounded particularly like Hotspur was yelling something about trust and unknown quantities. "Well, good. So what can I do for you?"

Jhaun crossed his arms and leaned forward. "It's about what you do. I think I can do it too. I've felt this… desire? For years. And now that you're here, maybe you can help me use it properly." There was a glow to the young man's features that warmed Ben's spirit. *Charisma.* Jhaun pushed away from the table, took a few steps farther into the room. "Even Cento, my strongest teacher, my mentor at school, shied away from it, but I can't just leave it alone." Jhaun shook his head, dark curls bobbing in the barely dawning light that slanted through the window.

For a moment he stood quietly, picking up a perfect sphere of black onyx from a holder on the table, staring into its shining surface. Ben wondered what it was that he saw there, or if the mirror of his eyes was enough. The youth's expression slowly changed from uncertainty to determination.

"Can you help me?"

Ben felt Jhaun's hope and confusion wash over him. So much felt familiar. So many of these feelings touched Ben to the core, touched him in ways he thought he'd forgotten. It overwhelmed any misgivings he might have had. It deafened him to the warnings of voices in his head. "Of course, Jhaun." Ben felt a rush of relief, and he wasn't sure where it was coming from. By helping the Lady's son he was actually helping himself. The young man who had all the talent and none of the encouragement was *him. Okay. This is why I'm here.* It was so loud, so persuasive, that he couldn't begin to focus on the older, wiser self that was shaking his head skeptically.

You're not thirteen anymore. It didn't happen to him, it happened to you. And it's long over. It was so compelling that he refused to hear even the newest voice in his mind, the character he was creating and had been cast into so abruptly. And then, as his subconscious pulled out all the stops, a voice that sounded strangely like his grandfather-

Boundaries, Benjamin. Know yourself!

Ben ignored it. Or rather, he didn't want to hear, so he didn't. This was all he had to do, teach the kid to act. Without being some kind of soul thief. No war, no standoff with Alious. Just this. Relief flooded him.

"Look, Jhaun, I'm glad to teach you what I know. There's a process -"

Jhaun cut him off. "I know what to do, I know how, I think. But I've never actually tried." Only a moment's hesitation crossed the young man's face.

Ben stopped and leaned back against the wall, his arms once more crossed easily on his chest. A ghost of a smile passed over his lips.

"Okay, then. Go ahead." Ben was curious as to what the kid could do. It would be interesting to see what someone from this world saw acting as. He opened himself to whatever came next.

That talent for openness, more than anything else, was his undoing.

He looked into the strong, obsidian eyes and waited. He saw the energy gathering behind them, and it startled and captivated him at the same time. It was like storm clouds gathering at midnight. Like lightning-

And abruptly, it hit him. Like lightning. Instinctively he threw his arm up to cover his eyes against the pain. Screaming, tearing pain. The door to his mind ripped open by a hurricane force, a vacuum drawing out everything it could reach. And then, nothing. An absence of being that could not be confused with simple emptiness. Nothing.

14

The minstrel sat in a room inside a stone fortress; grey, dark, imposing. Bars of golden light came through the slotted windows, easier to shoot out of than to see into. In the middle of the room was a circular platform of painted black wood raised a foot above the stone floor - a warm island in the center of a chilly and well-defended space. Connor was sitting on the edge of the circle playing his guitar, watching the sparkles of light he created as they danced around him.

A tall man with silver hair walked in, spoke urgently to him. Connor frowned up at the stranger, unable to understand. There was something about Ben, and then a distant scream -

Connor woke up. At first only his eyes moved, flashing open and darting quickly around for a sign that something was really happening, something besides a very odd dream. He took a deep breath and listened. Quiet. Calm. But something felt wrong.

He threw off the thick blanket of woven cotton, climbed out of bed and pulled a shirt on over the pants he had fallen asleep in. The more he listened for it, the worse it felt. Wrenching open his door, Connor made the distance to Ben's room at a run, his bare feet finding their way unerringly in the dark of the hall.

"Ben?" Connor yelled, feeling the adrenaline rise in his body. He shouldered the door open with enough force to break it, yet somehow he knew before he looked. The room was empty.

Scowling openly now, feeling the first flush of justified anxiety, Connor doubled back down the hallway to the Lady's room. Abandoning all pretense of formality, he pounded on the door.

"Yes?" The Lady's voice was quiet but wide-awake. Something about this dawn was disturbing everyone's sleep.

"Miran. Ben's gone."

The door opened abruptly on the Lady in a long robe, her hair spilling down her shoulders. Fine lines at the corners of her eyes, usually unnoticeable against the strength of her gaze, were obvious now. In all their discussions over the years, Connor had never before seen fear touch those peaceful, green eyes.

"Gone?"

"He's not in his room."

"Couldn't he -" The lady stopped herself as Cyrin rounded the corner on the run, her hair loose, her tunic disheveled.

"Lady." The girl stopped to catch her breath. "I can't feel him here. Anywhere. It's like -" Cyrin stopped, and frowned, her eyes abruptly focusing on nothing.

"Cyrin?" The lady spoke quietly, moving to touch the girl's arm, lending the apprentice her own strength. "What do you feel?"

The girl shook her head angrily as the sensation passed. "I don't know. For a minute, I could almost -" She stopped again, a light dawning in her eyes, and she flew down the hallway. Twice she paused, as if to recapture an elusive scent. As they reached the short corridor that led to Jhaun's room, she gasped. Leaping toward his door she suddenly stopped dead, fear forcing her back scant inches from the green starburst.

"Lady." Bright tears brimmed suddenly in her eyes as she pointed at the door. "He's in there. I feel it. But I don't know if he's - alive."

Connor watched the Lady make a conscious decision to push her own fears away. In the moment that took, Connor lurched forward and forced the door open.

Huddled on his back on the floor, legs bent and limp, arms curled up over his chest like a dead spider, lay the body of Benjamin Agante. His eyes were open, startled, but their sense was shut.

Nothing.

"Is he -" It was Cyrin who tried to ask, afraid to look too closely, feeling too many conflicting signals to figure out if he was alive herself.

"He's alive." Connor knelt beside him, feeling a pulse, weak and fluttering. "My God, Ben. What happened?" There was no response.

"He can't hear you. He doesn't know we're here."

"Can you feel anything from him, Cyrin? Anything at all?"

There was a pause, and the Lady's apprentice choked out a sob. "I can't. I'm sorry, I don't know why, but - I just -"

"Cyrin." The Lady's voice was firm, but she was holding the girl tightly. "It's all right. I wasn't able to feel him at all. You've done well."

The minstrel gathered Ben up in his arms and moved to lay him on the bed, then thought better of it and took him out of the room, carrying him back down the hallway to his own quarters. He whispered to him as he walked, quietly, as if to a sleeping child. "It'll be okay, Ben. I promise." Ben's eyes stared, unfocused, toward the ceiling.

Connor took a long overdue breath and began to sing. In a strong, gentle voice he sang of safety and hope as he made his way through the castle that was waking to a new dawn.

It's dark.

The mere articulation of the thought sets up a series of echoes, a reverberation that bounces back and forth in an infinitely large, infinitely small room. The echoes beat back and forth upon each other like a flock of birds doing early fall maneuvers with an insane leader, growing in intensity, increasing in volume, until the creature in the room with the thought cries out in pain.

The shredded wisp that is left of the man wants it to stop. Wants it to stop now. Wants more than anything not to think anymore, not have these loud, screaming echoes of thought hurtling at him, pounding against his very essence.

But it is his very essence that is struggling to think.

"We have to do something." Connor was sitting on the bed next to the gaping, twisted body of his friend. "There's got to be something."

"I don't even know if Ben's there. I can't feel him -"

"He has to be!"

The Lady spoke harshly. "If you can use your anger, Hawk, then do. If you can't, don't endanger Benjamin with your fear."

It's - dark. The creature forces out the thought, forces himself to know it. To know is to have some power.

The echoes redouble their efforts, the pain spasms within. The thing that is in the room, because it can't possibly express that concept anymore, keens quietly, huddled in the corner of this place. Stop. Pain. The wisp tries not to think. It tries to not be. Every thought, every moment realized, wrenches through it, louder, echoing, screaming in agony. Here, in this room locked so tightly from the inside, the man, such as he is, still exists. And there is something, even in this mere shred of what remains, that can't give up.

Help. Please. Someone help me -

Connor turned his anger and stared at her. "You know who did this." The Lady flinched away. "Why?"

Her facade crumbled abruptly. "I don't know why. And yes," she said, her eyes filling with angry tears, "It had to be Jhaun." The Lady of Anders Castle reached for the dresser to support herself as her strength failed. Connor stood to put his arms around her, and she breathed heavily into his shoulder, struggling to keep herself under control. "I swear to you, if I had known -"

"I know. I'm sorry. Not your fault." The minstrel brushed his hand down the back of her hair, twining his fingers into the curls. "And I have a feeling we have to save both of them to complete the circle. Am I right?" She pulled away and looked into his eyes.

"I think so. Hawk." She regained her composure slowly, but with elegance and grace. "We have to find Jhaun. If Ben can survive long enough," she said, looking at the figure on the bed, "Jhaun may be able to put things right."

"But will he?"

Her eyes clouded once more. "I don't know." Then her expression hardened, her voice became cold and sharp as a blade. "But I can make him." And in that moment, the Hawk had no doubt that the Lady Anders could make anyone do as she wished.

Help me. Please.

It happened slowly. Small bits of the man in the darkness filtered back to him. But not the part that had been so recently ripped away.

They came from a dozen homes - a dozen theaters, at least a world away. Blended, as they were, with characters he had created before - new souls that were individuals apart from him, that he was a part of.

Hotspur came, angry at the cowering fool who hid behind a locked door. Banquo, loyal and fearless, brushing off the metaphysics as if it were dust on his sleeve. Hamlet, understanding the desire to surrender, but driven by the desire to know more. Iago, curious, wondering if he could possibly take over while there was no one in control, already plotting revenge. Demetrius, petrified, but drawn as surely as the others. Characters the man had fashioned with the help of Shakespeare; the strongest of them were Shakespeare, but also Stoppard, and Chekov, Miller, Pirandello -

They rushed into the vacuum of a room that was suddenly milling with a multitude of character's shadows, gathering around what was left of the man like gnats around a piece of rotting fruit. With the combined energy of a hundred fragments of his own creations, Benjamin Agante remembered who he was. Barely. Remembered there was more, that if he could only hang on, help would come.

He looked up for the first time. It was no longer black, but a pearly grey nimbus that surrounded him, a foggy background for razor sharp personalities. In the crowd of characters that buzzed around him, he singled out a different but strangely familiar form, silver hair shrouded by a soft blue glow.

Hang on, Ben. No one can steal a man's soul.

Ben stared at the stranger, not knowing how to react, but feeling the words giving him a strange feeling... one that just might be called hope.

Connor looked into the Lady's eyes and saw the steel there, steel that he knew was always just under the surface. If she had to destroy her son to save the people that depended on her, she was capable of it. The minstrel shuddered inwardly, but reached out and took her hand.

It would cost her dear. The Lady pushed away from the minstrel and turned to her apprentice. "Cyrin. I think the Hawk should stay with Ben. Tell Wesp we need to know who saw Jhaun, which way he was headed. Tell him to send out groups of three, and make sure at least one in each party can create a warding on the move. We need to find him." The Lady turned back to Connor. "Can you stay with him? Are you able?" The minstrel looked down at his friend and took a deep breath.

"Hawk," the Lady said, "I know it's hard for you to sit still at a time like this. But if you can help him, reach him somehow, get him to hold on until we find Jhaun -"

The minstrel stopped her with a sharp nod. "I know. Yeah. I can handle it." He sat on the edge of the bed and untangled one of Ben's hands, massaging the stiff fingers. "I can handle it." Connor looked back toward the Lady. "It's my place." A resigned smile touched his glittering eyes, and the Lady put her hand on his shoulder.

"You are the Hawk," she breathed. "I've always known."

The minstrel nodded. Taking a breath and looking down at Ben once more, he said so that only she could hear, "It's hard to believe I wanted to be him so badly." The Lady stood by him for a moment as he blinked quickly, then ran a hand back through his hair. "Okay," he said more loudly. "I'm going to need my guitar, at some point."

Cyrin spoke from the doorway. "I'll get it, Hawk. As soon as I talk to Wesp. Lady?"

The Lady smiled at her, a feat of bravery on its own. "Go."

Cyrin left them then, and the Lady stood by Hawk's side as he sang softly to Ben. By degrees the minstrel focused more clearly on what he was attempting, but none of it seemed to affect the stiff isolation of the actor's mind and body. The Lady shook her head. "Do you feel anything?"

The minstrel spoke without changing his focus to look at her. "No. But I'm not giving up. If he can feel anything, maybe he can feel that." Connor paused to find a new song and carried on. The Lady took a deep breath, placed her hand gently on the minstrel's head for a moment, and then left him to his work.

A cold tremble passed through her as she walked down to her own quarters. Never had she missed something so obvious. Never had she suspected that this son was the danger that the prophecies warned of. That danger, she thought, had been dealt with long ago, and with pain she still felt.

"Lady." Cyrin, trotting toward her, brought her out of her reverie. "Wesp organized the search parties. He says no one saw Jhaun leave, but a horse is gone." Cyrin gave a weary shrug, her eyes tired but still exasperated. "He seems more annoyed at that than anything."

"Thank you, Cyrin." The Lady took a deep breath and exhaled slowly. "All we can do now is wait." She turned and walked down the hallway to her room.

Connor sat with Ben all through that day. Past midnight the Lady came and found him near exhaustion. "Hawk." The minstrel turned to her, a drained look in his eyes. "If you can last until I get to my rooms, I'll take a turn while you rest." Connor nodded heavily and went back to the melody he was picking out on his guitar. The Lady left for her rooms and played them safe until morning, when Connor was awake again and able to take over.

For two days they took turns guarding and trying to keep Ben safe, but nothing changed. They felt him slowly slipping away. There was little talk of sleep, and the food that Cyrin brought was left untouched as often as not.

There was still no word of Jhaun from the search parties, except for the vague idea that he was headed toward the gate. Connor felt the truth of it within him. He also knew that if Jhaun wasn't needed to help Ben, he would have the bastard shot on sight, Lady's son or no.

On the morning of the third day, when it seemed they had expended all of the energy in their stores, Cyrin came to the door of Ben's room, fatigue aging her youthful features. Even her steps in the hallway sounded old, and the tunic of pale blue and black was the same she had worn when she first found Ben. The Lady was there with Connor, checking in.

"Milady?" The apprentice looked very tired, and confused.

"What is it?"

"Lady," she hesitated. "There's… a man at the door. He says he knows both the Hawk and the One, and that he's ridden for two days without rest to reach them." She shook her head and frowned. "From the look of him and his horse I'd say it's the truth." She stared out at nothing for a minute, nodded, and then went on. "And it feels like the truth. He feels familiar, somehow." The girl shrugged helplessly. "I know I'm tired. But I'd say, Lady, that he might be able to help."

"Did he give his name?"

The girl hesitated once more, still feeling awkward about the stranger at the door without knowing why. "Perahn. Of Overlook."

Connor turned with a relieved smile just in time to see the Lady stumble back against the table. Cyrin made a startled noise and looked at the minstrel, who let go of Ben and helped the Lady up, easing her into a chair. "What's wrong?" Connor's concern, as usual, sounded more angry than anything.

Cyrin was more direct. "Lady?"

"Miran -" The minstrel dropped his voice to a more gentle tone. "You need rest. I know Per. He's okay."

"I know. I remember you speaking of him. I just -" The Lady of Anders Castle took a moment and organized her thoughts. Decided consciously what she wanted to do next. Turning to her apprentice, who was bleary-eyed with worry and fatigue, she spoke calmly. "Cyrin. Bring him here. And then get some sleep." As the girl began to protest the Lady raised her hand. "Please, Cyrin. I can't trust my own strength right now. Get some rest so I can lean on you again." Cyrin walked to the Lady and hugged her for a long time, her shoulders shuddering as she took a deep breath. Then she turned and left the room.

"Miran."

"I'm all right." She took several deep breaths with her eyes closed, and Connor held back his questions. He turned instead to Ben, and sat down on the bed next to the actor's motionless body. Only shallow breathing showed that his friend was still alive. After all this, to have come this far, to have it fall now... Connor felt someone else in the room before he turned, before he heard the familiar voice.

"Hawk? How is he?"

"Per." The musicians embraced before he finished saying his name. "I'm glad you're here. I think we're running out of time."

Perahn looked down at Ben, his eyes wide. "What happened?"

"Don't know. But it has something to do with the Lady's son." Connor motioned toward the Lady, who leaned silently against the stone wall, staring almost fearfully at the visitor. "This is the Lady Anders. Lady, this is Perahn. I've told you about him. He's a powerful musician, and my friend."

The Lady's eyes swam slightly in the dim light of Ben's room. "Yes. I've heard of you, - Perahn. Welcome." She stepped forward and extended her hand to him, and he kissed it respectfully. There was a strange stiffness to Perahn's movements that Connor didn't recognize, a strained energy between him and the Lady that he chalked up to the same kind of nervousness Ben had about meeting her.

"I thank you for your welcome." Perahn bowed and looked into the Lady's eyes. "I'm glad to meet you, finally."

The two stared into each other, the intensity of the energy that passed between them growing until it was nearly visible.

The minstrel looked back and forth between the two of them and shook his head. "Okay. What the hell is going on? And what does it have to do with Ben?"

"It has nothing to do with Ben. And maybe everything. I don't know, Connor, but I was with Tomas in Lintock when we felt something happen. And I knew I had to catch up, that I might be able to help him."

"Perahn -"

"No, Lady." Per spoke firmly to her, an edge of anger exposed in his voice. "Ben first."

The Lady backed away and bowed her head.

"Okay." Connor looked at the two of them, decided that whatever was going on would wait, and concentrated on Ben. "Per. What do you need from me?"

"Warding, I know that much. A safe place. I know Ben found me when I was lost. Maybe I can find him now." Perahn reached for the wooden flute that was tucked into his belt and ran his hands over it. Putting it to his lips, he began to play a delicate melody, a calm, centering song of search.

Connor nodded into the music. "You got it." Sitting on the edge of the bed, the minstrel picked up his guitar and began playing. First an echo, then a counterpoint, then unison. Perahn released the melody to the minstrel, took a few deep breaths, and put his hand on Ben's chest.

"All right, w'hentali. I'm here. Show me what's happened."

Perahn closed his eyes, concentrated, and opened the door.

Through a pearly grey mist he walked, trusting his direction by faith alone. For a bad moment he thought he was lost, but embraced the direction that Connor was giving him and felt the ground change. Felt, before he saw, a flagstone path beneath his feet. As the mist cleared he saw a wooden porch, steps leading up to it. Climbing them, he came to a door that was half ripped from its hinges. He stopped and reset the door, bending the metal with surprising ease, setting it so that it could at least be closed. It would require more to make it strong again, but that was up to the one who lived here.

Perahn rested a hand on the open door and waited. Nothing. Stepping over the threshold, he called softly into the main room.

Ben? Can you hear me?

It was dark, and difficult to see, but Per could make out jumbled heaps of debris. A smell like an abandoned root cellar.

Ben, what happened? I know you're here, I can feel it -

One of the doors off the main room caught Perahn's eye, and with good reason. It was the only one still closed. Part of the musician turned back to his physical body, long enough to check in with Connor.

His voice was barely a whisper. "I'm going to go farther-"

The Lady gave a plaintive cry. "Perahn, you could both be lost!" Either he didn't hear her plea, or chose to ignore it; the effect was the same. Perahn's physical body shut down again, breathing deeply and evenly. With a barely perceptible movement his hand crept a few inches over on Ben's chest, coming to rest on the pendant, a curved teardrop of blood red on pallid skin.

The sensation of fear was the first thing he felt, and the most overwhelming. Gently, Perahn pushed open the door, feeling the vulnerability and the pain as he did.

Ben?

The room was crowded with impressions that to Per looked like tendrils of fog intertwining, like thunderclouds heaped and marbled in a storm. Flashes of brightness, like lightning, chased across the clouds, tried to push him back.

Benjamin?

Suddenly Per saw him, the fetal bundle that was left of the man who was Benjamin Agante. There was no trace of the One here.

What has he done to you?

Who are you?

Ben? You're okay?

What do you want from me?

Benjamin. I'm a friend ...w'hentali.

The part that was left of Ben stared and frowned at Per.

Do I know you?

Yes. Be still. I have enough strength to ride us through. He opened his hand and held it out, facing Ben.

The thing that was Ben edged forward, put his hand curiously on Per's, and slowly smiled, like a flower opening.

Per. I remember.

Then the storm hit. With the force of a hurricane, the essence of Benjamin Agante swept back to its corporal quarters, with all the grace of a wounded buck bursting through a plate glass window. The effect was like a truck slamming into the house, a flood trying to wash it away. If Per had not been there to hang on, if the actor had not reached out to him, Ben might have been lost. Even so it was a close thing, as Per tried to stabilize it all, tried to figure out what the hell was going on.

"Lady?" Connor's voice was tight.

"I feel it too. What's happening?"

"Damn. I hoped you knew."

Ben's breathing had suddenly increased in depth and frequency. Per was holding on to him with both hands, one cradling the pendant, the other holding the actor's hand. The village musician looked startled by the intensity of whatever was going on.

"Per?" Connor waited for some kind of response. "What can I do? Talk to me!"

When the response finally came, it was as if it had traveled through the entire underworld to reach him. "Hawk. He's here, he's…"

"Per?" The minstrel shook his head and tried to concentrate on creating a safe place instead of trying to figure out what was going on. It took all of his focus, but he managed to do it.

Slowly, he felt Benjamin returning to them, although he couldn't quite describe how. By the time Perahn relaxed and was able to focus on the minstrel again, fully five hours had passed. The musician was drenched in sweat, and Ben looked twice his age, panting with the strain of exertion, eyes closed. Perahn opened his eyes, looked at the minstrel, smiled wanly at him. Connor stopped playing and reached out to his friend. "Is he okay? Are you?"

"I think so. He's going to need sleep."

"Join the club. What the hell happened?"

Perahn stopped and shook his head slowly, as if he was afraid of moving anything too fast. "I didn't do anything. I was just there when he came back."

"That's good."

"Hawk," The musician spoke in utter exhaustion, his head leaning down toward the bed, "I don't know what that means happened to -" he paused to find the words, "to the Lady's son."

"Don't worry about that now." The minstrel shook his head and staggered to his feet, resting his instrument in the corner. "We'll figure it out in the morning." He turned and saw the Lady standing near the bed. Saw her gently place a hand on Perahn's head.

"Miran. Is it safe?"

He saw her smile and nod to him, tears in her eyes, and that was the last thing the minstrel remembered clearly for a long time.

15

Two mornings later Connor and the Lady had recovered enough to talk. Perahn was awake by the second afternoon, although he still rested in the room that Cyrin arranged for him. Ben slept on, coming out of his twilight long enough to be fed some soup and wine before slipping into a healing sleep once more.

The ones who kept everything together while the balance was restored were true heroes. Cyrin took the Lady's duties when she could, and delegated the ones she could not. Wesp kept the search alive, and conferred with Cyrin when Jhaun was found unconscious and limp on the side of the road leading toward the Gate the day after Perahn arrived.

So it was that the traitor was imprisoned, held in the depths of the castle and warded by guards, while the ones who he had hurt so deeply slept on, too exhausted to even feel his presence.

On that third morning, Cyrin came to the Lady's chamber, where she was taking breakfast with Connor. "Lady." The girl looked so uncomfortable that Miran and Connor exchanged a look.

"Cyrin? Why aren't you resting?"

She smiled briefly. "Milady, Hawk. Are you feeling better? Are you up to…" Her speech failed her. Connor felt it first.

"Hey, 'Rin," he said with gentle concern. "Just tell us what's going on."

The girl sighed and plunged on. "We have Jhaun."

The Lady caught her breath. Connor's reaction was less obvious, his eyes hardening, his hand closing into a tight fist. "He's in the hold," the girl continued, answering unasked questions. "He was hurt when we found him, unconscious, but he's stable now. Still not talking, though. To anyone. Not even -" She stopped and stared at the floor, as if her speech was written there. "I'm sorry I didn't tell you sooner, but I was afraid that -"

"Cyrin." The Lady's tone was kind. "You've handled everything well. I'm sure this was for the best." She stood smoothly and walked towards the door.

"Miran?"

She looked back at the Hawk briefly. "I'm going to see my son." Connor pushed himself up from the table. "No, Hawk." The Lady tempered her voice carefully. "I need to see him alone."

Connor sat, his eyes still connected with hers. "You sure?" Miran gave no response, but turned and was gone, Cyrin following.

The minstrel sighed, picked up his cup of herb tea and stared into its depths as if it could divine for him what to expect. There was more to this, and it was too easy to blame the boy. He sipped the liquid, warm and slightly bitter, and exhaled a slow breath. There must have been some way to prevent this. Something he could have done differently. He was so absorbed that he didn't see the figure standing at the door.

"Con."

Connor turned, surprised, and looked up at Ben. His jaw tensed as he fought with the emotional interplay of relief and guilt. "Ben."

The actor spoke without preamble, not acknowledging the passage of time since they spoke last. "It wasn't your fault. I let him in." He paused, shook his head. "I didn't know. But don't worry," he leaned heavily on the doorframe. "It won't happen again."

The minstrel stood and faced him. "I should have warned you. I could have done something."

The actor's eyes widened. "You've got to be kidding. Per told me we wouldn't have made it if you weren't holding us together." His eyes were bright through the fatigue, but still held only a shadow of his former energy. "Thank you." Then, with a grin designed to let them out of an emotional scene, "I guess I owe you another one, eh?"

The minstrel saw through the ploy, stared at the floor briefly. "Right. I'll put it on your tab." They shook hands more seriously than their words would allow, and Ben felt something settle within him as Connor pulled him into a hug. *One more piece of himself in the right place, working properly. One more ray of hope against the fear.*

Abruptly, the minstrel stepped back and looked annoyed. "Do you know?"

The actor frowned. "I've been out for three days, and awake for what, an hour and a half? What am I supposed to know?"

"They found Jhaun."

Ben stared at the minstrel, then at the floor, shaking his head. Anger washed across his ashen features. Instinctively, the One reached out with his mind, knew the answer to the question before he asked. "Is he alive?"

"Yeah."

"What happened?"

"I don't know. The Lady's gone down to see him."

"Well," Ben said, turning to the hallway. "I guess she'll have company."

"Ben." The actor stopped without looking back. "She wanted to see him alone."

Benjamin turned back to the minstrel, his eyes flashing. "I really don't care. Are you with me?"

Connor looked into an anger he had never seen in Ben before. "Yeah, I'm with you." They walked the hallways with borrowed strength.

"Per!" Ben yelled before he actually reached the door, and it opened in his face. "He's here. Let's go."

Perahn blinked at him. "Here? Now?" A hard glint in soft brown eyes. "Alive?"

"Yeah. Let's go."

"Where?" That simple question finally stopped Ben's continuing movement with a shudder.

"Don't you know? The minstrel shook his head. Ben turned and yelled, his voice strident in the echoing hallway. "Cyrin!"

"Ben, calm down."

"Easy for you to say."

"No," the minstrel put his hand on Ben's shoulder. "No, not easy." Their eyes met, control against chaos. Chaos was winning. "Look, kid," he spoke quietly, willing Ben to calm. "I'm not sure you're up to this." The actor brushed off Connor's hand.

"Back off, Connor. You don't know."

Cyrin rounded the corner at a run just as he finished, and saw the two glaring at each other. Connor, tired but controlling his anger; Ben, anger the only thing keeping him on his feet.

"What?" She was breathless, concern stressing her features as she looked at them. "Are you all right?" Ben turned to face her.

"Where's Jhaun?" he barked.

"What?" She blinked and pulled back her head.

"Cyrin. Listen to me. Where the hell are you keeping Jhaun?" His tone, his feelings, hit her like a slap in the face. The girl stopped, stepped back, and stared at him. Somewhere inside of her, a door slammed, with a force that could be felt by the men standing around her. The voice that escaped after a moment of absolute silence was emotionless, words dropped from a fifth floor window.

"Where's Jhaun. That's what you screamed for."

"Look, I'm -"

The force in her voice stopped Ben. "That's it. And like a fool, I'm afraid that maybe you're dying *again*. Just worried that -" She stopped, caught herself. Her dark eyes narrowed for a moment, and she swallowed hard before she spoke. Her body tightened as she shelled herself in, and her fluid movements became stark. "Jhaun is under guard, a distance from here. If you feel up to it, I'll take you." Formality draped over her emotions like a tablecloth laid *over* fine china, and about as smoothly. She turned to move away when Ben caught her arm.

"Cyrin. Wait." She pulled away stiffly but turned towards him again, her expression painfully blank. Suddenly she was a seventeen-year-old girl. One who had, for the last three days, been taking care of this damaged and distracted mass of adults, trying and succeeding. And this was how he showed her how much it was appreciated? These were the first words he shared with her? Seeing the chaos within himself, reflected in her face, was too much. *I did this. I did this to her.*

A voice inside spoke quietly. *Perhaps you've lost more than you think.*

No. I just - I'm just not feeling.

Ben blinked a few times, closed his eyes tightly. With more effort than he would have liked to admit, he took a deep breath and tried to center himself. No good. He slid down the wall he was leaning on until he sat on the cold stone floor, freeing energy that he was using just to remain upright. He took another deep breath, tried again. This time he felt some semblance of being focused, connected to himself. It hurt. More than anything, he felt the pain he was causing. Breathing into it, he allowed himself to feel it for a time before he spoke. The others stood by quietly until Ben opened his eyes.

"Okay," he said softly. He rubbed his palms into his eyes before looking up at each of them in turn and shaking his head. "I'm angry. But I'll try to use it. Not let it use me."

Perahn nodded, understanding as always, and Connor shrugged, the incident already passed. He extended a hand to help Ben to his feet as Cyrin stared at the floor.

Ben stood, shakily, and stepped toward her.

"Cyrin?" He took her hand gingerly. Her eyes looked at him then, guarded beneath her brows. The actor looked away with a wince. The hurt and disappointment he felt coming from her was almost too much to bear. He took a breath and resigned himself to it, looked into her eyes once more. Drawing on years of technique, he offered her his most charming smile. The one reserved for beautiful women and huge mistakes.

"Forgive me?" She took another breath and stared at the wall for a while, as if it were giving her advice. He stepped closer, a faint wobble detracting from the smoothness of his words. "I'm sorry. Can we pretend I'm not quite myself yet?"

Cyrin snorted as if the wall had said something amusing. "I don't think we'll have to pretend much." She gave him a sidelong glare that was far beyond her years, while her eyes followed it with the promise of forgiveness that might arrive sometime soon, if he behaved himself.

Ben looked at her, and felt healing in the connection he had nearly severed. "Thank you."

He brought her hand to his lips before he released it. The actor turned then to Connor and Per. "Sorry."

Connor waved it off, anxious to move on to the next task, and spoke to the Lady's apprentice as if nothing unusual had happened. "Cyrin, can you take us there?" He gestured towards Ben. "Maybe he needs this more than we know."

The girl looked appraisingly at the actor, made a decision and headed down the hallway. The three men followed her, Benjamin at point, Perahn following thoughtfully, and Connor carefully guarding the rear.

They reached an archway that led down in broad steps to a lower level, below ground. Beyond there was a doorway, two men standing guard. One wore a sword, while the other carved a piece of darkly striped wood with a small knife. Ben looked curiously at what he was doing. In the guard's hand a wooden flower was slowly blossoming perfectly, petals overlapped and curled in a way that defied its material. He could feel the power in its creation.

"Who's with him?" Cyrin's voice rang with authority.

"The Lady, miss. And she wanted to be alone." The guard motioned with his chin towards the men behind her.

"I understand. We're going in." She started to move forward and stopped, looked back at the guard with a tight smile. "I take responsibility, Ian." The guard stared for a moment, then shrugged and went back to his carving, keeping the wards in place around the cell.

Perahn stood to the side. "I'll stay here. Don't worry," he said to Ben's concerned expression. "I'll know if you need me." He reached for the flute hanging at his side as they walked in and began a soothing melody, framing them in the depths of the castle.

Inside, it was dark. Nowhere in Anders that Ben had seen was truly oppressive, but this cell was as close as it was going to get. No windows here below ground, one lamp near the door. Against the far wall was a cot, which obviously was not part of the original cell. Clean linen and blankets stood out like jewels on burlap, although it looked as if it had never been slept in. Ben took in the details with an actor's eye, noting not only the details, but the meaning that could be found beneath them. This was Cyrin's work. He looked over at the girl, and even in his distracted state he could feel the concern rolling off her.

A dark figure sat motionless on the edge of the cot; face in his hands, elbows on his knees, still as a statue. Ben realized he was watching the man's chest, just to see if he were still breathing. Cautiously he reached out with his feelings. Nothing. Ben frowned. Standing opposite her son was the Lady of Anders castle, her arms folded tightly, standing stiffly in the cool of the cell. She turned after they came in, a regal frown flashing in the torchlight.

"I said I wanted to be alone with him."

"Yeah," Ben said. "So I hear."

The Lady shook her head and walked over to the actor, softening slightly. "Benjamin?" She passed her hand over his forehead, brushing back his hair. He felt the brush of her concern as well.

"I need to deal with this."

"It is your right." The Lady pulled herself up, looking only at Benjamin. He felt the draw of connection and looked at her, shook his head.

"I can't," he whispered. "Not now." There was moment of give and take, the Lady wanting desperately to trust his judgment, but Benjamin had no assurance to give. She stepped back, looked at her son for the space of a deep breath, and looked back into Ben's eyes, her decision made.

"You are the One." Her voice was strong, and only an actor would have seen how much it cost her to make it sound that way. "I give him to you."

Cyrin gasped, and Ben felt the reverberation of ritual within the cell. This was no casual remark. *His life is in your hands. Remember that.*

Suddenly Benjamin could feel each of them in the room. From Cyrin, shock; from the Lady, a wash of failure. There was less intensity from Connor, guarded but more concerned at the moment for Ben than the boy's fate. From Jhaun, Ben felt nothing.

"Thank you, milady." The actor turned and looked at the young man, so like a stone in the fluttering darkness. Sitting like a statue in a graveyard. Benjamin tried to sort out his feelings, now that he was able to do something about them. He took a deep breath and opened the door of a room filled to overflowing with pure, undiluted anger. Like moonshine at midnight, intoxicating, deadly. For a while Benjamin let himself roll in it, become drunk with the white-hot energy of it. *Now what?*

A voice then, the One. *You must speak to him.*

What?

You owe him that.

Almost against his will, Ben heard himself speak.

"Jhaun." His voice rang in the small cell. "Why?"

For the first time, the hands came away from his face. The boy's chiseled features were drawn and heavy with fatigue. He looked older, and burdened with guilt. Still, he looked at Ben with dark flashing eyes; eyes that could belong to a madman or a king. He spoke in a voice that was a bare whisper.

"Just do what you have to do."

Benjamin frowned. He was entitled to his anger. He was entitled to let himself hate. The actor shook his head without realizing it, not wanting to relinquish the fury boiling inside. *No. I'll have my revenge.*

Will you? Then see where you want to go.

With a wrenching pull, the One led Ben, leaving the bright, hot intoxication of anger to fall spiraling into hate. Deep, blood purple, like a glass of wine thickened with poison. Ben saw himself giving the order to kill the traitor, killing him himself, stripping the young man's mind of anything they could possibly use. It poured through him like hot acid. The sheer vile weight of it made him retch. He doubled over, grabbed the wall to support himself.

"Ben?" Connor was at his side instantly. Benjamin raised his hand to keep him back, shook his head. His body continued to react, trembling in the aftershock. Never in his life had he felt anything so bitter. There was no life in this, no power. It was draining the energy out of him.

What the hell-?

Is he so different from Perahn?

Ben dropped to one knee, connected with Jhaun's eyes, still listening to the conversation in his head.

Yeah, he's different. Per didn't want to -

The actor stared, saw the tormented soul of the man sitting in front of him. *Didn't want to.* Just because Per was attacked suddenly, did that mean that a person couldn't be affected over the years? Especially someone who was cursed with being able to walk into someone's mind, of being able to take anything he found there.

Yes. Per didn't want to do it. And Jhaun?

He wanted to.

Benjamin took a deep breath, and steadied himself with one hand against the floor, the cold stone stealing what little warmth he had felt.

Because he thought it would help. He did it, knowing what it would do to him.

With a gasp, Ben's eyes widened. There was something in that thought. Cautiously, he opened himself. Jhaun looked down and away, trembled slightly. He felt the One, felt Benjamin know the thoughts that were screaming too loudly for him to silence.

He thought it would help. He knew he was expected to be something special, but he didn't know what. My God, he thought he could go up against Alious alone, sacrifice himself and save us all. Both at once. Self-destruction and the fulfillment of the prophecies.

Jhaun risked a glance back into Ben's eyes, panic lying just beneath a stoic facade.

"Jhaun." Benjamin knelt to steady himself, took the boy's hands and put their palms together. Folding his own hands over them, he stared calmly into Jhaun's confusion, braving the storm like a hawk in a fierce wind. "I understand." Blue eyes kept their intensity, but softened somehow. "I forgive you."

The Lady's son pulled away. "No." It was the growling cry of an animal caught in a trap, laced with disbelief.

Ben felt the energy of the moment well up inside of him like the invigoration of standing beneath a waterfall, an elemental pounding baptism. *Yes. This is where the power lies.*

Light flowed in a soft liquid cocoon around his hands, glowing gently, warming the shadowy chill of the cell. Slowly the blanket of light crept up Jhaun's arms. The Lady's son shook violently, tried to pull away from Ben, found he didn't have the strength.

"No. Don't." He turned to the Lady. "Let them kill me. Make him-" His voice broke as sobs were wrenched from a broken spirit. "Mother. Please. If you can still care at all, let this end."

Tears ran down the Lady's cheeks, catching the torchlight and reflecting back in golden streams. Cyrin moved to steady her, and Connor nodded his appreciation, not leaving Ben's side.

The light crept on until it enveloped the Lady's son, surrounding him. Jhaun cried out. Great sobs that had no sound tore out of him, muscles that would not respond tried to push Ben away. But it was pushing against light, against warmth. There was no way to fight it.

Benjamin, with a calm strength that he didn't know he had, reached out to the man who had nearly killed him. Putting his hand on Jhaun's shoulder, he pulled him into his arms, and held him there. Healed.

"It's all right," he whispered. The light expanded to envelop them both, faded gently, absorbed into them. "Rest easy, Jhaun."

The Lady's son gave up. Ben closed his eyes and felt something akin to a door opening.

After some time passed, Ben released his hold and leaned back, shaking his head. Connor was watching, standing with Perahn who had felt the turmoil and stepped inside to join them.

"Ben? What's up?"

Ben turned to the minstrel. "He went after Alious. Alone."

Connor frowned. "Then why is he still alive?"

It was Jhaun who answered, in a quiet murmur. "I wasn't worth anything to him. He wanted the One, and I had him, or at least it looked like I did."

"But the One is part of me," Ben interjected, "and I was still hanging on."

Jhaun nodded. "When I got into the Castle of the Stone, it felt enough like the One that I was able to reach him. I could have killed him, but his guards got me first." His eyes became hard, and only Ben had a good idea why. Jhaun continued in broken pieces of sentences. "They brought me to him. I thought I could make a deal. He played with me for a while, then- he laughed in my face. Said that I had some power worth taking. Nothing compared to his. Said that he could use me to destroy the One." Connor looked at Ben, who nodded slowly.

"Just before he -" Jhaun stopped again, unable to go on.

"Just before he ripped into Jhaun's mind," Ben continued quietly, "Jhaun let me go. Nothing tidy about it, but it was that or I was gone for good." He pushed himself to his feet and turned to the Lady and Cyrin. "And maybe all of us were, if the prophecies ring true. He was doing what he felt he was supposed to do. Nothing more. No power to be gained." The actor looked over at Connor. "He just didn't know. And I understand that." The minstrel nodded, resigned. "And it seems Alious took his ability to, well, just walk in. To 'steal'. Which may be a good thing in the long run, but in the short run... he's lost a piece of himself." The actor looked down at Jhaun. "But he'll be okay."

"What about you?"

Ben actually laughed. "Just tired. What else is new?" His hand went to his pendant and stayed there.

Jhaun looked at him, rubbed his eyes, and tried to avoid looking at his mother. She saved him the trouble by stepping over and sitting next to him.

"Jhaun." His head turned in her direction, his eyes low. The Lady put a hand on his cheek and lifted his chin so that he had no choice but to look her in the eye. "I'm sorry I never shared with you what you were to be. I thought that it would make it harder. Now I know that you felt something, but without explanations, you had to invent what that was. I'm sorry," she whispered. "It won't happen again." The Lady rose, walked toward the door, touching Cyrin's arm with a weak smile as she did so. Then she paused, turned back to her son in a weary echo of her regal stance. "You, Jhaun, are the Inca'ti. The one who will lead."

Jhaun shook his head at her, incredulous. "That's impossible! After this?"

The Lady smiled. "Only the Artist knows what He is creating." Her voice held the bittersweet tang of memory.

"*In the time of decisions, a son of Anders will challenge the One, a son of Anders will save him. In the time of decisions, a son of Anders shall be torn away; a son of Anders shall be the Inca'ti, who may lead and guide the time to come.*"

"I only repeat what was said long ago." The Lady's eyes were solemn. "You are what you are. I know that. I only wish I had found the courage to show you your future." She turned away, ready to walk out. "Please don't think me a coward," she whispered, standing motionless at the door. "I wasn't sure. I knew that a son of mine was to be chosen, but..."

Jhaun spoke up, accepting his insignificance. "You weren't sure if you would have only one son. I do understand. And with me being what I am... not having any strong ability to create... you must have hoped for another." The Lady turned in shock, her eyes flashing, and then shook her head.

"No, Jhaun. I just couldn't know which son it was. It was guilt that made me doubt. I know that now." She stared for a moment at Jhaun, and then looked around the cell. "I had another son. Long ago. I was told that the darkness would use a son of mine if it could." She stopped and caught herself. "And I was told, by those who I trusted, that I should put an end to him. I couldn't. I thought that if I could get him away from here, if it was thought that he was dead, it might save him. Might save us. Might turn aside the prophecy." She blinked hard and looked back to Jhaun, who was watching his mother cautiously. "So I sent him away. I didn't want to." Her voice broke for an instant before she caught herself again.

Perahn spoke then, his eyes on the Lady. "Connor. You asked what was going on. I can tell you now." He took a deep breath. "I found a painting in Tomas' studio. A beautiful, dark-haired woman walking with two children." He swallowed hard, looked back at the minstrel. "I took it to Ahna and Taas, wondering who they might be. Ahna was overcome when she saw it, and said it was time I knew."

"Knew what?"

"The Lady Anders is my mother."

"What?"

Ben, close anyway, sat down on the floor.

"It's true, Hawk." She reached out for Perahn's hand, and he stared at it for a moment before taking it. "Can I explain?" Perahn nodded mutely.

"Even before my first child, I had been warned about the prophecies, the ones that said a son of Anders line could plunge us all into darkness, and that a son of Anders line could lead us out again. Against the advice of strong counsel, who said you could not be allowed to exist, including your-" she stopped, regained herself. "Including many who knew the prophecies, I let them take you away the day you were born." Her eyes spilled tears, while her voice remained steady. "My cousin Ahna disagreed with both the warnings and my solution, but left us to take you to a village where you would be safe. To keep watch over you. She was the only one who knew the whole story, knew which foundling child was the son of Anders." She rested against the wall, staring off into another world. "Ahna let me know how you were. It was more than I could take at times.

"By the time Jhaun was born, I knew I couldn't give him up. And the same counsel told me I wouldn't have to, that by breaking the sequence, I had averted the danger. Even Ahna, who came to see me when Jhaun was five, said that he was to be the Inca'ti. But she was worried." The Lady shook her head. "I didn't want to hear anything negative at that point. I couldn't. And that may have been my greatest failure." She brushed her younger son's shoulder and he grasped her hand.

"But I swear to you, Perahn." She turned, looked longingly at the man before her and seemed to see the child she had missed. "I named you. I loved you. I wanted you so much." Her voice broke then, great wrenching breaths that seemed to tear out of her heart and speak of a lifetime of sorrow. Her son's lifetime.

Perahn watched for a minute, then stepped forward and took her hands in his. "I know you did what you felt you had to do. I don't know what other forces were at work, but I don't blame you."

The Lady pulled him into her arms and held him until the tears slowed. They held each other for some twenty-six years, before Perahn pulled back and glanced at Jhaun.

"So." Perahn looked at him, unsure. "I guess that makes you my brother." Jhaun startled, then comprehension dawned across his features.

"Then it's you! It must be you." The sound of relief in his voice was overwhelming. "He's the oldest, he's heir, and he's the Inca'ti. You see?" He looked at them all, starting and ending with his mother. "You see now? I'm not what you think I am. I'm just -"

"No. I don't think so." Perahn cut him off, stood and walked two steps over to where Ben and Connor listened in amazement. "I am what I'm supposed to be. And you, in spite of, or perhaps because of anything that has happened, are heir and Inca'ti." He looked down suspiciously, an expression in his dark eyes that Jhaun found strangely familiar. "May the Artist guide you."

They stared at each other for a long moment, until Ben, still sitting on the floor, broke the silence. "I don't know about the rest of you, but I'm starving." He pushed himself to his feet with Connor's help. "Why don't we continue this over - what time is it - dinner?" He frowned at the minstrel who shrugged and looked at Cyrin.

The young woman gave them a grateful smile, and led the way into the hallway, where they slowly traveled up into the light together.

16

"He's coming with us."

Connor said nothing, while Perahn sat staring at Ben, hoping that he hadn't heard correctly. "You can't be serious." The musician's voice was level, at least for a moment. As he realized that Ben intended just what he feared, his composure vanished. "How could you possibly? After -" The stark memory of violation that he had felt in Benjamin sent a shudder through him. He snatched up his wine and walked to the window, resting a fist against the cool stone as he searched for answers among stars that were just beginning to jewel the velvet sky.

After they had eaten, the three of them had retreated to Connor's room. Jhaun and the Lady had remained behind, sharing long avoided conversation. Now, as the night wound down, the three men found themselves facing the journeys ahead of them, needing rest, and unable to relax enough to go to bed, or even to be alone. And now this.

Perahn looked to Connor for support, got none, and looked back at Ben. His tone was level, but the feeling behind his words was not. "Don't you see? It could color the creation of this whole journey. Even if he isn't *trying* to hurt you, his whole - "

Benjamin held up his hand. "Wait a minute, Per. He's your brother. Don't you feel anything from him? Anything you can trust?" The musician again looked out the window where he stood, abruptly sealed off. "Or is it just that there are other things he reminds you of?"

Connor cleared his throat and gave a warning look. Ben nodded, kicking himself for not acknowledging the strain Perahn was under, for throwing the term 'brother' out as if the man were comfortable with it yet. "All right. How about if we give him a chance. He deserves that much, yes?" Perahn turned to speak but Ben cut him off, knowing what was coming. "At least *I* feel he deserves that much. And don't worry about me." The actor favored him with an ironic smile. "It won't happen again. I won't let it." And then, quietly into his wineglass before the swallow, "And he can't." Perahn stood silent as Ben stepped up and looked out the window with him.

On the field in the moonlight, a lone figure in a gossamer white gown was dancing gracefully. Creating. They watched as she moved, feeling the power around her, feeling the focus of it lifting toward them. Ben blinked. "Is that Cyrin?"

Connor answered without looking. "If it's a tall girl dancing under the moon, it's Cyrin."

Ben felt himself drawn into her movements. An easy contentment settled over him as the figure spun effortlessly, her long dark hair gleaming in the moonlight. "Amazing. What's she dancing to?"

Connor moved to the opening and looked out, a fond smile softening his features handsomely. "The moon, the stars, the clouds. The wind. It's different every time. She just becomes part of it. Ask her sometime."

Ben watched for a while, then turned to Connor. Something in the dance had triggered another chain of thought. "Did I tell you?"

"Tell me what?"

"Well, you know this whole mind home thing?"

The minstrel raised an eyebrow at Ben's cavalier tone, wondering if his easily inebriated friend was still with them. "Yeah?"

"Well, guess what." Ben paused for another sip while Connor swirled the wine in his glass. "Jhaun doesn't have a door."

The minstrel frowned. "How can he not have a door?"

"I don't know how he can't, but he doesn't. It's, I don't know, a birth defect or something. There's an opening, a frame. But no door."

Connor shook his head as his voice darkened. "Alious?"

"No. This has been with him a long time, I could feel that much."

Perahn gave up trying to appear disinterested. He spoke quietly, the rich baritone of his voice framing the sincerity of his concern. "Did you see inside?"

"No. I didn't have to find him." Ben connected briefly with Perahn's eyes, grinning at the familiar energy.

"So how does he keep other people out?"

"That's the weird part," Ben said. "There's this - labyrinth, I guess you would call it, and I'm sure it's hell to get through if he isn't leading. But I think you can get into it at different places at different times, depending on how much he trusts you, how far he's willing to let you in. At least that's the feeling I had. I got in because at that moment, he was vulnerable as hell." Ben paused to think and sip from the goblet of wine. "That ability to protect himself shows a lot of power on his part. Probably that he doesn't acknowledge. And I may know more about it than he would be comfortable with. Hell, I may know more than he does."

Connor nodded in tacit understanding, staring at his wine without actually seeing it.

"Anyway. It's strange, isn't it? I mean, have you ever heard of anyone who couldn't close the door? Who had to use subterfuge to keep anyone from finding the entrance in the first place?"

Connor shifted his position against the wall. "A lot of people hide. Trou almost always did. And sometimes you have to protect yourself. But it's the door that gets me. He must be warding himself constantly." The minstrel tapped absently on the goblet in his hand, raising a series of concentric circles in the wine.

Suddenly Perahn turned, slamming his goblet down so forcefully that some of the garnet liquid slopped over the side. "All right. I'm coming too."

The sudden silence between the three of them was deafening. Ben spoke first. "You don't have to do this."

"I know." Perahn paused briefly, straining to make himself clear. "Look. I feel a need to come. Whether it's to do something, or to protect you from my erstwhile brother, I don't know. But I need to come." He took a breath, shook his head. "I *want* to come." In the blink of an eye, Perahn's tone changed, returned to his normal quiet reserve. "If you'll have me."

Connor looked at Benjamin, who was studying Perahn as if he'd never seen him before. The minstrel laughed soundlessly, and slapped Perahn on the shoulder. "All right, Per. I think we can handle you tagging along." He finished refilling his glass from the pitcher, which was emptying at an alarming rate. "So, Ben. When do we leave?"

The actor paused, not knowing what to do with the question. He looked at Connor, puzzled, and saw a sparkle in the minstrel's eyes.

You pick a fine time to defer leadership, Con. He took a swallow of wine and frowned, covering his confusion. Taking a deep breath, Ben looked for the One within him and began talking.

"We'll leave after midday meal tomorrow," he said, improvising. "If we make good time, by nightfall the second day we'll be at the base of the Gate rock. We can camp there, and make the ascent in the morning." Ben blinked and waited for one of them to ask how he knew this, or to tell him that he was mistaken, but they both kept quiet, Per nodding his head in agreement, Connor only raising his eyebrows as he recognized more than Benjamin's hand in this. "I know it isn't dawn, Con, but I think that tonight we should get as much sleep as we can. I'm a little tired."

Even Perahn grinned at that understatement, and Connor chuckled as he emptied the last of the pitcher. "Do you think Jhaun will be up to it?"

Ben looked thoughtful for a moment, seemed to be looking at something that wasn't there. "I hope so. We have to do this soon. Too much has happened." He frowned again, and looked toward the door just before Jhaun appeared, knocking on the frame.

The Lady's son looked like he had been running for weeks, more than tired, bone-weary. There was still a haunting depth to the obsidian gaze, but the fight with physical exhaustion was futile. Dark smudges in the fair skin under his eyes combined with slow, cautious movements to age the son of Anders tremendously.

"Sorry to interrupt." His voice was deep, and fatigue gave it a rough edge. "May I come in?" The Lady's son was obviously asking Benjamin, but never met his eyes.

"Sure, Jhaun. You okay?" Ben stepped forward and put a reassuring hand on the younger man's shoulder. It seemed to startle and reassure him at the same time.

"Yeah. I just-" He stopped, shook his head. "I am. Okay."

Benjamin glanced at Perahn, who continued staring out the window. "We were talking about when to leave tomorrow. A day and a half to get to the base of the Gate rock, camp there, and do the climb in the morning."

Jhaun stared at the floor as his gaze shifted into some other reality. He nodded. "That should work. It took me about half that, and Wesp is still complaining about the condition I sent the horse back in." In his fatigue he very nearly relaxed, caught himself. "But I was running. If you're saving your strength, I think that would be plenty of time." He looked anywhere but at the men in the room, leaning into a silence that could not support him. Ben raised his eyebrows at Connor, who began a shrug but nodded instead.

"Well then, you better get some rest for the trip. We can let you sleep until we eat, but then we have to -"

Jhaun's eyes shot up abruptly to look at Ben. "What?"

"I said, we can let you -"

"No. I mean - you want me to come along?"

Ben stared into the dark eyes and relaxed, willing Jhaun to do the same. "Yes."

"Why?" His voice was laid over a breathy, sarcastic laugh.

Ben felt the confusion of the young man before him. Felt the guilt, the fear, the lack of direction. Layer upon layer, shrouding his natural radiance. "You know why."

"Maybe you don't understand." Jhaun paused, trying to articulate. "I've got nothing to give. I have nothing to create." Connor broke in curtly.

"That's a crock, Jhaun, and you know it. You play, you sing, you dance and write - hell, Jhaun, you could do anything-"

Something deep within Jhaun snapped. Ben felt it from where he stood. "Exactly! Don't you see? I do 'everything'. Don't you realize that's the same as doing nothing?" The obsidian eyes danced with the light of a storm at sea, flashing only to illuminate a new danger. Even Per stepped away from the window toward his brother, drawn in by the force around him, the power blended with the anger. "Nothing!"

"I don't understand, Jhaun," Ben said softly. "How can you say you do everything, and - "

Jhaun stepped forward, eye-to-eye with Ben, practically shouting into his face as a lifetime of frustration burst through the dam of his defenses.

"I have no *maro w'elenti,* that's how." He broke off, suddenly, and backed away from them.

Ben reached out toward him, but Jhaun turned away, stepping across the room to lean against the table near the door. The actor paused, took a centering breath. Somehow, even in his fatigue, he was able to remain steady in the force of the storm. He suspected it was more than himself. The image of a graceful figure in white danced through his mind, and he silently sent his gratitude.

"All right, Jhaun. What's a 'maro w'elenti'?" Jhaun shook his head and said nothing, unable to trust himself enough to speak. It was Perahn who finally answered him.

"It means 'central focus'. It suggests that there's always one creating that can focus our power best, where our soul meets the Artist."

Ben nodded his thanks and continued to stare at Jhaun. "And you have none?" The actor frowned into the silence, trying to reconcile the contradictions he was hearing with what he felt coming from the man. "Could it be that you haven't found -"

Jhaun laughed ruefully. "No." His voice was small, no air supporting it. "Look at Cyrin. She's danced since she was what, six? I'm well beyond the age -"

Perahn found himself involved without trying to be. "Look, Jhaun. It's not unheard of. There are those who find their way later - " he stopped as Jhaun turned to him, and their eyes met. The gentle brown against the hardness of stone.

"But not the Inca'ti."

They stood, eyes locked, for a long moment.

"That is a possibility," Perahn said quietly. "But we don't know. Perhaps that's part of the path." His last word was barely audible. "Brother." Jhaun's eyes widened before he blinked several times and looked away.

Benjamin closed his eyes, felt the energy slowly shift into something calmer in the abruptly silent room. When he opened them again, Jhaun was at the window, staring out into the night. The actor took a deep breath and blew it out, feeling like he had forgotten about breathing for altogether too long.

"If you want to come, Jhaun, you are welcome. If you feel you should join us. If not, it's your choice. I can't -" Ben stopped, realized the truth with some amazement. "I won't force you." The actor evaluated Jhaun in a glance, his blue eyes glinting with starlight and confidence. "But remember. All you have inside is more than you will ever need." He felt Connor's smile without looking away from the Lady's son. "Trust me."

Jhaun stared at him, incredulous, then looked at Perahn more briefly, and back at the floor. When he finally spoke his voice was quiet, and sounded a little surprised. "I better get some sleep, then. Goodnight." He turned on his heel and was gone, leaving the three of them standing silently in the room, with a strange following sensation, as if a cloud had passed before the sun on a cold day.

Perahn broke the silence. "I'm still not sure about this." The actor nodded, still staring out the door. "But I felt something too. I understand, at least a little."

Ben turned and grinned at Perahn. "I know." His smile faded as he looked at Connor. "Part of me is afraid I'm setting him up."

The minstrel's eyes flashed with something Ben couldn't quite identify. "Really," he said softly, irony tinting his voice. Then he shrugged and emptied his glass for the last time. "We can't second guess ourselves, Ben. Just got to do." With that he stretched out on the bed and promptly fell asleep, leaving the two men to see themselves out.

*   *   *

Morning dawned bright and cool, the soft yellow spears of sunlight fading to peach and then blue, the clouds getting just involved enough to play at changing colors in the undecided light. There was a scent in the air of freshly mown fields, still wet with dew.

Sometime after dawn, Benjamin came down to the stables, ostensibly to check on his mount, but truly because he had run out of patience pretending to sleep. The lack of preparation went against everything in his training. But the Lady had been clear on that point; the One would have the answers he needed when he required them. Ben took a deep breath of the sweet air and sighed, realizing he was not alone. Wesp was up early, tending the horses. "Morning." Ben looked at the groom, not really expecting a response.

"Morning." Wesp turned and looked briefly at Benjamin before dismissing him. Then, thinking again, he turned back. "The passage to the Gate shouldn't be that bad if you use your heads. And be careful of them," he said, motioning with his head toward the horses. "Don't make them carry you in the gorge, those steps are tricky and it's not fair to ask them to do it. Not like that damn fool did."

"What?" Ben had only just figured out that Wesp was talking about Jhaun's flight when the groom went on.

"Wasn't even his horse, the idiot. Cyrin's Taliesin. And he only made it because she's the most sure-footed thing I've ever seen, not that he'd appreciate her. Can't believe the girl's letting him take her again." Wesp's expression softened in spite of himself. "The story around is that she taught that horse to dance as well as she does. She denies it, of course." He scratched Ben's horse and she rubbed her head roughly against him. "Good girl." Wesp shifted into talking to the horse, sounding quite a bit more natural than he had been speaking with Ben. "Make sure they don't do anything foolish."

Ben grinned at the two of them, and at the groom's sudden foray into communication. "Wesp?"

"Yep."

"What's her name?"

The groom shook his head disparagingly. "You travel with an animal for two weeks and you don't know her name? Did you just not talk to her?" A trace of real anger colored his words.

"Well, actually, " Ben said, a little embarrassed, "I just called her "girl", most of the time." The groom stared at him wide-eyed, and whether it was in amusement or outrage, Ben didn't know.

"Jasper. Her name's Jasper. Like the stone in her bridle." He pointed to an open triangle of stone on her forehead that shaded from light tan to dark brown, much like the horse's coloring did.

"Jasper," Ben said softly, and she turned to rub her nose against his arm. Ben brushed down her neck and smiled. Wesp looked at the two of them, and finally nodded.

"She likes you. That's enough for me."

"Oh?"

"Yep. You can't fool a horse. And she's a smart one. Trust her, she'll get you through anything."

The actor felt the truth in his words and nodded. "She's gotten me through a lot already." A memory flashed through his mind, registering with half a grin on his face. "Actually, she's the first one I met here. Scared me nearly to death." For a moment Ben felt himself back in the clearing in the forest, a crystal stream singing nearby, a stump of oak behind him, a sword shivering in the light through the trees, imbedded in ancient wood. How idyllic that seemed now.

"Hey."

Ben turned from his reverie to see Connor walking toward them.

"Morning, Con. Everybody up?"

"Yeah. How's the morning, Wesp?"

The groom nodded a near smile at the minstrel and retreated back to the stables. "I better get the dancer ready." Wesp walked away shaking his head and muttering.

Connor waited until he was out of earshot to continue. "What's with him?"

"I have no idea. Maybe it was his day of the year to talk." Benjamin scuffed at the ground with his boot.

"You sleep?"

"Some." Ben absently stroked Jasper's flank as they spoke. "I can't really expect to feel relaxed, can I?"

"Maybe not." The minstrel turned as his own horse pushed him from behind. "Kes. Hey. How are you, boy?" The horse whinnied, and rubbed up against Connor like a gatepost. "Yeah, we'll be on the move soon. We can run for a while." Ben watched in amusement. The minstrel seemed to share the groom's comfort with animals.

"You two get along, don't you?"

"We've been through a lot together."

"Connor?"

"Yeah."

"What does 'Taliesin' mean?"

Connor smirked. "Cyrin's horse? Literally? It means 'Wind Dancer', I think. Why?"

"I understand she's coming with us."

"Tal? Cyrin's letting you take Taliesin? Hell, she must really trust you. She loves that horse more than -"

"No. Not me. Cyrin's letting Jhaun take her."

Connor's eyebrows went up. Ben watched as several unidentifiable emotions passed through the minstrel's eyes. Eventually he shrugged and glanced at Ben. "That's a good horse."

"Yeah." The actor nodded. "So I hear."

Midday meal consisted of stew, heavy textured bread warm from the oven, and a bottle of garnet wine. Food to journey on. The four travelers ate together, joined by the Lady and Cyrin. The atmosphere was warm, although a little strained. Connor and Perahn focused the conversation around the last time they had traveled the gorge and attempted the climb to the Gate. They were so involved that Ben was able to keep most of his attention on them, even though he found the very quiet conversation taking place across the table much more interesting at the moment.

"Thank you." Jhaun's eyes darted around the table, settling back on the bread in front of him.

"For what?" Cyrin spoke as quietly as the Lady's son, not looking up. Ben realized that they must talk this way often. Both hiding while they connected with each other.

"Taliesin. I didn't think you'd let me take her out again."

Cyrin sighed. "She likes you."

The son of Anders looked down with half a grin.

"Jhaun?" she whispered.

"Yes?"

"Please be careful."

Jhaun shook his head. "It doesn't matter, 'Rin. It really doesn't matter." Ben peripherally saw the girl's hand come to rest on Jhaun's where it sat on the table's edge, give it a gentle squeeze.

"It matters to me." With that Cyrin got up and excused herself calmly. "Milady. If you don't mind, I want to check on the stores that were packed."

"Of course, Cyrin." And then, "Jhaun, if you're done, would you help her?" Her younger son looked at her for just a moment, then nodded and left, the walls in place, assuming she wanted to talk to the others without him present. Ben, noticing Jhaun's assumptions, also realized at that moment that he wasn't the only one who was watching without watching. As the two left the table, he looked into the dark green eyes of the Lady of Anders Castle, and they smiled.

"What's the deal with them?"

"I don't know yet. And neither do they. They've been friends since they were children. Teasing has grown into trust." The Lady shook her head and sighed, brushing her fingers against the broad white petals of the flowers that rested in a low bowl on the table. "I thought her bride bed to have decked, sweet maid." For a moment the actor frowned at the phrase as it struck a familiar chord in his mind. *Hamlet, of course. Gertrude. But which Gertrude was it that had green eyes? Was that-*

"And now, I may be sending him, sending you all-"

"Lady." Ben reached across the table, dismissing the search his mind was conducting, and took her hand. "You send no one. We're going of our own will and you, frankly, couldn't stop us. So play for us, keep us strong. I think we'll need it."

*　　　*　　　*

The sun, warm on their shoulders, danced sparkling lights in their hair as they set off. It could have been any pleasant summer outing, except that Connor insisted that they ride armed. Ben belted on his sword with trepidation that turned to a strange pleasure, with the now familiar weight on his thigh.

"How far are we safe?" Ben asked as they started off.

"I'm not sure. Her influence fades through the gorge, and between the gorge and the Gate itself is kind of a no man's land." The minstrel blew out a breath. "I think we'll be okay - I feel we will - but we need to stay on our tocs."

They navigated for hours through the fields and monumental stones of the place Ben couldn't help seeing as the Garden of the Gods, wending their way slowly toward the rust and grey mountains that provided an unyielding backdrop, somehow reassuring and unsettling at the same time. The discontinuity between the Rockies that Ben remembered and these equally majestic painted mountains made his head hurt, but he slowly adjusted. During that quiet, relatively peaceful portion of the trip, Connor and Perahn rode point, while Ben and Jhaun rode side by side, a short distance behind them. Conversation was lulled by the centering rhythm of the horses.

"So. I guess this is as good a time as any to begin," Ben said, his speech deceptively casual.

"Begin what?" Jhaun didn't look over as he asked.

"Begin teaching you about acting. I wish I had more time and some texts to have you read over, but we can start -"

Now the Lady's son jerked his head around in surprise. "What?"

"Frankly, you strike me as someone who would just want to jump in with a monologue anyway. Would you prefer a hero or a villain?"

Jhaun stared, his eyes searching for sarcasm in Ben's words. "Teach me to act? How? I lost any power I had -"

"Oh, please. That's not acting. That's more like... plagiarism. Acting comes from within yourself, nowhere else. Acting is a work of creation, and it can focus power, like any other creation. Like playing music - but with acting, the instrument is yourself." He thought for a moment and a speech learned years ago leapt into the front of his mind. *A villain it is.* "Okay. This character is the best bad guy in all of Shakespeare's work, as far as I'm concerned. I think you'll like him." *And maybe you'll be able to see what real malice is like.*

"Wait. You mean he's evil?"

"Oh yeah."

"And you will become him willingly?"

Ben sighed. "Jhaun, it doesn't mean I'm him. I'm playing him. I'm acting him."

Connor had slowed his horse, closing the distance between them. "Ben. Are you sure that's a good idea?"

Perahn had pulled up as well, and Ben took advantage of the sudden audience. Pulling his horse to a halt, he spoke quickly to set up the scene. "Trust me, Con, it's okay. I'm still in charge. I'm not going to lose control."

"Yeah. But is he?"

Ben stared blankly for a minute before the realization of what Connor was saying hit him. "I don't think he knows enough yet to get lost. It's an act of will." Turning his attention to Jhaun, he continued. "Now. Here's the thing. This character is pretending to be a friend of Othello, who they also refer to as the Moor. Othello trusts me. Let's see, what else do you need... oh, Cassio. He really *is* a nice guy, so I don't like him, either. At this point, Shakespeare has me talking to the audience, and I'm telling them what I'm going to do."

Jhaun was shaking his head in confusion. "I don't see what you think I can do with this."

Ben held up his hand. "I'm not thinking. I'm acting. Now shut up and listen, and after we'll talk." Ben took a deep breath and closed his eyes for a moment. When he opened them, a different character was looking through them. A superior sneer, unlike any expression they had ever seen on Benjamin, crossed his face. Even Connor was taken with the disdain that rolled off of Benjamin with the smooth verse.

"I hate the Moor;

And it is thought abroad that 'twixt my sheets

H'as done my office. I know not if't be true;

But I, for mere suspicion in that kind,

Will do as if for surety."

Ben went on, gaining momentum as he went. A part of him saw the expressions on the faces of his friends: Connor, with a certain admiration, Perahn, wary but fascinated, and Jhaun, completely absorbed. Feeling every word.

"He holds me well;

The better shall my purpose work on him.

Cassio's a proper man. Let me see now:

To get his place, and to plume up my will

In double knavery- how, how? - Let's see: -

After some time, to abuse Othello's ears

That he is too familiar with his wife.

He hath a person and a smooth dispose

To be suspected - framed to make women false.

The Moor is of a free and open nature

That thinks men honest that but seem to be so;

And will as tenderly be led by th' nose

As asses are."

Before he knew it, he was at the end of the speech.

"I have't! It is engend'red! Hell and night

Must bring this monstrous birth to the world's light."

The actor stopped. For a moment he held their eyes, then he broke character and was himself completely once more.

"So. That's Iago." He stared into the shining obsidian eyes of the heir of Anders, and saw utter amazement, excitement, and a portion of fear all fighting for the upper hand.

"He knows what he's doing is wrong, and he's trying to figure out how to do it in the most destructive way. He's - a monster." Jhaun stopped and his voice became deathly quiet. "Where do you get these words?"

Ben smiled at Connor and nodded for them to go on. The minstrel shook his head, turned his horse, and proceeded down the path. Ben turned to the young man at his side and felt the teacher within him stretching. They rode on, Ben talking about Shakespeare and acting theory while Jhaun asked the occasional question, absorbing what was said like a sponge.

"Hey." Connor interrupted them an hour or so later, as they came to a large clearing. "We're going to eat here, it's easier."

To their left was a wide stream, sparkling in the sun and crystal clear to the bottom. Ben and Perahn walked the horses over to the water while Connor sorted through their packs, and Jhaun gathered some wood for a fire. Perahn spoke quietly when he and Ben were alone.

"Have I been hearing you two right?"

"What about?"

"You're teaching him how to do that? How to act?"

"Yeah. As much as I can on horseback on a trip that we may not see the other side of. But I wanted him to know what I do. What it really is."

"Why?"

Ben paused and thought before he answered. "Because, Per, I think this is may be what he's really supposed to do. All those talents that he talked about, that don't focus - well, put them together and you've got a great set of tools for an actor."

Perahn stared at the horses as they drank and shook his head. "Maybe." He frowned thoughtfully, his deep brown eyes staring into the ripples on the stream. "Do you think?"

"Yeah," Ben said quietly, squatting down to get a drink himself. "I think."

Ben finished eating first, and was washing and repacking their cookware when he suddenly smacked his palm against his forehead and cried out. Connor was on his feet instantly, but Ben was already waving his hands at him. "I'm okay. It's okay. I just remembered something." He was fumbling through his knapsack, which was tied on over his saddlebags. "I bet I left them in here." He was rummaging furiously now, pulling out the clothes he had brought to the park that morning that seemed so long ago, finding his notebook, a pen, and, "Ha! I knew you were here somewhere." From the bottom of the bag he pulled a slim paperback book, followed by another, even thinner. "This is great! I can't believe this."

"What the hell are you going on about?" Connor stared with annoyed curiosity.

"The shows I was working on. I had them with me all the time! I completely forgot that I had Annie's in my pack, and I was supposed to give them back to her -" he paused and stared up into the trees. "Sorry, Annie," he yelled cheerfully. Then he laughed, like a little kid with a new bike. "This is great. I thought I'd have to do them from memory."

The other three men looked at each other, shrugged, and went back to finishing their food. Ben continued to page through the texts, occasionally making delighted noises. Perahn turned to Connor and gestured at the actor. "I understand the acting part of what he does, but what makes the books so special? Are they prophecies?"

Connor shook his head. "Words. They're an actor's bread and butter. It would be like me finding another set of strings when I thought I'd broken my last." Perahn stared at Ben for a few moments, then looked back at Connor and grinned.

"Whatever's in them, he's happy about it."

"Yeah. Shakespeare. His hero."

Jhaun's head had lifted at the last comment. He finished his meal and walked with his plate toward the stream, and coincidentally, toward Benjamin as well. Within minutes they were deep in conversation about the plays that Ben had been wrenched from so abruptly. Connor watched them for a while, finishing his mug of tea, and shook his head.

"He's got him. I've never seen the kid that interested in anything. Maybe Ben's onto something."

"I'd be surprised if he wasn't. This is his path." Perahn looked up at the sky and squinted. "How much time can we give them?"

"Maybe an hour. After that, we'll be finishing the gorge in the dark. Not a great idea."

"Okay." The village musician reached for the flute at his side and began to play. Connor nodded and walked over to his guitar. In moments the sunny glade was filled with the sounds of music and Shakespeare, mingled with the rushing of water and the wind in the trees. The air was absolutely crystalline with the energy of it.

Two hours and some later, as they started off, Connor was grumbling that they had tarried too long in the clearing, even though he had been as responsible as the rest of them for the delay. Perahn argued that the strength they gathered there might make all the difference in their journey. They managed to make up some time riding quickly into the forested foothills of the mountains.

The gorge itself opened suddenly upon them, a wooded rise that split apart, wounded by the flow of singing water that spilled and rested between the exposed rocks that looked and felt to Ben like the very bones of the earth. The entrance was bridged over with a stone arch carved out by the waterway in millennia past. They walked through feeling like they were entering an ancient cathedral, and perhaps they were.

Ben stared up and whistled softly. "This is beautiful."

"It is," Perahn said, looking as well. "And the safest trail up into the foothills. Even so –"

Connor swung down off Kes. "Okay, let the horses walk. I'm not going to answer to Wesp for them." They dismounted and began hiking up the ancient broad stairways that trailed along the waterfalls. Sometimes there were only five or six steps, then a stretch of gently rising ground, then a flight of twenty or more that curved against the rock wall. On their right the wall of stone reached to the sky, occasionally broken by some side stream, and on their left sang the voices of waterfalls, a veritable orchestral arrangement of sound.

"I thought Tal could make the ride through here." Ben looked at Jhaun as they walked together.

"I'm not going to take any chances. Not after Cyrin let me take her again."

"Good." Ben looked appraisingly at the young man beside him. "Let's talk about Hal."

"The prince in the story?"

"Right."

"The one that doesn't let anyone see what his powers are until he feels he really has to use them."

"Close enough." The kid was amazing. He was more than a quick study, he had a photographic memory. All he had to learn was how to shape what he had. And having Prince Hal as a role model couldn't hurt.

They were so involved in their conversation that they hardly noticed it was getting darker. The music of the water seemed louder in the gathering dusk, and Connor began to frown. The horses were slowing down as well, and the desire to get out of the gorge before nightfall was tempered with the necessity of caution on the increasingly slippery stones.

"Light a torch!" The call came from Perahn, who had taken the lead. "There's something blocking the way."

Connor found a branch and was trying to find a dry spot to start a light when a ghostly radiance lined the path in front of them. He already had his bow armed when a voice called out.

"Who's there? And what's your business?"

The voice was young, and from the little they could see belonged to a smooth-faced boy, probably younger than Jhaun, shoulder-length hair flying in the breeze. "What do you want?"

"We're just passing through." Perahn spoke for them, for some reason feeling no danger. "Is there a problem?"

The voice laughed cheerfully. "You could say that. A tree's fallen. Don't try to come across it here, the trunk is shaky and the whole thing could drag you in. Back along here." The youth crawled along the tree trunk like a monkey, completely at ease with the precarious perch, even in the dark. "You see, under this branch. The horses can do it if you lead them."

Following his voice, they moved with some difficulty through the branches that pulled at them and spooked the horses. It was Taliesin that made it through first, and the others seemed to take her confidence.

"Come on," the boy said. "There's a cave up ahead that was opened when the tree fell. It's good shelter for the night."

They followed through a small opening, barely big enough for the horses to pass, and into a huge subterranean passage lit by a small fire. In its way, it was rather cozy.

"It'll be safer to get through in the morning, although it's gotten strange here in the last few months. The gorge is falling apart." He moved a few notebooks, lay down on the floor, and pulled a blanket up.

Connor looked suspicious. "Is this place safe?"

The youth frowned, with eyes large and dark in a narrow face. "Yes, of course it's safe." When they waited for an explanation, he rolled his eyes and made an exasperated noise. "Can't you tell? I'm invisible."

Now Ben frowned. "He's what?"

"Invisible." Perahn stared for a moment and nodded. "Naturally warded. Can't be felt without knowing that he's there." The musician shrugged. "It's a gift."

"Great." Ben was already pulling a bedroll off of his horse. "Then goodnight." With a comfort that surprised even him, Benjamin settled down, and was asleep within minutes.

*   *   *

The next morning, Ben was the last one awake. He could feel something even before he was fully conscious. Walking out of the cave, he found Connor angrily confronting the youth who had taken them in the night before.

"It isn't safe, that's what the problem is." Connor's voice was furious. "I can't let you stay here. And you can't come with us. It's just not -"

"*Let* me?"

"Con, what's going on?" Ben looked from his friend to the boy who had helped them, and did a fast double take. The boy, it was obvious in the bright, sunlit morning, was a young woman. Slight but strong, her hair not much longer than Ben's. Her skin, which was fair with a scatter of freckles, combined with bright hazel eyes to give her the look of a youthful sprite. "Who - who are you?"

The woman looked into his eyes for a minute. She pursed her lips and squinted as if he were a painting in a museum that she was deciding whether or not to buy.

"Mekki." She looked at the four of them with a wry grin. "I've been waiting here for something to happen." Her eyes sparkled in the morning light. "Are you it?"

Ben found himself grinning. "I don't know. We have to find someone." Without thinking, the words came out. "Want to come?"

"No!" The minstrel exploded on Ben's left. "We can't take her. It's too dangerous -"

"For a girl?" The tone of Mekki's voice became chilly. "I've been taking care of myself for quite a while, sir, and I'll thank you not to underestimate me."

"Con. What's going on?"

"Yeah, right. How old are you?"

Mekki shook her head, and suddenly laughed. "Certainly older than the *boy* you're traveling with. Where's his nurse? Or would that be you?"

Ben held back a laugh at her tone and looked at Connor again. The feeling coming from the minstrel was strange.

"C'mon, Con. Is this about her or your-" The look on Connor's face made Ben glad he didn't finish the sentence.

"Never mind." The minstrel started to walk away, and stopped. Ben watched a sigh deflate Connor as he turned back to the woman. "Obviously you're quite capable of taking care of yourself."

Mekki, Ben noticed with relief, seemed to realize how hard it was for Connor to make that statement. She stepped forward and stuck out her hand. "Thank you," she said, her voice not sarcastic now but still strong. The minstrel nodded as he shook her hand and looked at Ben.

"So now what?"

Ben grinned, turned to the woman. "Are you coming with us?"

Mekki took her time in responding. "I have a feeling you're the reason I'm here." She glanced casually at Ben with disarming openness. "Yeah," she said slowly, as a smile blossomed on her face. "You're it."

17

"Careful, there!" Mekki's voice, now somehow quite clearly female to Ben, rang out against the stones of the gorge over the music of the water. "That whole section is soft. Mind the horses."

"Speaking of," Ben called to her, as he eased Jasper across the crumbling stairs, "do you have a horse, or travel by foot?"

The woman stopped, pushed her fine brown hair back over her ear and stared at him. Evaluating him again, with a strange expression that made Ben feel like he got a callback for some part he really wanted. Her eyes narrowed and he looked away as if he were checking the path.

"I have a horse," she said finally. "I wouldn't bring her into the gorge, though. She's up top." The criticism in her voice was modulated by the smile gleaming softly in her eyes. She turned, the movement tossing her hair in the breeze, and headed up the broad stone steps again.

Ben nodded at her back as she moved away, and felt a wave of disappointment. It took five minutes of walking and climbing for him to realize that he had been hoping she would have to ride with him. He chuckled, surprised and annoyed with himself. Connor, who had worked his way forward and was closer now than Mekki was, caught the feeling just as the surface of the stone beneath his feet crumbled into flat slivers. He regained his balance and spoke in his most concerned, accusing tone.

"What's wrong?"

"Nothing." Ben glanced at Connor and saw his eyebrows peak. "Okay, it's something, it's just - stupid. I mean, like I don't have enough to think about." He glanced up ahead at Mekki, and shook his head.

Connor frowned at the compact figure of the woman ahead of them, suddenly understood, and shrugged his shoulders. "So you need a distraction. Be distracted for a while. Don't let it throw you." He moved ahead of Ben, testing the steps as he went.

"Right."

The minstrel glanced back critically. "You're really not used to it when they don't fall all over themselves, are you."

"What?" Ben sounded confused, and a little hurt.

Connor shook his head in a dismissive gesture. "Come off it. Are you trying to tell me that most women you're interested in don't respond pretty quickly?"

The actor stopped his instantaneous denial before it escaped. He never considered himself a 'ladies man', but lately had been described as one often enough. He was comfortable with women, made friends easily with women – and, yeah, when he was taken with someone he had become accustomed to a pretty strong response in return. But he knew it was always a response based on seeing him play some character, not to the everyday, ordinary Benjamin Agante. "Okay, fair enough." Ben sighed theatrically and looked over at Connor. "So what should I do?"

The minstrel looked confused for a split second, then somewhat appalled. "What do you mean 'what do you do?' We're not on some pleasure hike. Have you considered we may not survive the day?" He shook his head. "For the love of -" The minstrel fumed for a few steps and Benjamin was framing some defense for hormonal thinking when a voice called from up ahead.

"Hey," Mekki's strong alto provided a counterpoint to the roar of the major fall that marked the top of the gorge. "Stay right up against the wall here. The horses aren't going to like the edge."

They followed carefully, single file, alternating men and horses. The minstrel was in front now, Per next, then Ben, with Jhaun bringing up the rear. Ben called ahead to Connor and Per. "Was it this bad when you were here?"

Per shrugged while skirting a suspicious looking pile of rubble. "It's always been difficult in places, but the damage evens out after a few years. This is the worst that I've seen it in a long time."

The minstrel agreed. "Yeah. I don't remember the top being this bad.

Mekki's voice from up above them called out. "All right. Be careful now, I'd hate to lose one of you after making it this far."

Ben looked up at her and shook the first four thoughts out of his head. *Get a grip, Agante. She's just something to obsess about, so you don't have to think about what comes next.*

As he turned to check on Jasper he saw Jhaun, who had been silent for nearly the length of the gorge, staring intently at him. "What?"

Jhaun blinked out of his thoughts. "Nothing." He paused, amending his automatic response with a conscious effort. "I was just thinking of -" Before he could finish his thought, a fist-sized stone broke free and fell down the wall on their right, narrowly missing Taliesin's head. She skittered back, prancing away from the fright and closer to the edge of the ravine. Jhaun was trying to calm her, when with a sudden shower of broken rock, her left rear hoof slipped. The stone crumbled beneath her feet, and she whinnied shrilly on the tight stone passage.

"Tal!" Without thinking, Jhaun put himself between Cyrin's horse and the precipice, a drop of twenty feet to the rocky waterway. He heard Ben yelling his name as he pushed against the struggling mare, his feet sliding precariously. The horse shifted, closer to the edge, and barely nudged Jhaun into the ravine.

For a moment frozen in time the Lady's son was floating, almost falling, his arms waving as he tried to find his balance. Benjamin watched in horror, his perception shifting everything into slow motion as he heard a chorus of voices shouting his name. Without knowing how, the actor had made his way to Jhaun and grabbed a handful of his shirt. Taliesin, at the same time, lived up to her reputation and danced out of harm's way, finding her footing once more some yards up the trail.

Ben jerked away from the edge as soon as the horse moved, landing against the stone wall with his arms wrapped around Jhaun, panting like a runner after a hundred-yard sprint. For a moment they leaned there, breathing, before Jhaun gasped in a strained voice. "I'm okay."

Benjamin had to order his muscles to relax in order to release his grip. He fell back against the wall and looked up the trail to where Perahn had caught Tal and was soothing her quietly. The Lady's son leaned over with his hands on his thighs, looking out toward the edge and slowly blowing out his breath. After a moment he let a word escape with the air. "Thanks."

Ben was nodding when the realization of the moment dawned on him. "Did I just see you try to stop a horse from falling over the edge?" Anger ran past his concern, slamming into Jhaun like a stiff gust of wind. "By *pushing* her? Do you think you outweigh her or something?" His voice, fueled by adrenaline, echoed off the walls, and Jhaun shrank a bit.

"All right, I wasn't thinking. But I had to do something." Jhaun looked at Ben, the obsidian eyes looking vulnerable as he pled for understanding. "'Rin would have killed me."

Ben slowly closed his eyes, rubbing the bridge of his nose in the hope that it would calm his brain. For a moment, he understood how Connor felt *all the time*. Finally he opened his eyes again, stepping close enough for only Jhaun to hear. "Somehow, Jhaun, I think I might have had the harder time, going back to Anders and telling Cyrin, not to mention your mother, that you killed yourself trying to pick up a *horse*. Think about it." Jhaun dropped his head back against the rock.

"They would both have killed me." He heard the words as he said them, and a nervous grin played across his lips. Then, in a voice and cadence that sounded suspiciously like Ben's, he spoke again. "I guess it's a good thing I would have been dead already." Ben, having played this game of trading personas before, proceeded to frame his answer as Jhaun.

"Maybe. But I know, somehow, it would have been my fault." He stared at the ground for a moment, then looked seriously into Jhaun's eyes until they both broke, and the resulting laugh dispersed the adrenaline they had accumulated. Ben wrapped his hand around the glass of his pendant.

He did it. Played with the reality just like Annie and I might have. One little moment, but he was acting. Ben felt amazement rolling off Jhaun at the realization that he could play at this without hurting anyone.

"Good. You see what I mean? All inside yourself, not in anyone else. Even when you're playing at someone you know. Everything you need is with you." Ben smiled. "That's power."

Jhaun held out his hand. The sincerity this time was uncolored by play, a little nervous, and Ben could feel it.

"Thank you."

"You're welcome. But for God's sake, don't make me do it again."

Connor and Per had taken the horses up top once they saw that everything was all right for the moment, giving the two men a chance to settle down. When Ben and Jhaun reached the top of the gorge, Mekki was waiting for Jhaun and glared up at him.

"Look. I don't care what you're supposed to be the heir to. You do something like that again and I'll tie you to a horse for the rest of the trip. Got it?"

Jhaun blinked, taken aback by her tone. Benjamin felt a wall go up around the Lady's son while the others exchanged curious looks. Connor started to speak, but Perahn raised a hand.

"Excuse me," Per said, his voice soothing in his normal soft baritone. "But I have a question or two. One, are we to assume that you've taken charge of this group?"

Mekki turned quickly and stepped up to him, her words powerful without being loud. "Come on. He could have gotten himself killed back there."

"Two," Per said, as if he hadn't stopped, "and I must admit, this is what I'm really curious about - what gives you the impression that he's heir to anything?" The others turned first to Per, and then to Mekki.

"Good point," Ben said uncomfortably, his hand dropping to the hilt of his sword. They certainly didn't make any concessions to Jhaun that would lead someone to assume that. "How do you know?" Ben felt a strange sensation in his chest, as if a part of him were locking itself away for safekeeping. *What do we really know about her? What if Alious sent her to get into this grouping? Or to tear it apart?*

The questions rattled in his mind as he looked at the face of the girl he had grown fond of in what seemed to be a matter of hours.

Mekki stood her ground for a minute, and then turned away. "All right," she said, letting go of the anger that had been bracing her and suddenly looking rather petite again. "I just know. And I thought you might need a drill sergeant for this crew. I could be wrong." She exhaled, with some relief. "To tell you the truth, I'm glad if I'm wrong." She stepped toward Jhaun and lifted her hand. Ben noticed that he flinched almost imperceptibly as she brushed a strand of wind-blown hair off his cheek. "I'm glad you're all right. You scared me to death." She connected with him for a long moment, her shining hazel eyes looking fearlessly into his confusion.

"Do I know you?"

"No. Not really." She laughed, a rich and mischievous thing. "But then, who does? I'm invisible." For a moment, so fleeting that he might have imagined it, Ben felt something from her. Sadness, perhaps, hidden beneath the facade she presented.

She turned with a whistle, and a coppery gold horse with palomino markings trotted from the woods. Pulling a soft bridle from her pack Mekki slipped it over the horse's head, greeting her softly. Then with an easy vault she mounted bareback, and almost as an afterthought turned to the Lady's son again.

"By the way, Jhaun. Cento sends his best."

Jhaun gawked at her. "You know Cento? You've been to the Core?" The emotions that flew across his face were too rapid to follow.

Mekki smiled down at him from horseback. "Of course I know him. I studied there, on and off, for three years. And no," she said in response to his blank stare, "we weren't in the same discipline.

Although we sure heard about you." She gave him a thoughtful frown. "Is it true?"

"Is what true?" The Lady's son was beyond lost.

"Is it true that you really didn't know the rumors? That you might be the One, or the Inca'ti?"

Jhaun shook his head, incredulous. "No. I didn't. I already had the answers that I decided were right." His tone became more thoughtful than self-deprecating, as if he didn't realize he was still speaking aloud. "Cento kept trying to warn me about that."

Mekki's voice was kind. "Well, you were wrong, obviously. And Cento felt that I had a place in all this, so he suggested I come here." She looked at their expressions, clearly enjoying the mystery she presented. "We should get moving. You do still want to make it to the Rock by nightfall?" Turning her mount she started off at an easy trot through the trees, not even looking back to see if they were following.

Connor turned to Ben as they mounted and urged their horses to catch up. "Nice."

"What?"

The minstrel nodded his head in the direction of the woman who was either leading them or just going the same way they were, but a little faster. "You can pick 'em, can't you."

They rode quickly through the flat fields of grass and wildflowers that led to the Gate Rock. The feathery greens grew only high enough to brush the soles of Ben's boots in their stirrups, and the small amount of real cover gave him a feeling of vulnerability. They followed Mekki for a couple hours, accepting that she knew where she was going, although occasionally Connor and Perahn would look at each other and nod, as if verifying their path.

Ben still had his doubts. He looked at her and shook his head, uncomfortable with the idea that he was unable to feel much of anything from her. Invisible. *And a week or two ago I wouldn't have thought that 'feeling' anything from someone was a normal thing to do.* As he was looking at her she stopped.

"What is it?" Connor, as always, was the first to sense anything that could be a danger.

She frowned, the expression on her face changing from annoyance to confusion. "I don't know. I can't tell. Can you feel that?" The rest of them turned, looked in the direction she was facing. Only Perahn nodded, his eyes closed in concentration. "What is it?" She looked helplessly at Perahn, feeling that he understood what she was unable to articulate.

"I feel it. Don't reach out. Your interaction with it will let him see you." She nodded, obviously uncomfortable, but tried to do as he said. Perahn turned and spoke in a low voice to the others.

"It must be his wards. I didn't expect them this far from the Gate, but I'm sure the Lady's go this far from Anders." Perahn turned and nodded toward Mekki. "It seems she's sensitive to these things."

They rode on more slowly, with Mekki now choosing to stay in the cluster of the group instead of riding ahead. No one commented on her sudden change of heart, and Ben, for one, was glad to have her where he could keep an eye on her, no matter the reason.

As planned, they reached the base of the rock by nightfall. The landscape had returned to a series of the monumental freestanding rocks like those near Anders Castle. They stood like the backbone of some impossibly huge mythical beast, in a straggling row across the horizon. Great triangular plates that joined and overlapped in a size that begged the mind to change the scale. The group set up camp at the base of the largest and Ben, taking his pack from Jasper's back, stared upwards in awe. He was absorbed by the stones, and overpowered by the unbroken mass of their presence.

"Ben. Stop being a tourist and give me a hand with the fire. There's plenty of dry weeds, not much wood."

"Right."

For the two hours before they slept, time was spent eating, unburdening the horses and repacking into the small knapsacks that they brought to make the final ascent. Ben and Connor took over setting up the camp.

"Wouldn't it be easier to climb up and between?"

"Not really. The Gate is lower than it looks. Besides, it drops you onto a path that leads straight to him." Connor stopped and shook his head. "Or so I've heard." Turning away, he called to Per. "Are you going for water?"

"Yes."

"Need help?"

"I'll take Jhaun." Jhaun looked startled for a moment, but put down the pack he was filling and followed his brother. They took the horses and the water bags, and in a brisk ten minute walk found a spring that Per had found in his earlier travels. After they stocked all the water they could carry, they took the remaining tack off of the horses.

"Is this a good idea?" Jhaun stroked Taliesin protectively after he removed her bridle.

"If we leave anything on them, it could snag and trap them. This way, if we don't get back - for any length of time - they'll be free." Perahn took his flute from his belt and played a soft melody. With water and plenty of grass here, he trusted that they would be fine. When Per had finished Jhaun took a minute with Taliesin before they headed back to camp, each silent in his thoughts. Perahn, with the occasional sideways glance at this sudden brother of his, had the distinct and uncomfortable impression that the horse wasn't the only one Jhaun had said farewell to.

"Look, Jhaun -"

"Don't."

"What?"

"I don't know. I don't know what to say to you. I feel guilty, I feel... cheated. I don't know." Jhaun paused for a moment, shifted the load on his shoulders. "You must hate me."

Perahn stopped. "Hate you?"

Jhaun turned back to speak to him. "Yes. You should be the one who's been living my life. And now, with all this..." He trailed off and shook his head, staring into the grass at his feet.

Perahn took a deep breath and closed his eyes. "What you're saying could be true if I hated my life. If I never found myself. Who you are is what matters. Where you grow up is just a place." They started walking again, slowly. "I've been surrounded by care all my life. I've been encouraged and trusted to use my gifts." Perahn looked at his brother. "Why would I be jealous? Why would I want your life when mine has been so good?"

Jhaun looked at Perahn, then down the path before him. "Maybe I'm the one who's jealous."

Perahn grinned at that, and clapped Jhaun on the shoulder. "You'll be fine, little brother. There's more to you than meets the eye."

Jhaun readjusted one of the bags as he looked back toward camp and shrugged. "Honestly, Perahn. What do you think of all this? I've heard the stories all my life, and this 'One' doesn't seem to fit."

"Actually, it fits beautifully. There are whole prophecies that describe the One in terms of playing his part, of becoming someone else while remaining himself, of things that all make sense when you hear Benjamin talking about being an actor." He shook his head and smiled wryly. "The way I read it, with what I know now from Ben - the one to defeat Alious is definitely an actor."

Jhaun looked down the path again, and nodded.

They reached the camp in a thoughtful silence, and found the others in a similar mood. Conversation was minimal around the fire, and when Connor and Per created music in the night, there were no words.

In the darkness it was difficult to make out the arch of the Gate high above them, but Ben could feel it there. With a conscious act of will, he pushed the concern of it out of his mind, and settled down to rest his body for the coming day, whatever it might bring.

As he lay down the last thing he remembered was looking up into the night sky and seeing a familiar constellation peering over dark clouds that covered it, a coat of fleece draped over a warrior's frame. Orion. The One. Benjamin sighed, held his pendant tightly in his hand, and fell into a deep, guarded, and strangely dreamless sleep.

*   *   *

The morning dawned with a feeble drizzle, the gray sky giving the minimum of light as the sun merely put in its hours, uninspired and uninspiring. The fact that they managed to get a fire going at all said something for their survival skills.

"This could make things a little more difficult," Perahn sighed as he looked up over his steaming mug at the side of the Gate rock. A pattern of dark wetness was falling in small streams down the broad plane of it, like tears on the face of God.

"A little more difficult?" Connor shook his head. "We never would have done the climb in this. It's just enough to foul the grips, the footing's never been that great to begin with."

"We wouldn't have done it, but that doesn't mean that we couldn't have made it if we tried."

The minstrel cursed softly, and placed a hand against the rock. "We don't really have a choice, do we." Connor turned to Perahn. "I hate to leave the guitar. I keep feeling like I'll regret it."

"I've seen you work without it."

"Yeah, but sometimes I feel like it can work without me."

"Can you make the climb with it?"

"I don't think so. I might lose it forever, that way. Not that forever may be much longer." The minstrel sighed and shook his head. "I think you should take the lead, you're the best on this kind of rock. What about Mekki?"

Perahn thought for a moment and looked across the camp for the young woman. She seemed to be the only one who was unbothered by the weather, and had spent some time after breakfast wandering off, gathering herbs and writing copious descriptions before pressing a few leaves in her notebook. "I'll go first. Then Ben, Jhaun, Mekki, and you." He paused a minute, picturing the lineup in his mind. "Does that work?"

Connor grimaced as if he were seeing the same picture that Perahn was. "Yeah. I think that makes sense." He looked at Per for a moment, shrugged. "It'll work."

"I feel it will."

The minstrel shook his head and looked around the camp, then over at Ben. "Hey. You want to go find the nature girl?"

The actor stood with his mug and scanned the field, when a sudden cry of 'Yes!' made them all turn. Connor snorted a laugh. "Sounds like she found some wonderwort, or whatever she's looking for now. Tell her to get moving."

Ben nodded with a grin and headed over to where Mekki was squatting over a small bush covered with nearly black round berries. She was giggling happily as she filled a sack.

"We're getting going," he said, squatting next to her.

"Okay, just give me a minute." She kept picking and he took one himself, staring at it. It looked pretty ordinary.

"They taste good?" He had it halfway to his mouth before she knocked it out of his hand.

"No! They're inkberries." She looked into his blank, slightly hurt stare and rolled her eyes. "As in ink. As in writing with."

"Oh."

"Also as in permanent, very lightfast, and fairly toxic. And a pretty silly way to die."

"Oh. Thanks."

"No problem."

*　　　*　　　*

Shortly after they had eaten Perahn began to climb. There were the occasional hand and footholds, enough for him to make it to a minor ledge a little less than halfway up. More like a fissure, a crack that had healed a bit off center. The plan was that he climb that far on his own and drop a safety line for the rest.

They stood, loosely grouped at the base of the climb, staring upwards into the drizzle as the figure of Perahn shrank in proportion to the rock. Mekki spoke in a voice filled with awe.

"How does he do that?"

Connor looked concerned. "You've never climbed?"

"Sure, I've done the gorge, but this? There's nothing to get your fingers into."

"There are holds. They don't show much. And there aren't a lot of choices. But you'll do fine - if you keep your wits about you." Mekki looked away from the wall of stone to glare at Connor. He lifted an eyebrow, making it obvious that he was trying to distract her, and knew it had worked. "Don't worry. We'll make it."

Ben stepped closer to the minstrel and nodded up the rock. "What do you think?"

"I just said we'd make it."

"You know what I mean."

Connor turned and looked Ben in the eye. "You mean, why do I think it's been so easy this far?"

"Right"

The minstrel scratched at his beard and looked up at Perahn, who had nearly made the ridge. In the gray light he was little more than a moving smudge on the rock face. "I don't know. He must know we're here. Am I right?" He looked at Ben again, searching for the One.

Ben blinked hard and looked away. "He's going to let us walk right in, if we don't kill ourselves on the way. He wants to do this man to man." Ben sighed. "God, Connor. I have no idea what I'm supposed to do when I meet him."

Connor grimaced. "Shake his hand and say hello. There's the line. Jhaun, grab that end. Ben. You're up next. Be careful." He clapped the actor on the shoulder as he passed by. "Don't count on him to pull you up. It's just a safety for now. Go."

Ben wound the rope around his belt and started climbing. Every time he got to a stopping point, he readjusted the tension on it, keeping some slack ahead, the rest of the line behind. Soon Jhaun was climbing too, and then Mekki, followed closely by Connor.

This is strange. Here I am, climbing, and I haven't mentioned to them that I've only done this twice, but I'm not nervous. Why?

Because you are the One. These rocks know you, are part of your path. There is nothing to fear from them.

As if to contradict what he had heard, Ben's right foot slipped off of the minuscule bump that had been supporting it. He felt the slack on the rope above him vanish as Per pulled it taut without pulling him off of his feet. He scrambled, nearly lost his grip, and slapped his fingers against the stone with enough force to push himself off. If Per hadn't been at least partially supporting him, he would have been a lump at the base of the rock. All of this happened as his foot moved aimlessly for a moment in time, and came to rest in another niche, this one more secure, safe, and, Ben was quite sure, one that was not there when he climbed past. Surely he would have noticed one of this size. He stopped, caught his breath, and called out, "I'm okay."

Where did that come from? He inhaled deeply, the wet smell of the stone twining in his nostrils. *The One can climb. It's just another part of the character. Use it.*

He stepped into the character's confidence and started climbing once more. Hand and footholds appeared like magic. More than once he heard comments behind him. The others were surprised, but they weren't complaining. Their comments were almost sarcastic in their cheerfulness.

Only Connor, bringing up the rear, remained wary. "Keep your eyes open." They reached Perahn and rested on the narrow cleft for a few minutes, regaining their strength for the last haul to the gate itself.

Ben turned to Per, avoiding looking down the sharp incline, and spoke quietly. "So. When we get up there. Is anything going to happen?"

Perahn shook his head as he coiled the line from hand to elbow. "I doubt it. The gate is an arch in the rock on this side. It's really only once we get to the Castle of the Stone that we're in for a fight."

Ben shook his head wearily. "How can you be sure?"

The village musician tied the spare line to his belt, nodded down the sheer face of the rock. "If he were going to kill us before then, he could have done it already. This has been ridiculously simple."

The actor looked down at his bruised and abraded hands and exhaled roughly. "This has been simple? Great."

Perahn laughed and twisted his head upwards. "Do you want to lead, now that you've found the way?"

Ben stared at him, and thought about it. "Okay. I'll go first. Stay close." He started up the climb to the broad low arch in the rock above them, carved, he supposed, by wind and water in ages past. At first he was too tense to trust the character. Then he stopped, closed his eyes, and took a deep breath.

"You okay?" It was the voice of Connor, who had not yet left the ledge they rested on.

"Yeah. I just - yes. I'm okay."

With a few moments concentration, Ben centered himself and reached up the rock face above him with every intention of finding a secure handhold. There it was. With a smile, the actor, the One, climbed up the last hundred feet finding holds wherever he needed them, and humming a random tune softly under his breath.

In just under an hour, Ben found himself at the archway in the rock. The Gate. He scrambled, exhausted, onto the flatter slope in front of it, expecting something to happen. Nothing. Getting a grip on himself, Ben hammered a spike into the floor of the archway and secured his line. Then he sat with his back against the smoothly worn rock, catching his breath and waiting for the ache to settle out of his arms. Benjamin Agante, the actor, closed his eyes just for a minute -

and walked out onto the stage. Annie was there, beautiful in teal velvet as Juliet. He breathed a sigh of relief. For a moment he had forgotten which show he was in, who he was playing. He turned to where Jim would be, Mercutio - and stopped. Jim was there. He was looking at him, waiting for Ben to do his line, concern at the pause showing only in his eyes - and he was wearing Horatio's black wool topcoat. Horatio and Juliet? What the - A noise behind made Ben spin around, and there was Evan, dressed in the fantastical period costume that he wore as Lysander.

"I will be with thee straight!" His rival yelled, waving a sword and charging off. Ben shook his head, trying to clear it, looked at Juliet, his love, who was weeping desperately - then at Horatio, his dear friend, who was clearly concerned about his well being, then out into the house - but it wasn't indoors, it was the stage in the park.

There were people as far as the eye could see, and they were waiting, waiting for him to do his lines, waiting for him to do something.

A familiar face in the front row. Several faces. The Lady. Perahn. Cyrin. Connor. Jhaun. Tomas, Ahna, Papa.

Ben began to shake. He tried to ask, "What do you want from me? Just tell me what part I'm supposed to do, and I'll do it!" But the words were choked off in his throat. He clutched the pendant at his neck, which slipped through his hand, now wet with sweat, wet with blood, and heard Connor's voice calling out to him from the audience. Suddenly the minstrel was on stage with him, grabbing him by the shoulders, shaking him -

"Ben."

The actor's eyes snapped open and he gasped for air. Connor, surprised, held on and stared into Ben's wild eyes. "It's okay. Ben. What the hell?" The minstrel stopped and took a deep breath. "We're at the arch. At the Gate. We're all here. We're okay. Breathe."

Ben followed instructions and inhaled deeply, standing unsteadily. Connor caught him before he got too close to the edge, and looked at him.

"What's going on? You were fine on the climb."

"I don't know. I'm tired, I guess."

The minstrel clenched his jaw. "Look, kid, I'm sorry." He spoke so quietly that Ben could hardly hear him, and certainly no one else in the group could. "We can't stop here. Really. Once we get to the other side, we can probably set wards and take a break, but -"

"I'm not going to put everyone in danger just because I'm wearing out. We'll be fine. I'll be fine. I'm just tired. I was dreaming. I'll live."

Connor stared at him, coming to some sort of decision in his mind. Then he swore softly under his breath and turned to the others. "Ben's in trouble here. I don't know what's going on, but I think we have to do something. Any ideas?"

Perahn spoke thoughtfully. "Is there anything physical we can give him?"

"You mean like a cup of coffee? I don't know."

"I do." Mekki stepped in front of Ben.

Connor grimaced. "I don't think we have time -"

"He needs something else to focus on. This place is trying to shut him down." Mekki looked into Ben's eyes, and searched their stormy blue for a long moment.

Ben looked back into her, and was wondering if it would help more if she slapped him, or kissed him. He was trying to figure out which was more likely to happen when her lips twitched to some internal monologue that made her frown, and then nod. She took a deep breath and began to speak.

"Thy spirit within thee hath been so at war, and thus hath so bestirr'd thee in thy sleep, that beads of sweat have stood upon thy brow, like bubbles in a late disturbed stream, and in thy face strange motions have appear'd, such as we see when men restrain their breath on some great sudden hest."

Ben's eyes widened and his mouth opened, although no words came out. Connor stared for a minute. "Oh, please. Tell me that's not Shakespeare."

Mekki shot him a look. "One Henry four. Lady Percy."

"Where did you learn that?"

"NYU."

Ben gawked, unable to grasp it. "What?"

"We come from the same world." She backed off a step and leaned against the inside of the arch. "I was stage manager for a student company in my third year. You're lucky." Mekki grinned and pulled out her hunting knife. "The only other one I know by heart is the dagger speech from the Scottish play, and I'm pretty sure you can do that one better than I can."

Ben continued to stare, completely confused. "Why?"

"Because you did the show. Too bad that you were the only good thing about it. 'A thoughtful and captivating Macduff', I said so myself."

Ben stared for a moment, then reeled back away from her, shaking his head. "No."

"Yes. And sorry."

Connor stepped next to Ben and looked curiously at him. "What's wrong?"

"She's a critic."

"*Was* a critic. I was also a very angry young woman at the time." She grinned and folded her arms easily on her chest. "I've done a little acting, but I'm more comfortable on the other side of the page. I was trying to figure out what I was supposed to do with my life." She looked out over the edge thoughtfully, running her hand through her hair. "I was working on some writing when I had the strangest experience. A passage came to me. Almost a poem, but - different. I felt like I hadn't written it, and I didn't know who had." Mekki stopped, sighed heavily. "I thought about it for the longest time… but to make a long story short, I ended up at the Core, with Cento. And here I am."

Ben stared at her. Thoughts fought for prominence in his mind and failed miserably. He turned to Connor and Perahn. "So do people move between our worlds all the time? What does it mean?"

Perahn's dark brows furrowed. "I have no idea, but I can't imagine it's that common. I think the Artist has a plan. That we're all in this together." He paused, a faint smile coloring his seriousness. "I hope."

18

Connor led the group farther into the rock, beyond the arch of the Gate. Abruptly the passage narrowed to a tunnel six feet across, leading upwards at an angle that Ben felt was too steep for comfort. If someone slipped and started rolling, their momentum would take them past the arch and send them flying down the side of the rock. He adjusted his safety line while there was still good light from the archway behind them, and took the opportunity to study the walls.

"Looks like someone made this wider."

"Yeah. And those were a good idea." Connor pointed at lines carved into the floor of the tunnel, making the traction better. "There was probably a vent here already, it was just expanded." They looked at each other for a moment before Ben took a breath and moved forward.

After traveling some twenty feet, the tunnel opened up into a cave once more, the floor leveled, and the air changed dramatically. What they saw in the dim light stopped them short. The minstrel swore softly.

"What the hell is that?"

Jhaun spoke for the first time in hours, his voice resonating in the tunnel. "That's the Gate."

Ben glanced at the Lady's son and felt a wave of barely controlled terror. He frowned at Connor. "Have you been through here?"

The minstrel's eyebrows peaked. "Not yet." They stared at what looked like nothing more than a film of mercury hanging vertically in their path, sealing off the passage. There was a faint light glowing through it, and they could make out their reflections in the gently waving surface.

"Can we go through without getting hurt?" Mekki directed her question to Jhaun, her voice quiet in the presence of mystery.

"We can get through."

She stared at him for a moment. "But?"

He spoke quietly. "It's what's on the other side, at the Castle, that can kill you."

"But is it just a skin, or deep? Do you know what I mean?"

"Thin. A hand's-breadth at the most." Jhaun shifted uncomfortably, looked away from the distorted reflections of the Gate.

Mekki was staring into it, her nose inches from the silvery surface, when she made a startled noise.

"What?" Connor moved toward her, his hand on his sword.

"Look." She pursed her lips and blew a stream of air at the wall. Nothing happened.

"Yeah?"

"But watch now." She closed her eyes for a moment and the reflection of her face rippled as if she had dropped a stone into a still pool. "I was trying to feel for what it might be."

Perahn pulled his flute from his side and played a few notes. As he swept into a song of warding, the film danced like a sail in the wind. He stopped to watch. "Creating affects it, but physically we don't. That's interesting."

"Right. Interesting." Connor stepped forward, hesitating at the boundary in the air, staring as if it were a wolf in the woods. "So we go." He looked at Jhaun briefly as he undid the safety, feeling the same waves of emotion from him that Benjamin did. Then, with a sudden movement, he passed through the wall. It rippled like a live thing as he pushed through, then bounded and settled again.

Ben shook his head. "I don't like this." He stepped away and then dove forward through the layer, executing a perfect shoulder roll. He found himself on the other side, crouching on the floor in the continuation of the tunnel he had just left. Connor was standing, illuminated from above by light that came through an opening in the roof of the cave.

"Nice entry. More points for technical difficulty then for execution."

Ben grimaced and took the proffered hand to stand up. "At least I stuck the landing." With a shiver he stared at the film. "Man, that thing is cold." He rubbed his hands on his arms, feeling like he was brushing off some kind of residue. "Are we still in this world?"

"We're still here. There are less dramatic ways to get to the Castle of the Stone, but the divide makes this is the only practical way we know of from Anders dominion."

"Less dramatic ways? They why did we -"

"Because we'd take another month to hike around the mountains, that's why."

"Ah. Can they hear us from the other side?"

"I don't know. Hey." He called at the film from a few feet away, unconsciously staying a distance from it.

The film rippled and bulged, and Jhaun passed through to their side. His movements were smooth, but fear screamed in his eyes. Ben wondered if they had grabbed him right here, as soon as he got through. "You okay?"

The Lady's son nodded. "Fine." Then he turned, seeming to wait for the others, hiding his expression from Ben and Connor. Not realizing in his distraction that the shimmering reflections of the Gate showed them all that they cared to see. Ben reached toward him but was stopped by a touch on his arm, the minstrel shaking his head. Ben nodded, took a deep breath, and waited for the rest.

In rapid succession Mekki and Perahn passed through. Mekki, shivering a bit, said, "Did that feel as strange for you as it did for me? What is it?"

"An energy gate. Like wards, but distilled to a physical film. There's no way anything can pass through without the person who set it knowing. Even you." Perahn looked at it and sighed. "But it takes a lot to keep up, and this one has been standing for years." Looking thoughtfully at the shimmering reflections, he moved into the light that dimly lit the tunnel opposite the Gate. "And I'm afraid I know where the energy has been coming from."

Ben frowned. "What do you mean?"

"The people he's been taking. That's one of the reasons for all the raids. He's able to redirect their energy to his own ends."

"But why here? Connor said there are other ways to reach him."

Perahn looked at Connor, who shrugged, and back at Ben. "The prophecies said that the One would come from Anders -"

"No." Ben felt adrenaline brush through his abdomen. "Don't tell me I'm the reason that people are being tortured." His voice rose with less control than he would have liked into the space around them.

"Ben." Perahn spoke gently into the cave that still hummed with Benjamin's protest. "You're not the reason they're being hurt. You're the reason this Gate is here. That was the question you asked, that was the question I answered. No more."

"That's a damn fine line, Per." Ben turned to the wall and rested his forehead against it, the cool of the stone draining the heat from his face. He took a deep breath and turned to face his companions again. "Okay. I'm okay. But it didn't stop us. Not at all. Why do this, just to know the exact moment we arrived? To make sure it was me? It doesn't make sense."

Connor looked from the Gate to Ben. "We can't expect him to make sense to us."

Perahn stared, frowning. "I'm sure he has his reasons." Something in the way Per spoke sent a shiver through Ben once more.

"Does this change anything?"

"I don't know. Do you?"

Ben stared at him for a moment, uncomprehending, and then looked at Connor. "Oh. No. I don't." He frowned in concentration, and walked back to the shimmering film of the Gate. "But I know there's a way to find out."

His hand was stretching toward the Gate when Mekki grabbed it. "Ben." There was a fierce urgency in her voice as she clutched his wrist. "Don't. If you open yourself to him, you can't know what will happen." Her eyes shimmered in the strange light. "We need you here."

The actor smiled slowly. "I'll be careful."

"Damn it, Ben. There's no reason to do this. It scares me." He turned to say something to her, and was suddenly captured by her eyes. They looked into him, and he felt himself open -

And he was standing on a path leading to a small cottage in a sunny wood, a path lined with wildflowers and singing with birds. A casual stone wall surrounded the house, with an arbor drenched in honeysuckle as a gate. Mekki stood at the door.

Ben?

She stepped down from the door of the cottage, and met him next to a small stone fountain. She held out her hand, palm first, and looked into his eyes. He mirrored the gesture, felt her tremble as their palms touched.

I didn't know we could do this.

She stepped closer and looked up at him, stroked back his hair gently.

I know you can't feel me normally. No one can. But I care. I wanted you to know. Now. Just in case.

Their palms touched once more and as she slowly pulled away, a faint glow narrowed to a bright golden thread that connected them. For a moment Ben could see all the lines that joined his soul to others - some stretching off through time and space, and some as near as this cave. It was a huge net of light, supporting him as he supported the others. It faded slowly, invisible, but still there. If he centered, he could feel it.

Be careful.

Ben blinked back into the more tangible reality and looked into Mekki's eyes. Resting his hand on her cheek, he felt the warmth of her skin against his stone-roughened palm.

"I'll be careful," he whispered. He glanced at Connor, nodded briefly. "Watch my back." The minstrel sat down and began a soft song in the echoing space of the cave, and Perahn joined him. Facing the Gate once more, Ben reached out his hand to make contact with the one who set it.

The character of the One was strong within him now, as comfortable as if it were the third week of a run and as easy to slip into. He had no doubt that the One knew how to use this shimmering field. He placed his palm flat against the wall, watching as it mirrored itself, until it merged with its reflection. His eyes closed.

Cold. Not like ice, but like water. Still and cold, lapping up around the edges of his fingers, melting around him and making room for his hand. He felt a part of himself reach out to the energy held captive there.

The connection was so sudden, so abrupt, that it took his breath away with a gasp.

So. You have come. The voice of Alious. Cultured, smoothly sarcastic.

Yes. The One felt no hesitation. This encounter was part of his destiny.

And you truly believe you can destroy me? His laugh was bitter and condescending. It left a bad taste in Ben's mind.

This creation will unfold as it should. You will not defeat us.

The reply carried a certain brittle shock. *Insolent boy! You know nothing! You are not the One. You are an impostor, a player at parts who thinks he can make a difference! Do you think these weak-minded fools who have brought you here have any concept of what I am? Of what they challenge? Death is all that you have come to meet. Now you are mine.*

A perfectly ordinary Benjamin reeled under the onslaught. The One had no such problem. The One was growing angry. With difficulty Ben opened to let the character work. He was an actor. The technique was still there.

You may lie to yourself and others, but not to me. I am the One. The foretold. This is my time. Until we are face to face, you are helpless, and you know it. You cannot fight me here. It is part of this creation.

A silence. Then, laughter once more. Forced.

And your company, your brave little band? What keeps me from killing them here, now, even as they stand?

You know you cannot harm them while I live. While they stand with me. Go. Prepare your worst, for I will fight you.

Ben jerked his hand free of the Gate. The last thing he heard was laughter, over the echo of his own words. *While they stand with me.*

Connor was at his side when he broke contact. "You here?"

"Yeah. He's waiting for us. We'll be okay until we get there." Ben looked at Connor and blinked, trying to clear his thoughts. The light was different. "How long was I gone?"

"Maybe half an hour. Maybe less. I was busy."

"I know. Thanks." Ben turned to Mekki and pressed her hand, feeling the reassurance of that connection sing just for a moment. He picked up his pack again as he glanced around. "Where's Jhaun?"

Connor looked back at the opening in the roof of the cave. "He went up a while ago. Couldn't sit still, said he couldn't focus enough to be any help. He was going to set a rope." The minstrel frowned. "Per, has he checked in?"

Perahn stood and slipped the flute into his belt. Then he looked up, took a leap that would have made any basketball player proud, and grabbed the edge of the opening in the ceiling. With easy athletic grace he pulled himself up and through. A moment passed.

"He's not here."

"What?"

"I think he's gone on ahead. Ben, you better come up."

Benjamin sighed and leaned against the wall of the tunnel for a moment, closing his eyes. Exhaustion was becoming too close a companion. He felt a hand on his shoulder and energy flooded over him, as if he were standing in the sun. Opening his eyes he saw the minstrel, concern softening the intensity of his gaze. Ben clasped a hand over the minstrel's forearm and relaxed for a few deep breaths, a faint blue-green shimmer visible between them. Connor squeezed his shoulder and released him. "Okay. Let's get moving." Ben nodded and accepted a leg up, scrambling through the opening almost as easily as Perahn had. He turned around and helped the others through.

"So. What now?" He regretted his tone as soon as he saw the expression in Perahn's eyes. "What's wrong?" Then the feeling hit him. *Jhaun's gone on alone. He's gone to try again. As the actor.*

"Oh, no." Ben looked down the incline, where Jhaun had indeed set a rope. "He's going to get himself killed." For some reason all he could picture was telling Cyrin. "We've got to stop him."

"We need to get this done. We can't waste time bailing out that kid's ass again." Connor cursed under his breath. He wasn't even fooling himself. "All right. What do we do?"

"I'll go after him." Perahn spoke as if his brother were a pet gone astray.

"You can't go alone." Connor turned to Ben who stared at him, trying to picture going on without the minstrel at his side.

"Con, I have no idea how this is supposed to go."

Mekki stepped in. "You're all crazy. Of course Per can't go alone after Jhaun. Of course Ben and Connor have to stick together. You're the Hawk, for God's sake. It would be wrong." Ben wrapped his arms around her tightly.

"Thank you."

"It makes sense. I know Jhaun from the Core. Probably better than Per does. Hell, maybe better than Jhaun does. Let's just get this over with so we can all sit down somewhere and tell great stories about it, okay?" She took a deep breath. "God, I'd give anything to be sitting at Dembee's over an ale right now."

The minstrel glanced at her, shook his head with a grin. "I'd join you."

Benjamin frowned at them. "Dembee's?"

"Near the Core. The best ale on Taela. I'll take you sometime."

The actor smiled and did the courtesy of following her distraction. "You bet. We get through this and the first round's on me."

"Deal."

"All right. We get to the castle and split up there. Who knows. Maybe this'll throw him off." Ben shrugged as he said it, hoping it might be true. In his mind all he could hear was an echo of sarcastic laughter. *As long as they stand with me. My God, Jhaun, what have I gotten you into?* He pushed the thought aside and turned to his companions. "Let's get going. The sooner we get there, the sooner we'll be finished."

They started down the line, rappelling in places, and reached level ground in minutes. The landing was higher than it had been on the other side of the Gate, and led off in both directions along the rock face.

Gathered at the bottom of the rope, the four remaining looked out over the scene in the descending darkness, and saw no sign of Jhaun. The huge rocks of the landscape, large enough to be mountains, rose out of a silvery lake.

"Is that the same as the Gate? It has that mercury look to it."

"No. It's dead water, or it's something like it."

"What the hell is dead water?"

"It's captive, drained. Water connects living things." Perahn stood like a statue looking out over the dead lands. "But this has no life. It can kill you. That's why we brought our own." He shook his head sadly. "All my life I've heard of this place. I expected it to frighten me. I didn't expect it to be so sad."

Ben nodded. "I don't like the feeling of this. Con. Which way?"

The minstrel looked out over the desolation, got his bearings, and pointed southeast of where they stood. "You can't see it from here, it's hidden by that peak. Down this way, to the left."

"How do you know?"

"I don't. But the Lady's told me stories."

"She knows it?"

"She did once. It was special to her, but she doesn't talk about it." He squinted back the way they came. "I think she had family here."

Silence shrouded them as they moved single file into the steadily deepening gloom. Their footfalls crunched against the crumbling slate of the rock, and even the clearing of a throat was loud as a clarion call. Connor hummed softly, just to break the silence, but couldn't keep it up. He turned to Perahn.

"What the hell is with this place? It's like it absorbs sound and throws it back at you at the same time."

Per stopped suddenly and pointed past a huge rock they had been winding around. "There it is."

The Castle of the Stone, Aumerle of the old legends, lay glowering in the dusk like an old man disturbed by a bad dream. Where Anders Castle was gracefully tall and lyrical, Aumerle was dark, squat, and oozed over the landscape like a fungus or a creeping vine, suffocating the land that it settled on. The walls were dark and streaked with lighter shades of brown. Ben stared at it, opened to it for a brief, cautious moment. What he felt startled him.

"It wasn't always like this."

"No." Perahn spoke without looking away from the Castle. "Not until he came. Aumerle was here for generations." He squinted at the rambling darkness of the structure, not so far off now, and shook his head. "It was beautiful once." A frown creased his brow, and he stopped in his tracks.

"Per?" Mekki had nearly collided with him on the pathway. "You okay?"

"I don't know. I'm fine. It just looks - I don't know. Familiar somehow. But I've never been here." He frowned again and started walking. The rest of the company exchanged concerned glances, and Ben nodded at Connor. The minstrel sang into the evening, ignoring the difficulty of the place.

"So are we really safe until we reach the castle? After all we went through on the road?"

"Yes." Ben was as surprised at the sureness of his reply to Mekki as the rest were. "He can't do anything until we meet on his ground, now that we've gotten past the Gate. I don't know why, but I know he can't."

"Honor among thieves?"

"No, more than that. Our energy ties us. A kind of - destiny." Ben frowned at what he was hearing himself say.

"So if someone gets to him other than you?"

Ben thought for a moment, nodded. "I wish I could worry about that happening." He stared down at the path. "But Jhaun doesn't have a chance." In a few minutes they came to a natural stone bridge spanning the dull silver lake below them. On the other side was Aumerle. "This is it. Once we're across, you and Mekki head for Jhaun. Can you feel him?"

Perahn closed his eyes to concentrate and nodded. "I do feel something of him, weak. But who knows how far away he is in a place that size?" He looked hopefully at Ben and Connor, who were unable to reassure him.

"At least he's still alive, Per. We'll deal with anything else as we come to it."

"This is wrong." Mekki was staring across the bridge at the huge open gateway of Aumerle Castle. "This is just wrong. Where is everybody? It feels dead. Is it just the place, or is something else going on?"

"I don't know. But I have a bad feeling about this." For the first time in days Ben drew his sword as he crossed the bridge. It shimmered softly in the night, and a symbol engraved near the hilt caught his eye, glowing brighter than the rest. A Celtic rune in the shape of an arrow. Sign of the Warrior. Ben felt the familiar confident wash of Hotspur and carried on. *Good. I'll need all the help I can get.*

The doors of Aumerle were thrown wide. Everything about the place was dark, as if centuries of fires had scorched the walls. Darker forms were mounded in the dim courtyard, piles of trash or debris. Nothing moved. They carried on carefully, watching for movement. Abruptly, Mekki gasped.

"Good God." She pointed at one of the dark mounds. "They're people." Connor stepped quickly toward it, sword drawn, and turned the body over with his toe. "Is he dead?" She held back as Connor hovered over the body.

"If he is, it wasn't long ago. Still warm."

"This is why the Gate was there, Ben." Perahn stared grimly at the body stretched out in front of them, looked around at all the others. "He sapped them all. Even he can't contain that much energy for any length of time. He waited until the last minute." Perahn looked at Ben, his face merely planes of darkness and shadow. "Maybe -"

"No." Ben cut him off before the words came. "We go on. Con, do we have light?"

"It looks like the torches inside are lit."

"Of course. He wouldn't want me to have any trouble finding him. Good. Per, Mekki, you find Jhaun. If he can be moved, bring him to us. If not, we'll meet at the Gate as soon as this is over." His tone was grim. "And look. If we don't make it out - get Jhaun back to Anders. He may be the One after all. But he'll need to practice." He clasped forearms with Perahn, and Mekki hugged him hard. "Teach him what you know, okay?"

"I'll do what I can."

Ben nodded and looked into her eyes for a bare moment, acknowledging the connection. "All right. Let's get this show up and running. And be careful. I'd guess that he's kept some guards functioning."

"Wait. Which way?" Mekki looked around at the entrances off of the courtyard. Only one had light seeping dimly out into the night.

"Circle," said Per. "Help me." They joined hands and calmed for a moment, focusing their energies on Perahn and his sense of his brother. "Good. This way." They broke the circle and Mekki followed Per off into the darkness. Ben watched them go with a pain in his chest, hoping the ominous words weren't absolutely literal. *As long as they stand with me.* He turned to Connor. "Let's go."

There was a dank and musty smell in the hallways of the castle. Torches guttered and smoked at intervals along the way, providing enough light to see scattered bodies as they went. Ben kept his sword in hand, its familiar weight reassuring.

How do I do this?

Do not underestimate the Artist. You were chosen with purpose.

But how? How do I fight him?

Be who you are.

An actor? Or a character I'm playing?

Ben argued with himself while he followed Connor, stepping gingerly over a prone form on the floor. Something grabbed his ankle in the dark. "Con!" He yelled as he turned, fear flowing almost instantly into fury at the attack. *You dare!* Hotspur flew into his consciousness. The prone guard had a sword, was swinging it wildly at Ben's leg. He parried, slashed at the hand still holding his ankle.

The sword hummed as skin and bone parted beneath its blade. The figure made no sound but stood, came at him again, blood running crimson down his chest where he cradled the stump of his wrist. He lifted his sword and charged, so quickly that Ben didn't have time to think. With a smooth motion he circled his blade around the other, pushing it off target, and continued in the familiar fencing parry, thrusting the point of his blade into the man's chest. His attacker folded with a little sigh onto the floor, the engraved blade sliding from the wound as he fell.

Ben gasped, lost his footing and stumbled against the wall, breathing heavily. Connor stood by, waiting and watching for another attack. There was none.

"My God." Ben shook uncontrollably in the dark. "I killed him."

"I know." The minstrel stepped closer. "He would have killed you."

"It happened so fast." Ben's voice cracked in the cold stone hallway of the castle. He shuddered and wrapped his arms around himself, rocking slightly. "How can I…"

Connor grabbed his arm and pulled him closer, staring into his face. "How can you what? Face Alious? Why the hell do you think this happened? He thinks you can't take it." The minstrel glared at Ben, who suddenly looked much younger. "The real question is, can you do what you have to do, or does someone else have to step up for you?"

Ben blinked at him. "What are you saying? That you'll just do it for me?"

"Damn it, I am if you can't. Someone has to *try*."

Benjamin stared at him for a long moment. Unreasoned fear snapped into resolve. "No." The actor stepped away, leaned against the wall. "He *used* me. He used that man to throw me, damn it. Damn him. It's not going to work. He won't win just because I wouldn't try. I won't give up that easily." His breathing was still ragged, but determination steadied him.

Connor nodded, a rather vicious smile crossing his face. "Good. I would have been disappointed if you did." He opened his water skin and handed it to Ben. "Drink. Not much. And get a firm grip on whoever you need in there."

The actor nodded, drank, and shuddered again.

"Stay close."

They followed the intermittent light of the torches as it led them deeper into the depths of Aumerle. Ben focused on staying in character. It was easier than remembering the brief throb of a heartbeat shuddering through his sword, that made him think of Per lying on the ground at Overlook - he still could see it clearly, as the image leapt to the forefront of his mind. The blood, the pain, the press of darkness, the cold stone walls - *what the? That's not Perahn* - "Con. Wait." The minstrel dropped back and stared as Ben closed his eyes. He looked carefully at the image, absorbing.

Dark hair, slashed black velvet, blood staining the rent edges of fabric. Dust of boots where he had been kicked. Blood running down into his ears, his hair. The side of his face bruised, swollen until his right eye, if it were indeed still there, was buried in flesh. Alive. Almost unrecognizable. The actor gave an angry gasp.

"What is it?"

"Jhaun."

"Alive?"

"Yeah. But bad. Really bad. Con, it's almost as if they worked him over as far as they could without killing him."

Connor took three furious steps down the hall, his sword outstretched. "The bastard's trying to get us so angry we can't think straight. And it's working." He pounded the stone with a fist, his eyes flashing.

"We can't let it. Mekki and Per will find him. We've got to stay focused." Ben took a deep breath. *Technique.* The One was who he needed now. And he was there.

Destiny will unfold as it should. Do not fear. That is, after all, his greatest weapon against you.

"Let's go." They continued to follow the torches on a circuitous route. "He's playing with us," Ben said, keeping his anger in check. "He's trying to make us use up our energy here. He must be more afraid than he's letting on." The warrior in Benjamin smiled, as Shakespeare came to his aid once again.

Now for our consciences, the arms are fair

When the intent of bearing them is just.

They rounded a corner. In front of them was a huge hall with doors thrown wide, a forest of torches and candles bringing the brightness of daylight into the darkened castle. A throne was set on steps at the far end, and a figure waited in royal blue and black silk, silver waves of hair pulled back and spilling regally onto one shoulder. A fair face, narrow and long, sculpted as of porcelain. Blue eyes that pierced to the bone, seemingly cut from the same fabric as his robe. A sword rested easily in his right hand, glimmering in the living light of torch and candle.

The Lord of Aumerle. Alious.

19

Per was moving so quickly in the darkness that Mekki grabbed the back of his shirt in desperation. "Hey," she shot the words forward. "I can't see in the dark." He slowed his pace, but not by much.

"I'm sorry. I'm following. I'm not sure how long the sense of direction the circle gave me will last."

Mekki made an irritated noise. "Why would it- never mind. Go. I'll hang on." Following the corridors of the castle was like navigating a labyrinth in the dark, and an unfortunate side effect of being naturally warded was the inability to connect easily with others. Mekki had no idea how Perahn was finding his way.

She exhaled emphatically, and took strength from the brief moment she connected with Benjamin. How easy that had been. She couldn't quite believe that the actor she saw onstage – one of the few she had admired in that admittedly bitter time in her life - was the same person. She was lost in thought when Perahn stopped so abruptly that she bumped into him.

"Here."

"What?"

"He's here. Nearby. There are guards." Per stopped and looked at her. "Can you feel them?"

Mekki shook her head and concentrated back into the here and now. "No." She frowned. "I don't know them. It makes it even harder for me. How far away?"

"Around the corner, down a short hall. I think. And there's some light coming from there." Per shook his head. "I wish you could tell. I don't trust my judgment right now "

She stared at him, surprised at the strength with which she felt his insecurity and something else. "What is it?"

"Nothing."

"Come on, even I can feel - what the hell's going on, Per?" Her eyes widened at his rising panic.

Perahn hesitated, staring at the wall. "I'm afraid." His whisper lingered in the corridor like a ghost.

Mekki gave it a few seconds to fade. Her voice, when she responded, was soft. "Tell me."

The musician sighed. "He had me once, Mekki. You weren't there. You don't know what it was like. What I did." Perahn shuddered at the memory. "What's to keep him from doing it again? Here, on his own ground? What if -" He broke off without finishing, shaking his head and staring down at the floor, suddenly looking very much like his brother.

Mekki stared for a moment, then forced a smile. "What's to keep him? Me. From what I understand, Per, if you're with me, you're as hidden as I am."

Perahn frowned at her. "Are you sure?" A spark of hope flickered in his dark eyes.

"It's truth, Per." She looked at him and considered a moment before going on. "Cento told me when he said I might be part of this. Because he knew the danger." She waved off his concern before he had a chance to express it. "I knew what I was getting into." Mekki looked into his eyes, as open as she was capable of being. "Come on. Didn't you ever do something crazy, just because you felt that it was the right thing to do?"

Perahn returned the intensity of her gaze. "I suppose I have."

She put a hand on his arm. "Then let's grab your brother and get the hell out of here before he finds some more trouble to get into."

Perahn nodded and closed his eyes briefly to concentrate, focusing on the guards around the corner. "Two of them. Nearly asleep."

"Good. I'll take the one on the left." Mekki pulled her knife from its sheath, stared at it uneasily and slipped it back. Looking around the corridor, she backed up a few steps and quietly wrested an unlit torch from its holder on the wall. The heavy handle felt reassuringly solid. Perahn saw what she was doing and followed her example. When they were both armed, he took a deep breath and looked at her with a nod.

They rounded the corner at a run, the soft leather of their boots whisper silent on the stone floor. The first guard, the one Mekki had claimed, was down before he knew what hit him. She turned to help Perahn in time to see him slam the butt of the torch into the man's stomach, and break it over his head when he folded in half. Per was shaking when he dropped the splintered, makeshift club.

"You okay?" He nodded, stared at the man crumpled at his feet. Mekki looked around in the dim light that came from the guard station. "I think they're going to be down for a while. Let's find Jhaun and move out." She lit her former weapon at the guard's torch and moved down the hallway to a heavy oak door. "This way?"

"Yes."

She tried the door, shook her head. "Are there keys on either of them?" Perahn nudged the guard closer to him with his foot, found a string of keys at his belt. Wresting them free, he turned to the door, found the right key in only three tries, and unlocked the cell. With a nervous look at Mekki, he stepped back.

"I'll keep watch."

Mekki searched his face in the flickering torchlight, and nodded. The door creaked open as she pushed the cold iron handle. Closing her eyes for a moment to let them adjust to the dark, she opened them again and moved slowly into the room, holding the torch in front of her.

It was barely high enough for her to stand upright. Without windows it seemed more suited for storage, preferably of something just as easily forgotten as kept. The stench of moldy straw rose from the damp floor.

"There." She looked into a corner, at a figure huddled unmoving on the stone floor. Mekki knelt at his side and felt the black velvet of his tabard. Damp, stiffening patches in the soft cloth made her shudder. She called his name gently.

"Jhaun?" When he made no response, she pulled his shoulder toward her, and he half rolled onto his back, his arms weakly rising to shield his face. At first she thought it was the light of the torch that he was guarding against, but quickly realized that he couldn't see it. His face was bloody, his eyes swollen shut. A clotted knife slice ran from his right temple to his chin in a curve that followed his jaw line. "My God, Jhaun. What have they done to you?"

A quiet sound escaped his bloodied lips, barely moving. "Mekki?"

"Yes." She looked away and swallowed hard. "It's okay, Jhaun. We're going to get you out of here." For an instant it seemed he was going to reach toward her. Then he pulled his arms back across his chest.

"No." He whimpered, his voice cracking. "You can't trick me again. You won't. I won't believe you again." The son of Anders curled helplessly on the floor, hugging himself, rocking. "Not *again*." He kept repeating, a grim mantra echoing over and over as he rocked.

Mekki's stomach lurched. She stood, turned to where Perahn was guarding the door of the cell. "Per," she croaked. "Get in here."

Perahn ducked through the door and moved surely in the dim light to where his brother was laying. "What is it? How bad -" He looked as he was asking, and stopped dead. So battered, so alien was Jhaun's face, that it took Perahn a moment to see that it was not the sole focus of the attack. Blood gave a dull sheen in patches on the dark velvet, stiffened the frayed edges of ragged tears. Horror turned abruptly to anger.

Perahn felt his emotions tighten in a way he had only experienced before with Aletia. Something entirely instinctive. Protective.

Mekki looked at him, at his clenched fists and flashing eyes, and put her hand firmly on his arm. He dragged his focus away from Jhaun to her, and she shook her head. Somehow he fought the feelings down, brought them under his control. He knelt and put his hand gently on Jhaun's forehead. "Someone will pay for this, brother."

Perahn stepped away to take a cloak off one of the guards and wrapped Jhaun in it. He swept his brother up in his arms as if he were a child, ignored the feeble protests, and carried him swiftly out of the dank cell. He whispered again, under his breath. "Someone will pay."

They moved quickly down the hallway, but not the way they had come. Mekki stopped. "Per. Is this the way out?"

"No."

"Ben said we should meet them at the Gate." There was no response. She grabbed his shirt and forced him to turn toward her. "Per. For the love of - where are we going?"

The torch she carried lit Perahn's eyes eerily, shining on a spirit in purgatory. "We're going to find them."

Mekki startled as she felt the anger pouring off him. She was glad, at that moment, that she couldn't feel the full force of his emotion. "Jhaun needs to get out of here." She stared at him, willing him to listen to reason. "We need to get out of here."

"No." Perahn's voice cracked in the stone corridor like ice breaking. "We're going to find Alious." He shifted his hold on Jhaun as he stared down the hall. "And if Benjamin doesn't kill him, I will."

*   *   *

In the great hall of Aumerle castle, Ben shrugged the pack off his shoulders, dropped it to the floor. "So. The time has come."

"Indeed." The voice of Alious slid over the word, caressed it, drawing out the vowels. Ben recognized the technique. He had used it himself. The actor knew the power that came from using language, and acknowledged his opponent with a certain grudging admiration.

There is a way to defeat him. It is within us.

But how?

You're the One. You were chosen for a reason. Find that within you which can conquer him.

Ben frowned at his internal dialogue as Alious rose from the throne and tossed his cape back, the royal blue shimmering iridescent in the flickering light. "Come forward, boy," the Lord of Aumerle said, drawing his sword, "and die."

The actor peeled off the deep green jerkin he was wearing, loosened the tied collar of the soft shirt beneath. It left him less protected, but in a fight, he always favored ease of movement. "I do not think," he replied, leaning on his words in the same style, "that it is my time to die." Ben drew his sword, felt the power singing through it. For a moment he saw it in his mind as the aluminum stage sword, a tool of his craft. The one always present in the other.

He held the grip in both hands, the soft red leather flexing under the pressure. It was clear to him that the actor was the one who had to fight this battle, but the warrior instinct of the One was still strong in him. He held that part of himself in check, surreptitiously scanning the hall.

It was a good set for a fight. The center was empty, candles and torches standing around the perimeter. Ben found it difficult to believe that this clear space was coincidental. Two steps the width of the hall led up to the throne, with no other furniture in the room. Clearly only one man's comfort counted here. The chamber echoed with footsteps as Alious crossed down to Ben's level, his sword draped from his hand.

It appeared that his every movement was deliberate, calculated, graceful. How one man could exude such delicacy and such malevolence at the same time amazed Ben. He found himself admiring the character before him, studying him. Alious knew it. A contemptuous smile played across delicately drawn lips as he approached Benjamin, studied the actor in turn.

"You?" He laughed. Ben shivered inwardly at the sound. "You are the One who will fight me?" Alious looked around the hall, mocking him. "Surely there must be more than …this." He stood within an arm's length of Ben now, and stepped closer. The actor stared into cold blue eyes flecked with silver, and felt himself being held there. It became more difficult to breath. With the lightning strike of a snake, the blade Alious held leapt forward, and Ben barely parried it in time, a surprised frown crossing his brow. The older man laughed.

Connor spoke from behind. "Careful, Ben." Alious turned abruptly at the sound of the minstrel's voice, as if noticing Connor for the first time.

"And you. Leading him here, to his death. How can you sleep at night?" The smile broadened, sarcastic.

Connor returned the ice-blue gaze without flinching. "I don't. I never know when the ghost of someone you killed will visit my dreams."

Ben felt a warrior's overwhelming desire to strike out, kill Alious, end this game once and for all; but somehow the actor knew that it wouldn't be that easy. Alious was purposely provoking them, had been doing so since they reached the Gate. Even before, when he had sent Jhaun back. That could only mean he wanted Ben to attack first, in anger. Without thinking, without using the skills of his creating.

If that's what you want, bastard, that's exactly what won't happen.

Benjamin Agante glanced around to check his field, stepped back and dropped into *en garde*. "I would salute, but that would imply that I expect some honor from you. I give you none."

Alious laughed again, as if a child were threatening him with a stick. He lifted his sword. "As you wish, boy."

*   *   *

Per and Mekki rounded a corner and saw light streaming from the great hall. Voices came from within, unintelligible in the echoes of the corridor. Perahn, still cradling Jhaun, stopped with a gasp. Mekki was at least three yards ahead of him when her momentum faded. "What is it?"

"It's him."

"Good." Mekki snapped off the word. "It's about time-" A guard appeared at the opposite end of the corridor, saw them, and advanced at a lumbering run. Mekki stared at him and avoided glancing back at Per in the shadows, still burdened with Jhaun.

Without thinking twice, she let out a feeble cry. Backing up against the wall farthest from Perahn, she weakly thrust the torch at the guard as he drew closer, keeping herself in the light. "Please, no, don't kill me."

The guard slowed, laughing as he reconsidered his options. "Oh, I won't," he said, leering at her. "At least, not right away." He took another step toward her, easily took the torch from her hand, grasped her roughly by the wrist. "Now. What do we have here?"

Mekki seemed for a moment to collapse into herself, then exploded out, kicking him full between the legs with enough force to lift him off the ground. His eyes bulged as he doubled over and she grabbed two handfuls of his hair, pulling his head into the stone wall with a resounding crack. He fell like a puppet with his strings cut. The torch went out as it fell to the ground and she kicked the still form once more, hard. It didn't move. "Idiot," she panted, shaking out her arms from the sudden exertion.

Perahn stepped forward, looking at her with renewed admiration. "Remind me to stay on your good side."

"I don't have a bad side. Remember that instead." She stepped gracefully over the guard's inert body, and into the great hall of Aumerle.

The battle had begun. Alious was toying with Ben, feeling him out before committing to an attack. Ben lunged forward, was parried, the swords locked together. Alious laughed. Ben stepped backwards out of the bind. *He's good. Could be better than me.* The actor stopped, re-centered himself at a safer distance. Alious' eyes shifted to the door of the great hall behind Ben, and he laughed again.

"Ah. So *more* of your friends have come to see you die." He frowned, so slightly that Ben wouldn't have felt it if he wasn't so close, if they weren't so involved. *Something caught his focus. What was that?*

Benjamin studied Alious in the merciless connection that fighting joined the combatants in. *Was it Mekki's invisibility that struck the Lord of Aumerle so? Or something else?* He dared not open himself more to find out. Ben didn't even take the chance to turn; he knew who was there. He called over his shoulder. "Is he okay?"

"No." Perahn's voice was solid ice. "But he will be."

"Get him out of here, Per."

"No."

The tone of Perahn's voice made Ben turn in spite of himself. He felt the anger streaming off of the musician immediately. "Per. This is my fight."

"And I would see you win. But if Hawk is your second, I am his." His eyes narrowed. "Alious will not leave here alive."

Benjamin stared at him, felt the barely controlled aggression pouring from this peaceful man. Fighting a flood of concern, Ben shied away from opening himself to Per's perceptions, trying to keep his head clear. Fighting angry was dangerous; it opened the floodgates of adrenaline, added strength - but it did nothing for thoughtful planning. If the first flailing attack failed, you were quite likely dead.

The actor knew that there would be more to this fight than brute force. In the brief moment of Ben's distraction, Alious attacked.

Target number three. Benjamin's mind registered the approach, and supplied the appropriate parry to defend himself. Abruptly there was something familiar about Alious' expression, the attack, even the blue of his cloak. In an instant Ben's mind spilled out the answers.

Kent. Lear. Good Lord, he looks like Kent, that show, four years ago ...it rained opening night. That was the attack that we worked on for so long, that he kept being late for.

Without consciously thinking about it, Ben swung his sword in a wide arc, the next move in the choreography of the fight he remembered. Alious parried obligingly, even pushed off the same way. A faint frown creased the man's brow, and he retreated a few steps. It took a moment for Ben to register what had happened.

Testing his hopes, Benjamin strode toward the master of Aumerle, circled him, and with a loud cry, attacked. Again, Alious responded with the movement Ben remembered as well as any monologue, the choreography of the show. Again, Alious frowned, this time more in anger than confusion. *Yes! I'm imposing the fight on him.* An important detail occurred to the actor, one his mind had neglected to bring up until now in the excitement of the random information flood. *And... in about two minutes he runs me through.* The realization threw him, made him step backwards.

So what I need is a fight I win... Dropping the choreographed routine and the character who would be dead very soon, Ben cast desperately about in his memory, trying to remember a fight that he won as a *hero*. Opening to a villain's role felt wrong, felt too dangerous right now. Even as Ben considered, his concentration on the fight before him faltered, and Alious, apparently unaware of what had actually happened, redoubled his efforts. Ben fought him off, the steel of their blades ringing echoes in the great hall. Slowly Alious pressed him back.

From behind him, Ben heard the sounds of a fight in the corridor outside the hall. The few guards remaining in the castle had arrived, and Connor was at them. Perahn left Jhaun with Mekki, and ran to the minstrel's aid while Benjamin was trying desperately to keep his focus on the opponent in front of him. Alious *knew*.

"Are you worried for your friends?" His sword carved a vicious low arc, and Ben leapt over it, stumbling slightly but catching himself in time. "You should be worried for yourself."

"Believe me," Ben said, breathing heavily and using the pause to circle Alious back toward the higher ground of the throne, "my friends can take care of themselves. So can I." Benjamin felt like he must have the weapon he needed in a sheath at his side. He simply couldn't figure out how to draw and use it.

Mekki cradled Jhaun's head in her lap protectively, not wanting to leave him alone but feeling helpless; anger sang in her veins. It would have been easier on her temperament to join the fight, but she felt the need to stay where she was. Jhaun murmured in a weak whisper. Mekki leaned into him. "Easy, Jhaun. We'll get you out of here soon."

"The actor… he's the actor."

"He knows."

"…but who *is* he now?"

Mekki looked down at Jhaun, unsure she had heard him right. "Save your strength." She brushed her hand gently over his head.

"…who is he? Is he a character… who can conquer the villain?"

"Character?" Mekki jerked her head up, saw Ben retreat again, barely holding his own against the age and experience of Alious. Turning to focus on Alious, she studied him like a hunter watching her prey. The silvery hair and handsome features, twisted by a malevolent smile. She felt like a critic again, like this was something out of a performance. Mekki gasped. "Could it be?" She reached out in her mind toward Ben.

She could, for an instant, *feel* what was happening. Feel the confusion, the frustration at his search for the right character. Feel his split concentration. Closing her eyes, she focused all her energy for a long, slow breath. Instinctively she clenched her fist, found her knife in her hand with some surprise. A dagger. *A dagger before me.* Her hazel eyes grew wide. Taking a deep breath she yelled across the great hall of Aumerle, her voice ringing clear and strong.

"Lay on, *Macduff*!"

Standing by the throne, Ben jerked his head up to stare at her. For a moment Mekki was afraid she had distracted him too far, done more harm than good. Then Alious turned toward her, furious, and she felt the connection sing between Benjamin and herself. Felt, almost saw, the fine gold cord that joined them as Benjamin's eyes widened.

Macduff!

The man who defeats Macbeth. The man who has the right of vengeance and conquers the villain, even when the prophecies make it sound impossible… but prophecies can cheat.

Benjamin looked at Mekki and Jhaun as Alious strode toward them, sword ready to strike. He closed his eyes, took a deep breath.

"No one opposes me here!" Alious glared at Mekki where she sat on the floor.

"Guess again." She was playing a dangerous game, trying to give Ben the time he needed. "*We* oppose you. Here. Anywhere. You're nothing but a coward, using other bodies to do what you can't."

On the edge of her vision, she saw Benjamin nodding, his eyes closed in concentration. Alious seemed aware that something was happening, but his anger distracted him. He took another step toward Mekki. "How dare you." He leaned into the words, pushing them on her. "Insolent, insignificant girl."

Behind the Lord of Aumerle, there was a strange sound as Macduff opened his eyes. The voice, as he called out, froze Alious where he stood.

"Turn, hell-hound, turn!"

Alious spun around to face Benjamin. His mocking expression died, and his already fair face went deathly pale. The man who stood with vengeance gleaming in his eyes was not Benjamin Agante. Not quite, not entirely. There was a faint echo of many voices in the air.

Alious stared at the figure before him. "What are you?" He growled.

"I have no words:

My voice is in my sword: thou bloodier villain

than terms can give thee out!"

Alious frowned. Confusion muddled his features for only a moment, then resolved. "I don't know who you think you are, boy." He walked forward, dragging his sword deliberately across the stone floor, the sound like a rattlesnake in their ears. "But you don't know who you're fighting."

Snapping out of his easy posture like a whip cracking, Alious attacked, swinging his weapon viciously down at Macduff's head. The Scottish lord brushed the sword away with his own, and parried quickly the cut to his left shoulder, his right, his left knee.

parry 5,4,3,1.

Alious snarled like a wild animal. With blade flashing, he thrust his sword at Ben's chest. Macduff caught it, forced the bind off to the ground at his right. *bind 2. retreat.* Ben backed off quickly. A part of his mind could still see the crumpled napkin that he and the choreographer had worked out this fight on, in a bar after rehearsal. *Why did we have to make Macbeth look so good here?* He frowned, clearing his head, and they circled each other warily, forming a mirror of each other, just as it had been on stage. *I remember. It gets worse before-*

Alious stopped his circling and began to advance. Now he was poking at him, mocking him, every thrust at the heart. Macduff backed up, knocking the sword away as smoothly as he could. It was close.

Okay, it should get easier from here - The point of Alious' sword caught Ben's shirt and tore part of it away as the actor parried. *That wasn't in the script.* The Lord of Aumerle laughed. It was Macduff that stared down at his shirt, and back up at his opponent. In an instant, unsteady fear changed to anger. The anger that the character felt, the anger that Ben felt, blending imperceptibly. Alious, unaware, continued to bait him.

"So. Growing weary, are you? Then despair." He moved in with his weapon tilted down just slightly. Just enough for Ben to remember his cue.

With adrenaline fed speed, Macduff began the cut to Alious' left shoulder, feinted to his leg and came back up to the same shoulder. Alious barely managed to parry. For the first time in their fight, the actor saw the man's age working against him. Alious felt it as well, and attacked in pure fury, a swipe at Ben's head. *Duck and roll. I remember.* Ben scrambled on the floor as Alious pursued him, his cape billowing sapphire across the floor. He stood over Benjamin, his sword lifted high.

"Now die, fool."

It was Macduff who kicked out with his leg and swept Alious' feet out from under him. The older man stumbled, caught himself, but not before the actor had regained his feet and cut at him again. The sword felt like it weighed twice as much as it had at the beginning of the fight, and Macduff's attack was slow enough for Alious to catch it, bind it against his own. The blades slid against each other with a screech of screaming metal, stopping when the two hilts hit, blades crossed, the men eye to eye over them.

For just a heartbeat, Ben felt himself being drawn in to those eyes once more. Then he remembered the writing on the crumpled napkin, grounding him. *Coeur à coeur. This was part of the plan.*

Alious cried out, angry and incredulous that he was being denied. He forced the blades down to his right, until the point of his own sword was touching the floor. Ben lifted his foot and kicked down, hard, against the blade.

In the stage fight, it knocked the sword out of Macbeth's hand. In the Great Hall of Aumerle, Alious was not a willing actor, and did not let go.

The blade shattered on the diagonal, leaving only part of a weapon, and an opponent in maniacal fury.

Connor and Perahn burst back into the great hall, panting, blood spattered. A dark stain was spreading slowly from Connor's left shoulder, but they were otherwise intact. Alious retreated a step, and Connor shouted to Ben. "We're clear." He looked at Alious. "It's over." It was too much for the Lord of Aumerle Castle. With an inhuman scream, Alious threw his broken blade at Connor.

The sword sang spinning in the air, a wild thing with a life of its own. The shattered edge sliced deep into the minstrel's thigh, and blood gushed so quickly from the wound that Ben knew instantly that an artery had been severed. "Connor!" Emotions collided within him, pulling him out of character. Every instinct, every nerve screamed *save him!*

"No." The minstrel gasped, clutching his leg as he dropped to one knee. "Don't waste it." His voice was harsh, his face pale. Benjamin felt as much as heard the minstrel's thought. *Don't waste my life.*

Ben turned to Alious and roared. "Enough!" It was Benjamin Agante who stood then, out of character, his sword point mere inches from Alious' chest. Alious stared at him, at the point of the weapon gleaming, ready to thrust. He looked into Ben's eyes, and Ben, unguarded and out of character in his anger, suddenly felt the draw again, felt the crackle of wind and lightning in his mind. With a small, desperate cry, Benjamin Agante was trapped – but with his last thought, instead of trying to break away, he lunged forward to meet his foe, *coeur à coeur*. Heart to heart. *I'll fight you, bastard. I'll stop you. Wherever I have to.*

Abruptly, Benjamin stood before the broken doorway of a stone castle. All around him was desolation and decay. A battle had been fought here, and the land had never recovered.

He stepped through the crumbling entrance, and heard a faint sound that became recognizable as someone crying out in pain. He ran through deteriorating hallways, following the sound until it led to a door, closed and barred. He lifted the beam that blocked it effortlessly, threw it aside, and wrenched the door open.

There, bound in chains, was a man writhing in the darkness. He was weak, emaciated, his long pale hair matted and lank. He looked up at Ben, and something like hope flared in his sapphire eyes. "Who are you?"

"Benjamin Agante." The actor stared at him for a moment. "They say I'm the One." He gasped as realization hit him. "Alious?"

"Then all has come to pass..."

Ben frowned, not understanding. "How is this possible?"

"And it was worth it. By the Artist, it was all worth it! He is safe?" Ben saw an image in the air before him, of an infant with dark eyes. Behind him stood a woman with long raven hair and eyes of the darkest green, radiant, smiling. Just as suddenly she was alone, her countenance full of sorrow.

"What are you saying?" Ben stared at the image, a younger version of - "The Lady?"

The man looked, pleading, into Ben's eyes. "Please. Do this for me. Tell Miran I love her. I always have. Tell her good-bye." His eyes were losing their bright edge.

The actor, shocked, saw a rush of images, felt a wash of hopes and dreams gone by, of decisions painfully made. "Then you - you're their father?"

"They?" The older man's eyes widened. "They?" Ben felt himself being searched, and surprisingly had no power to stop it.

"They! There was another! How could she keep it from me? Keep him from me?" Suddenly the image of Perahn filled the space between them. "The infant lives?" For a moment Alious laughed quietly, his face transfigured. "Yes. By the Artist, Miran. You did it."

Ben spoke softly. "Perahn. His name's Perahn."

The man frowned for a moment, then faded back into himself. "Yes. Of course. Tell Miran." His eyes were fading to gray in the suddenly dimming light. "Ask them to forgive me. To try. Tell them - good-bye."

"Tell her yourself! If you've broken away from this evil, why -"

"You can't understand. I can't ask that much. I've waited so long..."

Without warning the connection between them dissolved. Ben felt himself falling down a long shaft of light, and just as suddenly was himself again. The experience jarred him, left him disoriented. His eyes flew open and he saw, inches from his own, the eyes of the Lord of Aumerle Castle. Wide, sapphire blue, staring widely at him.

Dead.

The sword that had been pointing at Alious' chest now pierced him through, although the actor was sure he had never extended his arm.

A strange disturbance flooded through him, as if while looking into those sapphire eyes, he were looking into a mirror. Benjamin stepped back in shock, pulling the blade with him, and the lifeless body slumped to the floor.

"Ben." The actor stood frozen for a moment, staring. Then he turned to where Perahn knelt next to Connor, his belt tied tightly around the minstrel's right thigh. "I'm not sure he'll make it."

"No." Ben's voice was still thick. He looked at the body of Alious and back, trying to clear his head. In a few steps he was at Connor's side, his pulse racing, his thoughts spinning. The fight with Alious, the incomprehensible connection, had left him with more information than he was able to process. *Do what you must now. You can sort it all out later.*

"I can't help him in here. We'll have to get out. The castle is waking up, and some of these guards don't need anyone to give them a reason to fight." Ben thought frantically for a moment, slipped the chain of his pendant off and draped it over Connor's head. He felt strangely naked without it. "That should stabilize him enough for now." As he spoke, a soft glow emanated from the glass and seemed to be absorbed into Connor's chest. With a sudden shudder, the actor looked at the body of Alious again, walked over to it. Dropping to one knee, he opened the neck of the man's cape.

Shining in the folds of cloth was a blue oval of stone, outlined in silver, hanging from a silver chain. Ben cradled it in his palm, and stared at it for a long moment.

"Ben." Perahn was looking as concerned for Ben now as he was for Connor. "We've got to get out of here."

The actor nodded, closed his fingers around the stone and snapped the chain with a jerk. He looked into Perahn's questioning eyes and shook his head. "I don't know. Let's get them out of here while there's time." He blinked down at the minstrel's pale, unconscious face. *Damn it, Connor. Stay with me.*

Perahn scooped up the still form of his brother and turned to Ben. "Can you carry him?"

"Yes. Let's go." Ben folded Connor over his shoulder and regained his feet unsteadily. "If we can make the Gate, we'll be all right." He glanced sideways at the blood-soaked leg of the minstrel and breathed a silent prayer that he was speaking the truth.

20

Ben led them along the halls of the sprawling castle, ducking through labyrinthine passageways that seemed to appear from nowhere. They managed to avoid the remaining guards but Mekki, who had the packs as the others carried their fallen comrades, took Ben's sword from his side.

"I have a free hand," she said, in response to his questioning look.

He gave her a brief smile. "Good. I'm glad someone does." Suddenly his eyes changed and he frowned. "Down here. There's a passage that tunnels out to an opening not far from the Gate. It's our best chance."

Mekki frowned at him, but followed. Narrowing her eyes, she studied Ben from behind as they slipped through a narrow archway and into a small passage, barely wide enough for them to carry their burdens. A thought occurred to her. "Ben?" There was no response. She bit her lip and shifted the pack on her shoulder. The weight of Benjamin's sword felt reassuring in the darkness, and she felt the soft red leather caress her palm as she grasped it more tightly.

"Just a little farther." Benjamin was nearly running in the darkness, and they struggled to keep up with him. In a slow curve, the tunnel suddenly lightened. They saw an opening in the distance, and the light that came with it. The red light of dawn.

Mekki was about to call out to Ben again when Perahn turned and looked at her, whispering sharply. "Don't." She opened her mouth to respond and he cut her off, not unkindly. "I know. Wait till we reach the Gate. We need to get them to safety." Mekki stared at him in shock for a moment. Then she nodded, took one last look behind her, and joined in the dash for the light. In less than a minute they reached the mouth of the tunnel, burst into the ruddy dawn as it bounced between the rust mountains and reflected in metallic red on the dead water below.

Benjamin stared at the red sunrise and shook his head. "Ominous. Why?" He looked at Mekki as he asked, his tone strangely formal.

"I don't know." She stopped suddenly, as the echo of their connection sang through her. Something. *Something about a man with white hair.* There was a piece of Benjamin that this was important to. Mekki looked at Perahn once more, and his eyes begged her patience. She shuddered, frightened without knowing why.

"Let's get them past the Gate. Which way?"

Ben turned and squinted into the dawn. "Come. Follow me."

Mekki shifted her grasp on the sword and muttered under her breath. "Like we have a choice."

True to his words, they were at the rope in minutes. When they got there, Ben blinked confusion and stared up the wall. "How the hell do we get them up?"

Perahn squinted upwards. "If I go first, I can rig a harness to send down."

"Can you pull them up alone?"

"I think so. If I -"

"No. Wait." The actor was starting along the path away from the rope. Mekki stared after him.

"Ben. Where are you going?"

"There's another way."

For a moment Mekki and Perahn stood motionless in the red light. Then they looked at each other, and Mekki sighed. "What do you think?"

Ben stopped and looked back at them. "Come!" He paused a moment, and his eyes changed. "Please." She took one more look at Perahn and shrugged.

"Let's go."

They followed at a trot until they reached a crack in the rock at the side of the path. Mekki came to a stop next to Ben. "Now what?"

"Now this." He opened his hand and revealed the lapis oval that had hung around Alious' neck. Shifting it in his hand, he pushed the back of it into an almost imperceptible indentation in the wall. With a dusty crack, a door opened seamlessly inward. Ben looked at her and motioned with his head. "Go ahead. Keep to the right, one hand on the wall. There are a few steps down, so be careful how you walk." She stared at him, incredulous, but went on.

Inside the tunnel it was dim and cool, with a damp smell rising from the rock floor. "I have to close this. It'll be black as night, but we won't be followed. Just keep to the right wall."

The stone door swung shut, and they were immersed in darkness. "Go, keep moving." There was a strange hesitation in his voice, and a change of tone before he went on. "Mekki. Please."

They walked. Twice they stopped, checked on Connor and Jhaun as well as they could, caught their breath, and went on. The tunnel sloped gradually downward, and they walked until Mekki had lost all sense of direction. The only thing that kept her moving one foot in front of the other was the smooth cool wall to her right, the sound of breathing from the two who labored behind her, and the occasional weak groan that added urgency to her steps. The whole experience seemed unreal. Had there been a fight? Was Alious defeated? Had Ben gained something from him, or –

"Ow." She cried out sharply as her foot hit a step.

"Stop here. I've got to find the door." Mekki stood still in the dark as Ben found his way around her, still carrying Connor over his shoulder. He searched the dead end with his fingertips, whispering softly to himself. "It's got to be here. I know - *wait*, here it is." In the dark it was impossible to see what he had done, but a low door opened in the wall, barely large enough for them to crawl through. "I'll go first and pull them across."

There was light coming through the opening, and as soon as Connor and Jhaun were through, Mekki scrambled through herself, blinking against the sudden change. There was a stream, scattered trees and brush. A familiar whinny startled her, as a coppery palomino trotted her way. "We're on the other side of the divide!" She stared as Per joined them. "Then we're through? Safe?" Ben sat panting against the rock wall as Mekki ran her hand over his arm.

A voice carried through the trees in silken tones brushed with concern. "You're safe."

Perahn turned. "Lady?" A gasp from behind made him turn.

"Miran?" Ben stood, suddenly trembling, and walked toward the Lady of Anders. "*Miran*. It is you." He reached out to her. The Lady's brow creased. She took his hand and gasped.

"No." She shook her head. "It can't be."

The actor smiled. "Yes. Miran! By the Artist. How have I deserved this?" He closed his eyes and whispered. "Please. For a few moments, just..." A hush fell over the company as Ben stood trembling like a reed in the breeze.

"Ben?" Mekki moved toward him, but Perahn stopped her with a hand on her arm.

"Let him be. I think he's safe, and even if he's not, there's nothing we can do. This is his choice." Mekki stared at Ben as the breeze played through his hair, the rising sun shooting it with sparks of silver.

Silver. Long, silver hair, that fell in gentle waves to his shoulder. "My God." Mekki pushed her hand against her lips.

It was Alious that opened his eyes, standing before the Lady, holding her hands gently in his own. "My Lady. My Miran." He kissed her hands, afraid to do more. "I know you can never forgive me. I only wish -"

With a small cry Miran of Anders pulled her hands away, and then swept the man into her arms. "Why? Why?" She pulled back from him and looked into his eyes, sapphire flecked with silver. "Tell me. Show me. *Now*."

At her determination something like joy flared in his eyes, and the strength of the two joining filled the air with a shiver, as if lightning had struck nearby. "Alious," she whispered softly. It was all she said before she held him once more.

For a few minutes Perahn and Mekki stared, incapable of doing anything else. Then Alious pulled away. "I must go. I can't take any more than I have."

Her eyes sparkled with tears, but none escaped. "I know."

"My Miran." The Lady nodded, not trusting her voice. He shook his head solemnly. "The evil is defeated, not destroyed."

"Yes."

She stared into his eyes until Alious tore himself away and swept his gaze around the group. "The One must help the Hawk. I… will do what I can." He turned to the Lady once more, stepping close, breathing her fragrance as he rested his forehead against hers. Then he kissed her, gently. "I will see you again, but not in this creation." He smiled softly. "This I vow."

Miran nodded, laid her hand on his cheek.

Alious turned to Perahn. "And you. I thought you never were." He stopped, opened his mouth as if to say something, closed it again, his eyes tormented. "See that your mother is well."

Per nodded, not able to break his gaze. "I will."

Alious looked his son over, head to toe, one more time. "If you ever can, …understand." He turned then to where Jhaun lay on the ground, and knelt next to him. "I let this happen. The Artist forgive me." Placing his hands delicately on his son's face, he whispered a few words, too quietly for the rest of them to hear. Then he shook his head and frowned, the distress showing on his face. "It's been too long. I can't -"

The Lady said nothing, but stepped to Perahn and took the flute from his belt. She held it out to Alious. "Then play." Alious startled, but looked to Perahn questioningly. Per glanced down at his brother.

"She trusts you. That will have to be enough. Do what you can for him." The words tumbled over themselves as he struggled not to feel.

The Lady spoke quietly to Alious. "I can't help you. I can only give you my strength," she said, "and that is yours." He sat heavily on the ground and began to play.

He faltered at first. It had been too long. Then he found it, mastered it. Sweet and clear the sound rose, winding over and around and through them all. The horses grew silent and the trees whispered, rustling in a breeze that could barely be felt. He played strength and wholeness, and a plea to heal, to somehow make amends.

When the song ended, Jhaun looked like a week of recovery had passed. Still bruised, but whole. His face was serene at rest, and even Connor looked different. Mekki loosened the belt on his leg, as she had been doing from time to time, and gasped. "The bleeding's stopped. But he's -" She frowned, caught between tears of relief and anger. "Now what?"

Alious stood and nodded. "Now it is in the One's hands. The Hawk's needs are beyond my creating." He looked at Miran and smiled, reaching out to brush her cheek with his fingertips. Closing his eyes, a shiver shot through him as the energy shifted. The Lady reached for him and stopped.

It was Ben that opened his eyes, and promptly reeled backwards into Per. He gasped once or twice, catching his breath. "Ben?" Mekki's eyes shone with concern.

"Yeah. I'm okay. I think. Yeah." He remembered. "Connor." Moving to the minstrel's side, Ben looked more closely at the wound in his leg and swallowed hard. "Per. I'm going to need help."

"I'm here."

"I think the vessel's okay now, but - I don't know." He looked up at the musician helplessly. "I feel like he doesn't want to stay." Per was holding out his hand, and Ben realized he still held the wooden flute clutched in his fist. He handed it to Per quickly, with a little shudder. "Wards. Please. Mekki, what can you give me?"

Mekki looked at him and her eyes smiled. "Only my strength, and that is yours. Go." She grasped his hand briefly, and he knelt in the grass at Connor's side.

The Lady spoke from where she sat at Jhaun's head. "Benjamin."

"Yeah."

"He may not come back."

"He may not want to."

"It's his choice. If he feels -"

"Lady." Ben's lips tightened into a fine line. "This creation isn't finished yet. Is that not truth?"

The Lady looked down, stared at her unconscious son for a long moment. "Yes. But -"

Benjamin turned away from her and brushed Connor's hair back from his face. He took a deep breath and whispered softly. "Okay, Con. Let me in."

Ben closed his eyes, centered, and found the room within. Stepping out to the porch, he tried to see some sign of the minstrel. In the hazy distance he could make out a vast stone fortress, darkling in the mist. Fearlessly he strode across the space that divided them, pounded on the huge wooden door. "Connor." There was no response. "Connor, let me in." Stepping back, he stared up at the wall. Feeling for it.

There's got to be another way.

Ben walked along the wall until he reached its end, turned - and found himself staring at the backside of the same wall. As if he had walked behind a movie set.

A facade. Hiding what?

He walked in misty darkness for a distance, only vaguely aware of the danger of becoming lost, until suddenly another structure loomed before him. This one was wooden, contemporary by his standards, and finished to a honey glow. Trees surrounded it, and huge windows spanned the space from ground floor to roof. It was warm, beautiful, and dark. Ben ran to the door and called Connor's name. He tried it, and it opened easily, completely unguarded.

"Con?"

On the softly gleaming floor, Ben made out the form of the minstrel lying there, a guitar in his hand, just as he had first seen him in the woods.

It seems so long ago, and it seems like only yesterday. If this is the last time I'll see him, just as the first...

Ben shook that thought out and ran to the minstrel's side, dropped to one knee. "Connor." The still form did not move. The actor blinked hard and spoke more firmly. "Hawk. I need you. Talk to me."

The minstrel's eyelids fluttered open with a frown. Ben breathed a short sigh of relief. "Con. You've got to come back."

The minstrel stared lifelessly at him. "I'm done."

"No. We still need you. I still need you. Please."

"You don't need anyone. You did it. You're the One." His voice trailed off, his eyes closing.

"No. You don't have to die!"

Connor opened his eyes. "It doesn't matter, kid. Nothing matters now." Something fond softened the hard edge of his gaze. "I'm glad I met you, Ben. Take care."

"No. Connor, come on, don't do this." The minstrel was fading, Ben could feel it. Nothing he could say would change that. It was Connor's choice.

But someone else might change his mind.

Ben thought frantically. *Who?* A now-familiar voice answered.

There is someone. Not of this world.

With all his strength, with the strength of his companions around him, Ben called out. Across time, across space, across realities.

Light the way, begin the rhyme... and help me save him. Someone. Please.

A few moments passed before Ben looked up and gasped.

In a sparkling swirl of light, a young woman had appeared in the room. She was petite and strong, dark-haired, and the minstrel's eyes shone in her face. She blinked, confused, staring at Ben. There was no fear in her, but curiosity flooded the room.

"Where the -" She started, stopped. "And who -" She looked around the room and her eyes fell to the minstrel. For a moment she frowned, then gasped aloud.

"Daddy?" Instantly she was on all fours beside him, staring at his lifeless features. Angrily she raised her head and screamed to the heavens. "No!" She looked at Benjamin standing there, and her fury spilled over onto him. "I hate this dream! Why do I always come too late?"

The minstrel's eyes opened slowly. He blinked, frowned, stared up at her.

"Karen?"

The girl looked down as anger flushed her face, and yelled her concern in a way that Ben found oddly familiar. "Why? Why do I always find you dead? And why is there always someone telling me I'm too late? Tell me, Daddy, tell me now. I can't live with this. It's killing me." Her voice cracked, sorrow fighting with the anger. "Why did you leave? Did you know I couldn't help you? I would have tried, I swear..." she was trailing off now, sadness winning the battle. "Just tell me why I made you leave..."

The minstrel stared at her, incredulous, and then with growing fury at Ben. "Stop this. Stop it now." When the girl remained, he struggled unsteadily to his feet, grabbed Ben by the front of his shirt. "Stop it! Make this image go away." His tone dropped to a growling whisper. "This is my life. Leave it alone."

Ben shook his head and put his hand on Connor's arm. "I'm not creating her, Con. I promise. I only called for help. It's your choice, always, but don't pretend there're no consequences. Don't pretend your life - or your death – won't affect anyone else."

The minstrel turned back to the figure of the young woman, who was trembling with tears and anger. He swallowed hard and shook almost imperceptibly. Almost. "Karen. Sweet." He held out his arms, and she nearly went to him. Then anger returned, with shaking fury.

"No. You'll just die again. I know this dream!"

Connor staggered back and stared squinting at her, as if she were an over bright but nonetheless stunning sunrise. "My God, you're beautiful. You always were, but now..."

Ben looked at the girl and nodded. She was lovely, with haunted nobility in her dark eyes. The minstrel held out his arms again. "Karen. I won't die in this dream. Not now. I- " He glanced at Ben. "I promise." She hesitated for a moment. Then, with a little cry, fell into his arms, sobbing. He held her until the tears subsided, and spoke gently.

"It wasn't your fault. Nothing was your fault. I wasn't leaving you, I was following my own path. I'm still following it. I didn't think I could make anyone understand. There was so much to do. Such a long road. I'm sorry, sweet, so sorry..." The minstrel kissed her hair, holding her, and wept silently. For a time they stood there, until finally she looked up at him.

"I know I'm going to wake up." The strength in her voice surprised him. "Will I see you again?"

The minstrel stared into her eyes and brushed her hair back over her ear. "I don't know, Kari. Maybe not in this creation... but I will see you again." He gave a small grin in spite of himself. "This I vow."

She frowned. "Is what you're doing here so important? Can't you come back with me? Can't you stay?"

The minstrel laughed, seeing for the moment a much younger child. "Yeah, Kari, it's important. And I'm not quite done yet." His smile warmed and he held her tightly once more. "But remember, and take this home with you. I love you. I always will, no matter where I am, you got that?" She nodded, sniffing. "And nothing, nothing was your fault. Not anything between your mother and I, not me leaving. It was mine, okay? Mine."

From where he stood Ben could feel his truth flowing over her like a healing balm. "Okay." She smiled tentatively. "But I miss you."

"I miss you too, sweet. But I'm with you. Just like you're with me. That's what love is." The minstrel turned to Ben and spoke quickly, under his breath. "Send her back. I can't take it much longer." The actor had never seen the minstrel so vulnerable.

"I'll try." Ben closed his eyes and centered himself, focused on the One within him. It was the One who walked to the girl and placed his hand gently on her head. "Sleep, be at peace," he said. And then, *more quietly, "and always, always remember this dream." Her eyes closed, and she smiled in a shimmer of moving water light as she vanished. Ben relaxed, took a deep breath, let it out slowly.*

The minstrel turned to him, tears in his eyes. "Okay, kid. It's true. I want to be able to look my daughter in the eye someday and tell her I never gave up."

Benjamin nodded. "You're still a part of this, Con. Of the healing that has to come."

The minstrel shook his head. "I don't know if I have it in me."

Ben put his hands on the minstrel's shoulders and smiled. "All you have inside is more than you will ever need."

When Benjamin finally opened his eyes, he was kneeling next to Connor, who seemed to be sleeping peacefully. It was Mekki who realized he was back first. "Ben? Is he…?"

"He'll be all right. He needs to rest." Ben began to struggle to his feet, then thought better of it. "Which sounds like a good idea." He stretched out on the ground next to the minstrel, and did not so much fall asleep as lapse into unconsciousness.

*   *   *

Benjamin was back in his bedroom, sleeping under the quilt of greens and browns. He opened his eyes and saw his grandfather standing at the foot of the bed, his arms crossed, smiling. "Nice work, son. We're all proud of you."

"Papa? What happens now? Do I come home?"

His grandfather chuckled. "Choices. Opportunities." He gave him a warm and loving smile. "It's up to you, Ben. Always is. Remember, though," he said, looking suddenly very intent, very serious. "You have to be true to who you really are. What you really are. What you really need to do."

"How will I know?"

Ben blinked, and opened his eyes to the scene of a clearing in a forest, a sword trembling in a puddle of sunlight where it stood, embedded in an ancient oak stump. The stream nearby called him, and he stared into it. The face that stared back was barely recognizable.

It was his own.

*   *   *

The music of a wooden flute playing over a quiet guitar eventually woke Ben, along with the savory smell of sizzling meat. The view above, from where he lay, was a glorious spill of stars across a sky like black velvet. Closer to him was the reflected silver green of leaf bottoms, dancing gently in the firelight. He stretched carefully, feeling like his muscles might have forgotten how.

Mekki walked over when she saw him stirring, and squatted down to talk to him. "Hey. How're you feeling?"

"Okay, I think." He laughed as he tried to stretch again. "Unreal. How are they?"

She looked over to where Connor and Perahn were playing. "Connor's going to be fine. He's a little..." she hesitated. "He's a little something. I can't tell if he's ticked off or happy. You know Con."

"Yeah, in bits and pieces. Jhaun?"

Mekki nodded toward a stand of trees outside the circle of firelight. "He's quiet. Physically, he's good. The rest of him, I don't know. Maybe he's just afraid of how much he still has to learn." She stared into the darkness and shook her head. "Is he tough for you to read? Or is it just me again? He feels so different."

"He is different. He's the Inca'ti."

"Right. Any idea what that means?"

He grinned at her. "Not a clue."

Mekki nodded, let the moment pass before changing the subject. "That was quite a gift you gave the Lady."

The actor looked into the dancing flames. "I don't know how much I had to do with it. How did she end up finding us?"

"She said the feelings were so confusing that she couldn't begin to describe them... but she knew she had to come. Here." Mekki smiled sadly at him. "Are you really surprised by that, after what happened?"

"No." After a moment he struggled to his feet with her help. While the musicians wound to a close, the actor walked into the wood and leaned on a tree. Connor followed, limping slightly.

"So?"

Ben smiled at the minstrel's lack of preamble. It was a relief, and made what he had to say easier. "I think I have to go home." There was a long pause. Ben had a strange feeling that the entire group knew what he had said, even though he had spoken loud enough for only Connor to hear.

"Ah."

Ben waited for the recriminations that he was sure were in the minstrel's mind, the accusations. Surely, since Ben had convinced Connor to stay, he would expect the actor to stay as well. "It's up to you, Ben. You're the One."

Ben was speechless for a moment. "But - do you think it's right?"

The minstrel paused long enough to stretch his neck from side to side. "You're the only one who can decide. Just like I was. But feel it through, okay?"

"Okay."

Connor stood there for another minute. "I've felt guilty about dragging you into this. But it seems to have worked. It seems to have been the right path." The minstrel took a deep breath and cleared his throat, businesslike. "Listen. Why don't you sleep on it, until we get back to Anders, anyway?"

"Good idea."

In his heart, Benjamin Agante already knew he was leaving.

21

In an easy morning routine they broke camp, and by noon they were on their way. The guards that had accompanied the Lady took the lead, followed by Miran and Mekki.

A still exhausted Ben rode next followed by Jhaun, silent and unreachable; his defenses covering him like a dark and heavy cloak. At the end of the line Connor and Perahn framed them with music, sometimes singing softly, more often taking turns than playing together.

Light bounced in echoes off the ancient stones, and the horses wound along the path until they reached a stony clearing, the beginning of the winding cleft in the mountains where they had first met Mekki. It was getting late, and Connor called out from the back of the line. "Let's stop here. No point in pushing it." It was agreed easily, with no comment on anyone's obvious exhaustion.

Ben and Mekki were elected to water their horses while the others made camp, and the actor stood near her at what amounted to a little more than a spring-fed puddle at the top of the defile. "So."

Mekki turned and blinked at him, bemused. "So?"

He looked down at his feet, feeling foolish without knowing why. The grass around his boots was woven through with threads of golden brown, the beginning of the end of summer. He looked into her eyes again. "Will you be coming with us, or do you stay here?"

Mekki frowned at the abrupt question and suddenly laughed. "Is that what it is. You don't want the circle to break until *you* do it." She smiled at his expression and chuckled again, more quietly. "I was afraid it was something worse." With a sigh she squatted down to the water's edge, picked some mint that was growing there, and nibbled a leaf thoughtfully. "No, I'm not staying in the gorge. I want to pick up some things I left in that cave, but I'll travel as far as Anders." She stopped and drank a sip of water from her cupped palm, splashing a second across the back of her neck. "I was planning on heading south, back to the Core. There's still so much I want to know." She frowned off into the distance. "But right now, the Lady tells me that I should head for a town called Overlook."

"Overlook? I've been there. Perahn comes from there. I have to stop there -" He stopped himself before he blurted out the rest. *On my way home.*

"She said it was where Per grew up. There's a woman there who apparently knows more about healing and herb lore than anyone at the Core could teach me -" She stopped at Ben's expression. "What?"

"That's got to be Ahna." Ben squatted down to the water and rinsed his face, the cold water running down into his shirt and making him shiver. "And I guess that means we're stuck with each other. For a while longer, anyway."

Mekki offered him a mint leaf with a pensive smile. "I guess so."

Ben took the leaf, his fingers brushing against her hand in the process. A thrill of energy ran through him, and he looked deep into her eyes. He could get lost in those eyes.

Yeah, except you're leaving.

He blinked, shook off the feeling, stood and looked down the ravine.

From where he was now he could see only the beginning of a stream that would, some distance further on, turn into a spectacular display of falls, singing and sparkling as they sculpted the very fabric of the world. Where he stood now, most of that water was still hidden below the surface.

"And you?"

Her comment broke his reverie. "What?"

"You. What happens next for you?" Her expression was perfectly neutral. "Do you stay at Anders, or teach, or try to go home? You'd be quite the addition at the Core."

Ben sighed in spite of himself, and his response was colored with something that surprised him, a tone that he immediately regretted. "Haven't I done enough?" Mekki's expression didn't change, although Ben felt something shift between them. "I'm sorry. I didn't mean that. I guess -" He paused, waved his hand in a helpless gesture that startled the horses and made Jasper snort at him. "Cripe." He took a deep breath and started again. "I want to go home, but I'm not sure I even know how. And I know it's not done here, but I feel like I've done my part. I feel like I've done the things that the One was supposed to do, like the show's over, or I'm not in the third act." He trailed to a stop, laughing bitterly at himself. "Ah. That sounded just as foolish out loud as it did in my head."

He looked at her and found she was studying him intently, as if he were a painting, or an ancient carving covered with symbols of a language that she was only beginning to understand. "You have to be true to yourself, Ben." She took her horse's bridle in hand and slowly began the walk back to the camp, the other animals naturally following. "But don't underestimate your worth here. And don't be so sure of how you'll feel when you get home." She stopped, considering. "Do you think you *can* go back?"

"I don't know. I've got to try." He shrugged helplessly. "Do you understand?" She nodded, turned toward the horses once more. "Mekki." He called after her as she moved away, and she stopped to look back over her shoulder at him. "Do you ever think you were born in the wrong place? The wrong world?"

She frowned, but only for a moment. "I've wondered. But no. I think I need to be what I am, what my world made me. And I know I need to be here now."

"Will you ever go back?" His question was intensified by its immediacy, and she gave a wry grin.

"I don't know if I could. And if I did go there, and I couldn't get back here… well. I'm not ready to give Taela up. Not yet, anyway." She looked up at the blue sky above her and smiled. "But it's still an infinite universe, and this creation isn't finished." Walking away, she left him staring thoughtfully after her until Jasper nudged him in the back, reminding him that supper and sleep were waiting.

They took the ravine slowly. There was a new calm along the singing waters, and Mekki was even comfortable taking her horse through. She was in the process of retrieving a sack of notebooks from the cave under the fallen tree when her sudden exclamation drew the attention of the group. "Look!" They followed her gaze to a cleft in the rock. Bright in the sunlight, a seedling from the fallen tree was growing there, rearing its head like a miniature green serpent.

Perahn grinned as he placed his palm on his chest and then extended it outward, over the tiny plant. "The Artist is working still."

*   *   *

Only one incident on the road marred their travel back to Anders Castle for Ben. The Lady was sitting quietly near the fire, and he frowned as he felt the tension coming from her. "Milady? Are you all right?"

She forced a smile, taking a breath. "There is fighting still. I can feel it."

"With Alious gone? Why? What do they want?"

The Lady of Anders looked more sorrowful than angry. "There will always be those who lust for power, and those willing to follow." She moved to add another piece of wood to the fire. "The danger is that one could be strong enough for the darkness to take notice of, to use. That's the danger and the obligation that comes with power."

"This 'darkness' you speak of. Does it have a name? A face?"

The Lady looked at him, her eyes serious. "These things are not spoken of casually, Benjamin."

"This is not casual, Lady. I want to know." *I want to know what I'm leaving you to face.*

The Lady paused for a long moment before she answered him. "There are prophecies, but few answers. Perhaps you should talk to Tomas. Ask him what he knows when you see him on your way home." The casual way that she said it startled Ben. Everyone seemed to know that he was going to try to leave, and no one was going to attempt to talk him out of it.

He gave up trying to decide if he was relieved or disappointed.

*　　*　　*

As they approached the castle, winding up a road leading to the back of the keep, they spotted a tall girl walking out to meet them. Cyrin.

Ben, leading the line, dismounted to embrace her. "I thought you'd know."

She smiled, but her glance darted to the Lady's younger son on guard at the end of the file, still far off. A visible sigh of relief shuddered through her. "Is he – all right? Are you?" She reached out to Ben and grasped his hand for a moment. "I felt such strange things after you left."

"He'll need time. It hasn't been easy." The girl nodded, then remembering herself, gave a low bow.

"In the name of Anders, I welcome the One within our walls." She rose with a conspiratorial smile. "I told them all you were coming toward the front gate. This way I can see you to your rooms in peace. Wesp is waiting for your horses."

"Thanks, Cyrin. You're the best." He was about to turn away but stopped, bowed low. Formally, he took her hand. "The One thanks you, Cyrin of Anders. Your energy was with us. We could not have succeeded without you." With a quick glance to see just how far back Jhaun was, Ben nodded to the momentarily speechless girl and walked into the cool of the castle. The rest greeted her in turn, with the Lady taking a few minutes to make sure all was well. All were weary but glad to reach safe haven.

Cyrin was standing alone by the entranceway when Jhaun finally rode up, and she took the reins of his horse as he dismounted. "Welcome home, son of Anders."

Jhaun startled. He was so absorbed in his own thoughts that he truly had not noticed who was there. "Cyrin. I…" She stepped forward and hugged him tightly.

"I'm glad you came back." He nodded, shrugged. Her eyes narrowed as she felt the swirling feelings within him, some that he was trying to ignore, and others that he simply couldn't understand. It would take time, Ben was right. Cyrin smiled at him, glad of his presence, and felt the path clearing ahead of her. "Although I'm quite certain you did your best not to return." She ran her hand over the scar that ran from his brow to his chin, feeling some of what had caused it, showing none of it on her face.

"Cyrin -"

"Picking fights with people bigger than you, I'm sure. Getting in trouble without me being around to bail you out."

"Cyrin." Her unconditional acceptance of him, her lack of caution around him, took its toll, as it always had. She was the only one who left him alone only when she felt like it, not when his expression and bearing announced it. Jhaun smiled for the first time in days, a crooked half-smile. "I'm glad to be back. I think." He looked at her, opened his mouth and closed it again. She put her hand on his back and guided him toward the door.

"We'll have plenty of time to talk later," she said in a calm, businesslike tone. "For now, get some rest." Quietly she added, "I'll dance for you all. Sleep well."

He nodded, started to walk away, and stopped. Turning back to her, he leaned forward and kissed her cheek. "Thank you." His eyes said more than his words ever could.

She nodded, pointing to the door. "Go." He walked wearily into the castle courtyard, looking back over his shoulder once more to grin at her and shake his head.

Cyrin, for her part, trembled in the overflow of feelings she had grounded. Once the son of Anders was safely on his way, she turned from the door and walked, quickly, until she found a safe space to sit and weep the feelings away.

*   *   *

When the travelers awakened, a feast was ready. Not in the great hall, but on a quiet balcony overlooking the courtyard on the third level. After they had eaten, the Lady stood and waited for their attention.

"I thank you all. I believe this is the beginning of the change we've waited for." She looked at Ben with a warm smile. "As a small symbol of our thanks, I offer you this." She turned to the table behind her and lifted a long parcel, wrapped in green-gold fabric. "The House of Anders is forever in your debt, Benjamin Agante." She handed the package to him as he stood and bowed to her.

Ben gently unfolded the fabric and could not hold back a gasp. It was a delicately carved alabaster flute. He lifted it to the light, and veins of blue and white appeared in the translucent cream of the stone.

"It belonged to the Lord of Aumerle. The man you let me see once more." She hesitated for a moment. "I want you all to know, although perhaps Benjamin already does… Alious was not an evil man. He opened himself to evil because he knew that there was one in our line that would be used." Miran blinked hard and looked out into the sky above the courtyard. "He felt that he was weak enough to be defeated. It wasn't until too late that he realized that he was more powerful than he knew." She looked at Jhaun. "You see the danger of underestimating yourself." Turning back to Ben, she tried to smile once more. "I want you to have this instrument. I believe he would as well."

Ben felt a swelling in his chest that made it difficult to speak. "Thank you, Lady." He was studying it when a thought hit him, perhaps a memory. A promise made in exchange. "Milady," he said suddenly, "This is yours." He reached into the small pouch at his belt and drew out a blue stone on a silver chain. "I have kept my word." The change in his voice was not lost on the company, who exchanged quiet looks. The Lady took the pendant, stared at the lapis oval in startled recognition. Brushing her fingers against his cheek she looked deep into Ben's eyes, but all she saw there was the actor.

"Thank you," she whispered, when she found her voice again. "I will cherish this." Gently she placed it on the table where the flute had been, and taking a deep breath, turned to Connor.

"For you, Hawk. With all the gratitude I can express." She gave him a small wooden box, which he took with an uncharacteristically graceful bow. Inside was a finely wrought silver hawk on a black leather cord, wings spread, holding a sphere of malachite in its talons. Connor took it from the box and held it in his hand for a long moment before he raised his eyes to hers. "The House of Anders recognizes the protection of the Hawk." They stared into each other's eyes for a few heartbeats before the minstrel spoke.

"The Hawk will always answer your call, Lady." He took the pendant and held it out to her. She smiled, and fastened the clasp at the back of his neck.

"Wherever you may fly, Hawk," she said softly as she straightened the collar of his shirt. "Know that you are home here." He nodded without speaking, a gentle smile warming his eyes.

Miran turned her focus down the table. "My sons. I give you your freedom, and a place to return to. I hope you do so often." Jhaun remained seated, staring down at the table, but Perahn stood immediately.

"My Lady. *Mother.*" The warm brown of his eyes gleamed softly. "I thank you. There is a home and creations I must return to. There is one who depends on me for now, and I have already been gone too long."

The Lady nodded. "Aletia. I understand that she is almost of age, Perahn. Perhaps you can both-" she stopped, took a deep breath. "Your sister is always welcome here, my son."

Perahn smiled warmly at the formality, knowing that it was the only way she could face this good-bye. "Perhaps in the summer, if all is well." He hugged her, took her hand and kissed it.

"You've grown into a fine man, Perahn. I look forward to a future that you are part of. And if you should ever need anything -" He nodded, patting her hand gently.

As they parted, she turned to Jhaun. He felt her gaze, looked up at her, and finally stood. "Mother. I think it's time for me to move on." The Lady blinked, startled.

"And where will you go, Jhaun?"

He shifted, looked over at Cyrin almost apologetically. "It has been made clear to me in this quest that I do not yet have what I need. I am not master of my powers."

"Few are, Jhaun."

"I know that." Frustration gathered like storm clouds across his brow, quickly covered. "But if there's any truth to the claims of what I'm supposed to be, I can't see it." He looked around the group. "Everything I did on this journey slowed us down, or forced us into more danger."

"Knock it off, Jhaun. That's bull and you know it."

"Is it? Tell me, Connor. Tell me one thing I did to help. One thing that was right. One thing that could prove that I am what they say I am." His jaw tensed, pulling the scar along it to an angry white line. "I still think Perahn -"

Benjamin took a deep breath and relaxed. Effortlessly, the One was there. "What you need to recognize, son of Anders, is that you alone will rarely do something of note. You need to learn how to join a circle, to open to it. To accept your place as a part of something more. Only then will you be in a position to fulfill your destiny."

Jhaun face went dark, and there was a heavy silence around the table. "I don't overestimate my importance. I -"

The voice of the One chuckled, more like Benjamin. "You *underestimate* it. Without all parts, there's no circle. Without strength in each part, the circle breaks. You must trust, and be trustworthy."

"What about you? Are you saying the One is no more important than anyone else?"

"I am." Benjamin smiled. With a motion that encompassed the group, he went on. "I have done my part. But without this circle, I could have had all the power in creation and not been able to use it to its just end." He went on, more quietly. "You are the Inca'ti. That is clear. To isolate and blame yourself is to go against the natural flow of this creation. Accept what you are, who you are. Then find the way to be."

Jhaun walked to the balcony wall and stood silhouetted like a statue in black. "Then where do I go? What's the path?"

"Only you can find your way. Learn what you can about the Inca'ti, what has been prophesied, and find your own truth." There was kindness in his voice as he went on. "There are true companions all around you."

"Overlook." The group turned as one and looked at Mekki, who had been sitting quietly. It was Connor who questioned her with a frown.

"What about it?"

"Overlook. It looks like we're all heading there. Ben on his way home. Perahn, too. Me to study with Ahna. And now, Jhaun. If I've been listening right, it sounds like you need to talk to the teacher there, the prophecy expert." Looks bounced around the circle, starting and ending at Mekki. "Am I right?"

"Tomas. Of course. It feels right. Con?"

"It can't hurt to make sure the way is clear between here and there."

In moments several conversations were taking place at once. In the confusion, no one noticed that Cyrin and Jhaun were staring at each other from across the table, speaking silently with their eyes.

*   *   *

A week passed before they left, the injured using the break to rest and continue to heal. By the time they were ready to start out, the magical, intangible days that mark the change of season had passed, and autumn had a hold on the land. They gathered in the courtyard of Anders Castle once more, fortified for the coming journey. Jhaun was saying good-bye to Cyrin when she handed him a small book.

"Poetry," she said, "with blank pages in the back. Write what you feel."

He grinned and hugged her. "We'll see each other before long."

"I know. I can feel it. I just wish..." He hugged her again. She broke away reluctantly and turned to Ben. "Tell me there's a chance we'll meet again. You may lie if you have to."

He smiled at her earnest command. "Anything's possible, Cyrin." He kissed her hand and held it to his heart. "Be well."

"And you," she nodded, her eyes shining.

The Lady said good-bye to them all together, unsure of her composure. "I will play for you. Send word of what's happening in that part of creation."

"As soon as we can. And play well, Milady. We'll need it." Connor stepped closer to her and held up his hand, palm facing her. "I'll be back before winter. This I vow."

"The Artist willing. I look forward to it." She laid her hand against his and looked into his eyes, until he moved with a nod to tighten his saddle. She turned with a smile to Ben and hugged him tightly. "Farewell, Benjamin Agante. May the Artist guide you, wherever you go."

"Thank you, Lady. For everything."

Somehow, they broke away, and were off.

With nothing more than a lingering sense of deja-vu, they completed the trip to Lintock. Benjamin could still feel the energy of the places they had fought, and it gave him uneasy dreams. It was with great relief that he saw several horsemen on the outskirts of the town and among them, the unmistakably tall figure of Tomas.

"Welcome," the teacher called, his voice ringing through the wood. He spurred on his horse and rode alone to them, both to reassure them that it was a peaceful party meeting theirs, and to assure himself that it was the circle of the One. "Welcome in the name of the Artist," he said formally. "Will you be resting in this village?"

Ben laughed, but Perahn followed the ancient greetings. "We thank you for that welcome. We have traveled far, and long for safe haven."

"You have found it here." By now Tomas and Per had both dismounted, and embraced warmly. "Thank the Artist you're all safe. I see your circle has grown."

"It's a tale for the books, Tom. How've you fared?"

"Better than expected. I've only waited for you to start home myself. Are you all going on to Overlook?"

Benjamin broke in with a handshake. "We are. Tomas, this is Mekki. And Jhaun, a son of Anders."

Tomas greeted them both warmly. "Welcome. Let's get you settled. I'd hear this tale." They stayed that night with Berke in Lintock, telling the story over several bottles of garnet wine, anxious to be on their way at dawn.

It was a peaceful day with just a nip of fall cool that brought them close enough to hear the familiar whispering of chimes. Ben looked up at the sky that rose in a turquoise dome over them, dry-brushed with the barest hint of clouds. It was idyllic enough to make him sigh. Tomas, riding next to him, heard.

"The Artist must be pleased with his work today."

"Yeah."

The teacher caught the reason for his mood easily. "You're thinking of home."

Ben shrugged. "Sometimes it's like this. Not often enough." He turned abruptly. "Am I doing the right thing?"

The teacher looked off to the horizon, at hills beginning to jewel themselves with crimson and gold. "That's up to you. It's your path, Benjamin."

Ben sighed again. "I know."

When the six travelers rode into the center of Overlook, the noise started and did not stop until Taas called for quiet the third time. "I am Taas," he said, nodding to Jhaun and Mekki. "Who travels with the One?"

Mekki swung down off her horse. "I'm Mekki. This," she said, motioning to Jhaun behind her, "is Jhaun, son of the Lady Anders, who sent us here to learn." She smiled as he grasped her forearm in the traditional greeting. "Where can I find 'Ahna'?"

Taas laughed with his eyes and indicated the woman standing near him. She stepped forward. "I am Ahna."

Mekki nodded, her eyes thoughtful. "Miran of Anders sends her love. And me." Ahna's eyes sparkled as she greeted her. "I'd like to study with you."

The older woman bowed her head slightly. "Miran has only sent me good. I'm glad to share what I know."

The celebration moved to the great willow, where tables of food and groups of musicians waited. Perahn was greeted gleefully by the group that had missed him, and Tomas was surrounded by students who had two new questions for his every answer. Mekki and Jhaun were welcomed warmly, and Ben and Connor were given the awed space deserving of the stories that preceded them. At least, until the Hawk sang. Then the party began in earnest, and did not end until long after the stars were hung like diamonds in the sky.

*   *   *

Benjamin and Connor stayed several days. By the time Ben realized that he was stalling, Connor had packed their bags and had their horses ready. There was only one thing left to do.

"Mekki?"

The woman stood distracted in Ahna's herb garden that was being harvested for the coming winter. "Here. Oh, Ben, it's you. What's up?"

"I'm leaving."

She stared for a moment at the seedpod in her hand, made a note in her book, then looked up into his eyes. "I know."

"I mean, now. Today."

"Oh." Mekki frowned, stared into him. There was a flaring of energy between them, a cord that connected them. One that always would. Stepping closer, she brushed a speck from his shoulder. "Be well, Benjamin."

He sighed, exasperated, and drew her into his arms, burying his face in her hair. "I'll miss you." He pulled away, looked at her. "Very much."

"I'll miss you, too." She stood on her toes and kissed him softly. "Be careful. Come back someday if you can."

He leaned into her and pressed his lips against hers, holding her body snug against his own. For a moment they stood in the space between two houses, knowing each other completely. For a moment.

He backed away, still holding her hands. "Be well, Mekki." She nodded, a lone tear escaping to run down her cheek. He brushed it away with his palm and, turning slowly, took it with him.

*   *   *

The minstrel and the actor took three days to reach the woods. On the afternoon that they reached the clearing near the stump of an ancient oak, the sky was a somber shade of pearl gray. Ben slipped off Jasper and walked to the stump, verifying details. Yes, the cut was still there. A space just big enough to take the blade of his sword. Out of curiosity, Benjamin drew his weapon and held it over the cut. When he dropped it, the blade sank into the weathered oak with a sound like a satisfied sigh. Benjamin shook his head and smiled.

"Con."

"What?"

"I want you to keep this." With an abrupt movement, Ben yanked the weapon from the wood and turned to the minstrel.

Connor stared at him. "What are you talking about?"

"I want you to keep this. I couldn't bear to see it go back."

"Maybe it won't."

"I can't take that chance. And what would I do with it there? Hang it on a wall?" He dropped his shoulders. "Look, if you don't want it -"

The minstrel cut him off abruptly. "All right," he said carefully. "I'll give it to Tomas to hold for you. He can teach about it. About the One. All right? But we have to trade." He reached into his quiver and pulled out an arrow. "It's traditional."

Ben smiled and stuck out his hand. "Thank you." The minstrel grasped his forearm and pulled the actor into a hug.

"Keep in touch." Without another word, Connor handed him the arrow, turned and walked to the outer edge of the clearing. Then he took out his guitar, sat on the ground, and played a song of warding.

Ben slipped the arrow into his pack, stepped onto the stump and closed his eyes, taking a deep breath. Carefully he centered, focused on the character of the One. Concentrated on being able to do this. Without trying, he could see the vast web connecting him to all the people he knew, all the energies in his life. Some lines were bright and strong, some faint, but still connecting. Which led the way? He thought of the park, of his life there.

Wait. What about Annie?

A line flared into brightness. Several lines nearby began to glow more brightly in response. A network of light, a path outlined with streamers of stars on an indigo night.

Following the light, he went.

22

Ben scuffed his hands over his arms as he stood in the stiff breeze stirring off the park lake. It was cold, although the early hour and the fact that he was drenched in sweat weren't helping. He stepped down from the oak stump and nearly lost his balance, a queasy wave running through his stomach. He caught himself against a nearby tree and looked around.

Home.

The word didn't taste quite right on his tongue. Ben walked down the path from the clearing in the park, leaning on trees as he went. He saw the wooden skeleton of the stage loom out of the dim morning before him.

Home. Yeah. It's still the same.

No, not quite. He walked farther, until he could see that the stage had been redressed for the second show.

Good Lord, I really have been gone.

Turning back the way he came, Benjamin slipped back into the shelter of the trees and shivered. Shrugging the knapsack off, he opened it and pulled out his sweatshirt. It was only then that the actor looked down and noticed his clothes. Mossy green tunic over soft leggings. Shaking his head and digging deeper in his pack he pulled out his old jeans and shirt. Quickly, with an actor's efficient immodesty, he changed. When he was done, the only thing that remained of Taela was his leather boots, and he couldn't bear to give them up.

He repacked the outfit Ahna had given him as memories danced through his mind. With a resigned sigh, Ben unwound the bedroll that he had left attached to his knapsack, found a comfortable spot, and fell asleep.

When he woke several hours later, sunshine was flooding the clearing and voices floated on the breeze, children on the playground and musicians playing in the rose garden. Ben sat, shivered for just a second, and got up.

Walking to Dave's apartment was the first thing. Automatic bank payments should have kept up his end of the contributions to the bills, and that last commercial should have left enough in his account; but if his friends panicked, it could be trouble.

He worried about running into someone all the way there, but as it turned out the apartment was empty. Various notes about rehearsal times and leftovers covered the fridge. He slipped in, took the remains of his stuff that was bagged in a closet, and slipped out again. It was almost eerie, feeling like an intruder in his own life.

Crossing the street, Ben turned the corner and walked into his favorite coffee shop. A beautiful girl with onyx-shaded green eyes and a smile that often made men forget just what they came in for called across to him as she waited on the last of the morning rush. "Ben! Where have you been?"

"Hey, beautiful. Just got back to town." He leaned over the counter and kissed her on the cheek. She shot a look at the other customers as they wandered away, and spoke quietly. Concern made her voice breathy beneath a New York flavored accent.

"I heard you just *disappeared.* Are you okay?"

"I'm fine. But listen, Jamie, do me a favor? You didn't see me. Not yet, anyway."

She gave a deep laugh, but there was still a hint of concern in her eyes. "What, you knock over a bank or something?"

"Nah. Just trying to get some air. Okay?"

Her smile was warm and conspiratorial. "You got it, sweetie. How am I supposed to remember who comes in when, as busy as we've been?" She turned to the assortment of machinery behind her, and called to him over her shoulder. "Tall cappuccino, shot of chocolate, cinnamon, with a chocolate-dipped biscotti?"

Ben smiled. She never forgot anything. "Perfect." He reached for his wallet and she shook her head.

"It's on me," she mouthed. Smiling his gratitude, he grabbed an issue of an arts newspaper and looked for a review of the show he was supposed to be in as he waited for his coffee.

Evidently, an actor named David Virgil was given his roles in both shows, and was a huge success. There was no mention of his disappearance, but that wasn't surprising. People in the show would know. There would be plenty of talk over drinks, but it wouldn't be in the papers. Ben blew out a breath as Jamie called his order, and walked over to pick it up.

He hadn't really considered what would have happened to his reputation. Disappearing that way was beyond strange. It would take some figuring out, and a damn good story. He found a comfy chair in the back room, drank his coffee, and thought.

It seemed perfectly natural that he returned to the park early that afternoon and slept, rather than going back to the apartment. Waking up groggy a few hours later, his stomach grumbled and he took a walk down the street to grab a sandwich.

As the afternoon waned he watched from the tree line near the top of the hill as actors arrived for call. When he saw Annie, he waited fifteen minutes and circled around to the clearing behind the stage. She was there, as he knew she would be, doing her vocal warm-ups. *Some things never change. Thank the Artist.* Quietly, in a matter-of-fact tone, he called to her. "Annie?"

"Yes?" She was answering before she had turned all the way. When she saw him her jaw dropped. "Benjamin? Ben! Where in hell have you been off to?" She was hugging him furiously, relieved and angry in the simultaneous way of mothers everywhere. "Where were you, love? I was worried. We all were. If you didn't have a habit of takin' off out of nowhere, we would have called the police."

Ben smiled and hugged her tight. "I missed you, Annie. Lots."

She pulled back and stared at him, the Irish purr in her voice increasing. "Don't go thinkin' you can pull the charming act on me, Benjamin Agante. I know you too well." Annie spoke sternly, but her eyes smiled. "So, what happened? Was it a woman?"

Ben sighed and hugged her again, for moral support as much as anything. "No. Well… it's a long story. Are you doing anything after the show?" She paused for a moment to think, looking off at the trees as she calculated her schedule. "No, Sean's home tonight with the girls - I should give him a call, though. Meet at Flynn's?"

Ben thought for a minute before shaking his head. "No, I'd rather not be seen until I have a story together. Can we meet here?"

"*Here* here? Right here?" She asked, gesturing around the clearing. He nodded. "Whatever you want, love." She squeezed his arm affectionately. "I'm glad you're all right." Her eyebrows peaked as she frowned slightly. "But I think I knew you were."

"Of course you did. We're connected." He missed her expression as he looked around. "We'll talk later. Sorry to do this to you before curtain. Have a great show." He kissed her forehead and vanished into the woods as she stared after him.

Ben only half watched the performance. It was too hard watching someone else be Hotspur, the character that he had used so often. He realized for the first time how much he missed performing while he was gone. Certainly he had done his share of character work, but a show had a life of its own, one that he felt he understood better now. The life of a creation of many. He sighed, coming out of the fringe of trees and onto the hill, brightened after the show by harsh spotlights. After the audience cleared out even those came down, until the only illumination was from the ghost light of a full moon. Benjamin looked around, feeling like a tourist in his own backyard. The cars on the expressway and the occasional jet overhead didn't help.

He made his way up the worn hill backstage and found Annie sitting on the stump in blue-white dapples of moon cast shadows. She jumped up and hugged him. "I was beginning to think I made you up."

They sat down on the weathered oak stump, and Ben told her the tale. Most of it, anyway. From the beginning, where they sat, to its end in the same place. She listened quietly as the words spilled out.

When he finished she took his arm, and leaning her head on his shoulder, sitting quietly while the story settled between them. After a while he sighed, his fingers wrapping around the glass pendant at his neck. "Do you think I'm crazy?"

She shook her head, but sighed in return. "I don't know what to think, Ben. But I know you, and I know you're not crazy."

He shrugged. "Sometimes I wonder. But it was real. And some things - like the energy in this pendant - I can still feel." He stopped at her frown.

She frowned thoughtfully. "Oh? I think you left something out."

"It was in Overlook." He told her about the darkness at the edges of his consciousness, and the minstrel's insistence that they take care of it. Cupping his palm, he closed his eyes and described creating the pool of liquid white light. "You know, the exercise when you concentrate your energy? Try to make it tangible?" Annie made an affirming noise and suddenly gasped. Benjamin opened his eyes.

In his cupped hand was a pale white glow. Not well defined, but undeniable. As if he had scooped up a handful of mildly luminous fog. Without knowing why, Ben felt his eyes begin to water. The mist faded gently back into his palm.

"And how in the world did yeh do that?" Annie whispered in the presence of mystery.

"That was - that was nothing. Oh, Annie. You should have seen-" He stopped, his voice failing.

Annie held his arm for a few minutes, as he stared at his hand. When he dropped it to his leg, she waited. When his breathing had steadied, she spoke. "So when are you going back?"

"What?"

"When are you going back? I know you, Agante. This is part of you. You want to be there."

"But I should be here. Shouldn't I be here?"

Annie let it slide. "You can't possibly go by *shoulds*, love, not after all that." She stood and dusted off her pants. "Listen. You know my number. Let me know what you decide. Meantime I'm going to tell

Jan that I heard from you, that you… you'd had enough after losing the Hotspur role, and finally decided to make the trek to that monastery you're always talking about in Tibet. And then you found they had a month-long period where you couldn't contact the outside world." She laughed at his expression. "Oh, trust me, Ben. They'll believe it of you. And it buys you all the time in the world. Any world."

He stood up and hugged her again. Of course she would remember that they used to joke about Tibet. "Thanks, Annie. You're the best."

"I don't know about that, but at least I can handle a chore like you." Her eyes were shining when she looked up at him. "I've missed you, Agante. Be careful."

"I will be. I don't know how I'll get back, but I can't imagine… what the hell." He gave an exasperated shrug. "Maybe I really will end up in Tibet."

She looked into his eyes, suddenly all business. "Listen, if there's anything I can take care of, let me know. I still have those boxes of yours in the basement." She grinned up at him. "I'll hang on to those, just in case."

Ben shook his head. "Thank you." They smiled at each other again, and walked up through the dark to Annie's car.

"I do feel like I'll see you again, love."

"Same here." He hugged her and kissed her cheek. "Take care of yourself. And, Annie?" She paused expectantly at the door of her car. "Don't tell anyone, okay? I mean, other than Sean…"

She rolled her eyes. "Oh. Like I have the time or inclination to type it up and hand it out. Hmmm." She playfully looked like she was considering the idea, and Ben walked off into the dark with a laugh.

As the actor made his way across the park he stopped, stood under the trees, and closed his eyes. Listened. Felt. Somewhere in the back of his mind he heard an echo of another world. The actor took a deep breath and tried to fall into the character of the One. Nothing. *I'm trying too hard.* He relaxed, ran through all the technique he knew. Nothing. *Maybe he doesn't exist in this world. Or maybe he doesn't exist at all.*

Ben turned away from the path he had been following with a sigh and walked instead to the clearing on the hill backstage. There, in the dappled moonlight, he curled up against the oak stump and eventually, shivering, fell asleep.

Ben found himself standing under a huge oak. He looked up and could see the energy pulsing through it, feel the power there. Beyond it, the sky sparkled with stars. A noise pulled his attention, and he turned to see two women watching him.

Annie? Mekki? What the -?

A tall man with silver hair and glasses walked out slowly from behind the tree.

Hello, Ben.

Papa? What's going on?

You're no fool, son. Why'd you come back?

Isn't it the right thing?

Only if it is for you. Don't decide your life based on what anyone else has put in your head. Didn't you learn that?

Ben frowned, remembering. Jhaun's haunted expression danced through his mind. I'm doing the same thing? I'm living my life based on what I think is expected of me?

His grandfather smiled. Not always. Be true to yourself. Understand?

Yes, Papa.

Cheerful laughter erupted behind him. Ben turned and saw the two women working together, standing on opposite ends of a huge yellow fishing net, untangling it. They looked up at him, smiled, and disappeared. Ben was alone once more beneath the huge tree in the wood. Then, with a metallic shifting of the light, the tree itself vanished, leaving him alone with a weathered stump in the clearing.

Alone.

The morning was bright and warm when Benjamin opened his eyes. Birds sang as they fluttered between the trees, breaking the morning sun into patterns of moving light. A squirrel chattered noisily, and ran bouncing along a branch. For a few distracted minutes, Ben forgot where he was, although it felt like something was missing. He stretched and called. "Con?" Nothing. Concern creased his brow as he reached out, feeling - *Oh.*

In that moment he knew for sure. He had to come back, he had to see for himself and not just remember, because so many things colored his memories. He had to see it again, feel it again. And now he knew.

This isn't home anymore. The knowledge brought relief and a sudden aching dread. *What if I can't go back? What if I've lost my only chance?* He pushed those thoughts away and tried to formulate a plan. There were things that he wanted to do before he left, if he *could* leave, and it was better, more sensible, to proceed as if he was able. And if he couldn't... *I'll cross that bridge when I come to it. If I have to spend the rest of my life, I'll find the way.* With sudden resolve, he pulled out his notebook to make a list, and to write a letter to Annie. Tibet was suddenly sounding pretty good.

Cashing out his bank account was easy enough. Ben forwarded the money to Annie, with enough taken out for a round trip ticket to Colorado Springs. "Use it if you need it," he told her on the phone. "Tell everyone I've taken a vow of poverty, silence, whatever. And tell Dave thanks for the space to crash while I was here."

She was quiet for a moment before she responded. "Do you know for sure that you can go back?"

"Not yet. But hey. I'll improvise."

Annie sighed. "Ah. Well... be careful, love. And good luck."

*   *   *

The plane trip to Colorado was uneventful. Once he arrived, it was simply a matter of getting directions off the net at an airport coffee shop terminal. Her name hadn't changed. The garage door was opening as he walked up the driveway.

"Ms. Hawkins? *Karen* Hawkins?" The woman who stood at the door nodded as she looked distractedly at him.

"What can I do for you? I'm kind of on my way out here."

The voice, the eyes. Even that slight frown of concern. The similarities to her father made Ben smile, and she looked at him again, did a double take. "I'm sorry, do I know you?"

"I don't think so, milady." Ben bit his tongue and plunged on. "But I knew your father."

Her eyes widened. "When?"

He looked down and away for a minute, unwilling to meet her eyes and see how she was reacting. "Oh, a long time ago. I was in college. He played a coffeehouse there, and we got to talking." The actor had worked out the story well enough on the plane to make it real. "Seems like another world now, you know how college is."

"Yes, well." Her distraction was palpable, although her gaze remained steady. So much like Connor. "He's not here."

"Yeah, I heard. I'm sorry for what you've gone through. But I wanted to return this to his family, anyway." He opened his knapsack, reached down along the side. "I know it must sound silly, but when I heard about his accident -"

"They never found him. He might not -" She stopped, looked down, chewed her lip thoughtfully for a moment before looking up into his eyes again, rock-steady. "You were saying?"

"Right. Well, I felt like it was unfinished business, and you can do whatever you want with it." He pulled out an arrow, fletched with black feathers. "He was learning to make them, showed me this one, and I borrowed it to try to copy. Then I moved back east, and, well… I'd like you to have it." He held out the arrow and she hesitated.

Slowly, her hands lifted, and he placed it in her trembling grasp. "I know he was into archery in college, still did it once in a while, but I didn't know he actually…" She trailed off, studying the arrow.

"Yeah. You know, we used to talk a lot. A lot of coffee in the middle of the night. Your father was…" He paused, grinned at her, trying to find his way. "A good man." She blinked hard as Ben continued, softly. "And he talked about you so often, I would have recognized you on the street. Listen. I'm sure Connor loves you, wherever he is."

"Yes. I'm sure he does." She looked up into his eyes again, and made a little surprised noise.

"What's wrong?"

"I remember now. I had a dream." Her eyes narrowed as she thought. "That sounds weird. I had a dream about my father a couple weeks ago and you were in it - or someone who looked a lot like you." She stared for a moment, exhaled a laugh. "What do you make of that?"

"Nothing surprises me anymore." Ben smiled at her and picked up his knapsack. "I'll let you get to work. It was good to meet you."

"Yes... and thank you." She blinked suddenly. "Wait. Your name. I never got your name."

"Ben Agante. Be well, Karen."

"You too, Ben. Thank you." She stuck out her hand to shake his, but he took it and kissed it instead. Her eyebrows lifted for a moment before she smiled. "Good-bye."

*   *   *

He stopped next at the Garden of the Gods, and it was just as he remembered. Hiking through the park, he came to a place with a familiar feel, and looking up the steep face he saw an arch carved into the rock. A group of climbers were just descending and he called up to them.

"Hey - where does that tunnel go?"

"The hole? It vents up through the top of the rock. Good climb. You should try it."

"I think I did." They looked down at him strangely. "I mean, it was a long time ago. I remember the view was incredible. Thanks." There was no feeling of possible crossover, no draw. He camped in the park overnight before heading home.

Home. Benjamin stopped at Annie's and grabbed the few remaining things he could carry. *What do I need? What do they need?* Finally, he decided to take any plays he could fit in his knapsack after the Shakespeare. His complete works weighed a ton, but was as compact as could be. They'd be playwriting soon enough anyway, if Mekki and her inkberries had anything to say about it. *Mekki.* He left the house quietly, for what would be the last time. He hoped.

*　　*　　*

It was the very end of summer.

The air was fresh and crisp in the morning calm. Leaves fell in unexpected flashes of color: bits of red and gold among the green, still clinging to the promise of life. On the ground near the old oak stump, leaves already long dead curled like discarded parchment scraps.

Benjamin Agante, for the fifth morning in a row, took a deep breath and tried to relax into the character of the One. It was getting harder to relax, harder to believe. It had to be possible; he'd done it before. The One had brought him here. *Right. If you didn't make the whole thing up.*

No. He stopped himself again. *That way madness lies.* The actor sat heavily on the oak.

Again, he reviewed the first time he crossed over, and came once more to the disillusioning conclusion that the minstrel had been calling him, had been responsible for what happened. Now it seemed impossible to leave this world without that help. But - it didn't feel right. There was something that his brain just wouldn't grab onto.

A rustle in the grass startled him and he looked up, saw Annie. She smiled tentatively. "Ah. Still here, then?"

"Yeah."

"You okay?"

"I will be."

She looked at him with a motherly frown. "Have you slept lately?"

He shook his head and looked at her, the sun making a reddish halo of her hair. "It was real, Annie. I was there, it really happened. The One-" He stopped as his voice grew harsh, and pushed his hands through his hair. He wondered just who he was trying to convince.

She waited for a long moment, and then looked away with a sigh. "I believe you, Ben. But - maybe you're done there. And if, as you say, the One's a character... maybe it's someone else's turn to play him."

His stomach lurched a bit at that possibility, and he thought of Jhaun. "I don't know." Annie walked over and sat down next to him, leaning her head on his shoulder.

They sat that way for a few minutes. "D'you think you'll keep trying?"

"Yeah." He shrugged. "For a while."

Annie let out a long breath. "All right then. I'll be checking on you, just in case." She stood and kissed the top of his head.

"Thanks, Annie."

She walked away through the trees, and Ben felt exhaustion overtake him. He couldn't remember how much he'd slept in the last five days, but he knew it wasn't enough. Yawning, he slammed his palm down on the weathered wood. Tired and frustrated, Benjamin Agante lay back against the tree stump and slipped into restless doze. And dreamed.

The hallway in his grandparent's house. Honey-toned wood glowing in the dim light. A stairway that didn't exist in any reality he knew. Anxious, Ben took the steps two at a time until he reached the landing. Yanking the first door open, he called inside.

Connor?

Empty. Benjamin pounded the wall.

Wait... if there's a home here...my home...there has to be a door...

With a sudden gasp, he ran down the steps, jerked open the front door, leapt off the porch and froze, straining to see in the misty air.

There.

Through a field that led to a stone facade. Running now, almost flying, he was behind it, pounding on the wooden door of the house.

Connor! Damn it, Con, I can't do it. I need help. I want to come back. I need to come back.

He woke with a start, his fist hitting the flat top of the stump. Still in the park. Still hearing the sounds of traffic on the expressway nearby. Only a dream. No Connor, no help.

Standing slowly, Ben stepped up onto the stump, still a bit unsteady. He dropped his head and began formulating his stories to Annie, to the theatre community. The stump blurred below him as his eyes watered. No matter how much it hurt, he couldn't wait here forever. The weight of disappointment dragged him down.

Wait.

There, tickling in the back of his mind. A song. He took a deep breath, a moment to relax before panic could grip him. Benjamin centered himself, listening.

Connor?

A mildly sarcastic voice, faint, somewhere in his head.

What took so long?

You wouldn't believe, Con. Help me?

Oh, come on. You managed to find your way there.

I can't – I can't find the One here.

Right. When I called, had you even imagined the One?

But-

We're all connected, Ben. Follow the thread that connects us.

But I can't see it here!

There was a chuckle in the music.

Then make one up. That's what you do, right? Make things up? Light the way.

Ben opened his eyes and looked around. Make it up? Pretend that he could see the web of golden threads that he had seen so clearly on Taela. He looked down at the tree stump. Was it any different than imagining a sword?

"Why not." Exhausted, he closed his eyes without much hope and centered, imagining what it had looked like. He felt nothing, but stubbornness made him try harder. *Technique, Agante. Don't give up. Just -*

With sudden brightness, the image opened before him. A sparkling network of light connecting him to so many times and places. *Him.* Not the One. And all he had inside… was more than he would ever need. Ben found himself laughing.

This creation isn't finished yet.

Benjamin Agante, his path clear before him, leapt between worlds once more.

Made in the USA
Middletown, DE
28 February 2017